Only You

'90s Coming of Age
Book 3

LETA BLAKE

An Original Publication from Leta Blake Books (LB Press)

Only You ('90s Coming of Age Book 3)
Written and published by Leta Blake
Cover by Dar Albert
Formatted by BB eBooks

First Edition, 2023

Print Edition
ISBN: 979-8-88841-019-6

Other Books by Leta Blake

Contemporary

Will & Patrick Wake Up Married
Will & Patrick's Endless Honeymoon
Cowboy Seeks Husband
The Difference Between
Bring on Forever
Stay Lucky

Sports

The River Leith

The Training Season Series
Training Season
Training Complex

Musicians

Smoky Mountain Dreams
Vespertine

New Adult

Punching the V-Card

'90s Coming of Age Series
Pictures of You
You Are Not Me
Only You

Winter Holidays

North's Pole

The Mr. Christmas Series
Mr. Frosty Pants
Mr. Naughty List
Mr. Jingle Bells

A Boy for All Seasons
My December Daddy

Fantasy

Any Given Lifetime

Reimagined Fairy Tales

Flight
Levity

Paranormal & Shifters

Angel Undone
Omega Mine

Horror

Raise Up Heart

Omegaverse

Heat of Love Series
White Heat
Slow Heat
Alpha Heat
Slow Birth
Bitter Heat

For Sale Series
Heat for Sale
Bully for Sale

Audiobooks
letablake.com/audiobooks

Discover more about the author online

Leta Blake
letablake.com

Gay Romance Newsletter

Leta's newsletter will keep you up to date on her latest releases, sales and deals, future writing plans, and more from the world of M/M romance. Join Leta's mailing list today.

Leta Blake on Patreon

Become part of Leta Blake's Patreon community to support her indie publishing expenses and to access exclusive content, deleted scenes, extras, and interviews.

Author's Note

Here we are at the end of Peter's journey. As I said before, these books have been my love and my albatross for nearly twenty years. I published the first editions of *Pictures of You* and *You Are Not Me* in 2016 believing a few mistaken things about Peter's story:

First, that it would be a four-book series. I incorrectly believed that until spring 2022 when Peter appeared after years of absence ready to finally finish his tale. As it turned out, there wasn't enough material for four books. That had been part of the problem the whole time. In my very bad, no good, terrible drafts, I'd added too many characters and complexity, determined to stick to my plan. But, when it came down to it, everything that needed to be explored and wrapped up for Peter's long awaited happy ending could be handled in a single long book.

Second, that I'd be able to write the next book in the series quickly and easily. Whew, was I ever wrong about that. I've discussed the various reasons for the long delay in blog posts and interviews over the years, so I won't rehash them all here. But I want to say one important thing, something that I'm not sure I fully understood until very recently. Now that it's all said and done? I believe I couldn't have finished Peter's story a single day before I did. No amount of trying to force it, spending more time on it, or even additional financing could have resulted in *Only You* being completed any more quickly. Only time could bring me the skill, the information, and the inspiration I needed to bring this final book to fruition.

Over the last six years, I've felt a lot of shame and self-blame for putting the first two books out before having the last book ready and for not finishing the series quickly. I often told myself that I shouldn't have published the first editions of books one and two when I did. But now, with the last book complete and finally in readers' hands, I can reframe that narrative. I believe with my whole heart that I published those first editions when they were meant to go out into the world.

Since 2016, I can't tell you the number of messages I've received from our LGBT community letting me know how important reading Peter's story has been for them. I've received confessions of personal histories that were so like Peter's, shared heart wrenching memories of youthful first loves that went sour, and over and over the words "I'd have given anything to read a book like this when I was a young adult…" came up. Friends, readers, you sent so many messages! I'm grateful for every last one of them. Now I know Peter found you when you needed him. His story had to be out there, incomplete as it was, to reach your lives in the moment you were meant to have him.

Or maybe that's a fanciful story I tell myself to make up for the fact that I had an outsized idea, character, and story for my then-skill level. So I'll say it again: I couldn't have written *Only You* before I did. I'm sorry to everyone who waited a very long time for this conclusion, and I'm sorry to those who felt I was withholding the end from them. I assure you I wrote it as soon as possible, and I put everything else aside when Peter and the book finally came to me.

I suppose it's true: everything in its own time.

I'm so proud of *Only You*. I believe it serves Peter's story perfectly and sets him up for a future of happiness. I hope everyone who waited is satisfied with his ending as well.

As I write this note, I don't know how to feel about finishing this series. I mainly feel relief. Peter's books have been a constant companion, yes, but for the last many years also a source of grief and frustration. To be able to say, "Peter, I finished your story," and to feel so incredibly proud and happy with it? To know that this final book is satisfying, not only to me but to readers? To know that Peter is at last in a very good place? Friends, I just feel such deep and profound relief. Thank you, Peter, for coming back and helping me finish your tale.

For those readers who have loved Peter for years and never gave up hope for more, thank you. This book is for all of you.

Peter's so grateful you waited for him. So am I.

Twenty years. It took us *twenty years*, but, Peter, I'm so happy to say, unlike Michelangelo's *Prisoners*, you, my love, are finally free.

Dedication

For the readers who waited, for Cecily who's known Peter her whole life, and for me who's finally able to let him go

Part VII

Mid-August, 1991

Chapter One

I T'D BEEN LESS than forty-eight hours since I'd left Atlanta in the middle of the night, leaving Adam and our mess behind me. Once I'd reached home, I'd cried and slept before burning my pictures of him and washing the ashes of our relationship out of my life.

In some ways the end had come in a flash and a bang. In others, it'd been a slow wrenching break, one I'd tried to deny. But the bones of us had snapped, along with every lie I'd told myself. Adam and I were unsupportable. We were over. After everything I'd just been through, I should have been grieving, but the truth was I'd already done most of that before the end had come.

Now I just wanted honesty and comfort. I wanted something good.

Walking through the golden light of August to Daniel's open door, my heart was soft with hope and my mind was clear for the first time in ages. The light of truth had illuminated the differences between what I wanted, what I had, who I wanted to be, and who I was. None of it included Adam anymore.

Daniel's welcoming smile further confirmed this. He was a good person. He knew the truth of me, all the ugly, selfish parts, and yet still he was asking me into his home.

"I'm glad you came," he said, as I stepped over the threshold. Kennedy, Daniel's little sister, followed at my heels.

Carrying my Leica and Milky Way, our friend Bobby's pint-sized dog, I cleared my throat, looking around. When I'd started at Kingsley, the local private high school, I'd made it a policy to never mention how nice someone's house was. It just made it clear I wasn't living at the same level. But now, pausing in the foyer of Daniel's home, I couldn't help myself.

"You live here?" I asked, taking in the wide windows that showed off the river bending around the corner of their property, the water glinting through the fading green trees. Off to the right, the formal living room was opulently decorated. I felt underdressed in my jeans, T-shirt, and the light gray cardigan I'd put on to cover up my bruised arm.

Milky Way squirmed to be let down. I complied as I gaped at the broad, sweeping staircase leading up to the second floor. Milky Way scampered up it like she knew just where she was going, her tail wagging and ears flopping. "*This* is your house?"

I'd known his family's business was in construction, so perhaps I should have expected it, but Daniel was so down-to-earth, I hadn't.

"Yeah," Kennedy said, hands on her hips, a gentle frown creasing her brow in confusion. Her messy strawberry-blond hair stuck out around her rosy face. "Why wouldn't it be, Mister?"

"I just meant it's nice." I smiled down at her. "You can just call me Peter."

"Okay, Mister."

Daniel cleared his throat, the tips of his ears a little pink. "It's ostentatious, I know. Dad saw it as an advertisement for his firm."

Standing barefoot and handsome in his long-sleeve blue Henley and loose jeans, his brown eyes shone with amber highlights, and his dark blond hair glowed in the light from the windows. My heart tripped over itself just looking at him. "Don't let it put you off," he went on.

I regretted making a big deal of it at all. "It's great."

Daniel blew out a breath. He looked tired beneath his strength. "The location's not. Too far out in the middle of nowhere."

"But the view's awesome," I said, motioning toward the windows, determined to erase my mistake. Could I do the same about us? Make him forget how I'd hurt him? Probably not.

Kennedy took hold of my elbow and tugged. "C'mon, I'll show you the game room. Do you like to play pool? Or foosball?" She grinned, her dark eyes crinkling at the edges like Daniel's did when he was happy. "Dan kicks Paul's butt at foosball. It makes Paul so mad."

"I bet."

I'd never met Daniel's younger brother, but I'd had the honor of hearing him squabble with Kennedy over the phone. He'd seemed the type who'd get ego-invested in foosball.

Daniel removed her hand from my elbow. "Kennedy, go upstairs and tell Paul he can take a break from his homework. I rented movies. You can watch them while I hang out with Peter."

"Oh." Her face fell, and she shot a hopeful glance my way. "Can I hang out with him too?"

"No."

She narrowed her eyes. "Why?"

"Because Peter's here to see me, not you." He tweaked a tuft of fuzzy hair by her ear. "Besides, I got *NeverEnding Story II* and…guess."

Her voice rose an octave. "*The Muppets Take Manhattan?*"

"You know it."

Eyes bright, Kennedy darted past me and flew up the stairs shouting for Paul.

Daniel smiled. "Sorry about that. She's a piece of work." He put his hand on my lower back and moved me deeper into the foyer. "Was the drive over all right?"

"Yeah. It was pretty."

His eyes crinkled as he drew me into a hug. I couldn't resist tucking my face in against his neck to breathe in his comforting scent. All the tangled feelings I'd been fighting since our night in Nashville eased. This—him—us…? We could be good.

"I've missed you," I whispered.

"Me, too."

Can it be this easy? Surely, I don't deserve to be forgiven yet.

Daniel let me go, nodding toward a hallway leading to the rear of the house. "Come on. This way."

In the kitchen, windows lined the back wall of the room, revealing a stretch of gray river and green, leafy trees. Granite counters were tucked beneath dark wooden cabinets, and a matching table had been built into an alcove with bench seating—a breakfast nook, I believed it was called. The scent of fresh-brewed coffee and warm chocolate chip cookies filled the air.

"Want a cup?" Daniel asked, motioning at the steaming coffee pot.

"Sure."

"Cream or sugar?"

"Both."

"Go on, have a seat." He nodded toward the breakfast nook. "I put some cookies in the oven after you called earlier. Sweets always soothe awkward moments. At least that's what my grandmother says."

I smiled.

Putting my camera down on the table, I slid into the alcove as Daniel had suggested. The whole drive over, I hadn't been able to stop wondering what he meant by inviting me here, and what I could do or say to make things right between us. Now that we were in the same room, I wasn't any clearer on either question than I had been before.

He passed me a mug of coffee, and I busied myself adding cream and sugar while he headed back across the room to grab an oven mitt before pulling a sheet of perfectly browned cookies from the oven. Pillsbury brand, I guessed, based on the scent and shape of them.

Fidgeting with my coffee mug, turning it around in my hands, I watched as he grabbed a spatula to make a stack of melty, mouth-watering cookies on a large, white plate.

The silence had gone on too long. We wouldn't get anywhere without talking to each other. Cookies were great, but they wouldn't fix anything. Only words could do that.

Me? Eager for words? *Me?* Peter Mandel? The boy who'd always said words were hard and had hidden behind his camera? Even now I was tempted to pick it up and distract myself by snapping some shots of Daniel's kitchen, of the view outside, of Daniel himself, distancing myself from this moment. From him.

But as tempting as that idea was, deep down I didn't want to use that crutch with Daniel. I wasn't sure I deserved Daniel's forgiveness, and I didn't know how to get it, but at the very least, I knew I had to be honest with him—without hiding any part of myself behind a camera to make it bearable.

That? Would take words.

Gathering my courage, I started with the obvious. "How's Bobby?"

"He's at Baptist Hospital," Daniel said, leaning one hip against the counter. His whole body seemed to droop as his brows drew down low. On the phone, he'd sounded comforting and optimistic, but now he looked defeated. I didn't know if that was due to fear for Bobby, or from the sheer exhaustion of taking care of things at home. "I talked to him on the phone this morning. He seemed a little out of it from some of the drugs they're giving him for pain, but he was lucid enough."

"Are they allowing visitors? I'd like to go see him."

"I think so. I plan to go see him soon if I can get a break here." He rubbed a hand over his face with a sigh. "I just haven't had a chance yet."

Daniel looked so tired. I wanted to hug him again and take the burden from his shoulders. I'd just opened my mouth to ask how I could help when Kennedy's voice cut through the room.

"I told you Dan has cookies!"

She skidded to a halt next to Daniel with Milky Way crashing into her ankles. They both danced in place eagerly.

Paul, however, trudged over with narrowed eyes, all ready to pick a fight. Coming up to the middle of Daniel's chest, Paul's dark auburn hair was a mess, and his thin, freckled face was tight. I had no idea if he was a cute kid or not. I was leaning toward not.

Paul made a grab at the plate of cookies.

Daniel beat him to it, lifting it up out of reach. "What? I'm sorry?" Daniel cupped a hand to his ear. "I didn't hear the magic words."

"Hand them over." Paul glared at him.

Daniel shook his head. "That's not how you ask for things."

"I said—" Paul put his hands on his skinny hips. "Give me the cookies."

"Yeah, I'm thinking no."

Paul's lips curled in a snarl.

I'd seen enough sibling arguments between Mo, Sarah, and Adam to expect things to get ugly. My pulse fluttered in my throat, and I hoped I could score at least one cookie before everything went to hell. I moved my camera off the table and onto the bench next to me. It would be safer there.

"You're not our dad," Paul muttered.

"Nope. I'm not. But I'm in charge until Mom gets home." Daniel spoke with impressive patience. "And probably after, too.

Get used to it."

Paul's jaw tightened.

"Puh-lease," Kennedy begged, falling to her knees, hands clasped, and brown eyes wide. "Can I puh-lease, pretty puh-lease have a cookie, Dan?"

"Overkill, Ken." Daniel shook his head.

She grinned and stood up, dusting off her knees. "Dan, I'd like a cookie. May I have one, please?"

"How about two?" He put them on a smaller plate and handed them over to her. "Grab one of your lunch milks to drink."

Kennedy headed over to the fridge, while Paul crossed his arms and stared at Daniel.

"Fine with me if you don't get any," Daniel said, turning his back on his brother. He dropped the plate of cookies in front of me at the table and took the seat opposite. I reached out to take one, setting it on a small plate Daniel passed over.

"They're from an old family recipe," Daniel said, ignoring his brother's glare. "Pillsbury ready-made cookie dough roll."

I snorted. Suspicion confirmed.

I took a bite. The chocolate melted on my tongue.

Paul, with his arms still tight over his chest, stalked over to stand beside us at the table. Daniel continued to act as if he weren't there, biting into his own cookie and taking a sip of coffee without another word. By the fridge, Kennedy was singing a little song and trying to balance her carton of milk on the plate beside her cookies.

Seconds ticked past. No one said anything. I took a second bite.

Paul huffed. "Fine. May I have a cookie, please?"

The grudging tone was overlooked as Daniel handed him a plate with two. "By the way, this is my friend Peter," he said.

Paul's hazel gaze took me in.

"Say hello."

"Hey," he said, nodding his head once. He turned his back on us and headed to the fridge.

"Be nice to our sister," Daniel called, as he watched Paul grab a small carton of milk, too.

Paul rolled his eyes but took Kennedy's milk from her so she wouldn't spill it. They both disappeared with Milky Way through a door and down a set of steps to what must have been a finished basement.

"They're cute," I offered, wondering if it counted as a lie. I hoped not. I was determined not to lie to Daniel. I was through with lies. At least I felt confident the statement was half-true.

"Cute?" Daniel blew out a breath, shaking his head. "I guess. I mean, yeah, sure."

"You don't think so?"

"I'm just tired."

My heart lurched. This was what I'd come here for—to prove to him that I was worthy of being his friend, to try and repair what I'd broken.

He added cream to his mug and two spoonfuls of sugar. After shoving a hand through his hair, he took a giant gulp of his coffee. Closing his eyes and sighing as he set his mug down, he looked like he'd needed it.

I reached for my camera, the urge to fidget with the settings rising in me. I forced myself to leave it where it was and focus on Daniel. "Are you doing okay?"

"Not really. It's been tough. All this stuff with my mom." He met my gaze with a sad smile. "It's having a domino effect on my life."

"Yeah?" Maybe I'd been wrong. Talking *was* overrated. Listening was where it was at, and it seemed like he needed an ear.

Daniel scratched at his facial scruff. It glinted in the light from the windows, thick like he hadn't shaved yet today. Or in a few days.

"Yeah, because of the timing," he went on. "In order to deal with the repercussions of her relapse, I took this semester off and gave up the lease on my apartment. So, I'm officially living here now."

"Oh wow. I'm sorry. I didn't realize…"

He shrugged. "It's not good for me in a lot of ways. So, yeah. I could be doing better."

"I wish you'd have called me," I offered. "So I could've helped you."

Daniel avoided my eyes and took another sip of coffee. "You've helped enough. With Bobby, I mean."

And I'd helped with breaking his heart. I'd helped a lot with that.

I joined him in covering emotion with coffee. It burned my throat on the way down. "How long will it last, do you think? This problem with your mom?"

Daniel snorted. "What I wouldn't give to know the answer to *that*." He picked up his half-eaten cookie, frowned, and took another bite before focusing his gaze out the window. "I have no idea. Things are moving fast now, and I don't know what's going to happen next."

Something about his energy demanded silence. So, I ate the rest of my cookie and sipped from my mug, letting him think. He was as handsome as ever, but there was a fragility to him I'd never seen before. It made my heart ache as much as my bruised wrist still did. Again, my camera called to me, begging me to snap his expression and own it forever.

I gave in and lifted it, centering Daniel in the viewfinder. He didn't move, though he surely saw me out of the corner of his eye. I took that for permission.

At the camera's snick, Daniel turned back to me, giving me his full attention again. "You still know when to take a picture, don't you?"

With heat in my cheeks, I put the camera aside.

"I'm not complaining." Daniel reassured me before returning to the topic at hand. "All I know is I need to stay here at home for now. It's my fault she relapsed again. I should have known better than to move out in the first place."

I wanted to protest that he couldn't have known and that it wasn't his responsibility, but I didn't think he'd be open to hearing that right now. "I'm sorry."

Daniel's eyes softened. "You keep saying that."

"Yeah, sor—" I chuckled, catching myself. "I guess I don't know what else to say."

Daniel smiled. "I know. No one does. It's okay."

Caffeine and nerves made my fingers tremble, but I gave in and reached out to squeeze his fingers. I wanted to list *all* the things I was sorry about—Nashville, choosing Adam over him, being an idiot—but I knew that wouldn't be fair to him right now.

Daniel squeezed back and then let go of my hand. He put another cookie on my plate and took a second for himself.

"Already things are better than they were. She's going back to rehab in ten days. It could have been sooner, and I'd hoped it would be, but she wanted to return to the facility where she had the best experience in the past. They didn't have an immediate opening, so we had to wait. Cooperation is better than resistance, so I agreed," he said. "At least she's back in AA and not passing out drunk on the sofa."

"She's going to AA. That's good," I murmured.

"It *should* be," he agreed. "That's where she is right now. Nadine, Minty's mom, took her so the kids and I didn't have to wait in the car out in the church parking lot. Mom can't be trusted to drive herself there and back without stopping for alcohol."

I swallowed. I'd been thinking of bringing up my mom's dependence on Valium and how she'd used it to numb her emotions throughout my life, but this with Daniel's mom seemed to be at a whole other level. She suffered from a full-on addiction and not just significant substance abuse.

"At least the kids' teachers have stopped talking about getting CPS involved now that I'm back home. So that's something."

"Wow. I'm…" I trailed off so I wouldn't say "sorry" again.

Daniel shrugged. "Yeah, it sucks. I'm not going to deny it."

"Is there anyone else who can help? Your grandparents or an aunt or uncle?"

He met my gaze and the pain in his eyes made my stomach twist. "My mom's folks are gone already, but my dad's folks live in Florida." His lips twisted. "Mom didn't want me to ask them for help. The last time she relapsed, they threatened to file for custody and take the kids down to live with them in Florida. She doesn't want that." Daniel's eyes dropped. "So…here I am."

I noticed he didn't say *he* was against that outcome for his siblings, or that he'd never allow it to happen. He'd only said his mom didn't want it.

"It's okay to ask for help. You don't have to be a hero," I reassured him.

Daniel's jaw tightened. "I'm not a hero. I'm a selfish dick. You know what I keep thinking about?" His breath came in faster, and his eyes brightened with anger. "How pissed off I am about giving up my apartment. I *liked* living in my own place. I *liked* that there weren't any little kids running around asking me where I put their clean underwear. And I *loved* not having to parent my own mother." He rubbed a hand over his eyes. "Which is how I feel when I'm here. But shit, Peter. What else was I supposed to do?"

"I get it."

"It's not about being a hero. It's about necessity."

I reached out and touched his hand again. "Your friends can

help you. *I* can help you. Just ask us for, I don't know, anything. Everyone would be happy to chip in." I was overstepping by speaking for everyone. But if Minty, Windy, Antonio, Barry and Robert knew the whole truth, I knew they'd do whatever they could for him.

Daniel's gaze darted to the window again. "Everyone has their own shit to deal with. They don't need mine, too."

"But what if they want yours?"

Daniel let out a soft, disbelieving laugh.

"I'm serious."

He rolled his shoulders. "That's nice of you, Peter, but I don't need help. Not like that." Then he huffed a bitter laugh. "Well, not anymore."

"Why?" Was it because I'd let him down so much after Nashville that he didn't trust me? And why should he?

But that wasn't it at all.

"Because I didn't do what my mom asked. She's going to rehab. And the week after she goes? My grandparents are coming up for Ken and Paul." He glanced toward the door leading to the downstairs. "I haven't told them yet, and *she* sure as hell won't be the one to tell them. I won't let her. She'll twist it."

"Oh." I blinked. "Wow."

"Yeah. I'm not looking forward to breaking the news."

My heart ached for him. I couldn't imagine what he must be feeling. "How long will they have to live with them?"

"I don't know. A few months minimum? Maybe forever." Another bitter snort escaped. "Is it terrible that I hope, for their sakes, it's forever?"

"No."

"I feel like I'm letting them down."

"You're not."

"I am, but I'm not ready to be anyone's father. I'm just a kid myself. I love them both, but I'm not doing them any favors by trying to be something to them that I'm not." His voice grew husky. "Like Paul said, I'm not his father. I want to go back to being their brother. I want to go back to being *me*."

I put my hands out to him, palms up, inviting him to take them. "I understand."

Daniel took my hands, and we sat in silence for a few moments. When he tugged his hands back, he went on, "Also, I'm not helping either of them by letting them stay in Mom's orbit. My grandparents have the time and resources to dedicate to them."

Daniel sipped his coffee again, taking another bite of cookie. "Besides, my grandparents will be able to enforce good boundaries with my mother, too. When she's out of rehab, and she wants the kids back, they'll have the fortitude to fight her if that's not the right thing for Paul and Ken. I can't fight my own mother…" He gave a sad, aching laugh. "I can't do that. This is better. For everyone."

I still wanted to help if I could. "Until then, which days can I help you with Kennedy and Paul?"

"Thanks, but that's not necessary."

"I swear I'm good with kids. Maybe. Well, I can probably keep them from dying." Heat rose in my cheeks. "That's what a babysitter does, right?"

Daniel's mouth cracked into a helpless smile. He put his warm hands over mine this time. "It's sweet you want to help, but let's get real. Right now, the kids are angry and scared." He flicked a considering glance up at the ceiling. "Well, maybe not Kennedy, but Paul is. I can't put you in a position where you'd have to deal with the emotional fallout of what's going on in their heads. It wouldn't be fair to them or to you."

"But—"

Daniel didn't let me speak. "I need to stay close to home right now anyway. Besides, you're going to have plenty to deal with soon, aren't you? What with starting college and juggling your job." He sighed. "So, go be a college freshman and have fun, okay? I've got this."

I turned my hands around and captured his fingers in mine again. "Now you sound like Bobby. 'Don't want your help, kid. Go have fun. Kiss boys. Party down.'"

Daniel tugged his hands back and rubbed his face. "Peter, why are you really here today?"

Once again, hope peeked out of its hiding place in my heart. "You invited me," I reminded him. "And I want to help you."

Daniel let out a long breath. "I think we should cut to the chase. What do *you* want from *me?* Because I have nothing to give you right now. I'm running on empty, and if you need an ego boost after spending time with Adam, I'm sorry. I can't be that for you."

His words kicked the breath out of me. "No. That's not it."

Daniel's brow lifted.

My throat went tight. "I want to make up for what happened before."

I meant something so much bigger than that. I wanted to make up for the entire last year of my *life*, for who I'd been to him and Leslie, *and* for what I'd done to them both. But I also needed to find a way to prove it all to *myself*—not only to him, but to me. This wasn't just about Daniel. It was about being the person I wanted to be.

So maybe I *was* being selfish in a way. I wanted to be a better man, and, yes, eventually, I wanted to be with Daniel again, but I wanted to earn him.

"You don't have to make up for not wanting to be with me," Daniel said. "I'm a big boy. I can handle it."

"I want us to be close again," I said, hoping he could sense the truth in my words. "We had a good friendship. It means—*you* mean—a lot to me."

Standing up, Daniel carried the plate of uneaten cookies over to the counter and wrapped them in aluminum foil, tossing the bundle in a floral cookie jar. My heart throbbed. Was this my cue to go? Were we through here? He didn't say anything at all.

"You don't want that?" I asked.

Daniel let out a long breath, turning to me with a steady, honest gaze. "I appreciate what you're doing, but I don't have time to try to be friends again right now. If you want to take on Bobby's care when he's released, I'd appreciate that. But anything else—even offers to help—is more than I can deal with."

Sweat gathered at my forehead. A hot flash of embarrassment struck me, and with a sharp twist of pain, the hope hiding in my heart shriveled up and died. I'd ruined everything. I didn't get to just get it all back because I wanted it. Hadn't I learned that lesson yet? Hadn't Adam's selfishness taught me anything?

Still, some angry part of me wanted to ask why he'd invited me over then. If this was what he'd wanted to say, he could've said it over the phone. I opened my mouth to tell him he might not have time for his friends, but his friends had time for him. But I closed it again. Was this why Minty wasn't here supporting his "best friend?" Did Daniel push people away when he needed them most? Should I ignore his protests the way we often ignored Bobby's?

Still, Daniel had made his position clear.

Nodding, I stood. "All right, I get it. I'm sorry. I'll take care of Bobby for you, and that's all. I promise. I won't ask for more." The coffee had left a bitter taste on my tongue, and it tasted a lot like shame. I pushed up the sleeves of my cardigan and reached for my camera. "I'm sorry if I've made things harder for you. I should go."

As I started out of the breakfast nook and lifted my camera strap over my head, Daniel's gaze locked on to my left arm.

Chapter Two

Flushing, I rushed to push my cardigan sleeve down again, covering the mottled bruise, but he shook his head. "Don't." His voice was soft now, all the stern dismissal from before draining away.

I stood still, not sure what he wanted from me. I swallowed hard as he came around the counter.

Lifting my arm up between us, he pushed back my sleeve with gentle fingers, so we could both see the purpling bruises on my wrist. In the warm light from the windows, they looked worse than ever.

"What happened?" His voice shook as his fingers trailed over the evidence of Adam's angry grip. "Minty?"

I shook my head.

"Who then?"

My breath quivered. "Adam."

His jaw set in an ugly way I'd never seen before. "When?"

"Friday."

Then, with a gentleness that made my knees weak, Daniel's fingers traced over the marks, leaving tingles in the wake of his touch. Tension crept into my throat and chest as I huffed out a rough laugh. "It's nothing. If I hadn't made him…" I wasn't going to make my time here today about me. That wasn't why I'd come. "Never mind. I'm fine."

Daniel's eyes flew from my wrist to my face. "It's not your fault he hurt you." His voice was scratchy with anger.

Maybe not, but there were plenty of things that *were* my fault in one way or another. "I provoked him."

Shaking his head, Daniel pulled me into a hug. My camera dug into us, and I didn't wrap my arms around him in return. Daniel turned his head toward my neck and breathed in my scent, like I'd done to him before. I put my hands against his sides, ready to push him away, but I didn't. My breath quickened, and my head spun with confusion.

These mixed signals weren't like him. The Daniel I knew was straightforward and clearheaded. What was I supposed to make of the push-and-pull treatment he was giving me right now? I'd had enough of that kind of thing from Adam over the last year.

I pushed out of his embrace. "I should go," I said again, adjusting my camera and not meeting his eyes.

"Don't leave." I met his gaze, heart lifting to see real contrition there. "I'm sorry. I was being a dick just now," Daniel whispered, keeping a hand on my shoulder. "Call it a defense mechanism. I'm sorry." He touched my arm again, frowning at the bruises. "Stay, okay? Stay and talk to me."

"I didn't come here to dump my problems on you," I insisted. "I don't need an ego boost, or whatever you thought was the reason I wanted to see you. I came here because I want to help *you*."

Daniel stroked his fingertips over my cheek before sliding around to curl his fingers into my hair. He pressed our foreheads together. Another shiver went through me before he released his hold with a sad smile. "Thank you for wanting to help, Peter. I'm sorry about what I said. Stay longer?"

I hesitated. I *wanted* to stay, but I didn't know what to think of his sudden change of heart. "You really want me to?"

Daniel nodded, guiding me to sit back down in the nook. I slid in and removed the camera from around my neck again, placing it on the table by my half-empty coffee mug. I'd come here to get everything out on the table with him. Was he ready to do that?

Daniel scooted onto the bench next to me this time, instead of reclaiming his prior spot across the table. The place where our thighs touched captured my attention—we were *so* close. Memories of how it'd felt to press against him on the dance floor at The Slide and Tilt-a-Whirl, the scent of his skin, and the way he'd handled me that night in Nashville, taking care of me in bed without a selfish bone in his body, all rushed through me. I'd been an idiot to walk away from him like I had.

"Daniel…" I murmured, as he traced a finger across the back of my injured hand where it was stretched flat on the table. His touch sent more shivers over me, as he slipped his fingers up to skim the bruises marring my wrist again.

Would he think I was just here now because things didn't work out with Adam?

"I'm sorry. About what happened. The choices I made," I said. "I really am."

"You hurt me a lot in Nashville," he whispered after a few quiet beats. He kept smoothing his fingertips over my tender arm like he could erase the marks there with his affectionate touches. Meeting my gaze, the amber in his brown eyes glowed in the light from the windows. "I'm scared to trust you now. But that's no excuse for being unkind like I was a few minutes ago. That wasn't fair to either of us, and I shouldn't have acted like that."

My eyes stung. "I'm sorry. I know I keep apologizing for everything, but I'm so sorry about how things went down between us."

Daniel nodded, pulled his hand away from my wrist, and closed his eyes. When he opened them again, he spoke with that honest clarity I'd always admired in him, maybe even loved. "I *want* to trust you. It would be so nice to slip back into caring for you that way. It'd make everything I'm dealing with here *feel* so much easier." His lips quirked. "Feeling like that about you? Having you around? It'd give me something to look forward to, at least."

My pulse jumped. "I'm going to *prove* you can trust me again."

Daniel tweaked one of my curls and then sighed. "You have no idea how much I'd like that."

"Then count on it."

His gaze darted down to linger on my lips. His breath hitched, and I felt the familiar draw of attraction between us, urging me to lean in and kiss him. But kisses wouldn't make him trust me again.

Daniel's attention moved back to my bruised wrist. "This looks really bad, Peter. Tell me what happened?"

"It was fucked up down there." I kept the words quiet. "In Atlanta, I mean. Like, everything was *so* fucked up."

"What happened?" Daniel turned to cup my cheek. He examined my face as though looking for more damage.

The heavy memories didn't mesh well with the butterflies in my stomach. I moved his hand off my cheek but continued to hold it. He let me. "We had a fight."

"About his girlfriend?"

"No. About condoms. He didn't want to use one."

A dark expression slammed across Daniel's face. "But you did, right?"

"No." I closed my eyes remembering my cold rage, how the heat of lust had iced over.

"Peter—" Daniel's voice went tight with anxiety.

"No, I mean, we didn't even *have* sex. I told him no, and we fought about it."

Daniel cursed. "With AIDS, we have to be safe every time. No exceptions. How can he justify that?"

"I think it was a test. He accused me of sleeping with someone else this summer."

Daniel let out a sharp exhale.

Heat rushed through me, as I said, "I guess I kind of did. You and me at the motel."

"We made out, got off together. That's all."

"That's *all?*"

Daniel squeezed my shoulder. "Don't take it like that. What happened meant a lot to me. You know it did."

"I know it's too late for me to say this and for you to believe me, but it meant a lot to me, too."

"I believe you." Daniel cleared his throat. "Did he explain *why* he didn't want to use a condom?"

I choked on a laugh. "He said we were monogamous—me, him, and Leslie."

Daniel's brows rose. "Wow. That's one way to look at it. But I'd sure like to—" He bit off the rest of his thought.

"It's okay. Say whatever you want."

Daniel touched my wrist again. "I only care that you're safe. You are. Right?"

"I am. I'm safe."

"You didn't have sex without a condom?" he confirmed.

"No."

My mind flashed to the night Adam had spent with me the weekend before I went down to visit him in Atlanta. Despite his assurances, I still had a sick suspicion he hadn't used a condom the last time we'd fucked. I'd even counted the used ones in the trash, making sure they'd matched the number of times we'd had sex, and they had. But still… I couldn't shake the feeling.

Daniel and I were quiet for a few moments. The air between us grew humid with our shared breaths. I wanted to lean closer, and I wanted to move away. The push-and-pull was back, but this time it was on my side.

Daniel broke the silence. He shifted away, giving us space to breathe. "You said he accused you of sleeping with someone else while he was away. If he felt threatened by another guy—"

By you, I thought. *And he* should *have been threatened by you. You're everything he isn't.*

"—he might have seen going bare as a way to tie you to him."

"Yeah. I think that's what the condom thing was all about. A test. Like if I said okay and I let him, then I was still his."

Daniel nodded.

"But I'm not *his.*"

"No."

"And neither is Leslie. We're human beings, not possessions."

"Is he using a condom with Leslie?"

"No." I rolled my eyes. "She's on the pill. But she has no idea what he's up to behind her back."

Daniel's brows quirked. "Do you think you should tell her?"

I squirmed, remembering Mike's phone call insisting that if things weren't over with me and Adam, then he'd have to tell Leslie the truth about us.

Should someone tell Leslie? That was the question of the hour, and everyone wanted the answer. "I don't know. He loves her. I think now that we're over…" I thought it might sound arrogant, but I said it anyway. "I think it was just me he wanted. I don't think he's sleeping with anyone else."

Daniel's eyes softened. "So you still trust him?"

I shook my head. "No."

Lying for so long had stolen my ability to know who to trust. For that matter, could I even trust myself? I didn't know anymore. I'd walked away from Daniel for Adam like an idiot. I needed to prove I was trustworthy to myself as much as to anyone else.

"No, I don't." I covered my eyes with my trembling hand, and Daniel squeezed my shoulder again. I hadn't realized how talking about Adam would affect me, but my whole body shook.

"But you trust him with *her* safety?"

I dropped my hand. "With me out of the picture, maybe he can just be happy?" I had to believe it, for all our sakes.

"Why did he hurt your arm? Was it over the condom?"

I sighed. "No. After our argument about the condom, we went out with the group to Fusion."

"The gay club? Interesting choice."

"Yeah, Leslie wanted to go. I think she was trying to get me to out myself."

Daniel blew out a slow breath. "Damn."

"So—I did. I outed myself."

Daniel lifted his brows. "And how did you do that?"

"I didn't make out with anyone. I just danced with some guys. But you'd have thought I'd sucked them off on the dance floor with the way Adam freaked out. He was so angry." I swallowed hard. "He grabbed my arm and wouldn't let go. Dragged me off the dance floor." I rubbed the bruises. "Then he twisted it to keep me from getting away."

Daniel's eyes flashed. "Has he ever done something like that before?"

"No." I was back in the moment, back in the club. I could feel Adam's hand around my wrist, see his livid eyes. "Our friend, Mike, and some of the people at the club stepped in. It was over after that." I didn't want to tell him about the additional words we'd had back at Adam's dorm. The way Adam had cried. How he'd outed himself to Mike. The way he'd bargained and begged. That was Adam's pain, not mine.

"So, you left?" He pushed the mess of curls off my forehead.

I nodded. "I didn't just leave. I broke up with him."

Daniel put his arm around my shoulders and tugged me until I leaned against him, my head resting on his chest and his chin on the top of my head.

"I know I messed up with you," I whispered.

He squeezed me but didn't deny my words.

I took a tight breath. I didn't want to lean on Daniel. This wasn't what I was here to do. He needed someone to support *him*, not someone to weigh him down further. I pushed my fingertips against my eyelids and willed myself not to cry. I would *not* do that to him.

"Hey," Daniel said. "It's okay if you're upset. It'd be weird if you weren't."

I swallowed my feelings down. "I don't want to be," I said, speaking through a constricted throat. "He's *such* an asshole. Why am I so stupid?"

"You aren't stupid."

"Ha! I am!" I pushed far enough away from him to get a good look at his face. He gazed back at me with sweet compassion. "You and all our friends knew it was going to turn out this way."

Daniel's expression softened even more. "None of us wanted that. We care about you."

I yearned to tell Daniel how much I wished I'd made a different choice that morning in the motel parking lot in Nashville, but I kept my mouth shut. I didn't get to say that to him yet.

"Has he contacted you?" Daniel asked.

"No." But if I knew Adam, he probably would. I wasn't looking forward to that.

Daniel stroked my hair. It popped right back up into place as soon as his hand moved away. "Will he come up here? Force the issue?"

"Maybe? I don't know. He might." My stomach tightened. For all I knew, he was at my house right now banging on my front door.

"And if he does show up to beg forgiveness? Will you take him back?"

"No. It's over. I can't do it anymore." I didn't want to see Adam now or ever. "He never planned to break up with her, Daniel. I get that now. If he could have his way? We'd be living like this for the next fifty years. The two of them would make a nice, little family and I'd be the kids' Uncle Peter—the guy their dad fucks secretly. I can't do that."

Daniel wrapped both arms around me and held me close. A year ago, I'd sat in a booth in Chalky 'N' Joe's with Adam, and he'd held me in almost the same way. The memory bit into me, but I let the hurt merge with the old pain I'd already grieved. I also kept it to myself.

Daniel released me, leaning back and attempting to smooth my hair down again. I let him, but I was disappointed in myself for letting Daniel take care of me. I'd come here to take care of *him*.

"I want to be a better person than I have been," I whispered. "For a long time now, I've hated myself for what we were doing to Leslie."

"Peter, you don't need to hate yourself."

"But I'm not that kind of person!" I wanted him to understand this more than anything. "I'm not someone who betrays a friend like that."

"I know."

Words came out of my mouth so quickly I didn't stop to breathe. They'd been forming for days, months even, and I needed them out of me. "Except I *am* that person. And I *did* betray her. So maybe you shouldn't trust me, Daniel. I don't trust myself, even though I'm trying. I want to be a good friend to you, and, if I'm being honest, I want so much more than that. But I don't deserve it. I mean, look what I'm doing right now! Laying all this on you is selfish. *I'm* selfish. Just like Minty said."

"Peter, I—"

When he didn't continue, I looked up. He had so much affection in his expression, and I was ashamed by how grateful I was to see it there. I knew he cared for me. I didn't want to lead him on, and I *was* a mess, but I wanted to be near him. I wanted whatever he had to offer right now. I'd even take the door if that was all he had to give.

"So I know I'm a dick. I'm not delusional about that," I said. "Daniel?"

"Yeah?"

"You should listen to your friends about me. Everything Minty said to you after Nashville? It's true."

Daniel's lips twitched up. "Peter, you're so hard on yourself. Everyone makes mistakes. Remember what I told you about Margaret? How I slept with her to try to 'fix' myself? High school is a terrible time to be gay. It's a terrible time for almost everyone, I think. But for a queer kid? It's hell."

I blew out a long breath, not sure I wanted off the hook for any of it. "Yeah."

"Speaking of Minty, he was a wreck back then, too," Daniel offered.

"Back when?"

"High school."

"And he's not a wreck now?"

Daniel laughed. "Yes, but in high school, he wasn't even Minty. He was Mitchell, and it was awful what they did to him. He couldn't hide himself. He was always a target."

"So you took him under your wing?"

Daniel shrugged. "After how I hurt Margaret, I felt like I had a penance to pay. Then I kind of fell for him. Not like *in love*—he's not my type—but you've met him. He's pretty lovable."

I thought of Minty with his pink tank top slipping off one shoulder, his tight jean skirt riding high up his thighs, and his fists up, ready to beat me to a pulp for hurting his friend.

"He's kind of scary."

Daniel laughed again. "I'm sorry he threatened you."

I flushed. "Yeah, well, he needed to defend your honor, I guess."

"Makes sense after I spent all of high school defending *him*. And he *does* know Aikido, by the way. He's not harmless, but he is cute." Daniel's eyes clouded. "I'm sorry, though. He shouldn't have treated you like that."

"No, he was right. That's what I'm trying to tell you. I'm not a good person." I met his eyes and swallowed. "But I want to be. I want to be more like you."

"I'm not a good person. I'm a mess too." Daniel put his hand on the back of my head and dragged me forward into another hug. He kissed my temple, and whispered in my ear, "I'm proud of you."

"You are?"

"I am *really* proud of you. It's hard to leave your first love." Daniel let go enough to gaze into my eyes. "It's even harder not to go back a few times."

"I already did that last year. This time it'll stick."

He nodded. "Stay strong. You'll make it through this."

A woman's voice cut in, "Danny, I'm back. Oh, who's this?"

Daniel turned away and stood up, rubbing the palms of his hands against his jeans. "Hey, Mom. Where's Nadine?"

"She dropped me off."

"How was the meeting?"

"Good."

Daniel's mom had wavy, strawberry-blond hair and was the epitome of a wealthy, well-dressed woman. She was beautiful in the way of someone who'd had work done on their face, but her brown eyes caught my attention the most. They were weary and miserable. I wished I could snap them in a quick picture, but that would be rude. She approached, smiling, but it didn't seem to touch her pain. She put out her hand. "I'm Marlene, Danny's mother."

I stood to shake, finding her fingers cold.

Daniel introduced me. "Mom, this is Peter Mandel."

"Oh, your new friend," she said, and lifted her brow, giving Daniel a look. She clearly assumed I was more than just a friend. "I've heard Danny mention you. I see he's being a good host." She smiled down at the coffee mugs.

"He is," I agreed.

"Go on and ignore me, boys. Enjoy yourselves. Darling, where are the children?"

"In the basement, watching the movies I rented for them."

She smiled, kissed his cheek, and said, "Such a good boy."

His answering smile was stiff and lacked his usual warmth, but she didn't seem to notice. Marlene kicked off her high heels and picked them up, holding them clutched to her side, before going to the fridge to grab a bottle of Sprite.

Daniel watched her until she left the room. He wore another dark expression, similar to the ones that had crossed his face when he heard Adam had given me the bruises.

"Everything okay?"

"Sorry. Yeah." Daniel shook himself, and then slid into the breakfast nook across from me. I wanted him back on my side where I could feel him near. But it was more than just the table causing the distance. That was plain to see.

After a few seconds of awkward silence, he sighed. "I think she's still in denial about rehab. She acts like if she just attends a few AA meetings and drinks nothing but soda for the next week, we can all pretend she didn't fall off the wagon, Grandma and Grandpa won't take the kids to Florida, and everything can go back to normal again. But that's not how it works, and I'm not ready to make nice with her. I'm still pissed."

"Ah." Here was my chance to be there for him now. "Does she know that?"

He laughed, a sharp noise that wasn't like anything I'd ever heard from him before. It was almost nasty. "Yeah, she knows. I haven't exactly been her sweet, steady Danny since I got back. I've given her my uncensored thoughts." Daniel's mouth tightened. "To which she replies with shit like, 'At AA they say your attitude is to be expected, and I just need to be patient with you while you work out your anger toward me.'" His jaw snapped shut, and he snorted.

"My mom's therapist is always telling her stuff like that, too."

"She sees one?"

"Yeah. She's abused Valium for most of my life. There was an incident in her childhood, a trauma—" I grimaced. "You don't want the details. What I'm trying to say is my mom's a denial junkie." I smiled, trying to lighten the mood. It didn't work. "She used Valium to deny I was gay, but she's in recovery now."

Daniel's brows quirked. He huffed an almost-laugh. A few quiet beats passed. "As much as I don't want to say this, I think you should go now."

"Yeah?"

"Yeah, I'm sorry, but it's time."

I didn't want to go. I still hadn't managed to convince him to let me help, other than by taking over Bobby's care. But I'd stayed for over an hour, and it felt like his mom's interruption had broken the spell. Daniel was stiff again now, and his expression was guarded. If he didn't want me to hang out any longer, then I had to respect that.

As he walked me toward the front door, Daniel's hand moved down to the small of my back. "Excited for classes to start tomorrow?"

"I guess. Anxious more than anything. Got any advice for me?"

"Not really. You'll be fine." Daniel's lips set in a straight line, and he cast a glance over his shoulder back toward the kitchen. "One of the classes I needed to move forward with my degree is only offered in the fall. Looks like I'm going to miss it."

"What's that mean for you?" I asked.

"It means my graduation is pushed back. Again."

"I thought the board of your dad's company was eager for you to get the degree and start working?"

"They are. But, funnily enough, Mom's addiction doesn't give a shit about that." Daniel clenched his jaw tight. "Anyway, enough about her. I'm glad you came over today."

"Thanks for inviting me."

"Will I see you again soon?"

My heart jumped. "Do you want to?"

Daniel laughed, his lashes lowering on his cheek. "Yeah, I do." He took hold of my hand and twined our fingers together. "I think you're right. I do need people around that I can count on. Is that you, Peter?"

"It's me," I assured him. I'd make *sure* it was me.

Daniel walked me out onto the front porch.

About five hundred feet out from the house, a field stretched down to the bend in the river. Closer to the water, I could see a circle of benches had been cut from massive logs. In the center was a large black mark of scorched earth, marring the green lawn with the remnants of a previous night's fire. I aimed my camera and fired off a few quick shots.

Daniel noticed. "After this is all over—once Mom's in rehab, and the kids are with my grandparents—I thought I'd ask people over to have a bonfire night. Will you come? I don't know if you like that kind of thing."

A weird bubble rose inside me and burst. Relief. Everything had changed. I'd dumped Adam, and I'd promised Daniel to be his friend above all else. "Of course. Who doesn't like bonfires?"

"People who are afraid of fire?"

I laughed and ran my hand up his arm. His bicep was strong beneath my touch. "I'll be there. Duh."

Daniel smiled, and I took a few photos of of him with the sunlight in his hair, reflecting off the scruff of his unshaven face. I took one final snapshot of him looking simultaneously amused and sad, and then I let my camera drop. It was time to go.

"I'll be there," I called back to him as I headed toward my car. "I wouldn't miss it."

I meant that in more ways than one. I was going to be there for Daniel. I wasn't going to miss this opportunity to be his friend again.

In my rearview mirror, Daniel stood barefoot with his hands in his pockets. The hope in my heart came out of hiding and glowed like the late afternoon sun.

Bright and warm. Like him.

✦   ✦   ✦

FORTY MINUTES LATER, I was home, and the house was deserted. There was a note on the kitchen counter in my mother's handwriting.

Adam called three times. I told him if he called again, I'd have him charged with assault for what he did to you. That scared him good. Don't answer the phone for a few days. Let the machine get it. He'll move on. Your father and I are going out to dinner. We'll be back by nine or so.

I wadded up the note and threw it in the trash. I didn't want to ruin the glow of a possible new beginning with Daniel by calling Adam. I wanted to take my camera out and snap photos of beautiful things. But I knew Adam well enough to be certain he wasn't going to move on that easily. Unless I told him again, in no uncertain terms, that I was done, unless I added a threat to the mix, he'd just keep calling or coming around.

I steeled myself to dial his dorm room number. Pressing the

receiver to my ear, I slid down the kitchen wall to sit on the floor. I wrapped my arms around my middle to hold in my quivering, nervous guts, hoping to get the machine. I didn't ever want to hear his voice again.

"Hello?"

"It's me," I said.

"Peter! Thank you for calling me. Thank you, thank, *thank you*," he babbled, a wet edge to his voice, like he'd been crying. Had he ever stopped? "Please just hear me out, okay? We can—"

I squeezed myself tighter, interrupting him. "No. Stop calling me." I swallowed thickly. "Never call me again."

Adam plowed on like I hadn't said anything. "We can make this work, Eater. I know we can. Just listen to me. Please. *Please*. I love you, and—"

"Stop talking," I bit out. "We're done. Got it?"

He went silent, even his breath cutting off. I was torn between hanging up and asking if he was still there when he whispered, "How can we work this out if you won't listen to me?"

I closed my eyes, leaning my head against the kitchen wall. "*You* listen to *me*. I need you to understand this, Adam. We aren't working anything out. It's over."

"I'm going to change, Peter." Adam's voice broke, and he started to cry. "I'm going to be a better person for you. I swear. I just need a little more time, another year, and I promise to make this right between us."

I rubbed my forehead with shaking fingers. I had to stay strong. I couldn't let him get under my skin.

"Please, Peter, *please*!" Adam begged. The desperation in his voice embedded in my heart like a shard of glass. "I need you."

I remembered him grabbing and twisting my wrist at Fusion, Leslie's troubled blue eyes, and the sheer misery of the last time we'd been together. I hardened myself. "No. The thing is *I* don't need *you.* I'm happier without you. Understand?"

My throat felt tight, and my eyes burned. I'd been so in love with him once. I'd let him convince me to listen to and believe in him so many times before. It'd all come to this anyway. It'd all come to shit.

I forced myself to make it as final as possible. "I learned this summer I'm happier when I'm not with you. You make me *miserable.* You ruin things. You take love and make it ugly. I don't want you anymore."

"What does that mean? This summer you learned…" He whispered, "You fucked around on me?"

I gripped the phone. "Yeah, I did."

Adam's gasp of pain was guttural. "You *did?* With who?"

I didn't owe him details. I didn't want to mar the memory of my night with Daniel by telling Adam about it, but he had to know the truth. He had to understand. This wasn't just about him and me, anymore. Thanks to him, it never had been, and now, thanks to me, he'd get a taste of how that felt.

I spoke as steadily as possible, keeping my tone quiet and cold. "With a guy I met this summer. A guy I care about. A guy I want to be with instead of you."

The phone clattered on his end, and I heard retching noises.

My heart hammered. I hated the bright satisfaction that pierced a dark part of me. I considered hanging up, leaving him with those words as my final say on our disaster of a relationship.

Instead, I listened to him puke and cry, examining the nasty feeling in my chest. What was this miasma of sneering pride and wrenching pain? Did it have a name? How could I take a picture of it? It was so ugly, sharp, and mean.

Eventually, he came back on the line, his breathing ragged. I braced myself.

"Who?" he whispered, voice raw.

"It doesn't matter. I don't want you anymore. That's all you need to know."

"That's bullshit!"

My stomach twisted, and my heart tore open. "It's the truth."

"All this because of a fucking condom? Dammit, Peter, stop this, okay? This is ridiculous. You're being insane."

"It's not…it's not just because—"

"I'll use condoms with both you *and* Leslie from now on, okay? Just please don't leave me." More rough, broken sobs tumbled out of the receiver, and the ice around my heart started to melt.

I was glad he was in Atlanta, three hours away. If he'd been in his room down the street, I wasn't sure I could've stopped myself from running down there, taking him in my arms, and petting his hair.

"Please, Peter," he begged again, sobbing. "Please."

"Adam, it's not about the condoms. Be happy with Leslie. She's a good person, and she loves you." I cooled my voice to ice again. "We're done. Don't call me again. Ever."

I hung up before he could say another word. I had to get off the line before I let his love and my sick need for it pull me under.

Chapter Three

THE NEXT MORNING the sun rose early, and so did I.

I'd tossed and turned most of the night. Adam's broken voice on the phone haunted me, but I wasn't going to let him ruin more of my life. It was my first day of classes and I was determined to be excited, so I focused on that, with the occasional fantasy about what might happen with Daniel in the future creeping in as well.

My first day as a freshman at the University of Tennessee began at eight o'clock sharp. It started with Psychology 110 and continued until noon with Biology. I was most excited about my first college-level photography class after that, and then I'd head over to Robert's for a few hours of work, before calling it a day.

I showered and shaved before struggling for far too long to get my contacts in for some annoying reason. After dressing in comfortable jeans and a soft, green T-shirt I'd picked up at Target, I dithered over which camera to take. I decided on the Minolta. Checking out the window for an indication of the weather, I found a bright, cloudless dawn, so I popped in 200 speed film—good for daylight and decent for indoors with the right camera settings.

Heading downstairs, my nerves jangled with each step, a kind of electric anxiety built into the soles of my Chuck Taylors. I'd been on campus a thousand times over the years. I'd spent many sick days on the floor of my dad's office in McClung Tower. But this would be my first time as a student.

I chewed on my lip, biting back a nervous smile.

In the kitchen, Mom stood by the stove, wearing an old-fashioned white linen nightgown—she must have been working on a Regency romance novel—and staring down at the griddle pan. Her dark brown hair hung in messy hanks, and a cup of coffee steamed in her hand. Round tan splotches of batter indicated she was making pancakes.

"Morning," I said, crossing to the table. I opened my canvas backpack and fit my camera at the bottom. "What are you doing?"

Dad was the cook in our house, if you could call his microwave meals and Ragu spaghetti sauce cooking, so the sight of Mom using the griddle was unnerving.

"Making pancakes." She smiled at me, her eyes still sleepy. Then she turned back to the griddle and stared down at the pancakes with concentrated effort.

"Uh, Mom? I think those are burned."

"I know, Peter. I know."

She scraped them up and threw them into the sink. Then she turned off the stove and put the griddle on the back burner. Leaning against the counter, she rubbed a hand over her tired face.

I glanced at the clock. I didn't have time to offer to make them for her. I suspected she was trying to do something nice for me anyway. "I'm just going to have cereal," I said. "Stomach's too excited for more."

Yawning, she dumped the griddle in the sink and turned on the cold water. Steam billowed up, and she shut the water off fast.

"It's the thought that counts," she said, like she always did when she failed at being helpful. "You're excited, huh? It's going to be a new adventure."

"Yep."

Mom came to stand next to me as I poured milk over a bowl of Lucky Charms, yawning as she examined me from head to toe.

"You look nice." She ran her hands through my hair, trying to smooth my wild curls with her fingers.

"Leave it," I said. "It's going to do what it wants. I'm giving up."

Without protest, Mom sat down on the stool across from me, sipping her coffee. I thought about getting a mug for myself but decided a cup of anxiety was the last thing I needed. "So, Peter," she began in the tone of voice that let me know she planned to 'parent' me now. "Where were you yesterday? You didn't leave a note, and I was worried."

"At my friend Daniel's house." I met her considering gaze, holding it while I took several bites of cereal. I hoped my expression discouraged questions.

"Ah, Daniel."

I nodded.

"The boy from that phone call where you were all, 'Yes, I'll do *anything* you want, I'd *love* to, and when can I start?' That Daniel?"

I rolled my eyes. "Yeah."

"This is the boy from Nashville, right?" She waved a hand at her face, reminding me of the beard burn I'd sported. "Is he your new boyfriend?"

I shook my head. "We're friends."

"But you like him?"

"I just broke up with Adam three days ago. Give me a week or two."

"Mm. But hadn't you broken up with Adam in your heart a long time before that?"

I shoved cereal into my mouth so I didn't have to talk. I wasn't going to get into my relationship issues with her. When I had something to tell her about the guys in my life, I would. Until then, I wasn't going to gab to my mom about it all, like a heartsick kid.

I didn't have time anyway. Parking wasn't going to be easy to come by on the first day of classes. I should have grabbed a ride in with my dad this morning after all.

"You don't have to tell me about your romantic life," she said, sipping her coffee again, as if she hadn't just pried into it. "That's fine."

"There's nothing to tell, Mom. He's a friend going through a hard time, and I want to help him."

Her lips curled up at the edges. I reviewed my words and rolled my eyes. I was grateful she kept her mouth shut. I didn't want to hear what I knew she was thinking.

When I was almost done with my Lucky Charms she said, "I have something for you."

"A first day of college present? Tell me it's not another safer-gay-sex pamphlet."

She laughed, but it lacked any spark. "No. It's..." She rose and grabbed a big manila envelope from the edge of the counter by the toaster. With a nervous expression, she pushed it into my hands. "It's this."

I took in the size and shape of it, noting it was thick and rather heavy. "What is it?"

"It's everything I have from or about my brother George."

I started to open it, but she put her hand on mine. "I'd rather you looked at it with your father. I'm not ready to deal with what's in there."

"Why? Is it bad?"

Surely, she didn't have something awful like crime scene photos from his death or autopsy reports. But this was my mom, and she was weird, so there was no telling.

She shook her head. "No. It's just...I can't think about him too much." Her dark eyes grew wet as she touched my cheek. "You look a lot like him." Pulling her hand back, she tapped the envelope I was holding. "You'll see."

"Ah. Why now?" I asked, holding up the envelope. "I mean, why are you giving it to me now?"

"My therapist suggested it. She said we should look through it all together, but…" she shook her head. "I can't. I don't want to."

I didn't know what to say. Time ticked away, and I knew I'd need to leave soon. As I opened my mouth to tell her I had to go, she spoke again.

"This is the only way you'll ever know anything about your uncle at all, and, well… He deserves to be remembered." Mom leaned forward to kiss my forehead. "You're going to be late."

I glanced at the time. "Shit."

Shoving some of Mom's string cheese in my backpack to eat as a snack later, I paused on my way out the door. "Mom?" I held up the envelope. "If you ever do want to look at this stuff together, I'd like that."

Mom bowed her head. "Maybe one day. Now go. Don't be late to your first class as a college student."

✧　✧　✧

SITUATED ON THE outskirts of downtown Knoxville, the University of Tennessee campus was already bustling with commuters and students by the time I arrived and found parking.

As I walked to my first class, a few Humanities professors, friends of my father, called out to me. I waved but kept my head down. I didn't have time to chat, and I didn't want to be Abe Mandel's son right now. I wanted to be Peter, freshman on campus, lame for the usual reasons, and no one special at all.

Ducking into the Austin Peay building for Psychology 110, I sat down in the back of the enormous theater-style classroom filled with students.

As I readied my notebook and pencil, anonymity rolled over me like a blanket of peace. After the tiny classes at Kingsley, I'd forgotten what it was like to sit in the middle of a group of people and not have a single one of them know who I was or even give enough of a damn to find out. We were here to learn, not get into each other's business.

In an instant, I saw it all as a photograph: me in the center of the classroom, the focus tight, and the others blurred. Alone in a crowd. A different kind of quiet.

All at once the seat on my left was filled. I glanced over to find a small, dark-haired girl with glasses. She smiled, and as I opened my mouth to introduce myself, a very loud voice spoke directly into my right ear.

"Peter, you bitch!"

Jerking around and rubbing at my ear, I blinked in shock as Minty dropped into the seat on the other side.

He arranged a fresh notebook, four pencils, and a bottle of Snapple on his desk. Wearing a spring green, feminine-cut short-sleeve sweater and navy corduroy pants over pointy, high-heeled boots, he was a rainbowfish in a sea of plaid flannel gloom.

My fingers itched to dig into my backpack for my camera to capture his shine.

Glancing around, I found all eyes were now on Minty, and thus on me too. If I'd been treasuring my anonymity, it was gone. Still, I was relieved he was talking to me at all. The last time I'd seen him, he'd wanted to kick my ass.

"Uh, hi. Why are you in this class?" I asked, watching as he lined his pencils up lengthwise on his desk, each straight and perfectly sharpened.

"Same as you. Gotta have it to graduate, duh."

"But you're a Junior."

"You know I always arrive late to a party so I can make an entrance." Minty smiled and ran his fingers through his white-blond hair. Girls stared, boys squirmed. The discomfort in the room was palpable.

As nervous as the attention made me, Minty was undeniably a sight to behold. He reached into his own backpack and pulled out a compact mirror, checking his teeth, and then blowing a kiss to himself. I unzipped my backpack, but my camera was at the bottom. I'd have to empty everything out to get to it. I zipped it closed again.

"Who's your friend?" Minty asked, nodding to the girl on my left. He didn't wait for an answer, sticking out his hand, wrist limp and fingers dangling. "I'm Minty Arnold."

"Jennifer Alvarez." She took his hand and gave it a firm shake.

"Peter Mandel," I offered.

Jennifer's pink, lip-glossed smile stretched across the bottom half of her face. "Nice to meet you both." Her expression didn't waver as she asked Minty with no animosity or meanness, "I love your sweater. Did you get it in the women's section at Proffitts?"

Minty grinned. "As a matter of fact, I did. They're on sale now. Thirty-five percent off for fall." He darted a glance my way. "It was a splurge."

Emboldened, Jennifer leaned across my desk, her elbow resting on my notebook, and said, "I hope I'm not being rude—"

"Oh, the rudest questions always start just like that," Minty said. "I hope I'm not being rude, but are you a fag? *Yes.* Hope I'm not rude, but are you a fudge-packer? *You know it.* That kind of thing." Despite his words, he twinkled at her. "But go on. Scandalize me."

She cleared her throat. "I just want to get it right. My friend Narissa has a brother who's becoming a woman. I mean, I guess she has a sister." She nodded. "Yes, a sister." She focused on Minty again. "Are you like that?"

"No," I answered for him, but Minty put his hand on my arm and squeezed hard enough that I shut up.

"Not really," Minty said, looking thoughtful. "The country boy in me won't just lay down and die. Most days I feel girly, and I like exploring that."

"So you're called 'he?'"

"Yes," Minty said. "But if I look exceptionally pretty, 'hey, girl, you're looking hot,' is always fine with me."

I blinked, thinking about Jennifer's questions and his answers. I'd never thought to ask. I wondered if anyone else ever had. I'd known there were people who wanted to change their gender, but I'd never considered that for Minty.

Class hadn't even started, and I was already learning new things at college.

Jennifer and Minty left the topic of gender behind and resumed talking about fall sales and the best places to buy nice accessories for cheap.

I glanced at the clock, wondering where the teacher was.

Five minutes after class should have begun, a young, skinny Teaching Assistant walked in, looking harried and anxious. And a little green.

"About time," someone muttered a few rows down.

"Sorry, sorry," the TA said, coming to a halt in front of the podium. "Oh God." He cursed some more under his breath, turned around, and ran back out.

"I think he's gonna throw up." Minty picked up one of his pencils and twirled it around and around.

"He's as green as your sweater," Jennifer added. "Must be stage fright."

"Oh well. More time to gossip." Minty turned to me with a tight smile, different from the loose, friendly ones he'd shared with Jennifer, or even the sharp one he'd first given me. "So how did it go with your *boyfriend,* Peter? Was he worth breaking Daniel's heart over? Did you fuck like bunnies?"

Jennifer, who'd started skimming the first chapter of our text-book, closed it and leaned her cheek on her fist, settling in to listen. "Feel free to talk like I'm not even here."

Minty snapped his fingers in my face. "You heard the lady, go on. Did you ride the joystick of love, or what?"

I shoved his hand away. "Minty, just quit it. Okay? Not everyone needs to know my business."

Minty narrowed his eyes. "Are you going back into the closet for this guy?"

"What? No."

"Then why won't you spill?"

"We're in *class* right now. It's my private life."

Minty waved a hand at all the chatting people around us. "Show me a single person who's listening. Jennifer here doesn't count."

"Why doesn't she count?" I asked.

"Because you sat beside her."

That seemed absurd, and I *hadn't* sat beside her, she'd sat beside me. Even so, I didn't think he'd consider my opinion or arguments a valid reason not to give him the information he wanted. I went with, "I don't care. I'm not talking about it here."

Minty shrugged. "Fine, Heartbreaker. Be that way." He leaned over to whisper to Jennifer, "Peter's a little sensitive about his screwed-up love life, but he's an all-right guy."

I realized that was as close as I was going to get to an apology from him for threatening to beat me up. I was okay with that.

When the TA came in again, he managed to stay long enough to introduce himself as Donnie Huggins. He reviewed the syllabus, but kept his eyes down, not daring to send even a single glance up into the rows of students.

"Poor guy," Jennifer said. "He's a walking disaster."

"He's cute," Minty said, staring down at Donnie with glowing eyes.

I tilted my head, taking in Donnie's angular face and shaggy, brown hair. He was okay, nothing special, but Minty fell in love every day with someone new and today that someone was poor, still-green-around-the-gills, Donnie Huggins.

As soon as class was over, I swung my backpack on my shoulders and headed out. Minty clacked along behind me in his high-heeled boots, and Jennifer called a quick bye to us both before rushing off in the opposite direction for her next class.

"Where you headed now?" Minty asked, catching up.

"Biology."

"Do you have Kathleen Gregor?"

"No, some TA, I think?"

"Well, Dr. Gregor is amazing. She's my advisor. If you can drop whoever you've got and add one of her classes instead, you should."

"You're a Biology major?"

"Yeah, going into ecology. Rivers and streambeds are what I want to focus on when I get my Master's. I've got an internship pending with Dr. Gregor to be involved in her study of the flow-pattern disruption caused by dams and its effect on rare salamanders." He grinned, blue eyes shining. "God, I love pulling on some sexy rubber boots and wading out into the middle of an ice-cold mountain creek."

I imagined Minty doing just that. In my mind's eye he wore multicolored baby barrettes in his hair, a pink tank top, and massive wading boots. Would he wear a tutu, too, for extra glamor while doing science? I bet the other Biology geeks thought he was an alien from outer space. "How have we known each other all summer, and I didn't know this about you?"

"Aw, Peter, didn't you know? I'm more than just a pretty face." He batted his eyes at me before curling his fingers in a dainty wave. "Ta-ta! Off to the library to get some light reading on Aquatic Plant Evolutionary Morphology." He blew me a kiss. "See you Wednesday morning! We're going to make that sweetheart TA Donnie Huggins fall in love with me before this semester is done. Deal?"

I laughed. "Sure. Whatever you say."

The late summer heat seeped into me as I walked across the hill toward the Biology building. I ran a hand through my humidity-curled hair and knew I must look like a black-haired clown.

Five minutes into the next TA's boring review of the syllabus and after hearing her nose whistle with every other breath, I decided to look into Minty's advice to switch to Dr. Gregor's class. I didn't think I could take another hour of it, much less a whole semester.

As I watched the second hand tick around the clock on the wall, I wondered what Daniel's morning had been like. He'd probably woken early to get his sister and brother off to school, and then gone back home to make breakfast for himself.

I could picture him in his kitchen, the morning sun coming in and lighting up his face as he brewed coffee. My fingers twitched, wanting to take a picture of the image in my mind's eye.

I frowned. I had no idea what he'd do with the rest of his day. I didn't know any of his habits.

Now, Adam…

I knew all about him. I knew what to say to make him laugh until he snorted his drink out of his nose. I knew his dream car, the way he snored when he was conked out, and his favorite children's book. I knew what his mouth tasted like after he'd been sleeping, and I knew—stark and real—that I'd never have use for any of that knowledge again.

I put my head between my hands as the TA droned on.

I didn't want to think about Adam.

I didn't want to *know* him or miss him because he'd ruined it.

No. It'd always been ruined, right from the start—with the lies and the subterfuge and the bullshit. I had grieved it already. I was done. But at unexpected moments, like this one, it was still raw. It hurt to know what we'd lost.

Closing my eyes, I forced myself to think of something else. Something hopeful.

In my mind, I flipped through the photographs I'd taken of Daniel, beginning with the first, fuzzy one from the night on the hill by Ayres Hall, and ending with the as-yet-to-be-developed ones I'd snapped when I'd arrived at his house the day before.

The bell rang, and after running to the drop-add office to request that change, I was still free for twenty minutes before Photography.

Finding a pay phone near the University Center, I dropped in a quarter and dialed the number I'd already memorized.

The phone rang several times. When Daniel answered my stomach flipped over. "Hey, it's me, Peter."

"Hey, I was just thinking about you."

My smile came like an ocean wave breaking, uncontrollable and rushing with life. "Yeah?"

"Yeah."

"Cool."

Daniel chuckled, and teased, "Yeah, I think you're cool."

Blushing, I pushed ahead. "So, after I left your place, I called the hospital. They said Bobby's allowed to have visitors. Kerri's been in to see him."

Kerri was Bobby's other ARK volunteer. She lived in the same neighborhood and came over to his place four days a week, while Daniel had taken on the other three. I'd never met her, but she took good care of Bobby, so she had to be a nice person.

"Great. Tell him hi from me when you see him."

"I was thinking we could go together. Tomorrow?"

"I don't know. The kids…"

"They go to school, right?"

"So do you."

"My Tuesday-Thursday classes don't start until noon. We could meet at the hospital around ten. That'd give you plenty of time to make it back home before Paul and Kennedy's schools let out."

"But that'd mean leaving my mom alone all day," he said.

"Oh." I hadn't known that would be a problem, but now that he said it, I understood. I tried to keep the disappointment out of my voice when I replied, "Okay, I'll tell Bobby you said hi." It wasn't like Daniel didn't want to see me, or Bobby for that matter. He'd been thinking of me when I'd called. I'd hold on to that.

"Wait. Don't go yet."

"I've got class in a few."

He cleared his throat. "Okay, I can make it work."

"What?"

"Going to see Bobby. Meet me at Baptist at ten?"

"But what about your mom?"

"I'll take her car keys with me and hope for the best. It's a long walk to the liquor store."

We confirmed the plan again, agreeing to meet in Bobby's room, and when I hung up, I was smiling like I'd won a prize. Setting off toward the Art & Architecture building for my first college-level photography class, a warm breeze blew through my hair. My backpack was a nice weight on my shoulders and the clove-scented cigarette smoke of the dreadlock-wearing hippie dude walking in front of me drifted back, the aroma pleasant in the open air.

It'd been a good plan to call Daniel and ask him to come with me. He needed to see Bobby, and I still needed to find a way to help Daniel too. Two birds. One stone.

My heart flew.

Chapter Four

AFTER PHOTOGRAPHY, WHICH had been way too basic for me and a disappointment, I hung back to talk with the professor. After explaining my history and the depth of my experience, he told me I'd need to talk to Marta Neuheim about skipping ahead to the 200-level class.

"Marta is the Department Head. Normally this kind of thing isn't allowed—a prerequisite is a prerequisite—so I wouldn't get your hopes up."

"I understand," I said, though he must have sensed that I wasn't going to just roll over without trying. If there was one good thing that had come out of the last year's bullshit, it was that I was done with rolling over.

"If you decide to ask, she'll want to see your portfolio and camera, so be sure to bring those. Her office hours are posted on the first floor."

"Thank you," I said, extricating my camera from the bottom of my backpack. We hadn't needed it during class, but I wanted to show him that I had good gear.

Patting my shoulder as I swung the camera strap over my head, the professor said, "I hope she lets you in. There's nothing worse than being stuck in an unchallenging class, especially if it's a topic or skill you already love and excel in."

"Thank you, sir."

Leaving the Art & Architecture building, I headed down the leafy path toward my dad's office to meet him for lunch. I'd shot down Dad's request that I eat with him every day, but I'd agreed to once a week. If I ate with him today, then I'd fulfilled my obligation.

At the concrete steps leading up to the pea gravel deck around McClung Tower, a group of skaters surfed the handrails. One of them flew past, skidding to a halt in front of an occupied bench. The person sitting there looked familiar. My stomach tensed, and I put a hand over my brow to shade my eyes from the midday sun. Swallowing hard, I recognized the brooding figure sitting there alone with a small cooler and reading a tattered book.

As if he felt my presence, Mo's head came up. His gaze slid over the skaters and landed right on me. I was pinned in place with one foot on the bottom step, and one hand on the railing the skaters had just been riding.

He didn't look away.

Breaking eye contact, I took off up the flight. I didn't want to be reminded of Adam now or talk to his brother or have my day interrupted with the past. But a chiding voice in my head said the past wasn't going to go away if I just ignored it.

The smack and roll of the skateboards hitting the ground resounded around me. I turned around, lifted my camera and compulsively fired off a few quick, soothing snaps of the skaters. With a deep breath, I let the camera drop around my neck again, and walked back down the stairs, heading over to where Mo sat.

Biting into his sandwich, he raised his eyebrow at me. "What?" he said, when I just stood there in front of him, saying nothing and watching him chew. I almost snapped a picture in my anxiety, but I knew that'd just piss him off.

"I don't know," I shrugged. "I just didn't want to act like I didn't see you."

Mo glared at me before taking another bite of his sandwich. Behind us, the skaters risked their lives surfing the handrail again, and I considered just walking away. I licked my lips, trying for normal. "Can you believe those guys?" I jerked my thumb over my shoulder. "They've got some amazing tricks."

From his cooler, Mo retrieved an Arizona Iced Tea can and popped it open. "I heard you dumped Tad."

Cutting to the chase. Typical Mo. "Yeah."

"Awesome for you." He took a long draw of tea and wiped his mouth with the back of his hand. "Awesome for me, too."

"What do you mean?"

"Your orgasm noises? Good riddance."

Heat rushed over me, and my cheeks burned. "Fuck you."

"No, man, *fuck you*. That high-pitched hyperventilating thing you'd always do made me want to kill myself."

"You are such an asshole."

"Look, Tad may be a queer or whatever, but he's my brother, and you hurt him, so as far as I'm concerned you suck."

The sun glinted off the library's dark windows. "So, you didn't see anything wrong with what was going on?"

"*Everything* about it was wrong, asshole. But he's confused right now. I guess I thought you'd be there when all this crap blew up in his face. Catch him when he falls. All that shit. Instead, you're the first explosion."

"You think I should have stuck around and let him take me down with him?"

Mo sighed, threw his half-eaten sandwich back into his cooler and slammed the lid shut. "Fuck no. You did the right thing."

"But he's your brother. I get it." I was an only child, but I understood the concept of sibling loyalty.

"Exactly, shithead. So, go on and get out of here. I'm not your friend."

I nodded.

He was right. We'd never been friends, but it still hurt to walk away from him.

I managed to get all the way to the top of the stairs before I whirled around and aimed my camera. It was a quick shot, but Mo was right in the middle of it. Now I had something to remember him by. As if I could ever forget Mo in all his angry glory.

I got myself together, shaking off the discomfort and renewed ache, as I rode the McClung Tower elevator up to my dad's office. Walking into his familiar, messy, paper-filled room was a relief. Here was something that hadn't changed even a little in my entire life. I might've been with Adam a week ago and been at Daniel's house just yesterday, but my dad's office still smelled like dust and old paper. Even Elvis Costello's *My Aim Is True* was playing from his small tape player just like it often had when I was a kid.

"Ah, Petey-boy," Dad said, swiveling around in his chair and plopping two bagged lunches onto his desk. He was framed by the light from the window. I snapped a photo. He took a closer look at me. "What's up? English Literature got you down?"

"It's never been my best subject."

"But it's not your worst either."

"Adam and Dr. Landry taught me how to put together a paper, yeah." I conceded as I approached the chair across from him. "But no, it's not that. I don't even have English until tomorrow."

"How has your day gone?"

"Pretty well." I told him about how my day had gone as I put my camera in my backpack, and then opened my bag lunch to find a PB&J Dad had made for me, a small bag of chips, and some baby carrots. "So, if I can convince her with my portfolio that I'm worthy, she'll move me up to the next level."

"I have no doubt Marta will find you worthy."

"As for Biology, I hope the drop-add office accepts my request, because I can't take a whole semester of that nose whistle," I finished up, popping the straw into the Capri-Sun Dad handed me.

"Here's to a nose that sings praises to the Lord," Dad said, toasting his PB&J against mine.

I laughed as we took our first bites.

Chewing, Dad looked thoughtful, and I understood why when he said, "Since you brought him up earlier…"

Oh no.

"I've been meaning to ask about what happened with Adam."

"The inevitable."

"Your mother said he hurt you."

I held up my arm so he could see my still-bruised wrist. Of course, he hadn't noticed it yet. He was always too wrapped up in work and the saints and Mary Magdalene and everything else to pay too much attention.

"He did that?"

I nodded, sucking up more Capri-Sun.

"Do you want to talk about it?"

"Nope."

Dad frowned, and I knew the interrogation wasn't over when he switched tacks. "Okay, then how about we talk about this new boy your mother mentioned? What's his name again?"

"Daniel."

"The dust hasn't even settled from your breakup with Adam. He called the house all day yesterday."

"It's over with Adam."

"Right, as it should be." Dad ducked his head. "It's just that I liked him. I didn't like the situation, but I liked *him*."

"Yeah? Well, I *loved* him." My voice cracked. Clearing my throat, I went on, "It hasn't been easy to make this choice, but I know what I need to do. I can't be in a relationship with him anymore."

"But this new guy is different?"

"I've known Daniel all summer, so he's not new."

"And you love him?"

I groaned. "We aren't even dating, Dad. Get a grip. Look, I'm moving on. You need to move on, too." I popped a baby carrot in my mouth, letting him absorb that as I chewed. "Daniel and I are just friends."

"Do you want to be more than friends?"

I thought of Daniel yesterday with his vulnerability on display in the breakfast nook of his kitchen. His hands on my arm, his fingers trailing over my bruises. "I would," I admitted. "Daniel's great. He's generous and loyal. He's responsible, and an overall upstanding person. And he's careful with people's feelings, so that's a plus."

"Wow, Petey." Dad leaned back in his chair, crossing his arms over his chest. "That's some smile."

I shrugged, but my silly grin ruined my nonchalance. "Yeah, well, he's great."

"And when will your mother and I get to meet this young man?"

"I don't know." I picked up a few chips. "Like I said, we're *not dating*. We're just friends." My heart skipped a beat when I remembered I'd get to see him tomorrow morning, and that stupid big smile crept over my face again. It dulled some when I remembered we'd be seeing Bobby at the hospital, but even worry couldn't stop the excitement from welling up.

Dad snorted. "I *see*. Well, expect a renewal of the condom inquisition from your mother if you start dating this guy."

I rolled my eyes and took another bite of my sandwich.

"Watching the Detectives" began playing, and I bounced my head to the beat, hoping we could be done talking about my boyfriend situation.

"Speaking of your mother," Dad said. "Did she give you the envelope this morning? She was up all night thinking about it."

"Yeah." I pulled the manila package out of my backpack. I'd been so busy thinking about school and Minty and Daniel and Adam that I hadn't given it any thought all day. The paper felt old, fragile, and smooth in my hands. "I haven't looked yet. What's in it, do you know?"

"Pictures, his old journal, that sort of thing."

"It's been such a long time now… I know it was traumatic for her, but she still can't even look at his photos?"

Dad's brows bunched together. "Healing takes time, as much time as it takes. But AIDS certainly hasn't helped at all."

"How is AIDS connected to this?"

Dad picked through his remaining chips. "The dire warnings on the news, the skyrocketing deaths, the numbers of AIDS cases going up all the time… The suffering these men and women are faced with… The statistics are horrifying when someone you love is gay."

"But George is dead. He can't die twice."

Dad took a bite of sandwich and meditated on his next words as he chewed and swallowed. "Right, but you look very much like him, Petey. And at a deep level, she believes her brother died because he was gay."

"He died because of homophobic monsters."

"Right, and what is AIDS if not another monster that attacks gay men?"

"That's not all. HIV infects women, too, and IV drug users, and hemophiliacs, and—"

"Right, but can't you see how AIDS brought all those old feelings back up for her? Especially when it came to you. She can't remember George and his death without being gripped by fear for you. She's afraid she'll go through it all again, only worse this time, because no parent should outlive a child."

I stayed silent for a moment, a simmering anger beginning again. Hot. Not cold like my rage at Adam. I couldn't put words to it, aside from "selfish," and "wrong," and "*this isn't about her*," but I swallowed it all down with the nutty flavor of peanut butter.

She'd found his body. His brutalized body.

Of course the memory haunted her, of course it colored everything she did and felt and thought about homosexuality. AIDS would have reinforced those feelings for her. I should be kinder to her. More understanding.

But what about what I need from her and who I need her to be?

She was trying. I knew that, but sometimes I just wanted her to be further along than she was, so that I could lean on her when I needed her.

"I know what you're thinking," Dad said. "You're thinking she should have dealt with it all in some better way by now. But she's always preferred to stay in her fantasy worlds than to cope with the traumas of life. Why do you think she writes romance, Petey?"

"Isn't that what she's in therapy for?" I asked.

He nodded. "Therapy takes time, though, and you've got this envelope right now. She gave it to you, and I think she expects you to open it."

"No pressure." I set aside the sandwich, taking up the envelope again.

I struggled with the glued-down flap of the envelope before reaching across Dad's desk for the silver letter opener. I used to pretend it was a rapier when I was a kid. I wrenched the sharp side through the crisp paper. The scent rising from inside was old, dusty, and faintly reminiscent of tobacco.

As Dad watched, I poured the contents out next to my empty lunch sack. Old photographs, a journal, and some faded, folded letters slid across the small bare spot on Dad's desk. Most of the pictures were black and white, but there were a few early color-tinted ones.

"Ah," Dad said, picking up one photo. It was yellowing at the edges. "Here he is. George Robbins." He laughed, handing me the picture. "He was a handsome man. Like you."

I stared at the photo of a reed-thin man with curly dark hair that he'd clearly tried to tame with some sort of product that left it shiny. He stood outside an old white clapboard house, smiling for the camera, a cigarette dangling from one hand, and his gray eyes twinkling.

He looked *more* than a lot like me. In fact, the resemblance was undeniable. I had an uncomfortable new perspective on why my mother had reacted so badly to my coming out. I *must* have reminded her of him every day. There was no way I didn't.

"I'd guess he's about twenty-three in this one? Hard to say." Dad pulled another picture out of the mess on his desk and handed it to me. "There he is with your mom."

Mom had curly dark hair, too. I'd forgotten that she'd told me her hair went straight when she was pregnant with me and never curled up again. She was a tall kid, coming up to her brother's chest. She gazed up at him adoringly, and he rested his hand on her head, looking into the camera with a more serious expression.

"I'm pretty sure his wife, Beth, took that shot, and these ones too," Dad said, scooting a few more my way. "I looked through this envelope when you were a baby, but I didn't read the letters or his journal."

Grandma Robbins joined them in these, looking harried and annoyed. "Grandma doesn't look happy."

"Did she ever?"

I let out a stiff laugh. "I guess not."

Turning my attention to the letters, I examined the outside of them first. There were only five, all well-worn, and all from a man named Harold Seville. *They* were what faintly smelled of tobacco.

The first lines of the one I opened set my heart racing.

Dearest George, I miss our nights together, darling. I understand your need to care for your family, but I can't help but wish you'd leave them all behind and come home to me. It's just a fantasy, but one I entertain every day. If the world would let us, I know we could be so happy.

"These are love letters," I whispered.

"So I'd surmised, based on the return address and the fact that Beth gave them to your mother instead of throwing them away or keeping them herself."

I scanned the rest of the letter. It was painful to read the yearning in it. So full of longing and dashed dreams. I could tell my uncle had cherished the letter. Even after all these years, it unfolded and refolded easily. I wondered if he'd written back or if he'd ignored Harold's pleas.

Stuffing the letter back in its envelope and then into the manila one along with all the other things on the desk, I whispered, "I don't think I can read all this right now, Dad. It feels too sad."

Dad nodded. "What you do with this envelope and its contents is your business. Your mother said she wants it to belong to you now. When you read them, and I think you will, just know I'm here for you to talk about them. Whatever you find."

I put the manila envelope back in my backpack and finished my lunch. Dad turned around to flip the cassette over, and Elvis Costello welcomed us to the working week.

When I left Dad's office to head to Robert's house, I decided to forget about my uncle's stuff for a while. I didn't need to add a dead man's heartache to my own. I was carrying around enough right now.

I just wanted to heal.

And I didn't see how reading about my uncle's tragic life was going to help me do that.

Chapter Five

WHEN I ARRIVED at my job that afternoon, I was looking forward to a few hours of sewing sequins onto a new dress, or filing paperwork, or balancing accounts. The work was mindless, but satisfying, and I'd let myself indulge in optimistic fantasies. I'd see Daniel in the morning, and we'd visit Bobby together. Somehow, I'd find a way to prove to Daniel I was worth his time and affection. I could feel it in my bones. It was all going to work out: Bobby would get well, and Daniel and I would get close again.

There were only going to be good things ahead for me now. After ditching the weight of Adam, and all the shame and lies, now I was free to become the man I wanted to be. The kind of man Daniel could love. As I entered the house, I walked with more of a bounce in my step than I had in weeks.

I found Robert and Barry sitting at the kitchen table with paperwork from a local bank spread out all around them. Rolled up next to it all were the house plans for Barry and Robert's dream home, the one they were building on Barry's family's land in Strawberry Plains.

"Sweetie!" Robert waved me over. He wore a tiger-print leotard over red running shorts and was sipping from a big wine glass that was full to the brim with white wine and ice cubes. "You're early!"

"I wasn't sure how long it would take to get here from campus," I explained. "Besides, once classes are over, they're kind of over, so there wasn't any reason not to just head your way."

"Sit down," Barry said, indicating an empty chair. "We need to talk."

My step faltered. "We do?"

I couldn't think of anything I'd done that deserved a talking-to from either of them. Maybe they'd heard about Adam hurting me? Maybe they wanted to give me a lecture about abuse?

Robert chided, "Don't say it like that, Barry, baby. You'll scare him."

"Sit down, and don't be scared. We need to talk." Barry lifted a pierced brow at Robert. "That better?"

Robert blew a wine-wet raspberry. "You know it wasn't." Turning to me, he said, "Don't worry, Sweetie. It's nothing bad. It's just a change."

I took a seat, placing my Minolta on the table, and waited.

"I'm so glad I hired you last December. You've been a great help around here," Robert said, taking hold of my hand and squeezing my fingers. My stomach sank; this wasn't a promising start. "All the work you've done for us, the way you've been so open to learning new things, and the documentary, and the sewing! You were such a fast learner and so good with the sequins. I'm just proud."

Barry nodded in agreement.

"Uh, why does it feel like you're going to fire me?"

"Well…" Robert's brows tugged together, and he gripped my hand even tighter. "Because we are." My face must have given away my feelings because Robert rushed to reassure me. "But not immediately! We can give you a month to find something else. We don't want to leave you in the lurch."

I swallowed thickly. "Why though? If I've done good work for you? If you're happy with me?"

Robert glanced toward Barry and then went on, keeping his voice soft and gentle. "You know how I've been contracted to do weekly shows at the Slide in Nashville this fall?"

I did know this and had helped her get that opportunity. The Slide was a gay club that paid their drag queens more and had a much bigger stage than in Knoxville. The larger audience also meant a lot more in tips. The new contract meant that, starting this month, Renée was the one bringing home the bacon.

"Go on," I said. "Get to the firing-me part."

"Well, as you know, the documentary is finished. There are just a few small tweaks to make, and we'll be submitting it to the film festival circuits. I can handle doing that," Barry said. "So the documentary work is done now, and Robert's giving up the public TV shows since his schedule will be much tighter with all his trips to Nashville."

Robert went on, "You did a fantastic job straightening out our office, Sweetie. The filing's up to date, everything's organized and in order, and Renée has enough new costumes to last a year or two."

"Your work here is done," Barry said.

"And even if it wasn't," Robert added. "The new income from the Slide means Barry and I can move forward on building the new house."

I still wasn't sure why this meant they weren't going to need me anymore. Give Robert a few weeks' worth of mail and paperwork and the office would be a mess again, I was sure of it.

"So, here's the thing: in order to secure this building loan," Robert tapped the paperwork spread on the table. "We're going to need every last dime to prove our income. You understand, don't you, Sweetie? This isn't about you, or not wanting you around anymore. It's about Barry and me moving ahead with our future."

I understood, but it still left me reeling. I had my own financial obligations, and I depended on my rather generous income from Robert to meet them.

"Is this going to leave you in the lurch?" Robert asked, biting his lip.

"I don't know," I admitted. "My tuition is covered between what I saved this summer, the faculty discount my dad gets, and it turned out I qualify for the Pell Grant. I mean, I have car payments and my monthly insurance to cover, and I have to pay for textbooks, plus the extra cash I've earned from you is always good for film and gas. But I haven't tried to look for another job since I started with you. Maybe I can find something else… I just don't know."

"Like we said," Robert went on. "We won't let you go until you've secured another position. We wouldn't do that to you."

"Thank you," I said, my brain already making all sorts of calculations. I knew how much money I needed every month at a minimum, but I didn't know what kind of job to even look for or consider.

Last year, trying to get a job with the photography shops in town had failed, and I didn't see any reason to think things had changed there. Unless Renaldo from Foxx Photo had finally gotten busted getting a blow job from Robert in the back room.

"You look worried," Robert said. "Tell us your thoughts."

"I don't know where to look for work," I admitted. "I'd need a job that could fit around my classes." I didn't mention that I'd just promised Daniel I would look after Bobby for him after he was released from the hospital, too. I'd counted on the flexibility and leniency of my job with Robert to make all that feasible.

"University jobs are your best bet, depending on if the pay is enough," Barry said, leaning forward to put his elbows on the table. "In fact, the library's hiring. There's typically a waiting list for positions there—"

"But you just happen to know someone on the hiring team," Robert said, patting Barry's bulging bicep. "Barry here will put in a good word for you."

"Oh? Thank you."

"That means he'll hire you," Robert whispered with a grin and a twinkle. "Which do you prefer? Circulation or the Audio-Visual department?"

"Woman," Barry scolded. "Don't make promises I can't keep. I can pull some strings," he said to me. "But you'll have to apply, and I don't know if the pay is going to be enough for you. It's four dollars and twenty-five cents an hour and a minimum of fourteen hours a week of work. There's the possibility of taking on more shifts if you want, but that's all that's required."

"What's the job consist of?" I asked, wondering if there was a way to make additional money on the side. Selling my photos to a stock photo archive was something I'd been considering of late, but I was still exploring how to do that, and my initial investigation seemed to imply the payoff wasn't that high.

I listened as Barry explained the position. It seemed easy enough, and I agreed to apply the following day in between my classes.

"Just drop by the library with your application. I'll be there," Barry said, rising from the table and clapping me on the shoulder. "I'll vouch for you and tell them what a responsible and dedicated employee you've been for Robert."

"Do you think I stand a chance? Or should I start looking for other job opportunities?"

"I can't promise anything. Maybe check what else is available on the university bulletin boards until you hear back. But if you apply tomorrow, you should know within the week."

Barry disappeared back into the office, and I sat across from Robert, watching him sip wine and pet the loan paperwork like he needed to show it affection to keep it happy.

"I'm sorry to drop this on you out of the blue." He looked up at me with earnest, dark eyes. "I didn't expect Barry to want to start on the house so soon, but he made a good point: we never know when the Slide might cancel my shows, and if we have the money coming in now, and proof of it, that'll look better to the bank. We're in the best position we've ever been in, and maybe the best position we'll be in for a long time."

"I'm not upset," I assured him. "You've both done so much for me, and Barry's doing even more trying to hook me up with this library position. I'm going to be just fine."

"I know you will," Robert said. "You've grown up this year. I'm proud of you, and I just know you're going to keep on getting more amazing all the time, Sweetie. And this doesn't mean we don't want you around! Anytime you want or need us, we're here for you."

"I know." I didn't doubt Robert and Barry's affection for me. This was the right thing for them to do, both monetarily and personally. It wasn't about me or my job performance. But I would miss them. Seeing them most days, or at least having the promise of seeing them very soon, always made things better.

Robert put his elbow on the table and his chin in his hand. "Now, all that ugly business is handled. What's this I hear from our mutual acquaintances about you ending things with Naughty Boy?"

I didn't want to tell the whole story again, but I knew Robert wouldn't let it go until I did.

So I sighed, rubbed my hands over my hair, and filled him in. I left out a few important points—like the condom issue—because I didn't want Robert to think even less of Adam than he already did. I didn't know why I still wanted to protect him, but I did.

"He hurt you!" Robert exclaimed, grabbing my still-tender arm, and pulling it forward, tracing the lingering bruises with his long red fingernails.

I nodded.

And *then* came the "abuse is abuse" lecture—dotted with colorful language and bizarre examples. I listened to it and promised

Robert I was done with Adam. Once Robert had his say, he stood up, took hold of my hand, and pulled me into the living room.

"Now, how about we dance those blues away?"

Cueing up a song by Tony! Toni! Toné!, he swept me into his arms, and sang to me about how it never rains in California. Before long we were laughing, and Barry had come out to lean on the doorjamb, watching us with a fond smile on his face.

I was going to miss them, and this—dancing at work, laughing with friends and getting paid for it—but everything was new now. I had to get used to it. College had begun, I'd ended things with Adam, and started *something* with Daniel.

A new job wasn't so scary-sounding. It could even be exciting.

Here I was, dancing with Robert, at the start of a fresh new life.

Part VIII
Late-August 1991

Chapter Six

BOBBY WAS STAYING on the third floor of Baptist Hospital with a bright view of the river. He lay in the bed, with tubes and wires everywhere. He hadn't had any weight to lose, but now he was a skeleton, and my gut twisted at the sight. His red-rimmed, foggy eyes lit up when I walked into the room.

"Well, doggone if it isn't Peter," he croaked, smiling, but it looked horrible, like his mouth was crumbling into his chin. It was hard to believe that a little infection from cutting his foot on a bottle cap had taken him down this far in less than a week. That's what AIDS did to a person. I knew that, and yet it gave me chills.

I swallowed back my horror and walked toward him. "Hey, Bobby." I tried on a smile. "Why'd you go and scare us like this?"

He let out a rattling chuckle. "You know how it is, life wasn't exciting enough, so I thought why the hell not?"

My smile felt all wrong, so I tried to hide it by bending down to hug him. I was glad I'd left my camera in the trunk of my car. I didn't need to capture him like this. When I straightened, Bobby looked over my shoulder and grinned at the sight of Daniel standing in the doorway with a big bouquet of yellow and white roses.

Daniel smiled at us both as he stepped into the room. He looked as handsome as ever in jeans, a white T-shirt and an open, dark blue button-up. "Hey, Bobby. Milky Way wanted me to bring these for you."

"Did she now?" Bobby asked, and then looked between us with a raised brow. "Oh, I see, I *see*. Here I was expecting everything to get awkward now that you're both here, but it seems you two have zoomed past the apologies right into shaking-the-sheets territory, haven't you?"

"Not quite," Daniel said, laughing and placing the bouquet on a table with three other, smaller vases of flowers.

"We made up," I explained. "But we're not—"

"We're friends," Daniel said.

"Yeah, right." Bobby fixed his gaze on me. "And that other young rascal you were seeing?"

"Broke up with him." I busied myself by buttoning up my light gray cardigan. "It's chilly in here."

"Hospitals. Freeze you to death or kill you with secondhand germs. I'd be better off at home."

"What's the latest on that? When are they releasing you?" Daniel asked, and I smiled at him, grateful he'd changed the subject.

"Eh. Not soon enough. Seems I've popped a recurring fever, and they suspect it's a staph infection." He rattled a sigh. "If it ain't one thing, it's another. And not even one single beautiful boy here to take my mind off it."

"Until now," I quipped.

He smiled. "Yes, until now."

But Daniel wasn't as easily swayed from discussion of the serious issues at hand. "Staph. That's not great."

"Tell me what I don't know."

"What's the treatment for that given your compromised immune system? Is it—"

"Stop." Bobby waved Daniel's question away. "I don't want to talk about it. Don't deprive me of my joys in life by making me focus on miserable things." He turned to me. "So, how'd the ex take you dumping him?"

I wanted to know more about his prognosis given this complication, but I knew better than to push him. He'd talk when he was good and ready and not a minute before. So I indulged his craving for gossip. "Not well." I rubbed my wrist. "But he's stayed away, at least." I didn't mention the calls he still put through to the house. I wouldn't even answer the phone for fear it was him. I let my parents handle it.

"Well, he's got a good shoulder to cry on, doesn't he? In that pretty girlfriend of his."

"What good's a shoulder when you can't even be honest about the tears?" Daniel asked.

A lump rose in my throat. I hated feeling this way about Adam. How long would it be until it didn't hurt at all anymore? I didn't *want* him, but the pain lingered. It made no sense. Why couldn't he and the grief both be gone for good?

Bobby lifted a hand that was stippled with bruises from needles and pointed a skinny finger between me and Daniel. "You're jumping mighty fast into a new frying pan now. You like getting burned."

"Bobby…" I sighed.

"Just friends," Daniel repeated.

"Sure, and I'm just a little down-and-out." Bobby rolled his eyes. "I'm happy you two made up, but please throw caution to the wind and screw already. I haven't got forever to see you kids paired off and happy. Give an old man his dying wish, all right?"

My cheeks burned, but when I looked at Daniel, he just smiled at me and shrugged.

"Okay, Bobby. We'll see what we can do," he said.

I nodded. "Anything for you."

Bobby groaned and shifted on the bed. "Guess what? I missed Marlena telling Roman she's alive," he said. "They had me knocked out when I first got here, and I damn well missed it."

My stomach dropped in secondhand disappointment. *Days of Our Lives* was Bobby's favorite soap, and he'd waited all summer for that big reveal.

"Minty's mom might have recorded a copy," Daniel said. "She's watched *Days* for as long as Minty's been alive, I think. I'll ask her next time I see her, okay?"

"I won't count on it. That'd be a piece of luck, and I don't have a lot of those left to spend." Bobby smiled and let his head rest back against the bed. "When I was your age, oh my, I spent my luck every hour it seemed. So many beautiful young men. So little time." His lips twisted and he sighed. "It all went by too fast."

"Who was your first love?" I asked, sitting down on the chair next to his bed with my back to the windows. Daniel pulled up a chair on the other side, the sunshine pouring in to light up his dark golden hair.

"Oh, a big strapping boy named Tipton Fisher. We called him Tippy." Bobby sighed, remembering. "He used to take me out hunting for squirrels when we were kids." He wrinkled his nose. "I hated how squirrel meat tasted, greasy and like pine trees smell, but I loved watching him hunt. I didn't even mind watching him clean the animals. He was so respectful the way he did it, like he valued the life he'd taken, even the varmints."

"I didn't even know you could eat squirrel," Daniel said. "I guess I never thought about it."

"Oh, most folks don't these days. His family was poor. They needed the meat."

"What did he look like?" I asked.

"Blond, blue eyes. Pimply skin." Bobby laughed, again, a little clearer this time. "I didn't care. His ass was like an apple, and I stared at it so long I just knew he'd catch me one day. He never did."

"So, he was your first crush?"

"Yeah, I suppose that's a better name for what he was. A crush. He never even looked at me twice. Got a girl pregnant at sixteen and settled into a life of poverty like all his family before him. I bet he's got four or five kids by now. And maybe a second wife. And a kid or two with her."

The room was quiet as we all thought about Tippy Fisher and second or third wives.

"Do you have more stories for me, Peter? Something juicy?" Bobby asked.

I started to tell him no, but then remembered the envelope my mother had given me with information about my uncle.

"I'm not sure it's juicy, but I'll tell you about it anyway." I told him about my uncle first, leaving out the worst details of his murder, but giving enough information that Bobby wouldn't be confused about why my mother didn't talk about him or want to show me the contents herself.

"So you haven't read all the letters yet? Or his journal?" Bobby said. "What's the point of telling me all this if you don't even know what the men felt for each other or how it ended? Ah, hell, give the letters to me, and I'll let you know if there's anything important in them."

I laughed. "I figure I should be the one to read them first, if anyone does at all. That only seems right."

"Since giving up his life of deceit, this boy's bent on doing what's right, isn't he?" Bobby asked Daniel.

Daniel had walked over to the windows as I'd talked, adjusting the blinds and gazing out at the water. He turned now, putting his hands on my shoulders and squeezing. "He's figuring it out. I'm proud of him."

"Well, then, isn't that a pretty picture?" Bobby smiled. "If I die tomorrow, I'm happy since I saw you both here together."

"Don't talk like that, asshole," Daniel scolded. "You almost died last week!"

"Too soon to joke about it?" Bobby asked.

Daniel stepped away, the heat of his hands leaving my shoulders. "Way too soon."

My heart clenched. "It'll always be too soon."

✧ ✧ ✧

"IT WAS A good idea to come here together," Daniel said, leaning against Betty Blue in the hospital parking lot.

"I'm glad you could get away."

Daniel jingled his car keys in his jeans pocket. "I need to leave soon. The liquor store is a long walk, but it's not like she's never done it."

"I understand."

"I get it now, after hearing what you told Bobby, about why your mom took Valium to cope. I'm guessing she saw more than any child should have seen."

I nodded.

"I worry about that for my siblings. They've seen a lot too. Stuff no kid should ever have to deal with, like their mother passed out in her own vomit, too drunk to carry on a conversation or fix them dinner. That's how I found out she'd relapsed. Kennedy called me. Paul was trying to handle it all himself."

I touched his arm. "I'm so sorry."

"Me too. I feel guilty for having moved out and left them to deal with her. I was selfish."

"No, you're always doing your best," I reassured him.

He rubbed a hand over the back of his neck. "Maybe. I hope so." He sighed. "God, but Paul's going to be a handful for my grandparents."

"Do they know yet? Paul and Kennedy, I mean. About the

move?"

"I told them last night, and it was a mixed bag. Kennedy cried, and then begged to stay, and then got excited about living so close to the beach. It was emotional whiplash. Paul just went cold and silent."

"What'd your mom say to them?"

"She wasn't there."

My mouth fell open. Daniel just laughed bitterly. "She was locked in her room sobbing, making it all about her feelings instead of being strong for the kids. She's afraid she'll lose them for good. I hope she does."

I squeezed his arm and said, "You've got so much going on."

"That's just the start of it. I've also decided to sell my father's business."

"But that'll end your mom's stipend, right?"

"Yeah. And we'll have to sell the house." His lips twisted, caught between anger and hurt. "But I'm done trying to protect her." He squinted up at the clear, blue sky. The traffic on Henley Street rushed on by. "I'm doing what I can to protect the kids first, and then I'm determined to live my own life, my own way."

I knew what that meant, or at least, I suspected. "Nursing school?"

"If I can get accepted next term. I might have to wait until the fall. But I'm already so far behind. What's another year or two?"

"Just think," I said, reaching out to adjust the fall of his light-weight red jacket. "If you'd been on track, you never would have met me." I lowered my voice. "But, then again, maybe that would have been a good thing. Saved you a bunch of drama."

He tweaked the curl hanging over my forehead. "Maybe, but I sure would have hated to miss out on you."

The air between us grew thick with meaning, and if we hadn't been in public, and if we hadn't just committed to being friends again, I thought he might have kissed me. But he rocked back on his heels and broke the moment. "I should get going. What's your plan for the rest of the day?"

"I gotta see a man about a job, a professor about a schedule change, and then it's classes until the late afternoon."

"A job?"

"Yeah, I'm applying at the library." I explained about Robert and Barry. "I need to fill that financial void."

Daniel's eyes shone like warm honey as the sun moved out from behind the puffy white clouds. My insides buzzed like I'd eaten a spoonful of it, and I was on the verge of a sugar rush. He reached out like he was going to touch me but shoved his hand in his jacket pocket instead. "Good luck."

"You too."

"I'll need it more than you. You'll be a shoo-in for the job." This time he didn't resist reaching out to touch my hair again. His fingers drifting over my curls made me quiver. "Bye, Peter."

"Bye." I watched him climb into Betty Blue and turn the engine over.

As I walked across the parking lot toward the Volvo, I could still feel his touch tingling on my scalp. Just as I was keying open the door, Daniel's car slowed and stopped next to me.

"Hey, want to have dinner Friday night?"

More butterfly wings fluttered in my chest. "Sure. Where?"

"My place. It's the only option right now."

"I'd love to." I almost squealed with joy as I got into my car and shut the door behind me.

Betty Blue and Daniel drove away as I backed out of the parking spot. I felt as weightless as a cloud. He'd just asked me over for dinner, and it probably wasn't a date, but I still felt like it was more than I deserved.

If I was supposed to still have doubts or sadness about having left Adam, I didn't. I'd take a friendship with Daniel over a relationship with Adam any day.

Clarity felt amazing. I wanted to hold on to it forever.

Chapter Seven

THE UNIVERSITY OF Tennessee library was cavernous but quiet. Applications were available to students during the first week of classes, and I grabbed one and filled it out on one of the low round tables set up for studying.

When I was finished, I walked it up to the circulation desk on the main floor and asked the employee manning it if Barry was around. I knew he was, because I could see him in the back through the big doors and windows, and before the girl even had a chance to fetch him, he saw me too.

"Puker," he greeted me, emerging with his hand outstretched for the application. "Right on time." He nodded at the blond, chubby girl at the counter and said, "April, this is Puker. Puker, April."

The girl blinked at me and murmured, "Your name's *Puker?*"

"It's Peter. Puker's a bad nickname," I said. "One I hope won't carry over if I get a job here?" I asked Barry pointedly.

"No promises," he said. "All right. I'll run this by Ellie, and when she approves it, which I think she will, I'll call you to arrange for your first shift. Got any preferences?"

I shook my head. "Should I?"

"Mornings are the worst," April volunteered. "You have to be here super-duper early, and there's a ton of stuff to do before the library even opens. Afternoons are good, and night shifts aren't bad either."

"I'm open to whatever fits into my class schedule for now."

Barry waved me off. "Get gone then."

I smiled at April, and she waved as I walked away.

I still had over an hour before my meeting with Marta Neuheim, so I grabbed a cup of coffee from the library's vending machine and headed outside into the warm, leafy-green morning with the intention of hunting the wild photograph. My Leica was in my backpack, and as soon as I was finished with the coffee, I'd get it out.

Just as the sun burst out from behind a tree, almost blinding me, I heard my name being called. "Hey, Peter, wait up."

I blinked to see Millar Johansson from Kingsley jogging up the sidewalk. Wearing a blue sweatshirt and a pair of khakis, he was still reed thin and moving like he'd had five cups of coffee and a couple of No-Doz tablets. He stuck his hand out, and I shook it before he wrenched me forward into an unexpected hug. I had to hold my coffee out to the side to keep it from splashing us.

"Peter, wow, you're looking great." He pulled back and ran his hand through his short blond hair, his green eyes sparkling at me.

"You look good, too," I offered. "But I'm confused. What are you doing here? I thought you got in at Vanderbilt?"

"Financials fell through," Millar said, shrugging. "I had to pull out at the last minute." His lips twisted up in a gleeful smile as redness rushed up his neck and into his face. "Damn, that sounded dirty."

I snorted, surprised to see this playful, if embarrassed, side of him. He'd always been so businesslike at Kingsley. Of course, he'd been hiding his sexuality then. He had to feel a lot freer to be himself now. I knew I did.

"I'm sure there were plenty of people ready to fill your position," I said with a touch of innuendo, too, and we both giggled like twelve-year-olds.

"But seriously, you're really looking great." He waved at my face. "So confident and mature."

I smiled. "Thanks."

He glanced at his watch. "Hey, so what's your morning like? I've still got an hour to kill before Econ."

"Same for me, only it's a meeting with a professor."

His face lit up. "Awesome. What do you say you ditch that crappy vending-machine coffee—"

I tilted my head. "Is it crappy?"

"Have you tasted it? It's terrible."

"I haven't yet. I was waiting for it to cool off."

"Go on. Try it."

I took a sip, and my face twisted up in disgust. "That cost me fifty whole cents," I moaned.

Millar put his arm over my shoulders and steered me around. "C'mon. Let's get some *good* coffee and catch up. I know just the place."

"Catch up" was a strange way to put it since we'd never been friends, but I did want to find out what was going on with Millar. He seemed like a nice guy, and I admired the way he'd come out to the entire school last year.

On the walk down to Cuppa on Cumberland, the latest coffee place to crop up, Millar rattled on about the people we knew from Kingsley who he'd already run into on campus. I realized that for someone else in the future, I'd be on that list.

"That's about it, I guess," he said. "Oh, wait, I saw Travis Wilkins. Have you seen him?"

I shook my head. I'd never even known Travis.

"Well, he's looking hot. Put on some weight over the summer. I think he's trying to bulk up for sports. Wasn't he on the wrestling team?"

"Yeah, but don't you cut weight for that?"

"Maybe. Oh, and I saw Marie Donatello at Stella's Jazz Club the other night. She was holding hands with a chick. I'm pretty sure she's a lesbian."

"I didn't know her. Was she in our class?"

"Oh, right!" Millar said, holding the door to Cuppa open for me. "She was a grade above us. I forgot you were only there last year."

"Well, I'm sure there were plenty of queer kids at Kingsley," I said, thinking of Susan. The scent of coffee filled my nose, and I breathed it in. A cup of anxiety might not be what I needed before my appointment with Marta Neuheim, but it wouldn't hurt too much either.

"Absolutely. I wish it was a better environment for coming out. But it will be. One day," Millar said. "And we helped make that happen."

I'd reached the counter just as those words left his mouth. My mind hung and whirred, stuck on his acknowledgment that I was gay, too. I hadn't come out to the school or to him. How did he know?

The barista glared at me as I stared at the menu, unable to read through the din of alarms going off in my head. Finally, I ordered a latte and stepped aside.

Once we both had our drinks, I followed Millar to a booth in the back of the coffee shop. Twinkle lights hung down from the ceiling and he sat across from me looking almost handsome in their yellow glow, despite being too thin and way too jumpy. His eyes shone and there was an angle to his jaw that was attractive enough. I wondered if he had a boyfriend. Then I wondered if Antonio or Windy might be his type. Or even Minty.

If my camera hadn't been at the bottom of my backpack, I would have snapped a picture.

"So," he said, tapping his fingers against his cup and peering at me. "Let's cut through the bullshit and allow me to ask the thing I've always wanted to know. Are you still screwing Adam Algedi?"

I choked on my latte, burning my tongue. I wiped my mouth with my napkin, and when I threw it down on the table, my hands were shaking. "I'm sorry? *What?*"

"Well, maybe he screws you, but whatever the case, I have eyes, and I'm gay. Maybe no one else at Kingsley knew what was going on, but I did. I think Van suspected, too. He just didn't want to get involved."

I yearned for my camera so I could start firing off shots and put distance between me and Millar. I coughed some more, cleaning up the mess from the coffee I'd spilled.

But Millar wasn't letting it go. "So? Is that still going on?"

"Um, no." Numbness marked the answer. Shock wiped out my ability to feel anything at all. "I'm interested in someone else now."

"Oh? I can't imagine it's someone better-looking."

"It's someone without a girlfriend," I said. "That's pretty appealing."

"A definite improvement," he agreed, laughing. "God, your face. I'm sorry. I shouldn't have just hit you with it like that."

"It's okay. I just…we thought. I don't know."

"You thought no one knew."

"Yeah. How long have you known?"

"Since you guys joined the yearbook last year. He was pretty possessive of you, and you were gaga over him. I mean, that stupid Carpenters song was written for you, man. You heard birds singing whenever he was near."

I could get my camera out, take some pictures of the patrons of Cuppa, ignore Millar and my racing heart, but something held me in place. I toyed with the handle of my coffee mug. Taking another sip, I barely tasted it with my now-burned tongue.

"So, it went bad between you?"

"It was always bad."

"No, it wasn't. You guys were in love."

"We were. But we fought a lot. It was miserable lying to everyone."

"But there were good times, right?"

I didn't want to remember the times when it'd been just the two of us, and I'd been happy and in love. I didn't want to remember how it'd felt to be with him. It didn't fix anything, and it wasn't going to stop me from falling in love with Daniel.

Or maybe I already did love him. He was such a good person, and when I was with him, I felt safe. I wiped a hand over my eyes and thought of Daniel's smile, and my gut twisted with wild yearning and joy. Maybe I loved him.

"So, who ended it?"

"I did."

"Oooh, I bet he took it badly."

"Yeah."

"Adam was crazy about you. But it was clear he was crazy about Leslie, too. I can see how that would hurt."

"It sucked." I didn't know what else to say. Thinking about it made me feel sick and want to cry all at once. I'd much rather think about Daniel and how I might love him. Dream of convincing him to love me...

"I'm being a bit of a bastard about all this, aren't I?"

I shrugged and took another sip of my latte.

"It's just in high school I was so jealous that you got to be with him. He's so hot. That's why, when I saw you in the library earlier, I decided to corner you. I just had to get the scoop."

"I'd appreciate it if you didn't tell anyone from Kingsley about this."

"Peter, I kept my mouth shut all year about the two of you.

Now that it's over, why would I say anything?"

"Maybe you'd feel safer saying something now that high school *is* over? Because you'd think maybe no one could get hurt? But the thing is he's still with Leslie, and *she'd* get hurt. Now that we're broken up, she doesn't even need to know. He does love her, and I don't want her to feel…" I waved my hands around to indicate the mess of emotions she'd endure if she knew. "You know? I just want her to be happy."

"Got it. But don't you think he'll do the same thing again? Isn't it just a matter of time?"

"I don't know." I looked away from him, unable to meet his eyes as I admitted, "Call me an idiot, but I kind of think I was special to him. I'd like to think he wouldn't just start seeing someone else. I think he does love Leslie, and maybe without me in the picture he can find a way to be happy with her." I took a deep breath and met Millar's eyes. "I *want* him to be happy with her."

"That's generous of you."

"I loved him. I want the best for him."

"And *you're* going to be happy? With this new guy?"

I never liked the weird juxtaposition of thinking of Adam and Daniel in the same few breaths, but the reminder of the fact that Daniel existed at all lifted my heart. "Yeah. I am." If I could convince him to give me another chance at being more than his friend, I knew we could be good together.

"All right, good for you. Who is this guy?"

"You don't know him. His name's Daniel McPeak."

"Oh, the heir to the McPeak construction company?" He went on before I even confirmed, "Gay, wealthy, no girlfriend." He lifted his cup and toasted me. "Another jackpot. Congrats."

"Thanks?"

I was grateful when he changed the subject to classes and college life in general. He'd gotten a job working on the university paper—

"Don't worry! Not the gossip column!"—and was taking journalism classes because he'd tested out of most of his core requirements.

"What about you?"

"Photography is the only thing I could take extra right now," I said. "Otherwise, it's all required stuff."

"I'm glad to hear you haven't let that go. Your shots were always amazing. If you want a position on our team, just let me know, but, honestly, journalistic photography isn't for you. You're an artist. You've got a gift."

I smiled and thanked him.

"Where's your camera?" he asked.

"In my backpack."

"You used to have it out all the time. You took pictures of everything. Anything. Almost like a nervous tic."

It was as I said the words that I realized why I was holding back from getting the Leica out now. "I want photography to be a tool I use when I want to use it, not a compulsive way to process my life. I used it as a coping mechanism."

"Ah. You don't want to be behind the lens all the time."

"Right."

I'd used photography in the past to not only process my emotions, but to contain them, make them smaller and easier. Too often, I'd put my hardest feelings into the pictures, letting the camera separate me from the worst of it and keep me safe. As much as I loved photography, I wanted to confront my feelings head on. I didn't want to be the guy who used his art to hide from pain. Expose it, sure, but hiding from it had already made me complicit in too many bad things.

Millar's head tilted in thought, and he studied my face. "That's something I need to figure out how to do, too. Just live life. Not always be on the lookout for a story. My boyfriend says I need to learn to let down my guard, but I'm not sure how to do that yet. I spent a lot of years with my guard up, you know? I *had* to keep my eye on everyone around me, so I'd see immediately if they'd found me out. I guess that's made me distrustful, but it's also given me powerful insight into other people's behaviors and motivations. It gives me an edge in life."

"Then why does your boyfriend think you should change?"

"Because I'm lonely. Even *with* Billy, I'm lonely. I can't seem to let him in, you know?"

"Yeah." I did get it. The camera was my true love, but it was also a crutch. I needed to get out from behind it sometimes to truly live. "Your boyfriend sounds like a smart guy."

"He is. Pre-med." Millar looked smug but then he checked his watch and his eyes bugged out. "We need to go. If we don't, we'll be late. See? Hunting down a story fucks with my life. Gotta fix that."

I wasn't comfortable with being referred to as 'a story,' even if he meant it figuratively. But I accepted a hug as we left together, wishing him well.

We separated on the climb up toward Hess Hall. My mind turned over the revelation that Millar knew about me and Adam as I walked away. There was nothing I could do about it. The best I could hope for was that he would keep it to himself.

For the rest of the walk I focused on the trial ahead: getting Marta Neuheim to approve my class transfer request.

When I reached the sidewalk leading past the Clarence Brown Theater and the Circle Theater over to the Art & Architecture building, I paused at a concrete outdoor table nearby to free my Leica from my backpack. Taking a deep breath to calm my nerves, I framed the modern roof of the white building against the blue sky and took the shot. Ease seeped into my bones.

Zooming in on the bolted concrete walls, I snapped a few of the rugged mix and the dark holes. My breathing came easier, and my worries over Millar and the meeting ahead faded. I started toward the main entrance to the building.

As I passed the cubbies by the door, a place where Art majors left minor works to dry, I paused to peruse the creations with a curious eye. Some were no better than the art I'd seen produced at Kingsley by the more talented kids, but there were others that showed a genius of mind that I envied.

I took photos of those, as if I could steal their magic and infuse it into my own work.

Then I headed inside, taking in the mélange of odors: oil paint, graphite, stale air, and the acrid scent of photo-developing chemicals. Footsteps echoed behind me on the concrete stairs as I took them up a flight to Marta Neuheim's office.

Outside her door, I checked my Leica over. It was in good working order, of course. Then I knocked.

"Come in," a woman's voice called out, tinged with a faint unplaceable accent.

Marta had wild, loose, dark hair streaked with silver. She looked to be in her mid-fifties and was adorned in a colorful dress of green, pink, silver, and white, with a matching silver scarf around her neck. Her glasses were perched at the end of her nose. She looked at me over the rims of them, giving me the phantom urge to push my glasses up *my* nose, even though I'd worn contacts today, as usual.

"Hi," I said, when she cocked her head at me. "Um, I'm Peter Mandel."

Her eyebrows went up as if to encourage me to get to the point.

"I'm a freshman, and I'm taking Photography 110 with Professor Michaelson. I don't think it's a good fit for me. He said I'd need to talk to you about making a change?"

Sitting back in her chair, Marta took her glasses off and put them aside. "What kind of change were you thinking of?" Again, with the vague accent.

"I'd like to skip up to the 200-level."

She kept her eyes on my face as she shrugged her mouth. "Mm, I see."

I rushed on. "I brought my portfolio. And my camera." I indicated my baby. "I've been taking photos for years now and won several contests and competitions as a high schooler. I also already know how to use a darkroom and develop film. My art teacher taught me how back in high school."

"Your school made a darkroom available to students?"

"It was private. Kingsley."

"Ah." She motioned toward the chair opposite her. "Sit. Let's have a look."

As I held out my portfolio, she moved paperwork and staplers, as well as a flip-top storage box full of negatives, around on her desk to make room for it. She took it from me and placed it in the center of her desk.

My stomach trembled. To another person, having their work assessed to skip up a level might not be so anxiety-provoking, but this was the first time a professor would be evaluating my work. It felt like everything—the class, my future, my self-esteem—rode on her approval.

A very loud knock came at the door, and Marta looked up and over my head. "Ah, just a moment—Peter, did you say it was?"

"Yes."

"I need to speak with this student. I'll be right back."

"No problem."

She rose and walked with a flowing grace from her office, closing the door behind her. I heard her voice and another but couldn't make out the words.

While I waited, I checked the settings on my Leica, lifted it to my eye, and snapped a picture of Marta's desk. I looked around at the stacks of paperwork, the photos of family, and the walls covered in framed photos that I assumed were Marta's.

The majority portrayed young people of various ages and races speaking in sign language. The photos were alive with their vibrant facial expressions, wide eyes and hands moving so quickly they sometimes blurred.

Marta returned, and I picked up the smell of lavender when she passed me this time.

"Now, Peter," she said, seating herself and spreading the black cover of my portfolio wide. She put her glasses back on the end of her nose, looking over them as she said, "When you speak to me, please make sure I'm looking at you first. I'm hard of hearing."

That was when I noticed the hearing aids poking through her hair above her ears. I waited until she glanced up. "Yes, ma'am."

"Just call me Marta. Ma'am is too much." Her accent made sense to me now. I wondered if she'd had hearing problems her whole life or if she'd developed them later on. "Shall we?"

She motioned at the top photo, a shot I'd taken of Sarah last spring in all her tiger's-eye beauty.

I nodded.

As Marta flipped through the photos I'd spent hours selecting last night, I questioned my choices. Under her quiet scrutiny, most seemed far from good enough now. Too dramatic. Too juvenile. Way too many of me wrestling with my demons—the demons Adam had gifted me—in abandoned houses, along railways. I'd even included a few heartbreaking nudes.

My gut clenched. There was too much of *me* in these. They weren't art. They were an evisceration of my misery. And wasn't that what I'd just been saying to Millar? I'd used these photos to contain my ugliness. It was ghoulish.

Sweat popped up on my brow. I was tempted to lift my Leica and take photos of her looking through my photos. A meta moment of sorts. And she did so with no noticeable reaction to what she was seeing. Expressionless, she could have been looking at a black-and-white photo of a sunset.

Then she hit the second half of my portfolio, and everything changed. I remembered why I was here. I remembered I was damn good at this.

Photos of queer joy spread out before her. These pictures captured bright smears of color, laughter, lust, and friendship. I relaxed as I gazed across the desk at the upside-down prints. All those faces were so familiar to me, all the pictures were cataloged in my head, their details summonable at any moment. I should have started and ended with these.

Marta flipped the portfolio closed and sat with her head down, fingers stroking the back of it.

A fresh wave of adrenaline broke over me. My palms were wet from it.

When she looked at me, there was a sharp awareness in her eyes, as if she was seeing something rare. *Me*—not the photos. "Do you know how often students come to me with an overblown sense of entitlement, certain they're the next Cartier-Bresson or Helmut Newton?"

I shook my head.

"Too many." She cocked her head. "The name's Peter Mandel, you said?"

"Yes, ma'am. I mean, Marta."

"And you developed all of these yourself?"

"Most of them. Everything past the quarter mark."

She opened my portfolio again. "This one. Wide aperture or slow shutter speed?"

I leaned forward to see which picture she was referring to and answered once she looked up. "Both."

She snorted. "All right. Where do you store your film?"

Again, I waited until her eyes were on my face. "The refrigerator."

"Good." She flipped between a photo near the back and one near the front. "Growth. The photos at the beginning are amateur, emotional, and melodramatic."

I winced. Perhaps, but they were representations of my high school agony, so what else could they be?

"Doesn't mean they aren't good," she added. "You're willing to commit to capturing a raw and intense feeling on film. Most wannabe artists of any type—photographers, painters, musicians— are too scared to be that honest. Especially when it's about them- selves. Most are voyeurs. Happy to snap up other people's pain, but terrified of showing their own." She glanced up to see if I had anything to say or add. I didn't. "And that's why so many of them fail. They're cowards. You are not."

"Thank you." I realized she couldn't hear me, but she didn't look up.

She went back over the photos of queer joy. "These, though, are special. You can see a shift in spirit. These feel purpose-driven on a larger scale. It's no longer about just you and your feelings, right? You've grown to see the bigger picture. How you and your feelings fit into the scheme of things, and you've managed to capture not only the men in these photos, but the joy you, as a photographer, felt in witnessing them." She looked up for my response.

"Thank you. It's been a big year for me. A lot of changes."

"I like that, and I like these pictures." Looking me up and down, she laughed under her breath, "And I like you." She reached out with a gimme-gimme motion.

"I didn't bring anything else?" Then I remembered Professor Michaelson had said she'd want to see my camera. I held the Leica out. "Do you want this?"

She shook her head. "Don't be silly, hand over the drop-add and transfer forms."

"Oh." I had to dig into my backpack to retrieve the papers she needed to sign which would allow me to drop Photography 110 and add Photography 210.

"You *must* be in my class," she said. "I won't lose you to Boring Bob."

"I'm sorry? Who?"

She waved the question away. "Another 210 professor. So, if the timing of my class clashes with something else in your schedule, you'll have to submit drop-adds until you can make it fit. You don't have my permission to waste your talent, understand?"

I nodded, butterflies in my gut.

She filled out the form and signed it with a flourish. "I expect to see all that bravery of yours going forward, okay?"

"Thank you," I said. "I hope I can please you."

She shook her head. "No, Peter Mandel. You're going to please yourself. If you need to take self-absorbed photos of shame and misery, do it. If it brings you joy to capture a different kind of love and acceptance, do it. Just don't hem-and-haw over your talent. Don't overthink your photos. I can tell you haven't in the past, so don't start now."

"Thank you. I really appreciate this. I won't let you down."

"Ah-ah-ah," she scolded.

"I won't let myself down?"

"Correct. See you in class."

Stepping from the cool interior of the building out into the August heat was like walking into a mouth. I fanned myself with my hand as I leaned against the side of the building, laughing in relief. She'd said yes, but more than that—she'd *liked* what she'd seen. She'd called me talented, and she wanted me in *her* class. Wow.

I wanted to share the news, but I didn't know who to share it with. I could run over to McClung Tower and tell my dad, but a quick glance at my watch let me know he was already in class. I was tempted to find a phone booth to call Daniel with the news, but he might be busy with his mom or his siblings right now. Daniel had so much on his plate, and I didn't want to bother him.

I could call home and let my mom know, but I'd never done something like that before, and it seemed late in my life to start now. Besides, she'd just say she was proud of me, unless she didn't answer at all because she was lost on the prairie making a rancher fall in love with a preacher's daughter.

I decided to take care of another task I'd promised myself I wouldn't put off for too long. I walked to the UT Health Services Center.

Sitting down in a big cushy chair next to a low round table, I waited for my name to be called. Nerves flitted through my system, and I tried to think of anything else aside from the reason I'd come here. My brain offered up a memory of Millar's laugh earlier in the day.

He'd known about me and Adam. I wondered who else from Kingsley knew. I shook the thoughts away.

Everything Millar had talked about, our entire conversation, had been steeped in the past. The Peter he remembered was the Peter I used to be, the one who'd lied and cheated and hurt people. That person was gone for good. I was turning into someone new.

That was why I was here. To get the test that would put the final nail in that coffin of doubt. I had to make sure nothing from that past was going to follow me into the future. Beginning with the specter of HIV.

Cold anxiety whooshed through my stomach.

I remembered the last time I'd been with Adam, how even now I wasn't sure he'd used a condom. There'd been seven in the trash, but one hadn't seemed to have much cum in it, if any at all. But it'd been the seventh time! How much cum could he have had left?

Still, the fact remained: I needed to get tested. That's why I was here. Just to be sure.

Fidgeting, I tried to think of something else to center me. I pulled out my wallet, sorting through the small set of photos I had in there. One of my mom. One of Harry. One of my dad. And one I'd snatched from my pinboard just yesterday morning. It showed Daniel laughing as he bit into a slice of pizza. I'd snapped it of him over the summer at Robert's house, and I loved how carefree he looked.

I wanted that for Daniel all the time. That carefree laughter. The shine in his eyes.

I wanted it for me, too. I wondered what kind of photos I could take with a carefree, unburdened heart. What would they show of me? Of life? I hoped one day I'd find out.

Then that could be the real me, the one Marta would see reflected in my upcoming photos, and the one Daniel would consider his friend.

From now on, I was going to be the kind of man who took photos for the love of it, not because he'd die if he didn't, and I'd be the kind of man who fell in love with someone true and honest, like Daniel.

Someone who, if he ever did date me, would never hide me away or use me.

I was becoming a man I could be proud of, just like Marta had said.

"Peter Mandel?"

My head snapped up. "Yes?"

"Come on back."

Chapter Eight

AFTER WHAT FELT like days and days of pining and dreaming, Friday finally arrived. I woke with butterflies of anticipation in my stomach. The 4:50 a.m. alarm wasn't even hard to face, I was so eager to get on with my day.

Starting with my first shift at the library.

I'd gotten the news on Wednesday that I'd been hired in the Circulation Department, and they'd requested I come in on Friday morning to learn how to help open.

When I arrived, I was disappointed to find Barry wasn't there. Instead, a woman named Miriam was the manager in charge. As I waited for her to show me how to punch in my timecard, I could see the library's other departments were waking up and getting ready, too: Periodicals, Microfiche, Reference, and even Stacks.

As the morning shift started, April arrived, as well as a tall guy named Brad. While Miriam and Brad got the computers fired up and ready, April and I worked the book return.

"It's easy," she said, showing me how to re-magnetize the metal strip inside the spine of the books. "Then you put them in a pile here, and I wand them into the computer." She waved the barcode scanner at me. "After, we put them on that cart—" she pointed "—according to call number."

She was right. It wasn't hard at all, and I liked the rhythm of it once we got in the flow. It was almost like a dance. The catchy new

Spin Doctors song played in my mind as I repeated the same movements again and again. I mentally photographed April as we worked, and it was like a dull-but-satisfying internal music video.

After we'd checked in the dozens of books that'd been returned overnight, magnetized and wanded them, then put them on alphabetized carts to be returned to the stacks, we were assigned to the main floor front computers. I was instructed to sit with April and wait for patrons to arrive so she could show me how to check out the books. While we waited, April cleared off part of the counter to work on her homework, so I did the same.

All in all, it was easy work.

After my short first shift was over, I had class with Minty and Jennifer. I hadn't wanted to mention to him that I was having dinner with Daniel tonight, but when Minty wouldn't leave me alone about going to Tilt-a-Whirl for a first-week-of-college celebration, I had to spill the beans.

Minty's jaw clenched and released at the news, but he said nothing.

"Who's Daniel?" Jennifer asked.

"My best friend," Minty said.

"I thought Windy was your best friend." Jennifer frowned in confusion. They must have been hanging out together outside of class if she knew about Windy.

"He is. But so is Daniel." Minty turned to me, blue eyes burning. "I swear to God, Peter, if you mess with his head again, I will—" He clawed at the air with his painted, baby-pink nails. "I mean it. Dead. Deader than dead. Even if I *like* you. Even if I'd feel *sad* about it later. Dead."

"I'm not messing with his head."

"Dead."

"We're just friends."

"*Dead.*" Minty turned back to the front of the class, and after a tense moment, mused aloud, "When do you think my honey's going to arrive? He's ten minutes late again. He can't keep this up."

"He's the TA. It's not like he can get fired. Or can he?" Jennifer asked.

I didn't know. I supposed I could ask my dad what the protocol was, but I also didn't care. Whenever Donnie Huggins arrived, he'd proven to be interesting and provocative in his lectures, so I was willing to put up with his stage-fright-driven lateness.

Somehow, I got through the rest of my Friday classes without the teeming, wild mass of butterflies bursting out of my chest.

When I swung the Volvo into my driveway, singing "Don't Get Me Wrong" at the top of my lungs, I waited until it was over before hustling inside. I found two notes on the kitchen counter in my mother's scrawl. One read: *Daniel called and asked if you could arrive by six and if you could pick up a can of green beans on your way. They're his sister's favorite, and they're all out.*

The other: *Adam called. I hung up on him.*

Still singing under my breath, I picked up a pen and scribbled two words at the end of the second note: *Good, ugh.*

Then I nearly skipped upstairs to shower, dress, and figure out which camera to take with me. I was going to take lots of pictures this time. Joyful pictures. Excited pictures. I planned to take photos of Daniel, his house, his sister and brother if they let me, maybe even his mom.

I was going to document and claim these moments of happiness because I *wanted* to. Besides, I'd never had the chance to channel this kind of energy onto film before. Not even at the beginning with Adam. I'd always been so anxiety-ridden.

"Bye, I'm leaving," I called, gathering my keys, and settling the Leica around my neck.

Mom emerged from her office dressed in a red poodle skirt complete with a dog sewn onto the side of it. Looked like the prairie rancher had won over the preacher's daughter, and now she was working on a new romance set in the 1950s. "Do you have condoms?"

"Mom."

"Do you?"

"We're just friends!"

"No, you're not." She sighed, grabbed her purse from the sofa, pulled out a twenty and stuffed it into my hand. "You like this boy, right?"

I rolled my eyes.

"Then buy some condoms."

"Mom—"

"And take it from a romance author, buy him flowers, too."

With another eye roll, I took her money. She could be as annoying as she wanted to be. It didn't matter. Each minute that drew me closer to seeing Daniel again brought bubbly excitement chasing through my veins.

Almost an hour later, I rang Daniel's doorbell with a can of green beans and a bouquet of flowers clutched in my hands, a new pack of condoms in my backpack, my Leica around my neck, and a stupid, hopeful smile on my face.

"Mister! It's you again!" Kennedy swung the door wide wearing blue jeans, a sparkly hairband rather like one of Minty's, and a stained yellow T-shirt. She took one look at me, and whipped around to yell, "Dan! Your friend Mister is here! He has flowers! And green beans!"

"You can just call me Peter," I said to her.

"Sure, okay, Mister Peter. C'mon in."

I laughed as I stepped inside. "Just Peter."

At that moment Daniel appeared from the kitchen, wiping his hands on a small towel. He looked as glowingly handsome as ever, barefoot and laid-back in a white button-up and blue jeans. "Hey," he said, breaking into a smile. "Roses? Thank you." His eyes crinkled at the edges as his smile grew even wider. "Wow. I've never had a guy show up with flowers before."

"Me either." I let him liberate them from me.

He ducked his head to smell them. "They're gorgeous." He breathed in deeply again, closing his eyes. The golden tint of his hair picked up the orange tone of the flowers, and I lifted my camera to grab the shot.

Daniel's head came up at the snicking sound, his eyes searching mine. "Are they for me? Or my mom?"

"For you."

A flicker of emotion crossed his face, and I didn't know what to make of it.

"I got the orange ones—not because of UT, but because of autumn. It's coming up soon." A wrinkle of anxiety disrupted my joy. "And, uh, my mom said to bring them?"

Daniel turned to Kennedy, handing off the hand towel. "Take this and the green beans into the kitchen for me, will you?"

Kennedy fixed the sparkly headband in her messy hair before grabbing the can from my hand and darting off.

Stepping close to me, Daniel looked at my lips and then my eyes. My heartbeat picked up; my breath caught in my throat. I felt dizzy, like I'd eaten an entire cone of cotton candy and now I was on a soul-ascending sugar high.

Daniel licked his lips. I went up on my toes to make it easier for him.

"Tell your mom thanks from me," he whispered, a teasing grin spreading wide. "They're beautiful." Tweaking one of my curls, he turned to shut the front door. "C'mon." He started back down the hall to the kitchen without looking back.

My cheeks burned as I followed. Had he almost kissed me? I was pretty sure he'd almost kissed me. I wasn't delusional, was I?

"You can put your things there for now," he said, motioning toward the breakfast nook.

"How can I help?"

"You can't. Have a seat."

I heaved the backpack off and slid into the booth.

He bustled around the delicious-smelling kitchen, putting the roses in a vase with water and placing them on the table in the nook. I could smell their fresh scent even over the cooking odors.

"Where's Milky Way?" I asked, surprised she hadn't greeted me at the door with Kennedy. "And your mom and Paul?" I looked around. Kennedy had also disappeared.

"Downstairs watching TV. They ordered pizza earlier. We recently got Domino's delivery out here, and the kids are loving it. Milky Way, too. She's a big fan. That's why she didn't come greet you. It's not that she doesn't love you anymore. Don't worry." Back by the stove, Daniel put on oven mitts before reaching inside to pull out a bubbling pot pie. "We're going to eat on the upstairs deck for some privacy." He settled the pie on a metal trivet. "That okay with you?"

"Sure. But they're not joining us?"

"No. It'll be just you and me."

"Oh. I'd thought—" What was I supposed to say? That I'd spent the week picturing his mom and siblings being here in order to keep myself from imagining this was a date?

Daniel cocked his head and teased, "I mean, if you *want* to eat with my whole family, I can call them up here, and we can endure the awkwardness of me and my mom in the same room. It's intense and shitty, but I'm game if—"

"No!" I interrupted him before he could go on. "I'm happy for it to be just us. Alone." Daniel and I had almost never been alone. I could only think of a handful of instances in all the months we'd known each other.

"Good. Me too. I've been looking forward to it."

My pulse picked up again. "Me too. I mean, I've been looking forward to tonight. Seeing you."

Grinning, Daniel poked a fork into the pie, pulled it out, examined it and nodded. "That's done. Now, just let me throw these green beans on the stove to make Kennedy happy, and then we'll take the pie and anything else we need up to the deck. After that, it's possible, but not guaranteed, that we'll be left alone."

"She's going to eat green beans and *pizza?*"

"She's weird," Daniel said, like that explained everything.

I guessed it did. When I was a kid, I liked to mix Pop Rocks and mashed bananas in a bowl and eat them, so who was I to judge?

"What'd you bring?" Daniel asked, nodding toward my backpack as he stirred the canned beans over the heat.

I unzipped the bag and pulled things out one by one to show him.

"A folder of pictures from earlier in the summer. I thought you might like seeing them." I skipped over the new box of condoms. "Well, I didn't bring this so much as it was already in here. I don't know what to do with it." I pulled out the manila envelope full of proof of my uncle's life. I hadn't looked inside it since that first day with my dad, and most of the time I forgot about it. Except for when I'd accidentally grabbed it instead of the right notebook for a class.

"What is it?" Daniel asked.

"Remember how I told Bobby about my uncle's journal and stuff?" I waved the manila envelope in the air before returning it to my backpack. "That's what."

"Ahh. Bobby asked about that when I talked to him on the phone two nights ago," Daniel said. "He wanted to know if you'd read the journal or the letters yet."

"Such a gossip hound."

"He is."

The solemnity of Daniel's voice struck me, and somehow, I just knew. "He's not going home this week after all, is he?"

Daniel shook his head, his brow furrowed. "No."

"Do you think he'll…" How did I ask this without sounding morbid? "Will he ever get to go home?"

Daniel turned the stove off and strained the beans before dumping them into a bowl. "I don't know. We'll have to wait and see."

He came and scooted in beside me on the bench. Taking hold of my hands, he rubbed his thumb against the back of my knuckles. "I'm glad you're here. It's been a long week for me."

"I'm glad I'm here, too." My heart skipped a beat.

"You look…" He smiled and let go of my hands to run his fingers through my frizzed-out hair. Tingles broke out down my spine. "Well, to be honest, you look kind of a mess."

I huffed. "It's humid outside. My hair won't obey me when the weather's like this."

"It's cute. I love it." He blinked, as if he hadn't meant to say that. "I'm glad you didn't take Minty's advice about getting product."

"Yeah?"

"Mm-hmm. It's soft and never does what you want it to, and…" He leaned closer and took a deep breath. "It smells good."

"Pert shampoo. Pricey stuff."

He laughed and stood again, rubbing his neck. "Okay, let's see. The pie's done, I've got the…" He put up a finger. "And the…yeah." A second finger. "Okay. The green beans are ready for Kennedy. I'll let my mom know." He nodded at the door down to the basement. "Wait here?"

I agreed.

Once he disappeared, I rose to snap a few pictures of the view. Moving over to the counter, I grabbed a shot of the finished pot pie, and then looked around the kitchen.

Daniel's house was big, and not very homey in my opinion.

Daniel returned from downstairs. He looked grim when he first appeared, but his eyes lit up and then softened when he saw me. "That's done. All we need to do is carry the pie up, and we're done."

"All right. How can I help?"

Daniel grinned. "Grab your bag, bring the flowers, open the door, and follow me."

I held the door from the kitchen to the backyard, and Daniel balanced the pie on his oven-mitt-covered hands. Following him out and then up the stairs, I watched his bare feet climb the risers. Reaching the wide deck attached to the house's second story, my heart exploded with hope at the sight that met me there.

Everywhere were beautiful plants and flowers, as well as a rose-covered pergola with white twinkle lights strung through the shadowy interior. Cozy wicker porch chairs sat alongside a bar that seemed to be stocked with seltzer, ice, and some different soft drinks. In the center of the deck was a big picnic table dressed up with a black tablecloth and candles—not lit yet, but long-stemmed matches stood next to them ready to do the honors.

"What do you think? It's all for you." Daniel placed the pot pie on the table and took his mitts off. "Do you like it?"

I blinked again. "This can't be for me."

"Why not?"

"Because…you didn't…I mean…" I trailed off, not sure how to express what I wanted to say. Finally, I spat out, "Because this isn't a date."

"It can be, if you want."

"Really?"

He smiled. "It's up to you."

"I…"

Daniel's voice went tense with nerves. "Wait, let me explain first. So, um, I arranged the table, and put up the twinkle lights in the pergola, and set out the candles. I know it's maybe silly to have them when the sun doesn't set until later, but I thought it'd be nice anyway. The plants were already here. My mom almost killed them all with neglect during her relapse, but Paul, Kennedy, and I have managed to save them. But the rest...I did this. For tonight. Because, despite everything, I'd like this to be a date, Peter. If that's all right with you?"

"A date?" I sounded stupid.

He nodded.

"And you did this for me?" I gazed at the romantic scene Daniel had prepared. Adam had never, ever done anything like this for me. I'd never imagined anyone would.

"Well, for you *and* me. I like pretty things too. Like those roses. And you." Daniel spread his arms wide, encompassing it all. "It's not much. You deserve a lot more, but I hope it's enough."

Not much? I deserved *more?* It was beautiful. Amazing. With my heart in my throat, I placed the bouquet of roses on the table by the pie, noting that by some stroke of fate, they matched the yellow and orange patterned plates he'd put out.

"What do you say? Can this be a date?" he asked again.

"I'm not sure I'm dressed for all this," I said, letting my backpack fall to the decking, motioning all around and then down at my jeans and T-shirt. "This is all so fancy."

He gestured at himself—barefoot, in jeans, and that white shirt.

I laughed. "Okay. Yeah, this can be a date." The air felt carbonated, fizzing as I breathed it in. "I can't believe you took the time to do all this for me. I mean, for us."

Relief spread over Daniel's features. "Will it seem less special if I admit I had the kids help me?" He took up a match and struck it. "Paul was unimpressed, of course, but Kennedy thought it was a lot of fun." He lit the candles. "Even so, it took most of the day and I didn't have a lot of time for cooking afterward." Shaking out the burning match, he ruefully indicated the pie. "Maybe I should have focused more on food and less on atmosphere."

I waved that off. "No. It smells so good. I can't believe you made it. My parents don't cook. It's microwave dinners at my house or my dad's specialty: spaghetti noodles with Ragu sauce. So this is amazing. Believe me."

Daniel sat down and motioned for me to do the same. As we settled, I couldn't keep my eyes from straying to the twinkle lights, and then to the view of the river, and then back to Daniel's familiar smile.

Daniel opened a bottle of seltzer and poured it into our glasses, before handing me a plate with cut lemons on it.

"Um, Daniel?" I asked as I pressed against the sides of a lemon to squeeze the juice into my water. Some ran down my hand, and I licked it from the side of my palm before wiping the rest on my napkin.

Daniel's eyes lingered on my mouth. "Yes?"

"*Why* do you want this to be a date? I hurt you in July, and I haven't done nearly enough to prove you can trust me again."

Daniel began cutting into the pot pie, steam rising into the cool evening air. Even after he finished cutting the pie into sections, he didn't serve it yet. He seemed to be considering my question, and by the time he answered, I was sweating it, wondering if he'd changed his mind now. "Does it sound selfish if I admit that I've had a *really* bad week? And thinking of how I'd be seeing you tonight made everything a little bit better?"

My heart skipped again. "No. That's not selfish."

"Whenever I thought of you, it made me happy, and that just made me want to think of you more. At some point, I decided that if you, and everything about you, could make me smile during all this shit I've been dealing with, then I should take a chance. I want to be with you, even if, on the surface, maybe it isn't the most cautious choice."

I swallowed hard. "You want to be with me?"

"Yeah. Here, outside with these flowers, and that view—"

The river glinted in the sun, and the mountains trailed off in the distance.

"I wanted to see you surrounded by romantic candles and these twinkle lights." His voice went softer. "I wanted that a lot. And now I have it." A smile crossed his lips. "And, for the record, it's what I hoped it would be. You look amazing, by the way. You always look amazing. Ever since the first time I saw you. Every time I see you."

"Daniel…" I didn't know what to say. I was dizzy. If I'd had a sip of the seltzer water before he'd started talking, I'd think it was drugged. I hadn't felt so giddy and in love with the whole world since that asshole Jeremy put GHB in my drink. But this was different. This was because of Daniel. Because, somehow, despite it all, despite how much I'd screwed up, Daniel still wanted me.

"I've missed you," Daniel said.

"I've missed you too, and I'm glad it's a date." I reached out for his hand. His fingers were as comfortable in mine as I'd remembered. "To be honest, I wanted it to be too. All week I kept thinking of this as a date, and then I'd try to talk myself out of it. I didn't want to get my hopes up."

Daniel leaned close and pressed his forehead to mine.

My heart felt like a starry pinwheel in my chest, shiny and spinning with excitement, giving off sparks of joy. Our breath mixed in the space between us, and I waited for him to kiss me.

But he just pressed his lips to my forehead, like he had on my birthday, before sitting back to serve our dinner.

As he put a creamy, thick piece of pot pie onto my plate, he glanced at me. "Your hair in this humidity. My God. It's amazing."

I rolled my eyes. I could imagine how frizzed out it must be. "Glad someone enjoys it, at least." The affectionate glow in Daniel's expression conveyed the sincerity behind his words. He genuinely liked how I looked.

I liked how he looked, too: a warm, honest man who made me feel good. It could be love. It very well could be.

Daniel grabbed his glass of water and lifted it. "Wait, we forgot to toast."

Raising mine, too, we dinged our glasses together. "What should we toast to?"

"Hmm..."

Lights twinkled, and the sound of cicadas lifted into the air like a thrilled buzz. Instead of waiting for him to answer, I offered, "To our first date?"

Daniel nodded. "May there be many more."

We drank to that.

Chapter Nine

DINNER WAS WONDERFUL.

Inside, I was like Maria in *The Sound of Music*, running over internal mountains, happy with the idea that he'd done any of this, *all* of this, just for the two of us. I felt special and sparkling, or like I might burst into giggles and glitter, or maybe sprout feathers and fly away.

But I didn't want to fly anywhere. I wanted to be right here.

We didn't talk about anything serious as we ate. We looked at the photos I'd brought to show him. All shots of our friends from the summer. I told him about meeting with Marta Neuheim, and Minty's crush on our green-gilled TA. He told a few funny stories about the kids, but for the most part, he just wanted to listen to me.

As we finished our food, the night started to drop, and the air grew soft. Our moods softened as well. We breathed the fading light in, letting the evening sink into our skin. At some point, I took out my camera, and I fulfilled my promise to take pictures of Daniel—as many as I wanted, and he obliged.

I caught images of him in the dying sun and felt pleased to have cataloged his eyebrows and lashes, the angle of his cheek, and the curve of his chin. He seemed happy to let me.

After I'd satisfied my urge to press the night onto film, we took our dirty dishes downstairs to the kitchen, rinsed them off and loaded them into the dishwasher. Daniel put the leftover pie in the fridge. Then we went back outside.

Daniel took me by the hand and led me down to the river's edge to watch the sun set on the water. The colors were beautiful, and I'd have loved to get a few shots, but I'd left my camera behind on the deck. I'd nearly run out of film, and though I had another canister in my backpack, it was 400 speed. Better for inside pictures.

Milky Way's bark broke the quiet. Her white body streaked down from the house.

Daniel's mother stood on the back patio calling for her, but the fluffy thing wasn't having it. She raced toward us across the yard. When she reached us, I bent to scratch her ears and greet her. She was giddy with joy at seeing me.

"It's fine!" Daniel shouted toward the house. "We'll bring her back in."

His mom waved and went inside.

"She's been happy here," Daniel said. "The first few days, she seemed confused, but she's settled in. I think she'll miss the kids, though, when they go."

I picked Milky Way up in my arms and settled her down with a cuddle. She calmed as I petted her head, and the three of us stood, looking out at the water dancing with the coral, orange, and flame of the sky. Daniel surprised me by slipping behind me and wrapping his arms around my waist. He hooked his chin over my shoulder. "This okay?"

I leaned back against him. He felt strong enough to hold me forever. "Yeah."

We stood there, a little trio, breathing together and cuddling, until the remaining sunlight grayed, and Milky Way started to squirm. When I straightened from putting her down, Daniel was right there, looking at me. His golden hair had been tousled from the rougher breeze by the water, and his eyes glowed. My breath stuttered.

He turned his attention to my hair as he so often did, reaching out and smoothing his hands over it. I let the motion pull my head back, so my chin rose, and I was gazing up at him. He stepped into my space. The heat of his body against mine made my pulse pound.

His breath ghosted over my cheek. "Is it all right if I kiss you?"

"Yes."

"You'd like that?"

"Yeah."

His lips touched mine, and my knees shook. Because I did like it. I really, *really* did.

The whole of summer seemed to live in the moment—hot and bright between us. Lips to lips, my heart pounding, everything dissolving away except for what mattered most.

Us.

✧　✧　✧

AFTER WE KISSED by the river, Daniel took me by the hand and led me and Milky Way back toward the house. Neither of us said much, we were both too giddy, smiling and laughing together. Over nothing, over everything. Over whatever this dizzy pure feeling was called.

When we reached the stairs up to the deck, Daniel asked, "Do you want to go up to my room?" His hands sought mine.

"Your room?" I gazed up at him.

"Yeah, it's...it's up to you." He licked his lips, his breath hitching.

If I went upstairs with him, we'd kiss more, and we might even end up naked together. My heart trip hammered. *Yes*, I wanted that, but everything was moving so fast, too. I hadn't even expected this to be a date...

Daniel caught my hesitation. "Or we could grab some cookies from the kitchen and go back up on the deck to talk about whatever. Anything. It doesn't matter to me."

"No," I said, shaky excitement washing over me. "Let's go to your room."

Daniel's smile, as easy as it had been this summer, took my breath away. "Let's grab cookies too," he whispered. "Now that I've mentioned them, I want some."

I laughed.

Once a bag of Chips Ahoy had been retrieved from the kitchen, Daniel took my hand and led me back outside and then up to the deck. "We'll go in this way. My room's on the back side of the house anyway."

On the deck, I grabbed my backpack. Daniel escorted me through French doors into an upstairs living space that adjoined a hallway. Hand in hand, we headed down a long hallway with multiple open doors.

While the downstairs spaces were decorated nicely, the areas upstairs, like the hallway, seemed unfinished. It felt like there should be pictures or art on the walls, but they were bare. Like no one had ever taken the time to choose anything. Or perhaps after Daniel's father's death, there hadn't been enough money or inclination.

When we reached his room, he locked the door behind us and leaned back against it. I turned around, gazing at muted, calm blue walls, and the framed posters from bands I knew Daniel liked: R.E.M., The Church, The Waterboys, and The Cure.

"How long has this been your bedroom?"

"Since I was a teenager. The house I grew up in was different from this. It was large enough for all of us, but cozy. Like a big cottage."

"So this place doesn't feel like your childhood home?"

Daniel shook his head. "Not really."

Taking my backpack off and putting it on his big desk by the largest window, I looked at the bookshelf next to it. It was full of textbooks, and a few books containing information about architecture, sample designs, and building plans. Above the shelf, there was a framed blueprint. When I leaned closer to see it better, Daniel said, "My mom had that done. It was my first design for a class."

Stretched out on the wall above the window there was a colorful, framed banner that read, *Danny, are you okay?*

I laughed.

"Yeah," he said, smiling. "Kevin gave me that back in high school. It's still funny so…I keep it."

"It's great."

"C'mon," he said, motioning toward the bed. "Let's sit."

There was a beanbag chair by the window, and of course the chair at his desk, but he'd motioned toward the queen-sized bed. As I sat on the corner of it, I almost started chuckling. This was real, and it was happening. Somehow, despite everything, Daniel had forgiven me.

Daniel sat with his back against the headboard on his side of the bed, and he patted the space next to him before tearing open the bag of cookies.

"Not worried about crumbs, huh?" I asked, as I kicked my shoes off and crawled up next to him on the bed, sitting with my back against the extra pillow.

He tossed me a cookie. I caught it and took a bite.

I was transported to the last time I'd eaten Chips Ahoy. I'd been with Adam, studying at his house, and we'd eaten an entire bag of them before we'd played a game involving blow jobs and tickling.

I looked at the cookie. I didn't want to eat it anymore.

"Okay?" Daniel asked.

I cleared my throat. "The last time I ate Chips Ahoy, I was with Adam."

"Oh."

Saying those words, seemed to suck the air out of the room. "Sorry." I wiped a hand over my face. "I shouldn't have brought him up."

A beat passed before Daniel reached out to me. I handed him the half-eaten cookie, and he put it on the bedside table. "I wanted to hold your hand, not the cookie."

"Oh. Sorry." I let him take my hand in his, and he twined our fingers together. The heat of his palm against mine was reassuring.

"Don't apologize. He was a big part of your life. You aren't going to be able to just never think about him again."

But that was exactly what I *wanted* to do.

"When we're together, I don't want you to feel like you can't talk about him."

I sighed. "What could I even tell you about him that you haven't already guessed?"

"I don't know. What was his home life like?"

Oh, so we really *were* going to talk about him? I was surprised. I'd sort of thought we'd come up to Daniel's room so we could make out some more. But he was waiting for an answer, so… "Um, well, he has a big family too. Like you. Well, bigger than mine."

Daniel smiled. "That's not hard."

"Yeah. He has an older brother and a twin sister." I reached out for another cookie and Daniel handed one over. The taste wasn't as disturbing this time. "He and his sister used to fight a lot. Sometimes things got crazy with slamming doors and screaming. Once he searched her entire room looking for the pot she'd stolen from him. She'd stuffed it into one of her boots."

"Oh, yeah?" Daniel munched another cookie.

"Adam liked to smoke up. I did it once with him and hated it. I haven't done it since."

"Pot isn't my thing either," Daniel said. "I don't like anything more than a drink or two. I'm okay with feeling a little loose from alcohol, but I don't like getting *drunk,* and I hate even the idea of how other substances might make me feel."

"Because of your mom?"

"Yeah. When you live with someone who can't control themselves when it comes to stuff like that, you have a choice to make—mimic them or be nothing like them." Daniel popped the remaining half of a cookie in his mouth. After he'd chewed and swallowed, he added, "My dad used to tell me not to even start drinking because alcoholism is in my genes, but I figured out fast that being drunk wasn't for me."

"I like having a drink, but it turns out I puke easily, so I don't drink very much."

"I remember," Daniel said, laughing. "Barry's shoes remember, too."

"Well, I like to earn my nicknames."

I flashed back to Antonio and Minty calling me Heartbreaker. That wasn't a nickname I was glad to have earned. But maybe, since I was here with Daniel now, and my mouth was still tingling from our kiss by the lake, I could un-earn it.

"Do you miss him?" Daniel asked, sounding guarded, like he was protecting his heart. I didn't have to lie when I answered.

"I really don't. I mean, there are things about him that I still have feelings about, sad, mixed-up feelings, but that's not the same as missing him. The thing is, I realize now, Adam and I were always impossible."

"Impossible. What a word."

"It's true. It took me a long time to accept it."

"But you did."

I ducked my head. "Took me too long to figure it out. I'm sorry I hurt you."

"You hurt me a lot less than other people have, and we're here now, so—" He tweaked a curl again.

"You like doing that."

"I do." He smiled. "The thing is, I'm pretty sure I like everything about you."

"Yeah?"

"Yeah. So, tell me more about your first week of college," Daniel said, changing topics and settling back against his pillow again. I sat up and turned so I was facing him, sitting cross-legged on his bed with my back facing the foot of it.

"I told you most of it. What else would you like to hear?"

He laughed. "I don't know. I just like hearing how normal your week was compared to mine."

"I don't know that it was normal, but all right." I told him about the new job at the library, and what I thought of each of my teachers.

Daniel ate his cookies, handing me one occasionally as I talked.

We'd almost finished the whole bag when Daniel licked melted chocolate from his thumb, and I broke off mid-sentence.

He grinned at me, licking the pad again. "Go on. I'm listening."

"Well, I'm not," I said, laughing. "I don't even remember what I was saying."

Daniel sucked his thumb into his mouth.

I rolled my eyes. "Don't tease."

"All right, I won't," Daniel tugged me against him and then pulled me on top of him on the bed.

I went easily. *This* was what I'd come to his bedroom for.

His chest was firm and strong under me, as he wrapped his arm around my lower back, and twined his other hand in my hair. His lips were soft and warm, and his tongue slid against mine until a tide of want crested and we gave in to it, kissing desperately. Hands in each other's hair, we scooted down the bed to press against each other and grind.

Everything about touching and kissing Daniel felt so different from Adam. His skin had a different quality to it, his hair a different texture, and his tongue did things that Adam's never had. I pushed my hands under Daniel's shirt, and he moved his hands down to cup my ass. I groaned and pushed my hard cock against him.

"Shit," he gasped, rolling me over and moving on top of me.

Daniel was bigger than me, and with him on top, I felt covered and safe. His hands gripped me, holding me in place so that he could drive his cock against my thigh. I squirmed for more friction where I needed it.

My chin stung as his stubble scratched against mine. The taste of his mouth and the scent of his sweat was familiar from time spent under the blankets together in Nashville. The bedsprings creaked, the fabric of our blue jeans scraped together, and our sounds grew frantic.

A rapid series of hard knocks rattled the bedroom door. "Daniel!" It was his mother.

"Hold on," Daniel said, his voice breathless. "Just a second." He knelt up over me and peered down with lust-bright eyes. "Sorry. Just…hold on. I'm so sorry."

He stood up and adjusted his cock, tucking it up so it wouldn't be as obvious.

I wiped Daniel's saliva off my lips and scooted so I was sitting up with my back against the headboard, chest still heaving. My mind flashed to another time, another place, and another woman outside the door banging to be let in.

Daniel half-opened the door and leaned against the doorjamb, blocking his mother from my sight. His shoulders bunched up. "Yeah, Mom?"

"Why don't you move your little visit with your friend downstairs to the living room." Her voice was tight, and the tone of it made my stomach sink like a stone. I knew Daniel was out to his mom, but I shouldn't have assumed she'd be okay with us being in his room alone.

"No, we'll stay up here," Daniel said, his tone equally tight.

His mom switched to a loud whisper. I could still hear every word she said. "Danny, I don't want your sister to think it's okay to have a boy in her room when she's a teenager."

"I'm not a teenager. I'm twenty-two years old."

"Even so, you're not setting a good example."

Daniel laughed, sharp and bitter. "Setting a *good example?* Are you *kidding me* right now?"

"Daniel, I'm your mother, and you *will* listen to me."

He shook his head. "Mom, I'm the adult in this house, and you know it."

Silence strained from the other side of the door until his mother whispered, "I don't want your brother and sister thinking what you're doing in there is okay."

"What I'm doing in here? The being-gay part or the kissing part?"

I swallowed and sat as still as I could.

"Don't be like that. You know I have no problem with you being gay or with you kissing anyone at all. But you never flaunted it with Kevin and now isn't the time to start. The kids are already confused enough with me leaving and—"

"Flaunted it? Mom, Kevin and I had sex *everywhere* in this house. In my room, in the basement, in the hot tub, *everywhere.*"

"Seriously, Danny, that's too much information. A mother doesn't need to know things like that, and—"

But Daniel wasn't listening. "As for *now* not being the time to flaunt being gay, I think it's a *great* time. When's the last time I got to hang out with a friend without worrying about whether you were going to find a way to go get drunk again?"

"Danny, my problem is a private matter, and I don't appreciate the way you're speaking—"

"Mom, your problem stopped being private around the time Paul was born."

"Daniel James McPeak."

"Mom."

There was a silent stand-off.

"Fine. You and your 'friend' can visit up here in your room tonight. I give you permission."

"I didn't need it."

Another moment of silence and then she said, "Goodnight."

Daniel shut the door and turned the lock. Leaning back against it with his eyes closed, he shook his head.

"I'm sorry," he said, letting out a long, hard breath, and rolling his shoulders. "That was ugly, I know. She brings out the worst in me. That's one reason why I moved out to begin with, mistake though that turned out to be."

He took another slow, shaky breath and then stalked over to a boombox on the bookshelf, pressing play on the CD player. R.E.M.'s mandolin and guitar broke out over the room. The familiarity was soothing. Daniel scrubbed his hands through his hair before leaning back against his desk with a heavy sigh. "She just pisses me off so much."

I licked my lips. "Should we go downstairs? Or should I go home? I don't want to make anyone uncomfortable here."

"No, stay. I promise, it's not a big deal. If anyone's making things uncomfortable here, it's her..." He let out a sharp huff. "She's being ridiculous." Daniel crossed to the bed and crawled up next to me.

I wanted to make things easier for him, soothe him. So, I pulled him down and held him, with his head resting on my chest. It was strange and new having his weight on me. The spicy, sweet aroma of his shampoo and the warm scent of his skin filled my nostrils. I'd never held anyone but Adam like this. Tentatively, I kissed the top of his head.

Though I was still half-hard, even after the awkward interruption, I thought it was a good thing we'd been disturbed. We'd been moving way too fast. Despite having picked up condoms like my mom had demanded, I'd never hoped to do more than kiss Daniel tonight. But we'd been humping each other like we were bent on making each other come.

My blood cooled as I rubbed his back. I noticed a photo by his bedside of his entire family—his father, his mother, Kennedy and Paul, and a younger-looking Daniel. Daniel looked nothing like his dad. The man was rail thin with dark auburn hair and pale, freckled skin, like Paul. I wondered where Daniel and Kennedy got their sturdy builds, since Daniel's mom was also long and whip-like.

"Feeling better?" I asked when he sat up and ran his hands through his hair like he was scrubbing away bad things.

He smiled sheepishly. "Yeah, sorry. It's not healthy for me to be living here with her. I'm too angry this time."

"I understand."

He hung his head. "I know it's not healthy to treat her like that, but the problem is I don't fucking care. I'm so *fucking* angry with her. I want her to know how much she's hurt me, hurt *us*. Kennedy and Paul are about to be uprooted from their lives, and… God, I don't know how to stop feeling that way."

I thought of my mom, and how she couldn't stop her feelings either and what she was trying to do to solve that. "Have you ever thought about talking to someone about it all?"

"Like a therapist?"

I nodded.

Daniel closed his eyes and sighed. "I saw one. After my dad died."

"Did it help?"

"Sort of. She's the one who encouraged me to move out as soon as possible. And, aside from leaving Paul and Ken at risk, she was right. I'm happier when I'm not living here." Daniel looked down at his hands and then met my gaze. "When I get back to UT, I'll go see someone at the Psych Clinic."

"I just want you to be happy, you know? What kind of friend wouldn't want that?"

"Peter?"

"Yeah?"

"I don't want you to be my friend."

My stomach tightened. "You don't?" What had this whole evening been for then, if he didn't want me around after all?

"I want to be more than friends."

I exhaled hard. "Oh, I thought you meant…"

Realization flashed in his eyes. He touched my chin and slid his hand to cup the back of my head. "No. Despite what happened between us in Nashville, and how that might have looked to you, I don't make out with my friends."

Friends kiss sometimes.

"Yeah, I don't either."

Daniel's smile was a little heartbreaking, but he drew me into a hug. "Good."

Breathing in the scent of his hair, I murmured, "But are you sure? I messed up last month and—"

"I don't care anymore."

My heart didn't seem to care either. Because I'd always known deep down that friends didn't kiss. Not like we had tonight. And they didn't do all that we'd done in Nashville either—no matter what Adam had once said to justify his behavior with me.

"Okay, then," I whispered, my throat tight and that champagne feeling in my veins. "I don't care either."

Daniel kissed my nose and then my lips. "So we're going to try dating?"

"Yeah."

"Boyfriends?" His voice was breathy, and I could feel his heart beating as we hugged each other on the bed.

My own heart was pounding, too. "Boyfriends," I agreed.

Daniel grinned at me. "Your hair's a mess. I love it."

I ran my fingers through the curly disaster, trying to smooth it down, but I knew it was useless without water or some kind of product.

Daniel trailed his fingers across my cheek. "I remember the first day I saw you at Robert and Barry's, I thought, 'Steer clear of that one. Too young.'" He kissed me. "But then you kept showing up places. Like that night on the Hill when I helped you jump your battery." Daniel's expression went soft, and he touched his index finger to my lower lip before pulling it away. "I wanted you to think I had it all together back then."

"Well, you succeeded. I did think that."

Daniel sobered. "Are you disillusioned by the truth?"

I shook my head. "Neither one of us has it all together." He was such a better person than me, and I had a lot to learn from him.

"You won't go back to him?" Daniel's eyes flashed with vulnerability.

I stroked his back. "I won't."

"You love really hard, Peter, and even though I spent the summer jealous as hell, I thought your loyalty to him was beautiful. Fucked up and bound to end in disaster, but beautiful."

"Yeah?"

"Yeah."

Daniel pushed me down on the bed so that he was on top of me again. He placed his elbows on either side of my head, holding himself up to gaze down into my eyes.

He dropped kisses on my nose and jaw, straying to kiss the

lobes of my ears. I shivered and let him do it, reveling in his weight and touch. "All of that reminded me of my dad. He was flawed in a lot of ways, but he loved my mom so hard and so much that he did a lot of questionable things for her. He covered up her drinking and lied about it so she wouldn't be embarrassed. He was an enabler, but he loved her more than I've seen anyone love another human being."

I didn't know what to say. Was this a compliment? I wasn't sure.

"The truth is, I always resented how much he loved her. He never loved *me* half as much, and *I* sure can't seem to love her like he did."

"She's got problems." I stroked his back again, the weight of him making my voice sound strained. "Her choices make it hard for you."

"Yeah, that's true. But…" He sighed, his heart beating faster. I could feel it against my chest. "But when I met you, and when we started to get to know each other, I understood my dad more than I ever had before. I saw how messed up what you were doing with Adam was, how much it was going to hurt you and other people, too, and it was infuriating."

I stared up into his dilated eyes and felt his dick push against my stomach. "But even then, Peter, all I could *really* see was *you*. How gorgeous you are, what a kind, good-hearted person you are at your core. I wanted you then, and I want you now."

I tugged him down into a messy, urgent kiss, and this time, no one interrupted.

Chapter Ten

Daniel yanked my shirt off and I tugged at his, too. Our jeans were harder to get off when we couldn't stop kissing long enough to wriggle out of them, but we managed, and I got my first real glimpse of his dick.

"Holy shit," I whispered, grabbing hold of it as saliva flooded my mouth. I wanted to taste him. I wanted to see how much I could fit in my mouth and how deep I could take that monster. I'd known he was bigger than Adam—had felt it against me in Nashville and sometimes while dancing—but the reality of just how much bigger ignited me with lust and curiosity.

I didn't get a chance to try putting it in my mouth, because Daniel flipped me onto my back and set on me hungrily. He touched me everywhere, kissed me in places that made me writhe, and manhandled me so he didn't miss a single sensitive spot.

My cock thudded as he tongued my inner thighs, and then moved up to suck on the bend of my elbow, and then attacked my neck and mouth. He whispered my name as a constant undercurrent of connection, and I said his back to him, humbled by his intense display of physical adoration.

With a shaking hand, I gripped Daniel's cock. It flexed against the palm of my hand. Its heat was amazing, and it was slick on the sides from dribbled pre-cum. I swallowed hard looking at it.

Daniel reached under the pillow and pulled out a bottle of lube.

I watched him pour some into his hand and then down to slick himself. "I'm not going to penetrate you, I promise."

I was surprised by the wave of disappointment that engulfed me with those words. I wasn't ready for that today. His size alone was scary, and there were all the emotional repercussions of that kind of intense intimacy, at least for me. I didn't want to rush into penetrative sex—despite my brand-new box of condoms. But, still, when he'd said it wasn't going to happen, I'd realized how much I wanted it to…sometime very soon.

"Come here. Spoon with me. I want to feel you in my arms."

I didn't know what to expect, but I moved into the little-spoon position. His lube-slick cock rubbed against my ass cheeks.

"Lift your leg," Daniel whispered in my ear. As I did, he pushed his cock down below my balls. When I lowered my leg again, I could feel him there, hot and hard between my thighs, the head of his dick nudging my sac.

Then he began to move, and his slick hand came around to grasp my already-aching dick.

"I've wanted to hold you like this," he whispered, nuzzling the back of my neck, kissing my nape, and smelling my hair. "Oh, God, Peter…" He dropped my cock to run his hand over my stomach and chest. I looked down and saw myself as he did—thin, wiry, and taut. I guided his hand up to my nipple. He groaned as he rolled it between finger and thumb, his hips moving wilder, and his cock sliding faster between my thighs.

"Fuck," he whispered. "Want to take you this way. Want to fuck you just like this."

I turned my head, trying to see him, and he lifted up on his elbow to kiss me. His tongue and mine touched as we moved together. He played with first one nipple and then the other. It felt so good I whimpered. Squeezing my thighs together for more friction, he grunted, whispering against my cheek, "Yeah, like that.

God, Peter. This feels so fucking *good*."

The motion was almost exactly like being fucked on my side. When Daniel's breath stuttered, and his curses went quiet with the tension of approaching climax, I reached down and took hold of my dick.

"Fuck, you're so hot. I like everything about you so much, Peter," Daniel whispered, biting down on the back of my neck and groaning. "Oh, fuck. I'm gonna come." He went still and wet heat bathed my balls. "Peter, Peter, oh, *fuck*, Peter," he murmured as he gripped me and shuddered through his orgasm. His cum coated my thighs.

Before he'd even caught his breath, Daniel's hand joined mine, moving over my cock together. I felt the telltale tension of my balls tightening. His cock twitched between my thighs, and he whimpered, but I kept on thrusting and groaning, reaching for orgasm.

Suddenly, it was like I was over the bed and in the bed at the same time. I knew how I looked there with him, tangled up together, rutting against each other; I could see it like a series of photographs, and I turned my head, hoping for a kiss, and I got one just as pleasure gripped me, and I came.

Panting in the aftermath, we rolled to face each other, cum smearing between our bodies. We lay in the bed staring into each other's eyes, both of us flushed and laughing. I could sense in the far corners of my mind the buzzing pull of other people and their concerns, but I wanted to stay in our bubble longer.

Daniel reached out to run his fingers over my cheek, down to my chin, before leaning in to kiss my lips. Sighing, he smiled and peered at my face. "Was that okay?"

With my balls twinging from how hard I'd come, and my heart trip-hammering in my chest, I murmured, "Yeah. More than yeah."

His hands ran over me, and I trailed my fingers through his sparse chest hair. I touched his nipples, watching them peak and darken, a pretty reddish-brown against his chest.

Daniel's hand wandered down to my treasure trail, and then farther down to my cock. He trailed a finger along its length, and it twitched, wanting to get up again for him, but unable to manage it. Then he moved down to my still-taut balls.

"You're really hot," he murmured. "I love the dark hair on your pale skin. It's so sexy."

"You're hot, too." I licked my lips, feeling a zing of new arousal. "I love your eyes the most, I think. Your eyes make me feel—" I broke off, embarrassed at what I'd almost revealed.

"Feel what?"

I licked my lips. "Safe."

His smile was sweet, and I wanted to take a picture of it. "Given everything, maybe this sounds strange, but you make me feel safe, too, Peter."

This news brought tears to my eyes, and I cuddled him closer.

"You know, I think Nashville was a mistake."

"Why? I mean, besides what happened after, wasn't it good?"

"Oh, it was awesome, but think about it, leaving the last few weeks out of it. Let's say it had ended up with us together instead of…how it happened. It's just that…how it was today, just us, alone, seeing you naked in the light from the windows, watching your face when you came? *This* should have been our first time. Do you see what I mean?"

I slid my right hand down to his slim hip and then took hold of his dick. It stirred in my hand, growing and lengthening even more. I watched it avidly. "Yeah. Everything about today is more honest."

"There's nothing hanging over us." I knew it was as close as he'd come to mentioning Adam while we were naked together.

"This feels so good," I whispered, curling up closer, tucking my head against his neck.

I held his now-hard dick in my hand, feeling the rush of blood under the soft skin. I heard his heartbeat and felt his breath on my shoulder. He wrapped his arms around me, and I moved my hand lazily on his dick, and his hips moved in rhythm.

"No hiding, no secrets. Like, it's kind of creepy in one way, but it's also kind of cool that even your mom knows I'm here with you."

"Oh, God, don't mention her," he whispered, his cock now pushing hard against the palm of my hand as I jacked him. "Peter, please…will you…?"

I slipped down his body, and he flopped onto his back, spreading his legs so that I could kneel between his thighs. I rubbed my hands up and down his legs, feeling the hair catch and pull against my palms, and I looked up at him from where I sat on my knees.

My own dick was hard too, and I laughed. "I can't believe we're ready again."

He smiled and sat up enough to grip my chin and pull me up for a kiss. It didn't end for a long, long time.

✦ ✦ ✦

STANDING BY THE Volvo at nearly two in the morning, still shaking from the physical pleasure we'd shared, I leaned against Daniel and breathed in his scent. I wasn't ready to go yet. We'd just rekindled this flame between us, and it was burning so hot that my body roared with it. But it was the middle of the night, and I had the morning shift at the library.

"Peter," he whispered, stroking my back and burying his face in my hair. "I just want you to know that it's not just about sex with you. I should have held back, taken more time to get physical again, but things here are so…" He let out a horrible sound. "And things with you are so good. I rushed in."

"Don't be sorry. I wanted everything we did." I sighed and pressed against him. It felt like a role reversal—me reassuring him, when in the past he'd always seemed to be the one who'd reassured me. "Do you have regrets?"

"No. Not really." He rubbed his cheek against my hair again. "I'm sorry that we're starting something in the middle of all this personal chaos. My emotions are everywhere. I'm afraid I'll screw this up."

He was right, the timing was a mess all around, but I didn't want to wait. I didn't want to have some stupid rebound fling before coming back to him because this was "too soon" after Adam or wait for another year while things settled with his family. I just wanted us to ditch the past and carve a new future. We had the right. We could do this together.

"You won't screw it up," I reassured him. "Neither of us will."

"So long as we're honest."

"Yeah," I agreed. "That's the most important thing."

Daniel ducked his head and gave me a kiss. I sank into it, arms around his neck, heart fluttering as our mouths opened and our tongues touched. Somehow, in my time with Adam, I'd let honesty slip, but here, holding Daniel in his driveway with the midnight sky twinkling above us, all I wanted was truth from him.

Especially when the truth felt this beautiful.

Part IX

Late-August through
Early-September 1991

Chapter Eleven

TIPTOEING INTO THE house and up the stairs so that I didn't wake my parents, I showered and fell into bed. I'd get an hour and a half of sleep, and then get up and drive to work.

But, of course, I was almost too giddy to sleep. I kept replaying the night over and over in my mind, and when I did fall asleep, I dreamed about it, waking up rock-hard and flustered with my alarm clock shouting in my ear.

Once I'd grabbed another shower to wake up, I put on fresh clothes, and snatched up my backpack and some rolls of undeveloped film. As I passed through the kitchen, grabbing a granola bar for breakfast, I paused to read the note Mom had left on the counter yesterday.

Adam has called six times today. I hung up every time, but this is out of hand.

I picked up the pencil and scribbled, *Next time he calls, don't hang up. Tell him to fuck off and remind him that you'll call the police. Then actually do it.*

I didn't want to talk to Adam. There was nothing he could say that would make me reconsider or think of going back to him.

As I headed out into the pre-dawn morning, I drove to a Dunkin' Donuts and bought a blueberry donut and some coffee to help wake me up. I'd learned my lesson about the coffee machine in the library.

Finding parking was easy, which was a relief, and I made it to the library before whichever manager was responsible for unlocking the doors. The morning was cool, and I sipped the coffee to stay warm, hitching my backpack up on my shoulders.

Once inside, I was assigned the circulation desk near the front entrance. Being a Saturday, the morning crowd was slow to arrive, and when no one was around, I spun around in the seat, staring up at the high ceiling, listening to the echo of footsteps and the occasional burst of laughter throughout the library. I grinned like a loon remembering the night before with Daniel.

He'd put up twinkle lights for me. He'd cooked. He'd taken me down to the river to watch the sunset. He'd kissed me and touched me and made me feel all shivery and new. He'd asked to be my boyfriend.

I pounded my fists on my thighs, happier than I'd been in a long time.

Eventually, I managed to settle down enough to look through a book I'd grabbed from the returns, photos from the Galleria dell'Accademia in Florence.

Just before my mid-morning break, the morning's manager, a woman named Ellie, came to relieve me. "Hey," she said, passing me a list of call numbers. "When you're done with your break, would you mind heading up to the stacks to look for these? We've got a demanding professor saying she needs these books for a student of hers."

"Sure," I agreed. This was a part of my job I hadn't done yet, but April had explained it to me during the first shift I'd worked. Basically, you went up to the stacks and looked for the books where they were supposed to be, because people were often unable to successfully navigate the library, and if the books weren't there, then you got a little more creative about it. An M with wear on the far-right side might look like an N to a hasty shelver. Or a B with a worn-away lower curve might appear to be a P. An 8 with a worn-away middle could seem to be a 0.

April had said it was fun, like solving a puzzle. Sometimes you found the book in the wrong place, and sometimes you came up empty-handed, but it was a good way to spend ten or twenty leisurely minutes in the stacks.

For my break, I walked around outside. It was a warm August morning, and I fired off snapshots of sorority girls with bows in their hair, jocks in jogging shorts, and various campus citizens and buildings, especially the hot construction workers working on a new building by the Hill.

I ate some Laffy Taffy I'd bought earlier in the week from a campus canteen and stored in my jacket pocket. My mind wandered back to the night before. Daniel's smile, his laugh, his touch. Each memory was imbued with fluttery excitement and wistful hope.

When my break was over, I headed back into the library. Waving at Ellie, I went straight up into the stacks.

The first book was an easy find. It was right where it was supposed to be. Perhaps it'd been shelved shortly after the professor had looked for it. The second book seemed lost for good. I investigated a couple of different possibilities, but to no avail. Giving up, I looked at my list of call numbers again. The next book was supposed to be on the fifth floor, on the opposite side of the building.

After I'd taken the elevator up, I paused in the 71 Dewey Decimal numbers—books about area planning and landscape architecture—to double-check the call number. Putting the list back in my pocket, I looked up at the ceiling, and on impulse put my hand on the shelf next to me, grazing the edge of a book.

For some reason, I turned my head and looked at the spine.

The book was out of place. The call number started in the same way as the book I was looking for—77—so I pulled it from the shelf to take a closer look. It was a book of photographs featuring Appalachian wilderness scenes. The cover was of lush greenery alongside blooming azaleas and rhododendrons. No wonder it had been shelved in with books about outdoor gardening. I flipped it open, scanning some of the pages. They were nice pictures, tasteful and well-framed. Nothing groundbreaking.

Glancing around to see if anyone was watching me dawdle here and seeing no one, I took the liberty of reading some of the write-ups alongside the pictures. I nodded along. Yes, yes, all very standard. It was a little dated, but still good information. I'd reshelve it while I looked for the other book.

Snapping the book closed, I blinked, tilted my head, and read the photographer's name on the spine again.

Appalachian Dreamland by Harold Seville.

A flame of curiosity lit in me, I turned to the back flap of the book, looking for what I wanted to see. Bingo. There it was: a picture of the photographer, one Harold Seville. It was probably taken in the late seventies, based on the fashion, photo quality, and the publication date of the book. Harold was tall and blond with sparkling eyes, and in the photo he wore a khaki linen suit and held a Pentax K1000 in his hands.

I tucked the book under my arm, my mind buzzing, considering the possibilities as I went on looking for the other books on the list Ellie had given me. I found one more in a wrong section, but the others seemed lost or perhaps were out and about in the library and hadn't made their way back to circulation and their proper place yet.

I returned to the circulation desk and found Ellie yawning and doodling on a sheet of paper.

"Here you go," I said, handing over the two books I'd found

and the list. "This was the best I could do. Hope that's okay."

"That's great," she said smiling. "Thank you, Peter. Good work." She waved as she returned to the circulation office area just behind me, leaving me to man the desk alone.

Patrons were slim on the ground still, so I looked again through the photography book, interested to find two more photos of Harold within it. In both, he held his camera, and in the last one, he had his arm wrapped around a "friend" whose name was undisclosed. But based on the way the man was looking at him, I'd say he met Adam's definition of a "friend."

They surely kissed sometimes.

The write-up within the book gave little information about Harold's life, except the part near the beginning where he was quoted as saying, "Growing up in the South, near the Smoky Mountains, the area's flora was always near to my heart. I typically work in portraiture, but I wanted to honor these special scenes from my youth."

Portraits, huh? I wondered if the library had any of those books, too.

Turning to the computer, I typed in a search string for Harold's name and was surprised when fifteen volumes of photos turned up. All but one—a book titled *Robin*—were available to be checked out. And, based on their titles, all but the one I'd found by accident were books of portraits, just as he'd said.

Spinning around in my chair, head up, pondering the ceiling as I considered. I decided to go up to the stacks after my shift and look at them all.

What were the chances that this man was my uncle's lover? The one who'd begged him to return to him? Slim as hell. Perhaps this photographer was another Harold Seville. It was a common enough surname.

But what if…

I opened my backpack, dug out the manila envelope, and opened it up.

The contents were the same as ever, but this time I withdrew the letters and the journal both. I spent the rest of my shift reading them in between patrons. And that was why, by the time I made my way upstairs to look through the photography of Harold Seville, I already knew.

This man *was* my uncle's lover. George had written all about him in his journal, including about Harold's career as a photographer. That was, it seemed, how they'd met. Harold had been traveling through Nashville, run into George there while at a party of a mutual friend, and had found him beautiful. He'd asked George to pose for some portraits. George had complied.

As I reached the stacks, my hands were shaking.

I didn't know why. It didn't signify anything or make my uncle un-dead, but it felt fated for me to have placed my hand on that mis-shelved book and to have discovered it was full of photos by this particular man, the one who'd written the letters I'd been avoiding reading for too long.

It was as if my uncle's ghost had reached through the veil and guided me to pause just there, to touch just that book. Silly, maybe, but that was all I could think.

Sitting down on the floor in the stacks with all fourteen books—the one I'd found and the thirteen that were currently in the library—I flipped through the pages. For hours I was compelled to examine every picture, sliding my eyes over every write-up about the model, the camera, the film, the settings...

There were portraits of men, of women, of children and of pets. There were street photos, posed photos in studios, and photos that seemed like casual snapshots, but taken with the perfect aperture and timing, the right lens, and the ideal light.

Art. They were art.

Many of the portraits were of nudes. Mostly men, but a few women as well. I studied the choices Harold had made, wondering how he got these people to agree to disrobe for him. Wondering if my uncle had taken his clothes off for this talented man.

Photos of people naked inside, photos of people naked outside…

Naked in other ways, too, like the way their eyes shone up from the page, alive and young even twenty years out from the moment captured. Frozen in time at their most beautiful and most alive.

Harold was talented, and I was struck with both envy and wonder as I continued my journey through his work. There was one thing I hoped to find. One thing I saw no sign of yet…

I'd nearly given up when I came to the final pages of the last book in my stack. I'd learned a lot already, and admired Harold's work, but when I found what I was looking for, I felt transported.

My own face—or one very like it—peered up shyly from the page in full color. The portrait was a full-body one, fully clothed. A casual shot taken outdoors, seated in a wrought-iron chair, next to a wildly blooming rosebush.

My uncle was smoking a cigarette, legs crossed, and his hair was as unruly as mine. His head was half tilted down, like he was trying not to look at Harold or the camera but couldn't resist. There was a softness in his expression that'd been lacking in the other photos I'd seen of him, the ones in the envelope that still resided in my backpack.

It was a beautiful expression. A shy, embarrassed joy. I felt it myself in my chest, and I rubbed at it as a knot rose in my throat.

Beneath the photo was the title Harold had chosen for it: *My Robin.*

George. George Robbins.

Ah.

I sat the book down, peering into the depths of the stacks, remembering that the missing book, the one not in the library right now, had been titled simply *Robin*. Was it a book only of my uncle's portraits? Was that possible? Or was I making too much out of this? I didn't know, but I wanted to find out.

Rising to go research whether *Robin* was missing or checked out, I clutched the book with his portrait in the back to my chest, a smile starting in the corners of my mouth.

I didn't understand it. This feeling inside. But it was good to know my uncle's memory wasn't dependent on me alone. There were other photos of him. Other people who could carry his existence onward. I wondered if Harold still thought of him. If he remembered those letters. If he knew what had happened. If some part of him still burned, still yearned, still loved his Robin.

My heart fluttered.

Perhaps I had something new and exciting to share with Bobby after all.

✦   ✦   ✦

WHEN I RETURNED home, my backpack was extra heavy with the weight of Harold Seville's portrait book with my uncle's photo in it. I'd checked it out before leaving. Still zipping along on the high from the night with Daniel, and the unreality of having discovered this link to my uncle, I wanted to tell someone, but I didn't know just who.

The obvious choice, my mom, was in too good a mood to consider it.

Singing in the kitchen and pulling apart string cheese while drinking wine, she waved at me as I walked in. Dad was in the middle of making tacos and seemed to be struggling with it, which made Mom laugh.

There was no way I was going to burst her bubble with news about her brother. Even if it was exciting, and in my opinion, good.

"Hey," I said, dropping my backpack onto the counter and stretching my arms wide. I was exhausted. It'd been a very long day after a very exciting night. "How's it going?"

"Great," Mom said. "There's a message for you." She passed me a sheet of paper.

Call Daniel.

"Wow, such a long message. I see why you couldn't have just told me verbally."

"Aw, look at him," Mom called over to Dad. "All cranky after staying out half the night and getting up early this morning."

"But do I add the spice now? Or later?" Dad muttered.

"Either way, Abe," Mom said. "It doesn't matter. It's tacos."

I headed over to the phone on the wall, wishing for the millionth time I had an extension in my room. I'd love to tell Daniel about Harold's books and my uncle's portrait, but I couldn't have a conversation like that here, not with my mother listening.

I dialed the number and waited through four rings before Kennedy picked up.

"Hey Kennedy, it's me, Peter. Can I talk with Daniel?"

"Mister! It's you!"

"It's me, yeah."

Mom was watching me while putting string cheese pieces into her mouth.

"Mister, did you know Milky Way is Danny's dog for real now?"

"What?"

"Yes! Danny said she's gonna live with him forever!"

My stomach dropped. "Um, that's great, Kennedy." I felt sick. "Can I talk to Daniel?"

"Dan! Mister's on the phone for you!"

Apparently, I was Mister forever to Kennedy. I was all right with that. But what I wasn't all right with was the new anxiety that'd taken up residence in my gut. I hoped Daniel came to the phone soon. Hopefully, I was wrong. Hopefully, he'd reassure me that I'd only imagined the worst.

"Everything okay?" Mom asked, her brows drawing low.

I waved her off, rubbing my temple.

"Peter?"

"Hey." Relief fell over me at the steady sound of his voice. "My mom said you called?"

"Yeah, I did. That was earlier today. I was hoping you'd be home from school already because I was missing you."

My heart skipped, and I turned away from my mom, putting my forehead against the wall, smiling like an idiot. "Yeah, me too." I added in a whisper, "I thought about you all day."

"Me too." He paused, and my heart sank again. Oh no. "So that was the reason I called earlier, but I planned to call tonight, too." I braced myself against the wall just as he said, "Bobby passed away today."

"No. He was...he was..." My voice shook. "He was supposed to go home."

"I know," Daniel said, his own voice cracking a little. "I'm sorry. I wish I didn't have to tell you this. I wish we could have just talked about how wonderful last night was, and made plans for another date soon, and—" He let out a small sob. "Sorry."

"It's all right," I said. "Do you need me? I can be out there in forty minutes. I'll leave right now and—"

"No, it's okay. Stay home and get some rest. I'd just worry about you on the road. I know you barely got any sleep." He sighed. "I'll keep you in the loop about the plans. Right now, all I know is he's left his home and belongings to ARK. They're planning to auction them off and sell the property. There won't be a funeral, and his body will be cremated. That's it. That's all I know. I don't know what's going to be done with his ashes."

"Daniel, I'm so sorry. Let me come out there—"

"No, don't. Please rest. I care about you too much to have you driving around on country roads with no sleep. Besides, my mom goes to rehab Monday, and my grandparents arrive the next day. I've got a lot to accomplish between now and then preparing for all that. I'd love to see you. You'd make everything feel so much better, but I have to deal with all this first."

"If you change your mind, just call."

We talked a few more minutes about less horrible things, though the heaviness lingered. I agreed to see him again soon, and when we hung up, I could tell that my promises had lifted his spirits.

"That sounded like a tough phone call," Dad said, putting the already-stuffed tacos on the kitchen table.

I nodded, tears threatening. "Yeah. Bobby…" I cleared my throat. "The Person With AIDS I was helping Daniel with?"

They nodded.

"He died." I hoped this didn't set off a panic in my mother. I couldn't handle that tonight. "He was sick. So, it's not like it was unexpected, but it's still really sad. He was a good guy. I liked him a lot."

"From AIDS complications?" Mom asked.

"Yeah." I braced myself. This was her damage. This was what George's death had done to her and to all of us. She'd freak out now. I'd feel guilty. She'd drink valerian-root tea or maybe even go back to the dark side by taking a Valium.

Dad took hold of Mom's hand and squeezed, giving her a significant look. She took a shuddery breath, let it out, and took a big gulp from her wine before saying, "That's sad, sweetheart. I'm so sorry."

"Me, too."

"Are you okay? Do you want to talk about it?" Dad asked.

I shook my head, the heaviness pulling at me and making me so tired. "It's just strange. Earlier today, I found something at the library, a thing I knew would interest him. He likes gossip, and…well…" I sighed and rubbed my temples. I was starting to get a headache. The last few days had caught up to me. "I don't want to talk about it. Not tonight."

"Of course," Mom said, patting my hand. "Whatever you want. We're here for you."

We ate tacos, and I asked them questions about how they'd spent the day, and they asked me about my new job at the library. There wasn't that much to say. The most interesting thing that'd happened was something I didn't want to share right now.

Afterwards, when Mom had finished her wine, she broached the topic of Daniel and how our date had gone.

For once, it was the right thing to ask. Just remembering the evening before made me feel warm. I smiled as I told her about the twinkle lights, Daniel's delicious pot pie, and watching the sunset colors dance on the water. I left out everything about going up to his room.

"A romantic!" Dad said. "A guy after your mother's heart."

She smiled. "Aren't you glad you took flowers?"

I chuckled. "I am. Yeah."

"Well, he sounds like a sweet guy."

Finally, someone else was being called sweet for a change. "He's honorable, too. He's always doing his best by everyone in his life." Even now, even tonight, I could tell on the phone that he'd been wanting to do his best by Bobby—to do more for him, even in his death. "I think it must be exhausting for him. He puts so many other people first."

"Then you'll want to help him however you can," Dad said.

"I do, but he's not so great at letting people help."

"Keep at it," Dad encouraged. "Sometimes it's a trust issue.

Once he knows you're there for him, *really* there, he'll let you help."

I hoped Dad was right, but as it was, I was too tired and sad to think about it anymore. I went upstairs to prepare for bed.

Taking out my contacts, I washed my face and brushed my teeth, before staring at myself in the mirror. I looked the same as I had before I went to Atlanta to see Adam, but I felt like an entirely different Peter now. I was someone Adam would never know. I supposed I had been for quite some time now.

When I got in bed, I closed my eyes and ran through every photo I'd ever taken of Bobby—and there weren't too many. I hadn't wanted him to feel like I saw him as an oddity, or that I was using his illness for my art.

My favorite photo was of him holding Milky Way as she ecstatically tried to lick his face. I smiled. He'd seemed so alive in those moments, laughing and squirming, without any trace of the death that had been hunting him since before we'd even met.

I wondered if Milky Way would miss him. She'd already been living with Daniel for a few weeks and seemed happy there now. I didn't know what I hoped for. It seemed sad to think she wouldn't miss Bobby at all, but it seemed even sadder to think of a grieving dog. There was no way to explain to her where he'd gone or why he'd never come back.

But Daniel would take good care of Milky Way, the same way he took care of everyone in his life.

Tears stung my eyes. I wished I could have told him about the connection I'd found between my dead uncle and a living photographer. A man who'd written him love letters. I felt in my heart he would have been delighted by that.

I squeezed my eyes shut, willing sleep to come. This was the first time in my memory that someone I knew personally had died. I didn't know how I was supposed to feel, or what I was supposed to do to honor him.

One thing I knew for sure: AIDS was one hateful bitch.

Chapter Twelve

D ANIEL HAD SAID he had a lot to accomplish between now and Monday, but when I woke Sunday morning with nothing but him and Bobby on my mind, I decided to drive over and stop by. If he didn't have time for me, then I'd use the opportunity to take some photos of the Kingston area, and then I'd drive home.

But at least I'd get a hug from him, maybe a kiss, and we could give each other comfort and reassurance.

The day was sunny and bright, so I gathered my Minolta and several rolls of 200 speed film and a roll of 400 for good measure. I left a note for my parents and got into the Volvo.

Daniel's house was a pain to get to, and the weight of Bobby's death still sat on my shoulders, but neither could keep my anticipation from rising. Soon I'd see his face, get a hug, and hold him tight to soothe his grief. Our shared sadness would bring us even closer.

I parked next to Betty Blue, gathered my stuff, and rang the front doorbell. As I waited, I looked at the gray Lincoln Town Car that was parked next to Daniel's car. I wondered if it was his mom's or if they had visitors. Daniel's grandparents maybe?

Once again, Kennedy swung the door wide to let me in, but this time she was crying, wiping at her red, tear-streaked cheeks with her palms. No greeting, just wrenching sobs.

I looked around for Daniel or his mom or Paul. Anyone. But I didn't see them. I *did* hear loud banging sounds coming from the kitchen, wordless shouting between a man and a woman, and a smashing noise, like shattering plates.

My heart pounding, I knelt by Kennedy, and she came into my arms at once, crying against my neck. "Hey, where's Daniel?"

She pointed back toward the kitchen.

"Where's Paul?"

She shrugged, but sobbed out, "Upstairs. With Milky Way."

I hesitated, not sure what to do. Eventually, I pressed a kiss to the side of her head and whispered, "Wait here, okay?"

She shook her head, clinging to me harder.

"I need to go check on Daniel."

"Me too," Kennedy said, still crying. "Take me, too."

I didn't want to take her with me to the kitchen, because I wasn't sure what we'd find. Daniel's mom was screaming at him now, calling him names, and still breaking plates from the sounds echoing down the hall.

"You can't have them," Marlene screeched.

"Mom, you're just making things worse for yourself," Daniel shouted.

Another smash.

"Fuck!" Daniel roared. "Stop this! Now!"

Not seeing another option, since I knew Kennedy would just follow me anyway, I rose with her in my arms. She was heavy and dense, like she was made of sturdy material. When we reached the kitchen, I paused in the doorway, taking it all in. There was Marlene perched on a counter like a wild bird, hair a mess, face red, and her dark hair everywhere. She held two more plates in her hands, panting with emotion. Tears streamed down her face. She was poised to break apart.

Daniel stood next to the breakfast nook, arms crossed over his chest, and his eyes dark with rage. Next to him stood an older man and woman—his grandparents—wearing khaki slacks and loose,

Floridian-looking shirts. They looked to be about sixty, and both of them stared at Marlene, aghast.

Daniel's eyes swerved to me and then to Kennedy in my arms. He shook his head and motioned for me to go. I knew he wanted me to take his sister out of the house.

I nodded and backed away, heading to the front door and out into the sunshine. A fresh breeze raced up from the river. I cradled Kennedy closer and whispered, "Let's get out of here."

Clinging to me, she snuffled, "Where to, Mister?"

I didn't really know, but I put her in the passenger seat of my car, buckled her up as best I could, and took her away from the awful scene. We didn't go far. We stopped by several fields of Queen Anne's Lace, wild roses, and blue cornflowers. I let her pick bouquets in each field, and, at her insistence, showed her how to take photos with my camera. I let her waste a whole roll of film.

By the time I decided it must be safe to take her back home, she'd stopped crying and was singing a little song she'd made up. I was grateful she hadn't asked me questions about what was happening at her house.

Pulling up into the driveway, I was slow about getting out of the car, and so was Kennedy. The door opened and Daniel stepped out. This time I got a good look at him. He wore black jeans and a white T-shirt with Sinead O'Connor's *The Lion and The Cobra* album cover printed on it.

Kennedy ran to him, and he swept her up like she didn't weigh much at all. She pushed the bouquet she'd gathered into his hand and wrapped her arms and legs around him, hugging him like a monkey. Daniel rubbed her back, his eyes on me as I settled the camera in the abandoned passenger seat and shut the car door.

"Hey," I said as I approached. His eyes weren't dark with anger like they had been before. Now they were just sad and empty.

"Hey." He handed the bouquet of flowers to me so he could

hold Kennedy better.

Kennedy wormed in closer, and he kissed her cheek. Wordlessly, the three of us moved to sit on the white front porch swing together. Daniel started the rocking, and I joined in to help. No one spoke. Kennedy asked no questions, which seemed strange and worrisome to me, but after a good ten minutes of holding on to her brother, her breathing slowed. It was clear she'd fallen asleep.

Daniel sighed, transferring her so that her legs flung over mine, and her head was cradled against his chest. She looked even smaller and younger with her eyes closed and her mouth open.

"So…" Daniel began.

"Yeah," I answered.

Silence lingered a little while longer, and then he offered, "I'm glad you came."

"Are you? I thought you might be upset."

"No, it was serendipitous. Kennedy didn't need to see any more of that." She shifted a little, as if reacting to her name. After a few long moments, Daniel spoke again, but even more quietly, "They came a few days early."

"To get the kids?" I surmised.

Peering out over the yard, the sun glinted in his amber eyes. "She lost it."

I nodded.

"She thought she'd leave first, I guess. Say goodbye to the kids tomorrow and go to rehab. That way she wouldn't have to see my grandparents take them."

"Ah. She thought she had another day with them."

Daniel sighed. "She's had so many days with them that she squandered with alcohol. But, yeah, she wanted this last one." He huffed a bitter laugh. "But she's ruined it now, too. My grandparents aren't unreasonable people. She could have talked them into letting the kids stay until she left. They could have even gotten a hotel room, so they wouldn't distract the kids from her time with them. But she went berserk. It's been a long time since they've seen her…" He tried to search for the right word. "That angry."

I understood his hesitation in having chosen that one. She'd seemed so much more than angry. "What will happen now?"

Daniel looked down at Kennedy's face, a soft affection and sadness drifting over his features. "They're going to take them today. As soon as possible. Grandpa is cleaning up the kitchen. I told him I'd do it, but he wouldn't listen. Grandma is packing Kennedy's things, and Paul packed his stuff all by himself while we were in the kitchen fighting. He's ready to get away from this bullshit. I understand."

I swallowed hard, wanting to reach out to touch Kennedy's soft cheek. "How will she take it? Kennedy, I mean." After the hour or so we'd spent together, I couldn't bear to see her cry again. She was such a sweet kid. She should be always laughing.

Daniel shook his head. "I don't know."

We rocked some more. I knew I had no business staying here with him, but I couldn't seem to bring myself to leave, and Daniel didn't ask me to.

I reached out, taking his hand. We rocked some more. Kennedy snuffled in her sleep. We gazed out at the sunny sky, at the green grass.

"Tough week," I commented.

He laughed in that sad way, squeezing my fingers. "Between Bobby and this? Yeah. It's been a horrible week." Catching my eye, he added. "Another reason I'm selfishly glad you came. Just seeing you…" He trailed off, but his expression told me what he didn't say.

"Me too."

"Listen."

"Yeah?"

"This is going to sound like a terrible idea, and I'll understand if you aren't comfortable with it. You can always say no."

"What?"

"Nadine—Minty's mom—is coming over tonight to stay with my mom and make sure she gets off to rehab in the morning. That should be my job, but I just...I just can't."

I understood.

"Nadine's been friends with my mom since my dad died, and she knows how to handle her. Mom will be calmer with her, too. If I stay here, she'll start accusing me of planning this again."

"You don't have to justify not wanting to be here. I get it."

He hesitated. "So, I know this is morbid, but..."

"Go on."

"I have the keys to Bobby's place still. I'm going over there to spend the night. I need to say goodbye to him on my own terms, and I have to get away from her tonight."

A lump formed in my throat just thinking about Bobby's house. I'd never see the inside of it again either. I wouldn't mind saying goodbye. "What did you have in mind?"

"Come with me?" Despite his previous words, his eyes begged me to say yes. "You don't have to stay the night. It would just mean a lot to have you there with me. I mean, if you—"

"I'll come."

"Yeah?"

"Of course."

"You don't have to sleep there, but..."

"Would you want me to?"

Daniel swallowed hard, his eyes drifting to my lips. "I wouldn't hate it."

I nodded. "Okay, well, I have an early class tomorrow, but I'll think about it. And I'll go over there with you at least."

The front door squeaked open, and Paul appeared, holding

Milky Way. He looked pale in an almost sickly way, but he lacked all the anger he'd shown the first time I'd met him. He closed the door behind him, walking toward us as Milky Way panted and squirmed in his arms. He put her down, and she darted over to me, leaping into my lap and licking at my face, waking Kennedy.

"They're ready to take us," Paul said, and his eyes filled with tears.

"Okay, buddy," Daniel said, helping his sister to sit up. She wiped at her eyes, and then stared across the yard with a furrowed brow. It looked like she was gathering her courage.

I glanced toward Betty Blue and my Volvo. "Hey," I said. "You've got things to deal with before you can leave, and I do too. Why don't we meet there?"

He nodded, his focus on his brother. "Okay."

"Say around three-thirty?"

He agreed, and I rose to go. Milky Way jumped down and went back to Paul, who seemed grateful to hold her again.

"Bye, Mister," Kennedy said with a waver to her voice.

"Bye, Kennedy." I pulled her to my side and gave her a squeeze. "Bye, Paul."

He nodded at me but didn't say a word.

Daniel gave me a quick hug, saying, "Three-thirty. If I'm late, wait for me. I promise I'll be there."

"Sure."

Leaving Daniel and his siblings huddled together on the front porch broke my heart. Not because I wanted to be inserted into the middle of their mess, but because I was falling head-over-heels for him, and I cared about Kennedy, and Paul.

I hated that I couldn't take away their pain.

✧　✧　✧

SITTING IN MY car outside Bobby's house, I had a lot of time to ponder what it meant that Bobby would never return to it again. Daniel was late, but I didn't mind.

Things had been so chaotic at his house, there'd been no way he could have accurately pinpointed when it would wrap up. I could be patient. I'd waited on Adam to get his shit together for over half a year, so an hour or two of waiting on Daniel to tie up the loose ends of his mom's situation was nothing.

I thought about getting out and taking photos, but then I remembered how I used to walk Milky Way around this area after preparing Bobby's lunch and doing his laundry. The thought of walking into the house and finding it—How? Had Kerri gone in and cleaned it up in anticipation of Bobby coming home? Probably.

Betty Blue pulled into the driveway and parked behind me. We'd have to reshuffle the cars if I left. I glanced to the bags in the passenger seat. My backpack for school sat next to an overnight bag containing a change of clothes, my contacts kit, and the still unopened box of condoms. Just in case.

When Daniel exited, I got out, too, taking my camera but leaving my bags behind me. Bobby's house was in a safe neighborhood. I didn't think I needed to worry about it. Back at my house, I'd reloaded the Minolta with fresh film, marking Kennedy's roll, so I could decide if I wanted to develop it or not. I probably would. It'd be interesting to see if she had a natural eye.

"Hey," Daniel said, his own overnight bag slung across his shoulders. He looked worn down, like a bomb had gone off inside him, and he was too tired to even begin collecting the pieces.

"Hi." I put my arms around him, and we hugged each other close, despite my camera and his bag getting in the way. We didn't say anything, just swayed in the driveway as a breeze scented by freshly mown grass drifted over from Bobby's garden. Kerri must have been by to work on it. It looked as nice as it ever did. "Are you all right?" I asked.

"Yeah. No. I don't know. I'm just glad I'm here with you." He held me tighter.

"Me too."

We hugged for a long time.

Daniel broke the hug and took a step toward the front door, only to stop in his tracks, gazing at the house. "Oh."

I took his hand.

We stared at the house together.

Daniel's eyes shimmered but no tears fell. He nodded twice. "All right."

He moved forward, and I went with him.

Inside it was clear I'd been right. Kerry had tidied the place. That didn't stop the living room from smelling like Bobby—the medicinal scent and the smell of sickness. Daniel stood still, looking around. The fireplace, the coffee table, the chair Bobby liked best…

"It's…" He swept a hand through his hair and shook his head.

I didn't know what he'd been about to say, but I responded with, "Yeah." It was the best I could do when my own heart was aching.

"Let's open the windows," he said. He didn't wait for me to respond, going window-to-window and room-to-room, pushing aside the curtains and flinging up the sashes. Fresh air poured in. Sweet scents of roses from the garden. The green smell of grass.

Light came in too. The two bedrooms, the kitchen, and the living room all glowed with the sun, and the curtains and the fabric on the beds all fluttered with the breeze. I felt like Bobby would have laughed at Daniel's frantic airing of the place.

You can't get rid of me that quick! I'm inside you. Opening the windows won't chase me out of your heart.

A lesson I'd learned once before. Grief had to be gone through the hard way. There was no pushing it aside or wishing it away.

But Daniel had plenty of grief to process today. It wasn't just

Bobby. It was his mom and his siblings, too.

In the kitchen, opening the window over the sink, Daniel knocked into Milky Way's nearly empty water dish. It splashed onto the linoleum.

"Where is she?" I asked.

"With Mom and Nadine. I thought about bringing her, but I didn't think I could handle seeing her look for him."

My stomach knotted up. I couldn't have handled it either.

"She'll be fine with them. Mom's settled down." He turned back to me, leaning against the counter in exhaustion. "Sorry I was late."

"It's all right."

"I should have known it would take longer."

I approached him and took hold of his hands again. "It's all right."

"Peter…"

"Yeah?"

"Could you… Would you mind just…holding me some more?"

Without a word, I led him over to the sofa where we'd both sat when we chatted with Bobby. We turned to look at his empty chair.

"Not here." Daniel led me back to the guest bedroom. A place I'd rarely been in. It was spartan with only a bed, a bedside table with a box of Kleenex and a lamp, and a desk under the window. There were some paintings on the walls—forest glens with deer in them—but otherwise it appeared unused.

"The closet's full," Daniel said when I mentioned the emptiness. "Don't open it. It'll all fall out on you. Take a guess how I know that."

I laughed and he did, too, but it was faint.

I removed my camera from around my neck and put it on the bedside table. "C'mon," I said, pulling him down to the mattress with me. "Let me hold you."

This time I was the big spoon, and though Daniel was larger than me, he felt right in my arms. We didn't talk for a long time. The breeze from the open window blew over us, calming and soft. We breathed together, and at some point, I thought he'd drifted off.

But then he murmured, "I keep thinking about the next steps." Daniel turned over in my arms so he could see me. His hair was golden in the glowy light of the room, and his eyes were the sad, tired brown of fallen leaves in autumn. "If I can just get through these next few months, maybe it will be over." A pessimistic smile twisted his mouth. "But is that possible? Can it *ever* be over?"

"I hope so."

He sighed. "Me too."

"What are the next steps?"

"To sell our house. But that means I have to do a ton of other stuff first. It's not a single event. More like a series of steps that make up that big step."

"Where will you live?"

"I'm not sure yet. I might rent a place. I might take some of the proceeds from the sale—because some of them will be mine according to my father's will—and buy a place of my own. I don't know."

I hesitated before asking, "Where will your mom live once she's out of rehab?"

He tensed. "She can either buy a house with a lower financial profile here locally, or she can do the right thing and move to Florida to be close to the kids." His voice was tight. "Maybe buy a place near my grandparents there."

"The kids won't be living with her again?"

"I hope not. The legal aspects of it all are..." Daniel let out a long sigh and shook his head. "Even if she gets sober, in my mind there's no world where the right thing is to put them back in her hands. She's relapsed too many times. I can't—" he sighed and flopped onto his back, placing a hand over his eyes. "I won't adopt them or take custody. *I* won't be their father. My grandparents are the only option." He looked at me. "Does that make me an asshole?"

I shook my head. There was nothing to say, and there was no way Daniel was *ever* an asshole.

Daniel rolled toward me to cup my face. Gazing into his eyes, I felt dizzy with anticipation. Was it wrong to kiss here in Bobby's guest room now that he was dead? Was it disrespectful?

Daniel rubbed our noses together.

"Should we do this?" I asked. "In our dead friend's house?"

Daniel kissed the tip of my nose. "I kind of think he'd want us to, don't you?"

Tears pricked my eyes. "Yeah."

Daniel's mouth was hot and somehow full of sorrow. His kiss was sad and desperate, and I let it swallow me up. We kissed for a long time. So long that my lips ached, and I felt the beginnings of beard burn stinging my chin.

When Daniel shoved my shirt up and started kissing my chest, I didn't push him away or worry about Bobby anymore. Especially when he tugged off my jeans and underwear and then went for his own fly. Tugging off my shirt and casting it aside, I leaned back in the golden light from the open window. The breeze teased my nipples.

Daniel's body was gorgeous. He wasn't overly muscled, but he was strong, and he looked like summertime in the flesh. I wanted to get him over me, feel his weight on top of me like at his house, but when he moved down between my legs, I changed my mind.

"Is this okay?" he whispered.

"Yeah." I petted his soft hair. "It's good."

He nuzzled my thighs and pubic hair, taking a deep breath. "You smell so good." He kissed my balls, the insides of my thighs and slid his hands beneath me to grip my ass cheeks. "Can I suck you off?"

"Yeah…" I shivered as lust shot through me.

His mouth was amazing and well-practiced. He knew how to give a blow job, and he did it with passionate enthusiasm. Any niggles of doubt I might have had about doing this in Bobby's house were gone with the breeze. I threaded my fingers into his hair and whimpered at his skill. The twists of his tongue, the heat of his throat, and the perfect amount of suction… It didn't take long for me to turn into a sweaty, cooing mess.

When my legs started trembling and my stomach flexed hard, I knew I was close, but Daniel let my cock slip free of his mouth and lifted my hips up. His breath ghosted over my balls and then down farther.

Was he…did he plan to…?

"Wanted this so long," Daniel muttered. His eyes were dilated as he contemplated my anus, touching it gently. A shivery thrill raced through me. I grabbed my cock and gripped it hard. "Can I kiss you here, Peter?"

"Yes…yes…" My cock pulsed with pre-cum, and I slid my thumb through it, slicking it over my cockhead. "Please, Daniel."

I squeezed my eyes shut as he gave me what I'd begged for. The sweet, shocking, too-intense feeling of his tongue against my asshole made me shake all over. I'd always loved it when Adam did this, but Daniel was skilled. I didn't know who'd taught him—his ex, Kevin, or some other guy he'd been with—but I was going to levitate off the bed and my cum was going to hit the ceiling if he didn't slow down.

"Wait," I whispered. "Wait."

He stopped, gazing up at me from between my thighs with lust-glazed eyes. "You all right?"

"Yeah. I just…" I pulled my legs to my chest, exposing my hole even more. "Okay, go ahead."

His lips twitched in a helpless smile. "So you like it?" he whispered against my saliva-wet hole.

"Yes," I moaned.

"Me too." He drove his tongue into me.

I cried out.

What we were doing was so much more intense than I'd been expecting tonight, or even been ready for (despite those just-in-case condoms) but I didn't regret it at all.

Tears of pleasure stung my eyes, as I held my legs up for him. "Daniel, oh fuck…"

He doubled down with his tongue, teasing inside and out, making the nerves of my anus sing.

My hips moved of their own volition, twisting and jerking, but he took hold of them and held them steady as he licked over my hole one last time before moving up to my dick and balls.

Gripping my ass cheeks in both hands, he licked to the crown of my dick, sucked me in, and swallowed me down. I hitched up onto my elbows to watch. His cheeks hollowed out as he bobbed his head and sucked me hard.

My breath stuttered, my chest flushed bright red, and I quaked. I fought to keep from coming. Holding eye contact as he worked, a wave of intimacy flooded me with almost unbearable warmth.

Daniel circled his hips against the mattress in the same rhythm as he sucked me.

And, *God*, he sucked me. The soft, shocked whimpers and cries that hung in the air were mine. I gripped his hair, biting into my lower lip and groaning hard. Our gazes locked, his lust seemed to flow into my lust, and the sensations grew and intensified. "Daniel," I whispered. My nipples tightened, and my balls drew up. It was all too much, and too fast, and so very good.

My stomach quivered, and my breath came in short hitches that weren't deep enough, black dots swimming in my vision. Daniel didn't let up, stealing my breath again and again. Just when I was going to come, tension drawing tight over me, and pleasure spindling up in a knot that was just about to pop, he pulled off.

"No," I moaned.

Daniel grinned, before lifting my legs by the knees, and ducking down to lick my ass again. I trembled all over and flung my arms wide over the mattress, writhing and clutching the sheets. Daniel didn't let up. My hole fluttered and gripped at his tongue and words poured out of me without thought, without anything but desperate, horny need.

When Daniel took my cock in his mouth again and swallowed me deep, tears stood in my eyes, and I was heaving with shuddering breaths. My dick sliding into his throat made me almost black out with pleasure. He bobbed his head, rubbing his fingers over my twitching asshole. I couldn't take it any longer. My hips jerked up, and I fucked his throat, squeezing my eyes shut and tossing my head as the end approached.

"Oh!" I cried as my hips drove upward, and Daniel's gag reflex engaged. I convulsed, trying to pet his hair but instead gripping too hard, as bliss pumped through me. Daniel swallowed my first jet of cum, and then pulled off my cock to jerk me through the rest of my orgasm. "Daniel," I whispered. "Fuck."

Jerking and spasming through many convulsions and breathtaking spurts of cum, I couldn't catch my breath for several long minutes. Daniel's eyes stayed on me the whole time, taking in everything, and glowing with his own lust and pleasure. Then he ducked his head, groaned, and came against the sheets.

After we both calmed, Daniel moved up to cuddle me. I was sweaty, and I shivered in his arms. Daniel pulled the other side of the comforter over us, so we were wrapped up together.

Dazed and still buzzing in the afterglow, I could barely process how good it had all been. "That was…umm…" I trailed off.

"Yeah." He nuzzled my neck and kissed my shoulder. My mind whirled in blissed-out harmony. As I recovered, I curled against Daniel, hand on his chest, feeling his pounding heart. We were quiet a long time, just cuddling and kissing any available skin.

"Where did you learn to do that?" I asked.

"What?"

"Rim like that."

He laughed. "Do you really want to talk about exes right now?"

I shook my head. "No, but in case you ever wondered, you're very good at it."

He kissed my throat before shifting so that his elbows were on the pillow on either side of my head. He gazed down at me, pushing my hair back off my face. "In case you were wondering, your asshole is the prettiest I've ever seen."

I spluttered a laugh. "What?"

He chuckled too. "Yeah. It's beautiful. Have you ever seen it?"

"My own asshole?"

"Yeah. It's pretty."

I laughed again.

He blushed, but he insisted, "I'm not kidding! It's sweet-looking."

"If you say so. And no, I haven't ever seen it."

Daniel's gaze landed on my camera. I bit my lip. Was he thinking what I thought he was thinking?

He asked, "You develop your own pictures, right?"

"Yes."

"Can I take pictures of you?"

I caught my breath and felt a zing of new arousal. "Naked?"

His cheeks darkened more. "Yeah."

"You want to?"

"Absolutely."

"Okay."

"Can I take a picture of your asshole?"

I laughed. "Are you serious?"

"Yeah. You should see it. It's that pretty."

I laughed again, but then asked, "Okay. Can I take pictures of you, too?"

"Sure, but my asshole's not as nice. It's kind of hairy."

My heart tumbled hard in my chest, and I felt breathless. "Let me be the judge of that."

He giggled. "All right."

"I'd like to take photos of your whole body. Is that okay?"

"Yeah." Daniel bit his lip and then lurched up, stumbling over to the desk to pick up my camera. He glanced out the open window. "I don't think the neighbors can see in. There's a lot of woods out there at the property line."

"It's fine." At that moment, I didn't give a shit either way. "Set it on automatic focus," I murmured, watching him fiddle with the camera. My cheeks were burning, and a brand-new flush had started up my chest and neck.

"How?" He handed it to me, and I set it up for him before handing it back.

He took his role seriously, standing on the bed to get a photo of me from above, and then getting low to angle over my torso. After about four well-considered shots, he asked, "I can really take a picture of your asshole?"

A thrill vibrated in my core. "Yes."

Daniel laughed. "Roll over. Get on your knees and hold yourself open."

My dick filled and hardened again as I rolled onto my knees and buried my hot face in the pillow. Reaching back, I spread my ass cheeks. Heat raced over my skin making me sweat and burn all over when I heard Daniel's audible swallow.

The snap of the shutter punctuated my thudding heartbeats—one, two, three—and then his finger trailed down my crack, sliding over my sensitive anus, teasing over where his tongue had been earlier. I was dying to have it there again.

More shutter clicks. He was going through a lot of film on just my asshole. It was a roll of thirty-six, but still...

"It's so fucking perfect," Daniel said, his voice gritty and his breath coming hard. "Can I kiss it again?"

I nodded, gasping as his lips pressed to my asshole with a chaste kiss and then were gone. I groaned in disappointment that he hadn't used his tongue.

"Roll over."

I did, and he took several more pictures. "You're gorgeous, Peter. Your eyes. Your mouth. Every inch of you." He grinned and touched my hard cock. "Even your dick. It's beautiful."

I was achingly hard already and not sure what to do with the compliments. "Um, well, yours is...really big."

Daniel took another picture and then set the camera on the bedside table. "Sorry. I've heard. But I'm gentle." Daniel leaned in to kiss me again.

"I trust you." A rush crashed through me, breathtaking and intense. Tears pricked my eyes. I *did.* I *trusted* him.

"Give *me* the camera," I said, and he handed it to me.

I shot photos of Daniel until I ran out of film, documenting the shine of his hair, the angle of his shoulders, and the line of his jaw. I also collected his treasure trail, his dark blond bush, and his big cock. Biting my lip, I even considered asking him to show me his asshole, like I'd shown him mine. In the end, I didn't.

Daniel lay still on the bed, letting me take pictures. When I ran out of film, he sat up with his back to the headboard, and whispered with a shy smile, "I've never done anything like this."

"Like what?"

"Taking pictures, getting a little kinky."

I couldn't say the same, so I just put the camera aside and crawled up to straddle him. His cock pressed against the back of my ass and my dick flexed against his stomach. "Thanks for doing it with me, then."

"I just wanted you to see your own asshole," he whispered as I rubbed my lips against his.

I giggled. "There are such things as mirrors."

"Yeah, but this is permanent. Proof that we were here today. That we did this."

I wished I had one more shot left on my roll so I could have taken a photo of the two of us together. How could I have forgotten to do that? So we could be permanent too.

"I can't wait to develop them."

"You'll show them to me, won't you?"

"Yeah. Of course."

We stopped talking and started kissing again. Both of us chasing the intensity between us, sharing it, taking it in, and swallowing it down, until we fell asleep exhausted, the rustle of the breeze and the buzzing of an intruding fly our early evening lullaby.

✧　✧　✧

AROUND ELEVEN AT night, I woke to an empty bed. Rising, I found Daniel on Bobby's back patio, sitting on an outdoor slider-sofa that had seen better days, wrapped in a blanket and staring up at the moon.

"You okay?" I asked, putting my arms over my naked torso. I'd just pulled on my boxers before coming out to check on him. It was late August still, but it got chilly after the sun set.

Glancing over, Daniel opened his arms and blanket wide. "C'mere. You're shivering."

Sitting down next to him, I saw that he had just his boxers on as well. Skin-to-skin, he held me close and kicked the slider to make it move back and forth. I curled in closer, soaking in the heat of his body.

"What are you thinking about?" I ventured. With Adam, in the past, I might have feared he was thinking about Leslie, or worrying about telling me something else I wouldn't like, but I felt no apprehension like that with Daniel. If he was worried, I felt secure that it wasn't about me. Not tonight, anyway. "Bobby?"

He let out a sad sound and shrugged.

I didn't say anything, just hugged him tighter.

"I hate that he died alone." His voice sounded thick and tight, as if he were crying. I tried to see in the moonlight, but it was too dark in the shadows of the patio.

"Was he alone?" I asked.

"I don't know. Maybe some nurses were with him, but maybe they weren't." He wiped at his face with the heel of his hand. "I should have been there."

I shook my head.

"He was my PWA, and I should have been by his side."

"That's not in the job description." I knew that for sure, since I'd only read the forms and signed them recently. "Is it Kerri's fault that she wasn't there?"

"No, of course not."

"Is it mine?"

He snorted. "I see what you're doing."

"Then you also see that I'm right."

I could sense the tension in his body, his fight to claim responsibility for a burden that wasn't his to carry. After a few moments, his shoulders slumped in surrender. "Yeah, you're right."

"You did the best you could by Bobby, and he didn't want anything more from you."

"He didn't want that even," Daniel said, a wobbly laugh escaping.

"Not if we believed half of the protests that came out of his mouth, no. But he was grateful for you, too."

"I wish he could have seen Roman find out about Marlena."

My stomach twisted up with the unfairness of it all. "Me too."

"And I wish I could still tell him about this." He clasped my hand under the blanket. "Us."

"Me too."

A beat passed. Daniel raised my fingers to his lips and kissed them. "We could still tell him," Daniel whispered. "Right now."

"If there is an afterlife, I think he already knows."

"He might be busy right now greeting all his old friends and lovers and family in heaven."

I didn't share his idea of an afterlife, but given that his father had died while Daniel was young, he must have found it a comfort, and I wasn't going to ruin that for him with my skepticism. "Yeah."

"But he could take a break for a minute to listen to us."

It was my turn to kiss his knuckles. Whatever Daniel needed right now, I was prepared to do. "He could."

"Hey Bobby," Daniel called into the night, lifting his face to the stars and moon. "Hey, Bobby!" he shouted again, loud enough to disturb the neighbors.

My stomach tensed as I waited for lights to flick on through the trees. Nothing happened.

"You died, you son of a bitch," Daniel went on, glaring at the sky. "But I hope you're okay out there. I hope you're seeing all the men you've loved and lost, and all the people and pets you've longed to see."

I leaned my head on Daniel's shoulder. He smelled of residual sex-sweat and the regular scent of his skin. "Me too," I said.

"But you missed out on something important."

I kissed his bare shoulder.

"You always told me Peter was the one for me. I ignored you because I didn't think it was ever going to happen. But it did." He squeezed my fingers again. "You were right. I'm here with him now—"

"Hey," I said with a small wave at the sky.

"And I wouldn't want to be here with anyone else. He's good and sweet, smart and handsome. And you were right about something else, too. He's fantastic in the sheets." He snorted. "'Hot as a demon's balls' is how you put it. You were right."

I buried my face in his shoulder and laughed. "'A demon's balls?'"

"Yup. 'Get that kid in the sack, Daniel. He'll suck you like a Hoover and ride you like a cowboy. He'll be hot as a demon's balls.' That's what he said."

"Oh my God."

Daniel turned his attention from the stars onto me. His face was highlighted by the moon. Lowering his head, he brushed our noses together, so innocent compared to what he was saying, "And he was right."

"He told *me* not to let you get away."

"Did he say I'd be great in bed, too?"

"No? But he thought I was an idiot for not dropping—" I cut myself off. I didn't want to bring up Adam here. "For not being with you."

"He had *no* faith in my bedroom skills?"

I laughed. "I'm sure he did. He just didn't mention them."

"I'll have you know I'm great in bed," Daniel said to the sky. "Tell him, Peter."

"He's great in bed," I said, laughing.

Daniel snorted, too. "Tell him more. You know he loves details."

"He's great at ass-licking," I said, shyly. Daniel gave me a quick kiss. "And sucking dick."

"Mm-hmm, and?"

"And making me come like crazy."

"See, Bobby? You should have told him to expect great things from me."

"Bobby adored you," I said. "I wish I could have bottled up everything he ever said to me about you, just so I could uncork it, and you could hear it now."

"I'm going to miss you." Daniel spoke to the sky again. "But I promise to take care of Milky Way and this one—" he lifted my hand again. "Happy travels. I hope heaven treats you better than earth did."

"Hear, hear," I added.

Daniel moved so his arms were around me, and we slid back and forth slowly until I started to drift off.

"Let's go back inside," Daniel murmured, helping me to my feet. I rubbed at my eyes and realized I needed to take out my contacts.

As I did so in Bobby's hallway bathroom, using the kit I'd brought along, Daniel watched me with curiosity.

"What?" I asked, after I'd fished out the second contact and put it in the saline solution.

"You're great."

"You too."

"No, it's more than that."

I looked at him in the mirror as I slid on my glasses, packed up my kit, and got out my toothbrush. Tomorrow was going to be an early morning, but I was buzzing with new affection and post-sex bliss. Even though we'd lost our friend and were now staying in his house for painful and complicated reasons, my heart was still soaring. "How's it more?"

"It's bad timing, and it's too soon, but I'm falling in love with you."

I blinked at him. Turning around, I tugged him into a hug. A response was stuck in my throat. It wasn't that I didn't feel the same, but the last time I told a guy I loved him…

Everything had gotten so messed up.

That wasn't going to happen with Daniel, but I wanted to be safe and sure.

"You don't have to say it back," Daniel said, chin hooked over my shoulder and his arms around me. "Don't worry. It's okay."

I kissed him. Was I being like Adam, distracting from a potential problem with physical affection and sex? Maybe. But I wasn't ready to say I loved Daniel quite yet.

Adored him? Sure. Wanted him? Definitely. Admired him? Yes.

But when the day came that I told Daniel I loved him, I wanted there to be no doubt in my mind or his that I meant it with all my heart and soul.

So we'd both just have to wait.

Chapter Thirteen

THE NEXT MORNING, I arrived on campus early since Bobby's house was closer to UT than my own. In the peachy-orange morning light, I sat in my car sipping terrible coffee I'd picked up at McDonald's.

I fondled the film rolls in my backpack, hoping for a chance to develop them soon. I was dying to see the photos we'd taken of each other. So filthy, so intimate. My heart pounded, and I blushed just thinking of it.

I wished Robert didn't sleep so late. I'd have loved to call him from a pay phone just to hear his voice, but also to confide in him and express what I was feeling. The elation in my heart, the feeling that the world was spinning just a little too fast, and I was drunk-dizzy from it. I knew he'd hoot and tease me, but he'd be happy to hear it. Alas, given his schedule, he'd be asleep for at least three more hours.

I considered killing the extra time by going to see my dad in his office but realized that would be a bad move—because while he'd be better than my mom about me staying overnight with Daniel, he was still sure to ask questions I didn't want to answer.

I wondered what I looked like with this fresh influx of sweet hope and shiny adoration in my bloodstream. I pulled the rearview mirror over and noticed the glossy shine to my eyes, the flush in my cheeks, and the giddy energy beneath my skin.

I wished I had more film to capture myself and the echoing beauty of the sunrise still painting the sky.

At last, it was time to hustle to my first class of the day.

I didn't know if Daniel had talked to Minty about what was going on between us. I didn't even know if Minty knew about Bobby's death yet. I decided to say nothing about Daniel and me as I took my usual place next to Jennifer. She was studying, so I didn't bother her as I got settled.

The other members of the class drifted in, chatting with each other, creating a murmuring of voices and a rustle of paper.

Minty dropped down next to me wearing black ankle boots and skintight blue jeans that looked more like tights, all topped off with a pink baby doll dress. He chewed on a Red Vine as he arranged his pencils in his obsessive way, before turning to look at me.

His eyes narrowed. "Don't tell me. You made up with your ex." His voice was hard. He shook his head. "Why would you do that? In case you didn't know, you're a fool." He tossed a long red stripe my way, and I caught it.

"No. I didn't get back together with him. What makes you say that?" I put the licorice in my mouth.

Jennifer slammed her notebook shut, forgoing whatever note review she'd been doing in favor of eavesdropping on our conversation.

"Are you seriously going to try *lying* to me?" Minty asked.

"I'm not lying."

Minty shoved the rest of the Red Vine into his mouth, chewing loudly, as he measured me with his eyes.

I tried very hard to keep my face blank, but there was no disguising the redness of my chin or the fact that I hadn't shaved because of it. Daniel and I should have agreed before we went our separate ways on what we should tell Minty.

"You totally got laid, though," Minty said. "There's no hiding that." He gestured at my beard burn.

I rolled my eyes, but he wasn't going to let it go.

"Did you go back for a goodbye fuck? That it?"

"No."

Adam and I hadn't even *had* a goodbye fuck. Not like that. I'd let him fuck me seven times the weekend before we broke up, but we hadn't known then it was over. And the last time…

I shook the thought off.

Minty shook his head. "You had sex. So, if it wasn't your ex, who was it?"

Jennifer picked that moment to say, "I hate to interrupt this inquisition, but I was wanting to ask you guys a question before class started and *this* sounds like the kind of conversation that could go on for days."

"I'm not done with you," Minty said to me, before rolling his hand at Jennifer as if to say "out with it."

She smiled. "Is there any way my best friend and I can go with you to that gay club? The Tilt-a-Whirl or whatever?"

Minty looked her over appraisingly. "Have you ever *been* a fag hag before?"

"What?"

"Like, do you have hag credentials?"

"No?"

"Hmm, well, you're cute enough." He touched her hair, then slid his hands down her arms and lifted them up, examining her torso and limbs. "You'd make a pretty enough accessory without outshining me. So, I guess it would be okay. Well, wait, what does your friend look like?"

I rolled my eyes, but I was glad for the distraction. With any luck, Donnie would come in and start lecturing before Minty had a chance to get back to questioning me again.

"Her name's Bernie, and she's prettier than me," Jennifer said, fishing around in her purse and bringing up her wallet. She showed him a photo-booth picture of herself and a Black girl with a super-wide smile.

Minty considered the shot. "Why 'Bernie?'"

"Short for Bernadette."

"Okay. She a lesbian?"

"No."

"Because I don't truck with lesbians."

I rolled my eyes even harder and elbowed him. "Don't be an asshole."

"Fine, I'll admit that's prejudiced and hateful. I'll move on to something we can all agree is much more important than Bernie's sexual preference. Does she dress well?"

Jennifer flipped her hair. "Better than you."

Minty smirked and snorted under his breath. "What shoe size does she wear?"

"What? Why?"

"If she's such a snazzy dresser, I might want to borrow from her sometime. Hags do that, you know. Let their fags borrow their stuff."

She flipped him off, putting the picture back into her purse.

Minty capitulated. "All right, all right. The two of you can meet me and the gang at the front door of Tilt-a-Whirl at ten-thirty tonight. We'll see if we're party compatible."

"Thank you!" She clapped her hands together.

"No problem. Oh, and two rounds are on you. Got it?"

She rolled her eyes but nodded. "You'll be there, too, Peter?" she asked.

Part of me wanted to say no, because I was exhausted from the night before, and I had the opening shift at the library in the morning, but part of me yearned for the heat and smell and smoke of the club. I missed Antonio, Windy, and Renée. I missed the pounding music. I missed feeling gay and free.

But I had to work…

But I loved to dance…

Thinking of Bobby, I knew what he'd tell me to do. "Sure," I said. "Count me in."

Minty gave me a high five just as Donnie entered and the room fell silent.

"I'll talk to *you* later," Minty whispered in my ear. "I'll find out who you fucked."

Gazing down at Donnie Huggins's nervous mug, waiting to see if he'd run out of the class to throw up again, or if he'd manage to stick it out, I resigned myself to it. There was no way Minty was going to let it go.

Donnie began to discuss Bruno Bettelheim's relationship with the work of Sigmund Freud—even though that was decidedly not on the Psych 110 syllabus.

After class, I said, "It was Daniel. I was with him last night." I'd already gathered my things while Donnie had been wrapping up the lecture, so I stood, leaving Jennifer and Minty behind. There. It was done. I'd have to tell Daniel I'd told his best friend about us, but at least Minty wouldn't keep bugging me about it.

On the sidewalk, Minty caught up to me and grabbed my arm. He was strong. "You don't get to do that."

"Do what?" I said, pulling away. I started off toward my second photography class with Marta Neuheim. The first had been great. She'd laid out all the assignments for the upcoming semester, with the final being a self-curated exhibition of our best work.

Minty dogged me. "You can't just lay a bomb on me like that and walk away."

"If you want to talk about this, you can follow me," I said. "But I have a class to get to."

Minty glanced in the direction of his next class, which was in the opposite direction of the Art building, but he fell in step beside me.

Taking the many stairs that led us into the valley before we'd go back up another set of stairs to reach the side of campus nearest to the Art building, he said, "If you think for a second I'm going to let you fuck him up, then—"

"Why would I want to fuck him up?" I interrupted. "I care about Daniel. We're good. We could maybe work."

"Oh, that's really encouraging," Minty said, sneering. "'We could maybe work.' If that's not the declaration of love that Daniel deserves, then I don't know what is!"

I was tempted to stop on the stairs and face him, but I kept going instead. "I'm not going to fuck him up."

"You already know he's crazy about you."

I did know. He'd told me as much.

I remembered his eyes after we'd kissed goodbye that morning. He'd looked at me like I was the best thing in his life. It should have felt like a lot of pressure, but it didn't. I *liked* him looking at me that way. I hoped he'd seen the same thing when I'd gazed back at him.

"So you're going to just take what you want, and then—"

"You know, you sure think I'm a piece of shit for someone who calls me a friend."

Minty stopped for half a beat, and I got several steps ahead of him before he leapt in front of me. "I *like* you. I just don't *trust* you."

"I thought you wanted me and Daniel together? All summer, you and the other guys were practically shoving us at each other."

"You used him in Nashville."

"I didn't." I pushed past him.

"You hurt him. He *cried*."

I stopped, and Minty ran into the back of me, almost knocking me down the stairs. "What are you talking about?"

"He cried. After Nashville. He got really drunk—which he never does—and cried about you, and if there's one thing I won't stand for, it's anyone who makes Daniel cry."

"He cried?" I asked.

"We were at his apartment, that was right before he had to head home, and he drank more than he usually does. Next thing I knew he had tears in his eyes, and then one ran down his *cheek!* You had him one night, and you wrecked him." Minty glared at me. "He was listening to that shitty R.E.M. album he likes so much, and that dumbass 'Losing My Religion' song came on, and he cried."

Maybe Daniel had cried over me, but what could I do about it now? Only what I *was* doing. Being good to him. Taking his heart seriously. That was it!

"What I'm saying to you, Peter, is that I was around for Kevin, and every other guy he's ever gone on a date with. He's never looked at another person the way he looks at you. Why? Beats the hell out of me. I mean, you're cute and all, but you're a bitch."

"Again, I'm really feeling your friendship, Minty. I feel like we're brothers of the heart."

"Let's talk about hearts," he said. "If you break his, I'll kick your ass and bury you in a shallow grave for Dr. Bass at the Body Farm to find."

"I don't *want* to break his heart, and you can keep your threats to yourself. Besides," I said, smirking at him. "Unlike Antonio, I'm not afraid of dogs."

Minty huffed a soft laugh. "Antonio's such an asshole."

I smiled sideways at him. "Ruff, ruff, ruff."

Minty rolled his eyes.

After about twenty silent steps, Minty said, "So, you're not going to share any details."

"Nope."

Minty gave a sharp nod. "Fine. If he's happy, I'm happy. If he's not…you're dead. It's as simple as that."

"Okay."

We'd reached the Art & Architecture door when Minty pulled me to a stop, eyed me up and down, and stated, "You look good with some sex on you. I mean, color in your cheeks, shoulders relaxed. Keep up the good work, soldier." He saluted me, clicking his ankle boots together at the heels before walking away.

I could feel the eyes of the art students on us. Even amongst their goth, grungy selves, Minty looked like an alien.

At least, judging by their expressions, most were considering him as a potential model and not a potential piñata to beat to pieces.

✦   ✦   ✦

AFTER MARTA NEUHEIM'S class, I stood by the door, frowning at the sign-up sheet for darkroom times. The only times available were early in the morning, which was fine, but they overlapped with my work shifts.

"Problem, Peter?" Marta asked, coming to stand directly beside me, peering at the schedule too.

I waited until she looked at me to answer. "It's mostly full."

"Getting into the darkrooms is always competitive." She pointed at the open morning hours. "These are almost always available."

"I work at that time."

"Ah. At the library," she said. "I've seen you there."

I was surprised to hear it. I'd only been employed a week. "Yeah, Saturday, Sunday, and Monday mornings, Tuesday and Thursday afternoons."

"What if…" A sneaky smile passed over her lips. "You were able to sign up before anyone else?"

"How?"

"I put the new sheet up for the following week's schedule on Friday nights before I leave." Her wild gray hair shook with excitement at her own wiliness. "You work at the library on Saturday mornings. What time is your first break?"

"Around eight."

"You know who won't be up and around the A&A building at eight a.m. on a Saturday morning? Art students." She winked at me.

I laughed. "Thanks, Professor."

"Of course. Now, I get the impression you have undeveloped film burning a hole in your backpack, am I right?"

I nodded, trying not to blush as I thought about the nature of said undeveloped film.

"As it turns out, I had the darkroom booked for myself this afternoon, but I don't have time to indulge after all. My wife asked me to accompany her to a Tai Chi class, and one thing I never do is refuse my wife." She barked a laugh.

Her wife! Marta was gay, too? I smiled. "My father agrees."

"Smart man. That said, I'll make you an offer you won't get often: want my darkroom hours?"

"Yes!" I grinned. "I've been dying to get into a darkroom all summer."

"Excellent. I scheduled myself from three to six." She passed the key over to me. "It's yours. Enjoy."

I wanted to hug Marta, but that seemed silly. Instead, I said, "Thanks. I appreciate it."

"Of course. Just promise to show me something you develop today. I'm eager to see more of you work."

I swallowed, hoping that in the handful of rolls I'd grabbed there was a decent shot that wasn't utterly pornographic. "Yes, ma'am."

"Go on." She waved me out the door, her hair bouncing with the motion. "Off with you."

And off I went. I had another class to get through and then I'd have a darkroom all to myself.

For the first time since I'd left Kingsley.

✦　✦　✦

I GOT BUSY developing the film Daniel and I had taken of each other on Friday night. The nudes weren't Harold Seville quality, but they weren't too shabby either.

I made a contact sheet first, and then used a loupe to choose which I wanted to develop larger. The first picture of me that Daniel had taken showed me spread out on Bobby's guest bed. I was surprised to see that Daniel was right. I was handsome.

Deciding which I wanted to enlarge, I chose to develop them in black and white, despite having used color film. Both because it was easier, but also it would make for artsier-looking photos. I decided to make some five-by-eight, and a few others eight-by-ten, but the ones I was working on now were going to be four-by-six. Regular photo sized.

I used the tongs to pull a photo from the solution. I hung it up and as it dripped, examined the shot. In it, I was ass up on the bed, my hands spreading my cheeks open, exposing my hole.

I bit my lower lip, admiring the composition. Daniel was a surprisingly good photographer. The picture showed off my wiry back muscles and the heart shape of my ass. My buttocks were smooth, except for the dark hairs close to my thighs, and the shade of my anus was similar to my nipples.

I hadn't ever seen my asshole before, and I studied it. Vanity puffed my chest, and I couldn't help but smile. My hole was *pretty*, just like Daniel had said.

The next photo I pulled out of the solution was of more than just my ass. It was me, face-up on the bed, gazing lustfully at Daniel. I remembered the feel of the duvet on my back, and the aching excitement of Daniel standing over me with the camera, and the avid expression on his face.

I studied the photo—full-frontal naked—not well-framed, but not awful either. He'd cut my feet out—typical newbie mistake. But it was different seeing myself this way. It wasn't like looking in a mirror. It was more like looking at myself through Daniel's eyes, and the black and white of the picture only added to the stark reality.

Next: a photo that emphasized my gray eyes as I gazed up, naked, horny, and shameless.

I tilted my head. My cock *was* long with a good-shaped head. My pubes led up to a treasure trail that gave out right before my trim stomach, which didn't show a six-pack, but was tight and firm all the same. I wasn't *my* type, but I could see why I was someone's.

I wasn't just cute—I was hot.

I'd never thought I was ugly, but I'd never considered myself truly attractive before now. Now I could see what had drawn Daniel—and Adam—to me.

As I developed the rest of the rolls, I felt puffed up with vain pride. It was a new feeling, and in the privacy of the darkroom, I indulged it.

When I finished and all the photos were all drying along the wires above, I moved on to the second-to-last roll. It was the roll I'd let Kennedy play with. As I went through the negatives, selecting a few good ones to send to her as a gift, I hoped she was doing all right in Florida with her grandparents. I hoped she didn't miss her mother too much.

I paused over one that I'd taken of her. The sun in her eyes, the freckles on her face stark in black and white. I smiled. I'd give this one to Daniel when I asked him to mail the ones she'd taken down to her.

The final roll was full of pictures I'd taken the night before while Daniel was sleeping. *These* would be the ones I'd show Marta. There were three that were, in my not-so-humble opinion, spectacular. Daniel looked like a sleeping Adonis in them, moonlight dancing on his skin and hair.

Since our class assignment for the upcoming week was to capture images of "repose," these were pretty much perfect.

Just like my ass.

Chapter Fourteen

THAT EVENING AFTER dinner, with my mom clacking away at her word processor behind the closed door to her office, and my father listening to The Beatles' *White Album* and grading papers behind the closed door to his, I had the privacy to call Daniel.

The phone rang three times. "Hello?"

It was his mother. For some reason I hadn't expected her to answer, and for a moment I froze, a memory jumping into my mind of her perched on the counter, plate in hand and ready to hurl onto the floor.

"Hello?" she asked again, this time with a hint of irritation.

"Um, hi, Mrs. McPeak. May I speak with Daniel?"

There was a small hesitation before Marlene spoke. "This is Danny's friend? Peter?"

"Yes."

"Ah." Another pause. "Thank you for taking Kennedy away the other day." She cleared her throat. "She didn't need to see me like that."

"I was happy to help."

"I'm sorry you saw me like that too."

I noticed she didn't apologize for what she'd done, just that I'd seen it. I wasn't sure how to respond. I couldn't find it in myself to tell her it was okay. "Me too."

She let out an embarrassed laugh. "I'll find Danny for you." I heard her footsteps as she walked away, leaving the phone off the hook.

The wait wasn't long. Another extension picked up. "Hello? Peter?"

"Hey."

"Hold on a second. Let her hang up."

We both waited until we heard footsteps and then the clatter of the other phone being put on the base.

"Hey," Daniel said, his voice going gentle. "How was your day?"

"Good. How was yours?"

"Could have been better, could have been worse." A smile crept into his tone. "Starting it out seeing you next to me in bed was the best part of it by miles."

"I liked that too." I wanted to ask when we could do a sleepover again, but there were probably more important things on Daniel's mind, like: "How's your mom today?"

A low rumbling sigh came through. "She's embarrassed and apologetic right now, but when isn't she after an episode? When I got home, she and Nadine were having coffee and talking about the future."

"That's good, right?"

"I guess. Dreaming up scenarios where all the bad stuff she's done gets washed away in a river of roses is one of Mom's favorite pastimes right now. Nadine's an optimist and good at making other people feel hopeful too."

"You're not feeling as optimistic, though."

Daniel snorted. "No. After Nadine left we got a call from the rehab place. Her entry has been postponed. The individual they thought would be leaving today decided to stick around for another few weeks to make sure the 'sobriety would stick.'" Another heavy sigh. "I suppose that's a smart move for them, but it leaves us in a lurch. Worse, it leaves me here with her alone. At least when the kids were around, I had them to distract her and me from how much we irritate each other."

"I'm sorry."

"Me too." The echo of my brief conversation with his mother played in my mind. "There's not much worse than having to babysit your own mom. I can't trust her for a minute. I have to hide the keys in a different place every night before bed so I know she won't sneak out. It's…" He groaned.

"And the kids?"

"They called from the road. Grandma and Grandpa stopped just north of Atlanta last night. The hotel had an indoor pool. Ken was excited. Paul was…Paul."

"It has to be hard on him."

"It's hard on all of us, but maybe it's hardest on him. Living here he's helpless. I at least have some control. He's just on a roller-coaster ride and he can't get off. Kennedy's different. She goes with the flow."

I recalled her stricken face from the day before. "She feels it too."

"Yeah, of course. Being with my grandparents will be good for them. They love us to death, and most importantly: they *want* them. That's the thing, Peter. The worst confession I can ever make. Ready for it?"

"Yeah."

"I didn't want them."

"I know. It's okay. You love them. That's what matters."

"Being wanted matters a lot more, believe me. And the truth is I didn't want them." Daniel sounded ashamed, even though we'd talked about this before. This was a big hang-up for him. "And they knew it."

"It's all right. You're their older brother. You're *not* their dad.

Paul said so himself, remember?"

Daniel laughed. "Oh, yeah, he told me all the time."

I stayed quiet a minute, not sure what to say. Daniel's life was so much heavier than I'd known when I met him. But it was all worth it if I could stay in Daniel's orbit. If we could have more tender, exciting nights like last night, if we could grieve and laugh and play like that.

Daniel broke the silence first. "Anyway, yeah. It's been another day of trying not to hate my mother while being her little house-husband. Sorting laundry. Doing dishes. I never minded doing all that at my apartment when it was all my stuff. It's just—"

"She's your mom. She should be doing the parent-stuff."

"Exactly."

"But last night was great. It was just what I needed. Of course you showed up yesterday just when I needed you most. Like magic."

"Does it sound strange that I'm glad we went to Bobby's?"

"Not strange at all. I needed the closure."

"Yeah."

We hadn't spent a lot of time outside of the bedroom, but just being in his home, feeling his presence and, weirdly, his blessing had helped me accept that he was gone. A strange memorial, maybe, having sex in his guest room. But it'd helped me lay Bobby to rest and crown his memory with something I knew would make him happy: me and Daniel together.

"So..." I was sitting on the kitchen floor with my back to the wall, twisting the cord around my fingers. I wondered where he was and what he was doing. "What happens now?"

"I guess I have no choice but to wait it out here. Babysit her for a few more weeks. At least I've already set up a project for us to tackle together so we won't be sitting around making each other angry. The house will go up for sale soon, and I've got a list of things I need her to pack up for me to put into storage or decide how to otherwise handle. Even if I have to deal with the legalities of the sale all alone, at least I won't have to worry that she'll accuse me of thoughtlessly giving away or selling one of her prize bath mats or something."

"That's good." But that hadn't been what I meant. I was selfish, maybe, but I'd wanted to know what was next for us. "You'll be handling the sale? Alone?"

"I have an attorney on retainer and a real estate agent he recommended, but otherwise yes. She's given me her power of attorney."

"Wow." It was all so complicated.

"Enough about her. How are you doing? Really?"

"I'm good. Really."

"No regrets?"

"About what?"

He laughed, and the sound made my insides tingle. "About last night. How fast we moved. The things we did."

"No. Do you?"

"Not even one."

"Whew." I brought my knees up to my chest and hugged them with one arm. Twirling butterflies came to life in and around the vicinity of my heart. "I was worried since you asked."

"No. I was just checking in. I loved what we did."

"Me too."

"And that's one reason I think we should slow things down a little."

I blinked. "Slow down?" But we'd been wanting each other all summer. Did we need to go slower now that we could be together?

"I just mean that last night was the best. Being alone with you like that made me feel the happiest I have in a long time. And given everything—my mom, Bobby's death—that's precious to me. Sex with you is something I don't want to rush or ruin."

Could sex be ruined by rushing it? I remember Adam resisting moving on to full-on fucking, too. Was there something about me that made a guy want to slow down after he got a taste?

"But last night when I let things escalate—when I escalated them myself—I'd been thinking my mom would be gone this afternoon, and that, aside from dealing with the house, I'd have all the time in the world to focus on us, and on building something great together."

"Okay…" Everything he was saying sounded amazing, but there was something about his tone that gave me pause.

"But with my mom still here, and without even the kids to keep us away from each other, I just… I need us to slow things down."

I frowned. "All right. I don't want to rush you." I could hear the tension in my voice. "But I don't understand. If being with me makes you happy, why do you want to deny yourself a break from the situation with your mom?"

"Because it wouldn't be a break. It'd be…an interlude. I'd be using you as a distraction instead of giving you—and us—my full attention. You deserve all of me, not just scraps."

"I'm happy to take scraps."

Daniel chuckled, but he sounded serious when he said, "You shouldn't be."

"So what does this mean then? We still see each other, but we just kiss and keep our clothes on, or…?"

Daniel's silence was longer than I liked. I wasn't sure if that was because I was going to hate what he had to say next or because he was making up the answers as he went. "I think we don't meet up in person until she's gone. We can talk on the phone, and make plans for a few weeks from now, but until she's gone, let's not see each other."

"Are you…" I swallowed hard. "Are you saying we should break up, or are you—"

"No! Not that. Are you kidding me? I just got you, Peter. I'm not letting you go yet."

I laughed, but it sounded strangled. "Then what?"

"We're still seeing each other. Monogamously. But for a few weeks, we'll just keep our physical distance. We'll talk on the phone. Knowing that I'll have the reward of being with you once she's out of here will help keep me sane."

But not seeing Daniel would drive *me* insane. Especially now that I knew how good being with him felt. "But being with me while she's around could help keep you sane, too."

"I know this is hard to understand. You've just seen her a few times. I don't want her to taint us."

"I don't understand."

"She ruins everything, Peter. If she knew how much I care about you, she'd try to ruin us, too."

"How?"

"You'd be surprised."

I felt like the rug was being pulled out from under me again. I trusted Daniel, but this was shaking my tender heart. "I'm okay with surprises if it means I can still see you."

"Please, I'm still humiliated by what you saw yesterday."

"Her behavior doesn't say anything about you. It's her problem."

"I know. But I'm her son, and it's mortifying to have the guy you care about come over to find your mother throwing dishes and freaking out."

I didn't know what to say. I didn't want him to be embarrassed. The truth was, however, if it'd been my mom, I'd feel the same way.

Daniel went on, "I don't trust many people in this world."

"I understand."

"And, whether it's wise or not, I trust you more than most. But do I think you could see the full shit-show that is Marlene McPeak at her worst and not want to run away from me? I don't know. *I* want to run, Peter. Anyone would want to run."

I sat quietly, trying to sort through my emotions. Disappointment that I couldn't see him again soon—tonight! immediately!— warred with concern for his well-being, respect for his clear boundary, and hurt that he thought his mother could ever drive a wedge between us.

"Please let me keep one thing safe from her," Daniel whispered. "The most important thing. You."

"Just a few weeks?"

"We'll talk every night."

"You'll miss me?"

"I already do."

"What if I need to see you?"

"If you really need me, of course I'm here. This is just for me, not for you. I'm being selfish. But if you need me, Peter, come to me. Right away. Or call me, and I'll come to you."

That satisfied me. Daniel wasn't abandoning me. He was just trying to muscle through something he didn't want me involved in. There were things I hadn't wanted him involved in either, issues I'd had to deal with on my own—like getting Adam out of my life. I could understand not wanting the beautiful thing we were creating to get tainted with the worst thing in his life.

"All right. I understand."

"Thank you." With herculean effort, Daniel tried to change the tone of the conversation, forcing lightness into his tone. "Tell me about your day. What are your plans for the week? What's it like out in the land of the living-normal?"

I confessed that I'd told Minty about us being together-together, and Daniel laughed about Minty's various threats. Then I told him about Marta giving me the hours in the darkroom, and our conversation took a different turn.

"Describe them to me."

"I can't. I'm in my kitchen. My parents could walk in at any second." I flashed back to a memory of Adam demanding phone sex, and the frustrating way I'd given in to him.

"Ah, too bad." He sighed. "But your asshole, yeah? It's gorgeous, isn't it?"

I laughed. "Yeah." Heat roared into my face. "It's nice."

"So lickable."

"Daniel…"

"What?"

"Don't make me break my promise already."

"Which one?"

"If you talk about licking my ass, I'll get in my car right now and drive over there tonight."

He laughed again. "You like getting rimmed, huh?"

"Um, Danny, are you okay?"

Another long laugh. "Peter?"

"Yeah?"

"I'm falling so in love with you."

"New rule."

"What's that?"

"You're not allowed to say anything like that again until you can say it to my face."

Daniel hesitated, but when he replied he was serious. "Deal."

Maybe by then, I'd be ready to say it back.

✧   ✧   ✧

I BREATHED IN the smoke and forged through the room of dancing men and a handful of grinding lesbians to find my friends. I'd arrived late, having talked to Daniel for a lot longer than I'd expected.

But after getting off the phone with him, I'd pulled on some black jeans, a sleeveless black tank that I'd gotten a few weeks before at Repeat After Me and left a note for my parents not to wait up for me.

Tilt-a-Whirl was the same as it ever was, and my heart sang with the vibrant queer joy of it all. I'd brought my camera—a point-and-shoot so I wouldn't sweat leaving it with Barry behind the bar so I could dance—and I used it now to take a few photos. Now that I had access to a darkroom, I'd be able to fix up some of the limitations of the camera via the developing process.

"Hey you," a voice said in my ear.

I turned to find Millar and a tall, broad guy with the kind of all-American looks seen on movie stars. He was, as it turned out, the pre-med boyfriend Millar had mentioned earlier. I agreed to share a drink with them, but I stuck to soda water because the guy behind the bar wasn't Barry. Not that he'd serve me anyway.

Billy was nice and seemed protective of Millar, putting his arm around him whenever a guy seemed ready to make a move. It was sweet. But after a few minutes of yelling pleasantries at each other over the music, I was ready to move on.

"I've gotta go," I said, nodding toward the stairs. "Friends are waiting."

Millar gave me a hug, and I was surprised by how fierce it was. "I'm proud of you," Millar said before letting me go.

"I'm proud of you too."

Upstairs, I was greeted with a chorus of conflicting nicknames—"Puker!" "Heartbreaker!" "Sweetie!"—and within minutes I was surrounded by friends. Questions flew. Rumors had been spread. I was with Daniel, I wasn't with Daniel, we were just screwing, we were in love. I held back the news about Bobby because the night was too festive to bring everyone down, but I set them straight on what was real and what wasn't.

Daniel and I were together.

Yes, I was happy about it.

They were happy, too. Renée threw her arms around me, kissed my cheeks, and whispered, "I knew you'd do the right thing. I knew you'd see what was right in front of you the whole time."

I rolled my eyes, but her praise warmed me.

When Minty and Jennifer returned from the dance floor below, her friend Bernie in tow, the night was just getting started. By two in the morning, I had agreed to a drink or two, and I was on the dance floor. Friends on all sides, queer men all around, music pumping through my veins.

I had it all.

I had parents who loved me. A job that was rewarding and easy. A photography mentor who saw something in me. Darkroom access. A file of letters from my dead uncle's lover. Friends who supported me.

I had Daniel. Who was at home asleep and hopefully dreaming about me, the way I would dream about him in bed tonight.

Minty wrapped his arms around me and together we moved to the beat. Adam and Atlanta seemed far, far away.

College was off to a fantastic start.

Part X
Mid-September 1991

Chapter Fifteen

IT WAS AMAZING how quickly life could move on if you let it.

For the next two weeks, school and my new job at the library were good distractions from the lingering sadness over our loss of Bobby. The fast-and-hard tumble into a relationship with Daniel had eclipsed the confused hurt that still pricked me sometimes over the way things had ended with Adam.

To say I was busy was an understatement.

In addition to spending all the free time I could find on the phone "taking things slow" with Daniel, I also had my job and my schoolwork. Professors weren't like high school teachers. They didn't consult each other about when assignments were going to be due, in order to make sure you weren't overloaded. They just piled it all on. Which was good.

Classes were challenging but fun for the most part. Aside from Photography with Marta, my favorite class was turning out to be Psychology. While poor Donnie hadn't gotten any better at not puking before each class, he ran a fascinating—if not to-syllabus—class.

Today, even though he was incurably terrified of public speaking, he was gritting through it, and lecturing us on Freud's position on homosexuality. Namely that there was nothing shameful or wrong in same-sex love, and while Freud saw it as no advantage in life, many of the world's greatest minds like Plato, Michelangelo, and da Vinci had all been gay.

Many of the other students in the room were uncomfortable with Freud's take, but I was loving it. I glanced toward Minty to see how he was reacting to the lecture, but he was busy scribbling in his notebook—an ugly, squiggly ball of black pencil lead that grew larger and larger as the class went on.

I frowned. Minty had seemed off all morning, but he wasn't talking, and I wasn't asking. Sometimes, when it came to Minty, I wasn't sure I even wanted to know.

After class Jennifer asked us to meet up with her later for lunch and gossip—supplied by her, because I didn't have anything I was willing to share. I was game, and while Minty still seemed crabby and distracted, he said he was in, too. Unsurprisingly, because while he wasn't as much of a gossip hound as Bobby had been, he was still a big fan.

I stepped into Marta's classroom, unprepared to find the walls covered with photos. A quick scan proved it to be student work, and when I located some of my own in amidst the chaos, I had a sinking feeling that I knew what was in store.

"Surprise!" Marta said, standing at the front of the room with her hands on the hips of her swishy skirts. Her silver jewelry sparkled in the sunlight sliding through the big windows. "It's class critique day."

A groan went around, and my stomach wrung itself into knots.

"Ah-ah-ah," she scolded, wagging a finger at us. "None of that misery please. This isn't meant to humiliate you, but to grow your eye and your skills."

We all ranged out at the various tables and chairs, a few of the other students looking almost as green-gilled as Donnie. Marta walked around slapping packets of papers down in front of us. Each page of the packet had a number on it.

"Each number corresponds with a photo. For the first fifteen minutes, I'd like you all to go around the room, taking notes on each of the photos. What do you like about them? What are their strong points? What weaknesses and room for improvement do you see? This isn't an opportunity to bash your fellow classmates. This isn't even *about* your classmates' pictures. It's about you, and *your* relationship with the camera, with framing, light, and development. Not your classmate' actual photos. This isn't personal. Do you understand?"

That all sounded fine and dandy, but I felt certain everyone in the room was going to take every criticism personally.

"Let's begin."

Walking around the room, looking at the photos and jotting down my thoughts was the easy part. I had enough opinions to fill an ocean. It was a question of whether I had the guts to share any of those less-than-positive thoughts with anyone.

"All right. Time's up." Marta waved us back to our seats. "Who wants to go first?"

Heads turned, gazes bounced around the room landing on nothing. No one seemed to want to start.

"All right, I'll choose," Marta said, pulling up a chair and sitting on it backwards. Her silver hair shone as she peered around the room. "Peter."

"Me?" I pointed at myself.

"You're the only Peter in here."

My palms went sweaty. "This is my first college-level photography course. Maybe someone with more experience should go first."

She clucked her tongue. "I think you know how to say what you like and don't like about a photograph." She rolled her hand in the air. "Stop stalling."

I cleared my throat. "All right. Um." Choosing a photo I'd written down positive things about, and something innocuous for the suggested improvement, I steadied myself so that when I spoke, my voice sounded stronger than I felt. "So, for Photo 9…"

The room tensed. I didn't look up from my notes for fear of meeting the gaze of whoever had taken the shot of the bird in a cage coated with uncleaned droppings.

"The composition was good. It pulls out emotions of empathy and sadness, as well as illustrating the beauty of the bird against the ugliness of the cage. The depth of field was handled well. I think it was taken on 200 speed film, and maybe it could have been pushed to 400. But otherwise, it's a good shot."

"Okay. And why did you think they should have pushed the film speed?"

"To grab the shadows."

Marta nodded. "Anyone else have notes to share on Photo 9?"

No one did. So that was that. No one screamed. No one cried. I'd said my piece and now we were moving on.

"How about Photo 5?" Marta asked.

That was one of mine. I sat up straighter, bracing myself.

"Todd, you're awfully quiet today. What did you think of Photo 5?"

"It's bullshit."

My flinch was instant.

Marta's brows went up, and I expected her to scold him. She'd stated this wasn't an opportunity to bash your fellow students. Gaze drifting over to my photo, I wondered, was it bullshit? I'd taken it at Tilt-a-Whirl, capturing Barry behind the bar as Minty and Windy did shots. Their faces twisted up at the burn of the liquor while their skin shone with sweat and glitter. Two guys kissed in the background. Barry cleaned a beer stein, the sheen of sweat glistening on both the glass and his dark skin.

"All right. Strong stance. Why's it bullshit?" Marta asked. "You've got a vocabulary. Use it."

Todd, a solid, burly guy with a patchy beard, bristled. "It's a political agenda. Not art."

Marta went over the photo, brought her glasses down from the top of her head, and made a show of looking at every inch of my photo. "Hmm, I'm not sure I see where it tells me to vote for any candidate. What makes this political, in your opinion, Todd?"

"The guys kissing."

Marta squinted harder. "Oh, in the background. I see. Hmm. Well, putting your homophobia aside, what do you think of the photo? The framing, the choices?"

Todd's mouth worked hard. I thought he might spit. "The framing is good. The shadows pop. The whites shine. It's dynamic. The composition goes beyond textbook."

Marta nodded along, peering at the photo as Todd bit out the compliments. "I see, so your only suggestion for improvement is for the photographer to cater to your delicate sensibilities?"

Todd's jaw flexed. "Yes."

"All right then. I have one thing to add for improvement."

My gut tightened.

"Learn to embrace the lens flare a bit more. It's not always your enemy." She pushed her glasses back up and moved on. "Photo 12."

After class, as I packed up my things, Marta crossed to me after Todd had left the room. "You handled that well."

I hefted my backpack onto my shoulders. "Homophobia is par for the course around here."

"Exactly. But you're not going to just take it, are you?"

My lips twisted into a small smirk.

"I thought not. I fully expect photos of *naked* men kissing to be in your next batch for class critique. I'll be disappointed if I don't get them."

"I'll have to learn to live with your disappointment, then," I laughed. "I can't submit naked photos for an assignment."

We exited the class together.

"I notice you didn't say you don't have any naked photos," she teased. "Do what you think is best, but I'm a fan of challenging small minds. I'd be happy if over the course of the semester you blew Todd's."

"I'll do my best."

On my way to meet Minty and Jennifer, I swung by McClung Tower and rode the elevator up to my dad's office. He wasn't there, so I left a note on his desk for him.

Stopped by, but you're teaching. One day I'll learn your schedule. Just in time for it to change. Love, P

In the UC, after locating Jennifer and Minty and finding an empty booth in the back of the cafeteria, we picked at our soggy French fries and soy burgers. I'd just taken my first bite when Jennifer burst out with, "Guess what!"

"What?" Minty asked with less enthusiasm than Jennifer's injunction begged for. I had assumed his mood would have improved by lunch, but he still had a brittle air about him, like he might snap.

"Bernie and I went to Tilt-a-Whirl last night on our own."

Minty shrugged. I took another bite of soy burger and waited.

"So...we kissed." Jennifer went on, describing how after a night of dancing and drinking, she and her best friend had ended up kissing and touching and sliding fingers into vaginas.

"Oh my God!" Minty exclaimed, covering his ears. "That's disgusting!"

Jennifer rolled her eyes. "Well, you came out of one, you know. They're beautiful things. Givers of life."

"My mother most certainly *does not* have one of those," Minty insisted. "She's like Barbie. I was delivered by a fairy in the middle of the night. Covered in fairy stamps."

"Fairy stamps?" I dunked a fry in ketchup and tossed it into my mouth.

"Glitter. Duh."

Jennifer waved her hands around. "Whatever. Forget about that. The important thing is I made her come like four times, but this morning she didn't say anything about it. What's up with that? Do you think she's mad?"

"How would I know?" Minty said, flapping his hands around like he could wave away her words. "Ask *her!*" He rubbed his temples like he was getting a headache.

"Peter, what do you think?" She turned to me.

I finished chewing before I spoke. "In my experience, friends don't do that stuff together…not if they really are *just friends.*"

"That's crap," Minty said. "Gay guys do it all the time. I've had sex with most of my friends."

"I said in *my* experience."

Minty huffed. "Your experience is invalid."

"My experience is plenty valid."

"Stop arguing," Jennifer said. "This is about me."

"Right," I said. "Are you worried she didn't want to do what you two did?"

"Oh, she wanted it last night. She wanted it so bad. She was *soaked* when I was done with her."

Minty spit out his bite of soy burger. "I can't." At first, I thought he meant he couldn't eat the burger, and I empathized, but then he stood up and walked away with his tray.

"I had no idea he had so much internalized misogyny." Jennifer mused as she watched him go. She didn't sound hurt at least, just mystified. "I figured he'd be a feminist given the way he dresses."

"I don't know. He's being a dick. Forget about him." I watched Minty dump his tray and leave the cafeteria. Something wasn't right with him, but if he didn't want to talk, I wasn't going to push it. I changed the topic back to the one at hand. "Anyway, so how are you feeling about all of this?"

"I don't know. Excited, but also confused." She bit her lip, looking worried. "Does this mean I'm gay?"

I shrugged, dunking another fry before eating it. "You could be bisexual. Or maybe you just wanted to experiment?"

She tapped her fork against her tray, thinking. "I don't know if I could have a *girlfriend* or fall in love with Bernie. I mean, sex is one thing, but making a life with someone? That's another. You may not know this, but I like penises. A lot."

"Me too."

Jennifer poked at her burger's bun with the fork, putting holes all over the top. "What if I fell in love with Bernie? Would I never be allowed to have a penis again? That's depressing."

"I think there are strap-ons," I offered.

"Could it be the same? Plastic versus flesh?"

"I don't know." Being a fan of penises myself, her worry made sense to me. "You won't know if it matters until you try it."

"Oh, God. Am I going to try it?"

"You should."

"Do you think she's thinking the same thing?" Jennifer's eyes were pleading, as if I knew the answer and refused to tell her.

"Minty's right about one thing. That's a question to ask her."

"And how do I do that? Just call her up and say, 'Hey, so, are you worried that we're gay now or something?'"

"Maybe it would be better to talk about it in person," I suggested.

Lunch with Jennifer went on longer than I'd intended. We brainstormed and practiced various conversations. I played the role of Jennifer, and she played Bernie. Eventually she had to get to her next class, and we went our separate ways.

Later that evening, after studying for a few hours in the library, I came home to find our house quiet. There was a note from Mom and Dad saying they'd gone out to dinner with Mom's agent. That meant I was on my own for food, but, in better news, I'd have all the privacy I could want for a long phone call with Daniel.

I flung open the cabinets and fridge. There weren't many options. All right, a homemade pizza bagel would be just fine. After my carefully constructed bagel with Ragu and American cheese on top was heating in the toaster oven, I noticed an envelope addressed to me on the counter. The handwriting was familiar.

With a sinking sensation in my stomach, I tore it open:

Dear Peter,

I understand why you're not taking phone calls from any of us. I can't imagine how you must feel. I was appalled by Adam's behavior at Fusion, and I wanted to come up to the dorm room with you both that night, but Sarah said it was best for you guys to work it out alone.

I'm so sorry, Peter, for everything. If I hadn't chosen Fusion, if I hadn't suspected you were gay and decided to push the issue, maybe you guys would still be friends.

Adam is getting help now to deal with his anger issues. There's a college counselor he's seeing, and it's going great. He says the counselor has helped him understand that he reacted the way he did because he felt betrayed by you because you'd kept being gay a secret from him.

But I know he'd want you back in his life if you'd just forgive him. Now that he's getting help, I think things might be even better between the two of you if you'd give him another chance. Think how good it will feel to be honest with your best friend and have him love you for who you really are?

Whatever happens, Peter, I love you. I always will, and I'm always your friend.

Truly,

Leslie

I sat down on a stool and rested my chin on my hand, the letter still in my hand.

Todd's comment about my photo came to mind. *It's bullshit.*

My photo wasn't. But this? This was. I wanted to yell, to scream, to find a way to cast this crime off forever and for good. But it kept coming back to me. The disgust over my choices, the shame of what I'd done and who I'd hurt. Didn't Adam feel it too? Why didn't he? How could he keep on lying even now?

The phone rang just as the buzzer on the toaster oven went off. I hissed as I tugged the pizza bagel free and dropped it, steaming, on a plate. Rushing to answer the phone next, anxiety roiled inside me. What if it was Adam?

"Hey, you."

Daniel.

The peace his voice gave me was like absolution. No matter what I'd done in the past, somehow, I'd ended up here with Daniel on the other end of the line. Everything was going to be all right. Everything was fine.

Daniel would never lie about me, about us, or about who he was and what he wanted. He'd never be like Adam. He'd always be what he'd been right from the start.

Honest.

"Hey," I answered, a smile on my lips. "I've missed you."

"Me too."

"My mom leaves Saturday morning. For real this time. Are you still up for that party I mentioned?"

"Yes."

"Good. Because I've missed my friends, but most of all, I've missed seeing you."

"Daniel?"

"Yeah?"

I didn't know what I'd been about to say. Was I going to tell him about Leslie's letter? No. I didn't want to burden him with that. "Nothing. I just wanted to be sure of you." I didn't know how else to explain that I'd wanted to confirm that we were together.

"Be sure of me," Daniel said, pitching his voice lower. "Saturday night, I'll show you just how sure of me you can be."

"Is that a promise?"

"Petey, are you okay?"

I laughed. "You're such a goofball. And, somehow, that's just not as good as 'Danny, are you okay?' Doesn't have quite the same ring."

Daniel snorted. "No, it doesn't." He paused. "But yes, it's a promise. You can be sure of me, and also...*are* you okay? You sound tense."

I fingered Leslie's letter and then wadded it up and tossed it into the trash. "I'm good. Just needed to hear your voice."

"And I needed to hear yours, so we're even."

"Yeah." I took a bite of pizza bagel. "I love that about us."

That was as close as I'd come to telling him I loved him. Maybe one day soon.

For now, just being on the phone with him was enough.

Chapter Sixteen

THE NEXT SATURDAY afternoon, after hours of distracted studying for upcoming midterms, it was time to head out.

Before I left, as I crammed some string cheese into my mouth so I would have the strength to make it to Kingston, I fielded a few questions from my parents about Daniel and the plans for the night.

"So, you're happy with this new boy?" Mom asked. She was at the stove watching a can of soup heat, like she might burn it. Knowing her, she would find a way. "Actually happy?"

Dad sighed and rolled his eyes from the kitchen table where he was chewing on what looked like an over-microwaved Lean Cuisine.

Mom's attitude toward Daniel had shifted after I'd spent the night with him at Bobby's house. She was suspicious of him now. I could practically read it on her face whenever Daniel came up— which was every day. She thought he was just in it for sex. "Yes. I'm happy."

"He's nice?" She'd asked me this several times before.

"Super nice."

Then came the next expected question, the one I'd been avoiding answering for a couple of weeks now, because the reasons behind why the answer wasn't "today" were none of her business. "When can we meet him?"

"Soon."

"When is 'soon?'"

"I don't know."

"That's not a good answer."

"No. It isn't," I said with a cheeky grin.

Alas, that wasn't the end of Mom's interrogation. I finished up the string cheese as my mother reminded me about safer sex, requested my wallet, checked inside for a condom, and handed it back to me after confirming its presence.

Deciding that was enough indulging her new overbearing-mother persona, I grabbed my bag. "I'm headed out. Don't wait up. I might stay over at Daniel's if the party goes late."

The truth was, I *planned* to stay at Daniel's. His enormous house was empty—well, empty of *people*—and there were plenty of rooms I'd never seen, and lots of surfaces he might want to see me spread out on…

After two weeks of just phone calls, I was down for any and all of it.

"Be careful," Mom called, as I kissed Dad's temple. "Don't drink and drive."

"Don't drink at all!" Dad amended. "You're not twenty-one!"

With a sigh of relief, I stepped out the back door and walked around the house to my Volvo.

When I was on the interstate, driving toward Kingston, I popped in a new mixtape Daniel had mailed to me the week before. It'd come complete with a letter explaining why he'd chosen each song, how they made him think of me, or what they meant to him. To say I'd almost swooned was not an overstatement.

"The Whole of The Moon" by The Waterboys was the first song on the tape, and as the thrumming opening began, a helpless grin took over my face. I couldn't wait to see him. I knew a number of our friends would already be there when I arrived, but just being in Daniel's company, seeing his smile would be…so good. I felt like I could fly.

The nights were falling earlier now that we'd passed into September, but there was still plenty of evening left. Heading west into the blinding light of the falling sun, I almost didn't notice the Easter-egg green Mercedes in my rearview mirror.

But once I did, my soaring heart plummeted. Adrenaline hit my veins, and a roiling sickness started in my gut. Squinting, I recognized Adam in the driver's seat. The passenger and back seats seemed to be empty. I couldn't make out his expression because he was squinting into the sunset, too. He drove fast enough to be right up on my bumper, aggression in every lane switch and curve. If I slammed on my brakes, he'd hit me.

Violent anger twisted inside. Jamming my foot on the gas, I got some space between us. Was he trying to scare me? It wasn't working.

That was a lie.

He wasn't even close enough to touch me, but Adam already had me reverting back to lies.

I pulled off at the Lawnville exit and swung into the parking lot of a brick Baptist church. Adam pulled in right behind. I parked in the middle of four empty spaces, near the back of the lot, before getting out and slamming my door hard.

Adam was out almost as quickly. He smoothed out his dark sweater and then hooked his thumbs into his dark jeans, leaning against his car's hood. The white spire of the church cast a shadow between us. I'd have thought he looked handsome, despite how much I hated him now, if he didn't look so sick.

"What the fuck do you think you're doing?" I yelled. I hoped he didn't notice I was shaking. I didn't want to give him the satisfaction of knowing he'd frightened me.

Adam lifted his hands as if in surrender. "I just want to talk to you." He made it sound reasonable, but his voice was trembling, too. "You won't take my phone calls."

"Because I don't want to talk to you!"

He sighed, as if I were being unfair. "We have to work this out, Peter. Face-to-face. You and me. It's the only way."

I laughed in shock. "There's *nothing* to work out, Adam. Nothing at all. We're over. Done. Finished."

He shook his head. "No. You love me."

"Not anymore."

He laughed, disbelieving and delusional. "That's impossible." His hair shone reddish in the orange light of sunset. His dark eyes looked deeper-set than usual, and his cheeks were sunken, as if he'd lost weight.

"Are you sick?" I asked, sudden fear gripping me.

"No." He tilted his head in confusion.

"You look horrible."

"Because I'm sick, yes," he said, catching on to the term because it'd made me go soft for a moment. I toughened up. "I miss you like a sickness. Please. I need you."

I let out a huff. "No. I'm not having this conversation with you. We're done."

He shook his head and repeated more desperately, "That's not possible. We can't just be *done*."

It was my turn to shake my head. "We can. All I felt for you is dead. You killed it." My throat felt tight, and my eyes were hot. It wasn't entirely true. I'd felt something when I thought he might be ill, when I thought he might… But it wasn't enough. What I'd felt at that moment wasn't nearly enough.

But Adam wasn't getting it. He took a step toward me, and I backed up until I was pressed against my car. There were still several yards of space between us, but I didn't feel safe near him. "You want me to break up with Leslie?" His voice was the usual mix of pleading and determined. Like I was asking something very unfair of him. "You've always wanted that. If I did that for you? If I cut out that piece of my heart? Would you come back to me then?"

If I'd been scared before, now utter rage roared up from my feet. I almost growled as I gritted out, "No."

"No?" How could he still sound so surprised? Why was this so hard to believe? After all he'd done to me, and all he'd convinced me to do?

"I don't love you, Adam."

His face twisted. "That's a lie."

"It's not." I was surprised by how calm I sounded now. Like I was talking to a child. "You need to accept it. Don't follow me. It's stalking. It's sick. And it won't make me love you again."

He reached out his hands. "Please. I love you so much." His voice wavered as he stepped toward me again.

"Stop."

Surprisingly, he did. Standing there helpless looking, he went on, "I love you *both* so much," he amended. "Why can't you understand that? Why is that wrong? It doesn't *feel* wrong to me. I love her, and I love you, and I just want to keep you both forever. Why can't I? Why won't you let me?"

My mouth opened and shut on replies like: it feels wrong to *me*, or why don't you tell *her* about us, then, and see what *she* has to say. But in the end, I went with the simplest response that I could. The one that would be the final retort to any comeback he might have had to my other comments.

"I don't love you. Go back to Atlanta. Be happy with Leslie." I turned and opened my car door, putting one foot inside. "Don't ever come near me again."

I got in and slammed the door shut behind me. I locked the doors before I started the engine. I pulled out of the parking lot, leaving him in the shadow from the church spire. Turning back toward the interstate, I gunned it hard so I'd have a good lead on him if he tried to follow me again.

The rest of the way to Kingston, I kept one eye on the interstate ahead of me and the other on my rearview mirror. As it grew darker outside and evening descended, I tried to ascertain if the headlights behind me were shaped like a Mercedes, or if I was being paranoid. After a few more miles, it seemed evident I'd left him in the dust. Or else he'd chosen not to follow me after all.

At the Kingston exit, I pulled over onto a side street and parked outside of a stranger's house for a minute, just to get my breath. I was determined not to cry or feel anything except anger. But the image of Adam's face when I'd said I didn't love him kept flashing through my mind.

I didn't love him. Not anymore. But I didn't like hurting him either. Why did he have to keep coming around? Why couldn't he let me go?

Fuck him.

A telltale tightening started in my throat. I swallowed around it. I was *not* going to cry.

I moved back out into the street and began driving toward Daniel's again. It was easier to put Adam behind me when I was moving.

✦   ✦   ✦

DANIEL'S DRIVEWAY WAS cluttered with the gang's vehicles. I found a spot next to Barry's car on one side and Minty's tough-as-nails truck on the other.

The first time I'd seen his truck, I'd done a spit-take, it was so unexpected. Minty, wearing a pink T-shirt and a blue jean skirt over leggings, had glared at me and said, "What? I'm a country boy, asshole." And I guess deep down he was.

It was a lucky thing Robert and Barry could be here. They both had a rare Saturday night off from the clubs, and they'd chosen to spend it with Daniel. I'm pretty sure it was because they knew how hard things had been for him lately, and not because they didn't have better things to do than to hang out with us in the countryside burning wood and staring at the stars. It wasn't Robert's usual scene.

The sunset was dying, casting a pink glow behind the house, and from the driveway I could smell the bonfire smoke in the cool evening air. It seemed steeped with the promise of the upcoming fall weather, and I took a deep breath. As I let it out, I released the rage that'd pooled and boiled in my gut after Adam's stunt.

As I walked toward the bonfire—a big ball of orange and red— and my friends, I took my time, letting the anger ease out of me into the night. I scanned for Daniel and found him standing beside Barry with a soda can in his hand, listening as Minty told a story requiring a lot of hand gestures. Windy and Antonio sat on the wooden benches pulled up around the edges of the bonfire pit, and Robert stood by them, talking over Minty with equally dramatic gestures.

Daniel saw me and lifted his hand. I raised mine back.

This, *this* was what I'd chosen when I walked away from Adam in Atlanta and again tonight. This sweet, swooping feeling.

When I was about twenty yards away, Daniel ditched his stick with the marshmallow still attached, and ran toward me. The smile and the sparkle in his eyes were enough to push away any lingering ugliness.

When he reached me, he swept me into his arms, lifted me off my feet, and twirled me around. It was silly, it was giddy, and it was, as always, honest.

"Hey," I said, when he put me down, one arm still around my waist.

"Hey." He plucked one of the curls that'd fallen into my face. "Boing."

"You're ridiculous."

He grinned again. "I've been dying to see you."

"I could have come over at any time."

"This was worth waiting for." He nuzzled my cheek, kissed my nose, and then picked me up again, hands on my ass. I wrapped my legs around his waist, and he kissed me.

His kiss wasn't gentle, but it was still sweet. He put all of his joy at seeing me, all of his pent-up eagerness into it. It wiped away everything but a clarifying sense of wonder in me.

Fuck Adam. Fuck everything but this.

Here was a man who wanted me in a way that was healthy and good. If "healthy and good" was kissing me senseless right here in this field while our friends hooted and hollered from over near the bonfire. And it was.

"Well, hot damn," Antonio said, when we joined them, hand in hand, my lips aching from the happy force of Daniel's kiss.

"Hopefully that isn't how you greet each other all the time." Barry rolled his eyes, the sclerae looking whiter than usual in the glow of the fire.

"And I hope you do, darlings!" Robert clapped slowly. "Bravo."

"Jesus, guys. Heartbreaker, you don't have to suck him off right here to prove your love, you know," Minty said, sipping his Coke and giving me a half-hearted glare. He seemed in better spirits than he'd been in recent days at school, at least. Though that wasn't saying much. He still seemed crabby. "No one needs to see that."

"I need to see it," Robert said with a giggle. He dropped into a green lawn chair that was set out next to Barry's. "I've heard rumors. I want them confirmed by my very own eyes."

"It's big," Minty said. He was wearing boy-drag tonight, including some cowboy boots. He almost looked like the country boy that drove a pickup truck, but he still had his hip thrown out, and wore a sparkling headband in his short hair. "I'm talking about his dick, in case I need to be clearer. Seriously. Really big."

Daniel elbowed him.

"What? It's not a secret."

Daniel ignored him and turned to Barry, "I'm getting another soda from the cooler. Do you want one?"

"Caffeinated," Barry said. "I've got a long way to drive home tonight."

I could see Daniel opening his mouth to offer to let them stay, but then his eyes swerved to me, and he clamped his lips shut again.

If he wanted time alone with me in his huge empty house more than he wanted to be a good host, I agreed one-hundred-percent with his priorities.

"There's news, darlings," Robert called out, when Daniel returned with colas for me, Barry, and for himself. "Come over here," he yelled across the bonfire to Windy and Antonio. "I've got big news."

"What news?" Minty asked.

"Patience is a virtue," Robert said, and Dr. Landry came to mind for the first time in months. His voice rang in my head, and I remembered everything about him from the way he stared out the window at odd times, to the way he'd been so kind to me and Adam.

I wondered what he'd think of how that had all turned out. "Inevitable," I guessed he'd say. I wondered what he'd think of Daniel. "Does he light up the poetry in your soul?" I thought he'd ask.

I gazed at Daniel's face, shining in the light of the bonfire. Yes. He did.

Antonio whapped me on the back of my head as he passed by.

I winced. "Hey!"

He huddled up with us. "Hey, Heartbreaker."

Windy draped his arm around my shoulders and pressed his cheek to mine. "*Bonswa*," he murmured. Then he slid away to cuddle up with Minty, who kissed his cheek and whispered, "Bon sugar."

"So?" I asked, eager to hear what Robert had to say. "Did you get an even better contract with the Slide?"

"No," Robert said with a preening smile. "Guess again!"

"The building has started on the house?"

"No."

Barry interrupted. "Let's not get distracted with guesses. Tell the people the news, woman."

Robert stood and twirled around flapping his arms. "My baby bird has left the nest! Now we just have to see if she can fly!"

We stared at him and then at each other, the glow of the fire licking our skin, hair, and clothing, trying to process what he'd said.

"For fuck's sake," Barry barked. "Don't speak gibberish." He turned to us. "The documentary is done and dusted. We submitted *Drag Dolls* to the Atlanta film festival yesterday."

We all smashed our cans against Robert's with cheers and congratulations, drinking to the film. I hadn't seen the final cut yet, but based on what I'd worked on this summer, I thought it had a strong chance of being accepted.

"I missed the deadline for a lot of the others," Robert said. "But I can submit *Drag Dolls* elsewhere next year. It's Atlanta that I wanted most. If my film does well there, it could open all kinds of opportunities for Outrageous Video. God only knows where we could go from there!"

"To the stars!" Minty exclaimed.

"Don't you mean to the moon?" Antonio said, poking his dimpled cheek with a finger. "Mr. Everything's-Made-of-Moonbeams."

Minty smacked his finger away, grumbling, "I'm never going to live that down."

"It's all happening so fast," Robert said, fanning himself like he might faint. "It seems like just the other day *Drag Dolls* was only a twinkle in my eye, and now she's all grown up and out fending for herself."

"I'm not ready to call it a done deal yet," Barry said. "We have to wait and see if it's accepted."

"I know you're just trying to protect my feelings if it's not, but dream with me, Barry." Robert wrapped his arms around Barry's middle and kissed his jaw.

"I dream with you all the time, woman. I gotta hold your feet to the earth now and again."

Robert rolled his eyes, but there was that eternal fondness. He and Barry were a forever thing. It made my heart warm to watch them bicker.

I glanced toward Daniel. Could we have that kind of relationship one day? I hoped it wasn't too much to ask.

The fire crackled behind us. "The fire needs more wood," Daniel said, putting his hand on my shoulder. "Peter, come help me carry some from the shed?"

"Sure."

The hoots and hollers that followed us as we crossed the field were slightly embarrassing but mainly ridiculous.

"What do they think we're going to do? Fuck against the piles of wood?" I asked as we rounded the corner of the shed.

"They probably thought we'd do something like this," he said, grabbing my hand and pulling me close. He kissed me and slid his cool fingers underneath my T-shirt, skimming up to rub his thumbs against my nipples as his tongue tickled against mine.

My heart leapt and a smug sense of satisfaction ripped into me. Daniel was mine to kiss and have. He was my *boyfriend*. And everyone here knew it. Even better, Adam was *not*. Adam was driving back to Atlanta right now because we were over, over, *over*. Thank fucking God.

"I can't wait to get you alone," Daniel whispered. "You're the only good thing in my life the last few weeks, and I want to wallow in you."

"Me too."

He huffed. "What was I thinking inviting them at all? It should have just been me and you. Alone."

I shivered. "I don't know, but you did invite them, so now we have to live with your mistakes."

He laughed.

A new round of noises rose from the group. "God, keep it in your pants, Daniel!" Antonio shouted.

"Yeah, guys, enough!" Minty called out. "It's making me wanna puke up my entire life."

"We're not even doing anything!" I called out, as I hauled an armload of wood around the shed and toward the bonfire.

"Sure you're not!" Antonio and Minty started making kissing sounds and dry humping the air.

The rest of the night was awesome. We talked and laughed, we drank soda and made plans. I took photos of them all with the beautiful glow of the firelight dancing over their skin and in their hair.

It was easygoing after so many days of stress for Daniel and so much abrupt change for me. The evening encapsulated the one thing I'd never had in my entire life before this past summer: friends who knew me for who I was, and who loved me anyway.

As the moon made its way across the sky, the celebratory mood dried up. Once the bonfire was on its last leg, Daniel threw one last log on to keep the fire from going out, but it seemed the party had run its course. Barry and Robert were getting ready to go and so were the others.

"It's such a long drive," Daniel said to Barry. "Are you sure you don't want to stay?"

I felt awful about it, but I really hoped Barry would say no. I was also grateful that Daniel had spoken quietly enough that Minty, Antonio, and Windy hadn't heard. They'd have jumped at the offer.

"I've got to open at the library tomorrow," Barry said, standing with a big yawn and stretch. "Or else I'd take you up on that."

I winced for him. It wasn't that late yet, but opening shift was so early, and he'd be getting by on a less-than-ideal amount of sleep. As for me, I'd traded my opening shift with another employee, a nice guy named Graham. I had no reason to rush away tonight.

"Next bonfire we'll stay over, baby," Robert said, patting Daniel's cheek. "Promise."

"I don't think there'll be a next time," Daniel admitted. "I'm pretty sure the house will be sold by the end of next month." He shrugged. "Besides, you're a little on the elderly side for sleepovers anyway."

Robert smacked his arm. "Barry, did you hear that boy insult us and call us *old?*"

Barry just grunted and lifted his cooler full of snacks and sodas.

"Well, if they're leaving, Antonio and I are leaving, too," Windy said, standing up and brushing off his jeans. He pulled Antonio up. "It's early enough we might still hit the club tonight. Want to come, Minty?"

Minty shook his head, spitting out the piece of grass he'd been chewing on. "Told my mama I'd stay with her this weekend. Gotta be bright-eyed and bushy-tailed for my crucifixion tomorrow."

"Church?" Daniel asked.

"I've even picked out my nicest dress for it," Minty said, winking at him and preening a little.

Daniel's face went dark. "You better be joking."

Minty sighed and wrapped his arms around Daniel in a hug, patting his chest. "Don't worry. I'm not an idiot. I wouldn't give those assholes the satisfaction of killing me in the parking lot like the sacrificial lamb I'm destined to be. I'll be wearing my old, ugly brown suit like a good boy."

"I wouldn't put it past some of those assholes to attack you in the church itself if you wore a dress," Daniel muttered.

"But that wouldn't be very Christian, now would it?" Minty snarled. "Besides, I'd just like to see them take me." He puffed up his chest.

Right. Aikido. How did I always forget?

Antonio took up barking and Windy joined in, until Daniel told them to shut up. Laughing, Windy threw his arm around my shoulders. "Akita. Damn, Antonio is such a dumbass."

Daniel was still lecturing Minty. "Be careful. Use what you've learned in theater classes. Spit on the ground and grab your dick. Pretend you're an old redneck dude with a truck full of shotguns."

"I've got the truck. Just need the guns."

"Feel free to beat Pat Morrison's ass if you see him there. Just kick him in the balls. Tell him it's a gift from me."

"Oh, Patty, he's not even worth it," Minty said, shaking his head and laughing. "I'd like to kick Pastor Newsom in the balls the most. That fucking prick told my mama he'd *pray* for me to *change*. Said I had demons in me." Minty spit on the ground and then with the rubber sole of his tennis shoe ground it into the dirt. "Prick."

"I hate that guy," Daniel said. "He smells like cinnamon gum."

"Yeah. Ruined Big Red for me forever."

"At least he's not your father," Robert added.

"Oh, are we playing 'who's had it worst' now?" Minty asked. "Believe me, I'd win." An uncomfortable wave moved through the group, but it passed when Minty turned to Daniel and said, "Daniel would definitely lose. Your folks took *you* to the snooty Episcopal church where no one ever talks about burning in hell."

"When they took me to church at all."

"If I didn't love you so much, I'd hate you for being such a lucky fuck."

Daniel cleared his throat, and everyone could see the weight of all the very unlucky things that had happened to Daniel land between them. Minty cast his eyes down, ashamed. "I mean, I know you've had bad things happen. I just—"

"I know what you meant," Daniel said. "Dead fathers and drunken mothers don't negate that I was lucky not to be raised in a hellfire-and-brimstone church. Don't worry about it."

Minty stood on his tiptoes and kissed Daniel's cheek. "See? You're the best person ever."

Daniel rolled his eyes.

Minty turned to me, then. "Guess you're staying?"

I nodded.

"Okay, well," his eyes sparkled in the light from the dying bonfire. "If you find after this weekend, you'd like some tips on how to take a really big dick, give me a call. I'm always happy to share my wealth of experience."

"Uh, thanks. I think I can handle it," I said, blushing when I realized how that sounded.

"Oh, I doubt you can. First you need to make sure that you lube up—"

Daniel put his hand over Minty's mouth. "You are *such* an asshole."

Minty pried his fingers away and went on, "Lots of lube. Lots of it."

"Lube *is* very important," Robert said, chuckling. "And be sure to take your time with it."

"Right. It's best not to just let him ram it in," Minty said. "And if you need to take a break in the middle to get your breath and stop crying, that's okay, too. Oh, and be drunk. Be really drunk. It helps to loosen up all over. But...I guess then you might puke. Huh, Puker?"

"Thanks, Minty," I said, not sure if I was annoyed, humiliated, or amused. Maybe all three. "You're generous to want to share these tips."

"No problem." He stuck his tongue out and then shrugged, feigning an innocent expression. "Anything to help our Heartbreaker."

I rolled my eyes. Of all the nicknames, I really didn't want that one to stick.

"Stop harassing him. What we do is none of your business," Daniel said with a hint of real irritation.

"Right," Antonio said. "Like we didn't *all* hear his high, breathy moans when you made him come in the hotel room this summer. That pretty much made it our business."

My face burned, but Daniel wasn't having any of it. "Drop it. Now. I'm serious."

"Consider it dropped," Minty said, lifting his hands. Antonio raised his hands in surrender as well.

As we said goodbye, I gave Robert and Barry hugs and high-fived Windy. I didn't say much to Minty or Antonio, still annoyed with them for being pricks.

Not that I didn't understand it, especially with Minty.

I knew that while he and Daniel had never been a couple, Minty's treatment of me was based in overprotective jealousy. I got it. Daniel was his oldest friend, more like a brother. I was the interloper who'd let Daniel down once already. Minty would have to get used to the idea that I wasn't going to dick Daniel over again, and then he'd stop needling me so much.

Minty stomped away from the bonfire in his cowboy boots, leading the group back up to the front of the house. Daniel followed to see them off closer to the driveway.

Hanging back, I remained by the fire. I hunted down a stick from the pile by the side of the benches and stabbed a marshmallow on the end. The night had been fun but exhausting. I was eager for our friends to be gone, so it could be just me and Daniel alone. Nervous excitement thrilled through me. What if it didn't feel like it had at Bobby's house? What if it was different tonight?

I picked up a wedge of chocolate, and maneuvered my smoldering marshmallow, gooey and hot, onto a graham cracker and mashed them all together. And just like that, my entire night mashed together, too.

My mom's skepticism and interrogation, Adam's appearance—was he dangerous? Was he losing his mind?—the comfort of friends, followed by the annoyance of being teased, and most of all the delicious anticipation of being with Daniel. I wasn't sure what to expect tonight. Were we going to have anal sex? Was I going to need Minty's advice after all?

I didn't know. It made me feel shaky inside to imagine it.

Marshmallow smeared over my lips as I ate. With sticky fingers, I added two more marshmallows to my stick, and held it over the flames while I took another bite of the s'more I'd constructed.

Daniel walked the gang halfway up the hill and then stopped, gesturing back toward me. I saw Minty turn to hug Daniel with both arms while Windy patted Daniel's shoulder, and Robert waved. Antonio high-fived him goodnight, and Windy did a silly, fancy bow. I could almost hear him bid Daniel *bonswa*. Barry just nodded his head.

It'd been such a fun night, and much as I just wanted to enjoy the rest of the night alone with Daniel, there was something I had to get out of the way first.

I had to tell him about being followed by Adam. I didn't *want* to tell him. Mainly because I wasn't sure what Daniel would say. Or do. Now that it was done and I'd calmed down, I realized I was more sad than angry. What I *really* wanted was to have not seen Adam at all, to be allowed to go back to the flawless, joyful feeling

I'd been swimming in before I'd seen his car behind me on the road.

"Everything good?" Daniel asked, panting from his jog back down the hill.

In the dying firelight, his dark blond hair glowed like a halo, and his eyelashes were like spun gold. I wanted to press myself against him and smell his now-familiar scent. I knew it would lift off his skin in the warm juncture of his neck and shoulder. All I had to do was bury my face there, and I'd be enveloped by it.

Instead of answering his question, I pulled the marshmallows out of the flames, still burning like tiny torches. "These are for you."

Daniel blew them out and then peeled the black skins off, raking the melted centers onto a graham cracker and topping it with a piece of chocolate. He took a bite and the soft, pleasurable sound he let out left my knees a little weak.

"Is everything okay?" Daniel asked after he swallowed. "You seem stressed now. Was it what Minty said? I'll talk to him. He and Antonio can't tease you like that. It's not right."

"They're dicks, but lovable dicks," I said.

"But something's on your mind." Daniel took another bite of s'more.

"Yeah. It's, um, Adam," I said.

Daniel choked and coughed up the hunk of s'more into the fire. When he next spoke, his voice sounded breathy with panic. "Adam? What about him?"

I stroked his arm to soothe him. "On my way here tonight, he followed me for part of the way."

Daniel's jaw tightened. "He's stalking you now?"

"I don't know. He followed me until I pulled over. I asked him what the hell he was doing, and he said he wanted to talk to me since I hadn't taken his calls."

He tossed the rest of his s'more into the fire. "He's an asshole."

"Yeah, he is."

"So, what did he say?"

"The usual. He wants me back. He begged. He said he'd leave her." I frowned. *Had* he said that? I tried to remember. He hadn't. Just implied it. Typical Adam.

"So…"

"So, I told him it didn't matter. I said I never wanted to see him again." I gazed at Daniel in the firelight, the tension in his shoulders, the fear in his eyes, and I wanted to make it go away. I wanted that warm, happy, excited feeling that had been filling me up for days now to come back. And I wanted him to *smile*, because it made my heart melt when he did, when he looked at me with eyes full of affection.

"I don't want to talk about him anymore. I just want to be with you and feel happy."

"*Do* you feel happy when you're with me?"

"Yeah."

Daniel swallowed and took my face in his hands, his fingers cupping each cheek. "You…don't look happy right now."

A smile started at the left corner of my lips. "He's a bad topic. Brings up bad feelings."

Daniel searched my eyes and then leaned in, kissing me. I wound my hands around his neck, feeling the short hairs stick to the marshmallow residue on my fingers. I tangled my other hand into the back of his hair, deepening the kiss.

Daniel broke the kiss, but he wrapped his arms around me. He buried his face in my neck, taking deep breaths and letting them out. "I hate that guy," he murmured. "I've never even met him, but I hate him."

I didn't say anything, a strong urge to defend Adam welling in me. *He's not a bad guy. Just messed up.* I ran my hand through

Daniel's hair. "You don't need to worry about him."

I forced the defense down until it disappeared.

He is *a bad guy. Being messed up is no excuse.*

Daniel snorted and whispered against my throat, "I've heard that kind of thing before."

I made a soft noise of confusion, and he shrugged in my arms, explaining, "From my mom. 'You don't have to worry about me drinking, Danny.' 'It's over, Danny.' 'Never again, Danny.' I've heard every version of that you can imagine. Addictions are hard to break."

I pulled out of his embrace and touched the underside of his chin, forcing his eyes up so that I could gaze into them. I said nothing, not sure what I could say.

I'm not sure what he saw in my eyes in the low light from the dying bonfire, but whatever it was, he ducked his head again. "I'm sorry. You're not my mom. Adam's not alcohol."

"I told him I never wanted to see him again," I repeated. "And I meant it."

Because Adam had hurt me, he didn't understand, and he wouldn't ever change. It was too late even if he did. Because now I had feelings for someone else. For Daniel.

Daniel nuzzled my cheek, his stubble scraping mine. "I'm sorry."

"I know."

"Sometimes I'm scared to trust you."

I nodded, turning my face to take a deep breath of his hair and neck, before rubbing our stubble together again.

"But that's my problem," Daniel said. "Not yours."

"You can trust me," I said. "I'm done lying. It ruins everything. That's why I told you about running into him. I don't want secrets between us."

Daniel kissed my neck. "I believe you," he whispered.

That was the thing. I believed in Daniel, too. We could believe and trust in each other.

That alone was worth more than I could ever express to him.

✧   ✧   ✧

LATER THAT NIGHT, after the fire died and the air grew cold, we returned to the big, empty house together. We were greeted at the door by Milky Way, who snuffled at us and licked our hands before rushing outside to do her business, and then trotting right back to her dog bed in the kitchen.

"She's an early-to-bed-early-to-rise kind of girl," Daniel said. "I think Kerri trained that into her with those morning ARK visits…" He sighed. "I can't believe he's gone."

Milky Way ruffed and turned her butt to us, scowling at us over her shoulder.

"All right, all right," Daniel laughed. "We'll let you sleep."

He turned off the kitchen lights, took my hand and pulled me back into the front hall and up the stairs. I was surprised—although maybe I shouldn't have been—to see the boxes standing packed or half-packed in every room.

The size of the empty rooms with no one in them was impressive, and I thought about how it must feel to be Daniel. Until recently, these rooms had had two kids running around in them, and, for better or worse, his mom had been here, too.

I'd only been to his house three times before, and even I felt something was missing without Kennedy there to call me Mister.

"You've packed up a lot," I said, as we passed by what appeared to be a crafting room, and then another room that looked like an upstairs living space with beanbag chairs around a TV.

"Keeping myself busy," he murmured, squeezing my hand. "That way I don't think so much about what I'm doing and why I'm doing it."

He pulled me into his room and shut the door. The familiar space where we'd been alone together once before now felt like a haven. I saw he hadn't started packing his own stuff yet. The oasis of his room remained sacred and untouched.

"You're having regrets about selling?"

"No," he said. "This house has been a burden for far too long. And with it gone, maybe my mom will do the right thing by the kids. It remains to be seen." Daniel walked over to his boombox, turning it on. "Did you listen to the mixtape I sent you?"

"The first half."

"The last song on it is my favorite. 'Only You' by Yazoo." He held up a glossy CD showing two people sitting across the table from each other under dramatic lighting.

"The pop song? From when we were kids? I thought the group was called Yaz."

"In the UK and the rest of the world, they're known as Yazoo. Some sort of legality made them have to go by Yaz in the States."

"Weird."

"Yeah, but I love the song." He popped the disc in the player and clicked through to the seventh track. "I keep listening to it ever since my grandparents left with the kids. It makes me happy." He turned back to me as sweet, rhythmic synth sounds filled the room. His expression went shy. "I put it at the end of the mixtape, because…" Reaching out for my hands, he pulled me against his body, and he whispered in my ear, "It makes it too obvious how I feel about you."

"You haven't kept your feelings much of a secret," I murmured.

"No, but when you hear the song, you'll really know how you make me feel inside."

The contralto voice of the singer broke over us like shivers, and Daniel pulled me into a slow dance with him. Pressing my head against his shoulder, the sound of his heartbeat merged with the pulse of the song. The lyrics were sweet, perhaps too sweet, and yet he was right. If this was how I made him feel, then Daniel was a goner.

I was a goner too.

We danced, and as the drum machine came in, I touched Daniel's nose with mine. I breathed in his familiar scent mixed with the lingering woodsmoke from the bonfire and teased our lips together. We fell into a sweet, delicate kiss. Breaking it, Daniel wound his arms around me, bending me back as he breathed the lyrics of the song into my ear. Slowly, he walked me backward toward his bed.

He must have set the song to repeat because it started again as soon as it ended. He lifted my T-shirt off, rubbing his face along my neck and chest, taking a deep breath against my skin before pressing kisses along my collarbones.

I gripped his strong shoulders, clutching the fabric of his shirt in my hands and tugging as he nosed against a ticklish spot behind my ear. "Take your shirt off," I whispered.

He pulled free long enough to grab the back of his shirt and pull it over his head, tossing it to the floor. His body was strong and tanned, and I ran my hands over his chest, before leaning in and smelling him like he'd done to me. I loved the scent of his skin, and I pressed kisses wherever I could reach.

Daniel's hands moved on to my jeans. I helped him take them off, kicking them, along with my underwear and socks, to the floor. Daniel's jeans and boxers joined mine in the heap. We inched up the bed together, hands everywhere, and mouths too. The sweetness of the moment far exceeded any expectations I'd had for the night. I was drunk on us, floating away in Daniel's embrace. We thrust against each other, kissing like the world began and ended in each other. We chased orgasm gently, moving with the music as the song began again.

Only you.

"Peter," he groaned in my ear. "I want you so much."

I whispered, "I'm here. You have me."

Pre-cum slicked our stomachs. He ground down against me, cuddling me close as we moved together. "Want you even closer."

"I'm here," I whispered, kissing his neck, drowning in the size of him. Bigger than me, bigger than Adam, he covered me completely with his body so that I felt safe, protected, and owned.

As he kissed me again, I gave my mouth up to him. Our chins scraped, beard burn starting already.

"Want to fuck you," Daniel confessed.

"All right," I whispered. "Fuck me."

We kissed and dry humped each other, our urgency increasing with messy nips, licks, and sucks on necks, jaws, lips, and cheeks.

"You want that?"

"So much."

Rolling us to our sides, he moved his hand down, sliding his fingertips over my hole in teasing, frustrating strokes. "Damn, Peter," he whispered. "I want to open you up."

I groaned, humping against him to get more friction on my dick. "Do it then."

Daniel brought his hand up to his mouth, sucked on two of his fingers, and then moved them back down to slide wetly over my asshole.

"You make all these hot little sounds," he whispered in awe.

I whimpered.

He groaned. "Do you want me closer too?"

"Yes."

The blood rushing under my skin was like a river heading south, making me harder and harder, needier and needier with every beat of my heart. I pushed my cock against the soft treasure trail on his belly, whining as his fingertips danced over my hole. Soon I was shaking, and so was he.

He tossed his head back, a bead of sweat dripping down the side of his face. "God, Peter, you make me want to do so much."

"What do you want?" I whispered. "Tell me. I'll give you anything."

"We can't," he said, shaking his head.

"Why not?" I kissed his neck, pressing my lips to his pounding pulse. "Tell me."

"I want it *all* with you, Peter."

"Mm," I murmured. "Me too. I want all of you."

Daniel rolled on top of me, buried his face in my neck and choked out, "I wanna fuck you bare and come inside you." His hips thrust down against mine. "I wanna be that close to you. Joined together, skin-on-skin…" His stomach tightened, and he whimpered as he went hot all over. A fine sweat broke over his skin, sliding beneath my palms. "Oh God, *fuck!*"

He groaned, juddered, and convulsed with his orgasm. His cries were loud, and his intense pleasure left him shaking, whimpering, and panting next to me. His hot cum slicked between us, coating my dick and smearing all over our stomachs.

"Daniel," I whimpered, still strung out. "I know we can't have it, but I want that too."

Daniel kissed my neck and rolled off me, taking hold of my cock. He went up on one elbow, still panting, pupils blown wide as he took me higher and higher, closer and closer to climax.

"Daniel!" I cried, knotting one hand in the sheets and clinging to him with the other. "Fuck!"

And *fuck* barely covered it.

I went taut as a bow. Images of what he'd said he wanted to do to me wrecked my mind. Me on my back with his bare cock in me, me stretched raw around his dick, me with his cum up my ass, leaking out onto my thighs. "Fuck!" I cried, as jizz shot over my belly and covered his fist.

I subsided against him, panting and breathless. When I opened my eyes, Daniel was staring at me with such intense adoration that my heart turned over in my chest. I kissed his chin, his jaw, and the hollow at the base of his throat.

"Are you all right?" His voice sounded raw.

"Amazing." I slumped against him, shivering. He held me and kissed my hair. We stayed silent and trembling, the world outside our bubble of lust and new love had gone hazy.

Minutes ticked by as I basked in the afterglow. Daniel rolled up onto his elbow, peering down at me as he stroked my cheek with the backs of his fingers. "You know that wanting to do something doesn't mean we can, right?"

"I know."

Daniel nodded, his eyes drifting down to my lips.

The song started again. So did our kissing.

I knew that wanting didn't mean having, but if I were going to do something like that, I couldn't imagine doing it with anyone except Daniel. He was the only guy I trusted enough to even consider letting myself be that vulnerable with.

The sweet lyrics rose around us.

As we moved together again, I murmured in his ear, "Only you."

Chapter Seventeen

I'D TRADED THE opening shift at the library for Graham's afternoon shift, so the next afternoon, I drifted into work still high as hell from the night and morning I'd spent with Daniel.

As I went through the handover rituals with Juan and Ellie, I sipped the coffee I'd picked up on the drive in, and hummed under my breath, smiling when I realized it was the song we'd made love to last night.

Because that's what we'd done. Made love.

We may not have fucked, but every other way we'd pleasured and pleased each other had felt profoundly intimate. I shivered remembering how Daniel had peered into my eyes, how he'd kissed me like I was someone he cherished, and then how he'd held me like he just couldn't get enough.

And the things he'd said! About what he wanted with me!

We both knew we couldn't do it. Not in today's world. Not with AIDS. There was no way. But it was romantic, wasn't it? For him to want that? And for us both to know we wouldn't be able to have it, that our love couldn't be expressed like that... I sighed. That part was hard. But just the way things had to be. Because otherwise our love could make us sick.

Unless we were loyal to each other. Unless we were true.

I shivered again, imagining it. We *could* do that. Daniel and I, we could be true. Honesty and truth were what we were building our relationship on, weren't they?

I magnetized the spines of the returned books, thunking them against the magnetizer a little harder than necessary as I replayed memories at will: Daniel holding me by the bonfire. Daniel dancing with me, kissing my neck. Daniel telling me, "This song makes me happy," when he meant "you make me happy." He made me happy too.

On my break, I went to the audio-video section of the library to see if they had the Yaz album there. I wanted to hear the song again, even though it was already earwormed deep into my brain. They did have it, and I spent the remaining fifteen minutes of my break listening to "Only You" on repeat.

"Oh, Peter," Ellie said, stopping by the circulation desk later, holding out a big book toward me. "You put a hold request on this, right? It was returned this morning."

My heart leapt, and I took the book from her hands, turning it over to see the front. The word *Robin* was emblazoned in raised white letters on the cover, and the underlying black-and-white picture showed a man's naked torso and nothing more.

"Thanks," I said.

Ellie nodded. "No problem."

I put the book aside, eager to be allowed to look at it in peace. But, alas, there was no peace that shift. The semester was in full swing. For hours we were swarmed by an endless glut of patrons wanting to check out research books.

But when the line did die off, and after Ellie went into the back, I was left alone. Laying *Robin* on the circulation desk, I examined the front of the book before flipping it over to read the back blurb.

Robin *is an extraordinary collection of a photographer's most intimate works. Every photo comes alive as we peer at it, bringing us closer and closer, until we, too, are worshiping at the divine trough of beauty and passion that is his lover, Robin.*

Intense. Okay.

I opened the book and within a few pages, I decided the blurb didn't lie. The photos were stunning, far superior to the other portraits of Harold Seville's I'd seen. I ran my finger over one of them: my uncle George, Harold's Robin, by the stove, lighting his cigarette from the pilot light. It was breathtaking—the glowing elegant bend of his body, the strength in his shoulders, the way his mouth puckered and his cheeks sucked in...

I couldn't explain it, but it was as if I were there and *I* had taken this picture, like *I* had been the one in love with George. How was it possible Harold had captured that adoring feeling of romantic love so that I, a stranger to both these men, felt it in my heart just by looking?

And in such a common sort of photo. There was nothing overtly romantic. Nothing sexual.

Not that there weren't pages like that, too.

I hadn't wanted to see my uncle's cock, but Harold Seville had had other plans. Because there were photos of it alone, photos of George submerged in a bubbleless bath, shots of him wetting his naked body down with a hose outside in the middle of summer...

My uncle's body was nice. I could understand why Harold had taken so many pictures of it. Of course, it was a lot like my own, and I noted that this was how Daniel saw me. How Adam might have seen me, too. Through this lens of love and passion.

I thought of the English Literature paper I had coming up. More poetry. If you asked me, not a single poem we'd read in class this semester, or even in Dr. Landry's class back in high school, came close to the intimate beauty and demonstrable love of the photo Harold had taken of my uncle sleeping in a rumpled bed, his hair a mess and his mouth open and drooling.

"Wow," I whispered to myself, closing the book as I spotted a patron coming toward me with a stack of journals, followed by a small army.

I didn't have time to think about the photos after that as I dealt with students desperate to finish papers and cram for midterms. It wasn't until after midnight, when I got back home and found myself alone in the kitchen, sitting at the counter while I talked on the phone with Daniel, that I remembered the book again.

"Do you think he'd want to meet you?" Daniel asked after I'd told him all about it.

"Who? My uncle? He's dead."

"No, the lover. The photographer. Harold Seville. Maybe he'd like to meet you."

I was quiet. The thought hadn't occurred to me. "Why would he?"

"Well, you're a photographer too, so that might be one reason. Also, you're the nephew of the man he loved so much he documented his feelings in this way."

"I don't know," I said. "How would I even find him?"

"There's this cool thing called a phone book."

I snorted. "He doesn't live in Knoxville."

"Right, but you work in the library where they have all of the phone books for the entire state, the entire country maybe." Daniel laughed.

"What if…" I sighed.

"Yeah?"

"What if it hurts him to meet me?" I remembered my mother's refusal to truly see me for all those years. I thought about the whys of that. "I look a lot like George."

"How did they leave things? In the journal?"

"I don't know. Hold on. Let me get it out." I slid my backpack over from where I'd left it on the counter. I pulled the envelope and the journal free. "I haven't read all of this stuff yet." I flipped to the end of the book.

"Why not?"

"I don't know. It just seems so sad. With Bobby, and AIDS, and…everything else. I guess I'm tired of thinking of gay men being sad."

"I know. Me too."

I skimmed from the end of the journal back toward the beginning, looking for mention of Harold. George called him "H" and was surprisingly honest about their relationship. What if his wife had found this? I supposed the fallout couldn't have been worse than what had actually happened to him.

Maybe it would have been better if he'd been caught. Maybe he would have left his wife, or she'd have told him to go, and he could have spent his years with Harold instead of…

I shook the thought away.

Coming to the last entry that mentioned "H," I grimaced. "They fought. That's how they left it, I think."

Daniel sighed. "What did they fight about?"

I read the entry to him. "'H and I fought last night. I think it is finally over with him now. He asked me to divorce Beth and move in with him. He's asked this of me many times, but I told him, once and for all, to stop asking. It won't happen. I won't leave Beth. H says it's her or him, and I choose her.'"

"Wow."

"He goes on to say, 'It breaks my heart to the point I feel like death has already snatched my soul, but I won't turn my back on my family. I'll have to turn my back on H instead.'"

Daniel made a sad noise.

"Yeah." I sighed, rubbing my eyes. I needed to take out my contacts and put on my glasses. They were feeling gritty. "Plus, if I reached out to Harold, I'd have to tell my mom about him. Especially if I met him, right? What if it upsets her so much that she goes back to Valium?"

"Take it from me, you can't protect her from her worst self. Only she can do that."

"I know." We were silent together a few moments.

"Speaking of our worst selves…" Daniel ventured.

"Yeah?"

"What I said last night when we were…"

My heart twisted. "Don't take it back."

"It wasn't right," Daniel said urgently. "I need you to understand that wanting something doesn't mean I need it from you. It's just a fantasy I have. That's all."

"It's all right," I said, my throat thick. "It's a nice fantasy."

"Yeah?"

"I liked hearing you say it." I hesitated. "So please don't take it back. I don't think you're trying to pressure me into doing it like that." I huffed a small laugh. "I mean, we haven't even 'done it' at all."

A beat of silence came down the line before Daniel asked, "Do you want to?"

"If you do." My heart rate doubled, and my voice sounded breathy.

"I think we should both get our test results back first."

I smiled. So reasonable. So steady and obsessed with doing the right thing. That was my Daniel. "Yeah. Okay. The UT Health Center said it could take six weeks."

"Right, my family doctor said the same."

"Your doctor knows you're gay?"

"He does now."

"Daniel?"

"Yeah?"

"I miss you," I whispered, feeling silly. I'd seen him just yesterday, but I'd wanted to be back in his presence, if not his arms, from the moment I left him and Milky Way on the front steps of his house.

"Me too." A sharp bark sounded in the background at his end. "Little Miss Milky Way wants to go out back. Talk tomorrow?"

I frowned and calculated. "I've got work and classes, and a test the next day, but yeah. I want to talk to you if I can. It might be late, though."

"If not tomorrow, then the next day."

"Definitely."

"Later, baby."

Baby!

I wanted to twirl around the kitchen, dance on my tiptoes, sing and throw confetti. Instead, I said, "Later."

TUESDAY AFTERNOON, AS I strolled through the UC, I stopped and pulled out my camera to snap some photos of a few cute couples holding hands and some eager football fans already waiting in line for a chance at student tickets.

Exiting into the September sun, I stopped in my tracks. Minty was lying down in the middle of the courtyard, wearing a pink tutu skirt over his jeans, and holding a melting ice cream cone above his head. The ice cream dripped down to the tip of the cone and then plopped onto his face. The vision he presented was surreal. And messy. And he'd drawn a small crowd.

As I approached with my camera, I asked a girl, "What's going on?"

"He says it's a performance piece."

"It's titled *Cream My Face*," Minty said, opening his mouth wide as five more drops fell from the cone. He caught them all on his tongue.

"Faggot!" someone yelled from across the courtyard.

"No," Minty replied calmly and much too quietly for the guy to hear. "It's not titled *Faggot*. It's called *Cream My Face*."

I shook my head and snapped some pictures, before sitting down a few feet away on a bench to do my Spanish homework. I wanted to make sure Minty made it through his performance in one piece. If he didn't, Daniel would be upset, and Daniel had enough bullshit in his life.

The crowd around Minty came and went, but over time, the ice cream melted all over his face and neck. It looked sticky, uncomfortable, and too much like cum. When all that remained was the melted-ice-cream-filled cone, Minty said, "Peter? Get your camera ready."

I rose, aimed, and focused just as he yelled, "Cream my face!"

With a flip of his wrist, he dumped the remaining liquid cream into his wide-open mouth and all over his face. I took a few more pictures.

The people still gathered at the climax applauded and laughed. A few cheered. Some groaned. But nearly all had dispersed by the time he sat up. Gazing around, his expression suggested he felt a strange mix of disgusted and pleased with himself.

"Wow," he said as I approached with my stuff. "I feel sticky and gross. But admit it, that was awesome."

"Totally." I didn't know if it was, actually, but it was definitely weird.

"Did you get any good pictures?"

"Probably."

"Cool. I'll need copies."

"For what?"

"For flyers. A repeat performance of *Cream My Face* could bring in a few bucks, and a few bucks could get me some good X."

"Why do you need cash? Don't you have that job at Nature's Foodway?"

"Fired. They said I flirted with too many customers." He wiped at his face, licking the stickiness from his fingers afterward.

"You could get another job." I realized that I'd just suggested Minty get a job so he could buy illegal drugs. I rolled my eyes at myself.

"Jobs are for losers, Heartbreaker. Real queers make their money via the world's oldest profession."

"Prostitution?"

"Wait—is that the world's oldest profession?"

"Yes."

"Oh, I thought it was theater for some reason." He stood there covered in ice cream, with his arms straight out from his sides, like he didn't know what to do with himself. "I should have brought another shirt. This wasn't planned well. I'm going to reek of rotten milk by the end of the day."

I put away my camera and Spanish book. "Let's go to the bathroom so you can clean up. I have a T-shirt in my bag. You can borrow it."

"I'd rather stink of spoiled milk than wear *your* hideous boy-drag."

"Minty," I said, maneuvering him into the University Center and toward the men's room. "Let's just wash your face, then you can go back to your dorm to shower. You look like someone jizzed all over you."

He grinned. "That's the whole point!"

Three guys were washing their hands at the sinks, and they stared at us like we'd just come from some wild on-campus bukkake party. Of the three, one of them looked more *angry* than freaked out, and my heart kicked at the flashing rage in his eyes.

I forced Minty over to the one empty sink. He needed to clean his face and get his tutu off before we both got beaten up.

"Hurry," I whispered.

At that point the tallest guy left, but the angry-looking one and his friend both lingered. Rage-face couldn't seem to tear his eyes away from Minty.

Sweat popped out at my temples, and my stomach began churning. A cowardly part of me wished I'd just minded my own business outside and left Minty to deal with his stupid sticky problem by himself.

"Let's just go," I urged. "You can wash up in your dorm."

"Nah, no way. I'm not going anywhere with all this cream on me." Minty wiped at his skin again and licked his fingers. He noticed my anxiety. "What's your problem?"

I glanced toward the guys who had now moved to block the door with their big, built bodies.

"Oh, yeah," Minty murmured. "Good taste. Hot."

I glared at him.

He ogled the guys as tension escalated in the bathroom. It was like electricity on my skin. I couldn't stop myself from staring back, breath caught, horror freezing me in place.

Rage-face asked, "What the fuck are you looking at, cocksuckers?"

Minty smiled winningly. "An ugly son of a bitch. What are *you* looking at?"

"A faggot with a big mouth."

"It sure is. Very big. And your daddy likes to use it." Minty moved his hand in the universal blow-job motion and smirked.

Rage-face snarled, lunging forward. His pal grabbed his arm to swing him around. "C'mon, Kyle. It's not worth it. They're not worth it."

Minty laughed. "Oh, yes, we are. Our asses are worth a *hell* of a lot more than either of you can afford. But since you're so keen to try, Kyle, I'll let you try mine for half price."

Kyle whirled back around. "Shut the fuck up."

"Oh, free then? A hard bargain, but..." Minty pretended to

think. "All right."

Kyle's jaw clenched.

"Admit it. You want it," Minty crooned. "I saw you watching me outside. You are so hot for me."

Kyle struggled against his friend's hold.

"Oooh, sexy," Minty purred. "How did you know I like it rough?"

"Shut up," I gritted out, cringing back against the wall. My throat felt so tight I could barely pull in a breath, and my vision had gone hazy.

Kyle broke free and came toward Minty, his eyes bright with anger, and his hands outstretched—to grab or choke him? I wasn't sure. Whatever was about to happen, it wasn't going to be good.

The bathroom door swung open, and a middle-aged professor strolled in with a grad student at his heels. Coming to a halt just inside, their wide-eyed faces shifted between Minty, still covered in what looked like cum, and the heaving lump of muscle that was Kyle.

"What's going on in here?" the professor asked.

"Fuck this," Kyle's friend said, leaving.

"Is everything okay?" The professor looked at me, and I shook my head.

"You," Kyle said, pointing at Minty. "Watch your back." He pushed past the grad student and out the door.

"Hope you're on my back soon, baby!" Minty called after him, as he turned back to the sink and started to wash off.

The professor's eyebrows went up. "Want to explain that?"

"It's fine, sir," Minty said, splashing water on his face and neck. "Just my boyfriend being a bitch."

The man glanced to me, and I shrugged, still shaking and sick. I hadn't come that close to being beaten up since I *had* been beaten up.

"All right. If you say so." With a curt nod, the professor ducked into a stall, and the grad student pissed at a urinal. "Be careful, boys," the professor added after they'd both washed their hands. "Guys like that can be dangerous."

"He's a teddy bear, really," Minty said. "I promise."

Both men left, neither looking convinced by Minty's story. Scrubbing my hands over my face, I collapsed against the wall for support. With my blood still running cold, I stared at Minty in the mirror.

"What?" he asked, meeting my gaze.

"Fuck you. That wasn't funny. Why did you provoke them?" My voice was rough with fear.

Minty's eyes took on a harsh sheen. "Because I have terrible taste in men. Didn't Daniel tell you?"

"Minty…"

"*What?* He was hot. He wanted to fuck me. I'd have let him."

"Raped you, maybe."

"It's not rape if I want him to do it." He groaned. "Don't look at me like that."

"You don't want me to look like I care about you?"

"No! Don't look all *judgmental!*" Minty tore off his shirt, washing it out in the sink, and then used the wet material and the hand soap from the dispenser to scrub at his neck. "As if you've had such great taste in guys? I mean, Daniel is awesome, of course, but you spent *how long* screwing that other piece of shit?"

"Leave Adam out of this."

Minty rinsed his shirt again. "Still protective of him?"

"No. But Adam isn't some Neanderthal who threatened me and my friend with physical violence."

"Right now? You and me? We aren't friends."

More of this again? "Yes, we are!"

He scrubbed harder at his pale skin until it was red and mottled.

"You can't be serious about wanting someone like him," I murmured, coming closer to put my hand on his bare shoulder. "You can't want that."

Minty shrugged me off and didn't meet my eyes. "You don't know what I want."

"Minty, *this* scared me. *You're* scaring me."

He met my gaze in the mirror again. It frightened me how tired he looked. It was like he was suddenly a hundred years old. "Christ, Peter. I wish I had your life."

"Meaning?"

"You have no idea, do you?" Pulling on his wet shirt, he waved me off. "Go on. Leave. It's fine. *I'm* fine. And if I see that guy again, I'll make sure he treats me nicer before offering him my ass, okay? Happy?"

"Minty, please."

"Stop. I don't want to hear it. Just go."

I went, but my heart worried over him for the rest of the day. My classes went by in a blur. I couldn't stop replaying the moments in the bathroom over and over again.

THAT NIGHT, ON the phone with Daniel, I had planned to tell him about Minty's performance piece, the upsetting encounter in the bathroom, and Minty's odd behavior afterward, but Daniel had his own troubles and needed an ear.

"ARK is asking me back. There are new PWAs every day, and they're running out of volunteers. There's even a person out this way—over in Rockwood—who could use support. I feel like such an asshole, Peter, but I don't think I have it in me yet. Not so soon after Bobby."

"You're not an asshole, Daniel." He was never an asshole, and I didn't know how to get that through his head. He was always so sure that he was both the problem and the answer to the problem. The hero and the villain all at once. "You're getting the house ready to sell, and you're still grieving."

"It's a full-time job cleaning this place out. There's a lot to arrange. I've made God knows how many trips to the dump, and that's just dealing with the stuff in my dad's old garage. There's still the entire basement to sort through. I've got a half dozen boxes to send down to the kids. And I've got to meet with the estate sale company next week…"

"Daniel, if you can't do it, or just don't want to do it, it's okay."

"But they need help."

"And so do you."

He sighed. "Nadine's been coming over to help sometimes after her shifts at the diner. But she's not able to move anything heavy. Still, I got her to pack up my mom's room. I didn't want to go through her things. It felt wrong somehow."

"I understand."

"The kids are miserable."

"Oh no." The idea of little Kennedy miserable tugged on my heartstrings.

"Well, that's an exaggeration. They miss Mom, and they miss me, but Grandma says it's getting better every day. Paul's causing trouble at school, though. What if I did the wrong thing? Maybe I should have kept them here with me and—"

"Daniel, breathe."

He sucked in a deep breath.

"You couldn't keep them with you. For all the reasons you told me before, none of those have changed, and also because you deserve to live your life for you." I took a small breath and ventured an addition. "For us."

He didn't miss it. "For us?"

"Well, we're a couple, right? We're building something together, aren't we?"

"We sure are."

"Okay, well, it'd be hard to do that with your brother and sister around, and if you'd wanted that, if that was something you felt called to do, then okay. That would be one thing, and, if that was the case, we'd still find a way to make us work. But it wasn't, and it isn't. You're allowed to be happy."

"I'm allowed to be happy," he repeated, like it was a mantra to drill into his heart.

"Yes, we're both allowed to be happy." It'd taken me far too long to figure that out, and now that I had I wasn't going to let Daniel bring us both down with his anxieties about it.

"We're allowed to be happy."

"Yes."

"*You* make me happy."

My heart tightened and released. "You make me happy too."

"In fact, I'm happy right now just hearing your voice."

There was no way in hell I was going to mention Minty to him now. He deserved so much more joy than just this moment, but if talking with me now made him feel better, then I wasn't going to bring him down.

"I miss you." I whispered the words despite being alone in the kitchen.

"I miss you too. I could drive to you. Right now."

I was tempted, so incredibly tempted to tell him yes, to do that, but I had an early morning and a test. "I wish you could."

"The test," Daniel said with a sigh.

"Yeah."

"I can't wait until midterms are over. I'm going to take you out on a real date. Do things right."

"Do *things* right? Or do me right?" I teased.

He laughed. "Both. When it comes to you, I want to make sure everything we do is right."

"I'll settle for good and honest. That's all I want."

He laughed again. "We can do that. That part will be easy."

I smiled, my heart in my throat.

Easy. Just the way honesty should be.

Imagine that.

Chapter Eighteen

O N FRIDAY MORNING, I noticed signs posted around campus for a performance-art piece called *Cream My Face* to be performed in the University Center courtyard that afternoon at three o'clock. A sick feeling started in my gut as soon as I saw it.

Nothing I said to Minty before class started could dissuade him, and I sat next to him, a ball of anxiety, through Donnie "Green Gills" Huggins's entire lecture about the psychology of sexual intimacy—yet another thing that I was pretty sure was not on the typical Psych 110 syllabus.

Jennifer was absent, and I'd agreed to take notes for her, so I did my best. It should have been easy enough, but the subject matter had unexpectedly turned graphic and lurid. At least it pulled my attention away from my worry over Minty's plans.

"Researchers find condom refusal goes up among a certain subset of gay men despite the current risks associated with HIV and anal sex. Can anyone make a guess as to who this subset is comprised of, and why they refuse condoms?"

A beautiful Indian girl in the front row raised her hand. She answered questions a lot in the class, and I think Donnie had a thing for her because he got greener and gulped hard every time he called on her.

"Yes, ah, Aditi?"

"Committed partners," she said with a toss of her head.

Donnie looked surprised but nodded. "Correct, and why do you think that is?"

"Intimacy," she said, her voice going a little high-pitched, like maybe she'd just figured out that she was going to have to talk about sex stuff to respond. "Earlier in the lecture, you said that humans are driven to attain intimacy with each other—emotional, sexual—to promote reproduction."

Donnie took over from there. "That's right. Some researchers are arguing it's instinct, and evolutionarily to our benefit, for the human animal to have unprotected sex that leaves a deposit of semen in the receiving party."

"But gay men can't reproduce," some idiot guy offered with a nasty laugh. "So that's stupid."

"It's not stupid, it's *instinct*," Donnie said again. "Instinct is neither smart, nor dumb. It serves a purpose that goes beyond logic."

"But how does just a little barrier between you and your partner reduce intimacy?" an older student asked. "Surely pleasure is pleasure. And even if our mind *can* tell the difference, there's no way we would notice it consciously."

"We can and do notice it," Donnie Huggins said. "This is exactly why heterosexual men try to talk their girlfriends into letting them go without a condom—claiming it'll feel better to them. Is it true? Physically, negligible, but emotionally? Yes. Is it logical? No. Do they do it anyway? Yes. We can surmise that for gay men it's the same thing."

"But that's not true—"

"That's debatable," Donnie said, cutting her off.

It was interesting to see him getting some real confidence as he spoke on this subject. I suspected this might be what he was doing his grad school thesis on.

He went on, "Research is beginning to indicate that male bodies and minds are hardwired to perceive penetration of, and ejaculation within, the body of the person we're engaging with sexually as *more* pleasurable, *more* satisfying than any other kind of orgasm. In heterosexual relationships, you can see that men prefer to achieve orgasm while fully inside the woman. Withdrawing before climax leaves a sense of a failure to connect, a lack of satisfaction, and a lack of intimacy."

"That's what I'll tell my lady next time we bang. 'No condom, honey, because I want you to feel my loooooove.'" Guffaws sounded in the room.

Donnie shrugged. "It might sound manipulative, but these illogical urges seem to be backed by some degree of science. But, let me also state that this so-called 'love' and 'sense of intimacy' is *chemical*, cooked up by hormones and neurotransmitters. Dopamine and the like. A logical, reasonable, *unaroused* love is going to say of course it's more loving to protect your partner against pregnancy or disease by using a condom. Right? That only makes sense. But that chemical love? It's driven by another kind of logic—the logic of 'reproduce at all costs.' It's not the smartest kind of logic, of course. It can't see that a man leaving his semen behind in another man will inevitably fail in the evolutionary directive that's causing these feelings in the first place. Instinct only knows that *that's* the key. He must put his semen *inside* someone else and *leave* it there. Anecdotal evidence implies that instinct rewards us for following those commands by giving stronger, better orgasms and a heightened sense of intimacy, affection, and love."

"Is that *true?*" one of the women near the back of the room asked.

"Science isn't about true or false; it's about theories that are more or less challenged," Donnie hedged. "These are currently more challenged, but I have the journals in my office, and I'll be happy to lend them to you for photocopying or reading purposes."

He stood up straighter. "This is *not*, however, a license to have unprotected sex. It's not permission to pressure your girlfriend or boyfriend into it either. It's simply an explanation of how human beings make choices in the heat of the moment when under the influence of powerful internal chemicals."

"Bad choices, you mean," the first guy muttered.

"Bad or good isn't the prerogative of instinct. Maybe it's more accurate to say that understanding our instincts might help us have more empathy for choices that we perceive as having risky outcomes—teen pregnancy, HIV. Possibly, by having understanding, we might find more compassion for those who do follow that instinct, and in so doing take on risks that maybe we don't like or understand. It doesn't have to be a blame game, folks. People don't *deserve* bad consequences for doing something we're nearly all hardwired to want to do."

"We're nearly all hardwired to eat sweet things, but that doesn't mean we should eat candy all the time," another student, also named Jennifer, pointed out.

"And you don't, do you?" Donnie agreed. "But you do eat sweet things sometimes. And those times are very enjoyable, maybe even more so for not doing it 'all the time' as you put it."

Both other-Jennifer and the first guy hushed.

"But doesn't HIV change the risk-and-reward balance?" an older student with a gray beard asked. "How does it remain evolutionarily sound to go with an instinct that might expose you to infection?"

"Evolution moves both quick and slow," Donnie said. "In this case, it's too slow to alter the instinct of men alive right now today. But, perhaps, if things stay as terrible as they are now—God, let's hope not—then we might see a change in our sexual instincts in the future." He shook his head. "But it's unlikely. Semen deposit is key to human survival. The human animal is *always* going to feel driven to do that.”

“What about women? Do they want that too?”

Donnie smiled. “Good question. Our data is anecdotal for the most part, but many women report that sex is more pleasurable for them when their lover doesn’t withdraw before ejaculation.”

“Aw, hell no, he can just leave *all that* in the condom,” a lady in the back of the room called out. “Who needs that mess?”

Titters broke out and some real laughter as well.

“Nothing’s a hundred-percent, across-the-board accurate for all people. That’s what makes human beings so fascinating to study. We’re all different.” Donnie sighed and looked at the clock. “And we’re out of time. We’ll talk next class about the chapter you were supposed to read for today. I got off topic again it seems. Apologies.”

I sat back, stunned, and confused. I didn’t think Psych 110 was the right forum for this kind of discussion. I was pretty sure the frat boys on the other side of the room were *not* going to heed Donnie’s warning that this wasn’t permission to pressure their girlfriends for raw access. I wasn’t even convinced they were smart enough to see how, by pressuring them, they’d be engaging in the same behavior many people got angry at gay men for: deciding that pleasure was worth the risk.

“You hear that?” Minty whispered in my ear as soon as class was over and everyone else was putting away their stuff. “Wanting jizz up my ass is normal, natural, and evolutionarily sound.”

“That’s *not* what he said,” I muttered, following him from the room and out into the autumn sunshine.

“Yes, he did.”

“Okay, he kind of did, but HIV changes that.”

“He said it *didn’t* change it, actually.”

“Minty,” I said, grabbing his arm. “Please, don’t do anything dangerous.”

He batted his eyes. "You and Daniel, *my God*. You're always so worried about whether I'm using condoms. I am, all right. Mostly. Almost every time."

"What is *almost every time?*"

"Every time," he corrected. "Don't worry about me. I can take care of myself."

"I don't think you can," I muttered as he skipped away, purple tutu shimmering in the breeze, and his black leggings showing off his slim legs and pert ass.

I had to get to my next class, and then I was going to need to hustle to the UC to keep an eye on Minty as he performed *Cream My Face* again.

I didn't know what I'd do if that asshole Kyle, or guys like him, showed up and tried to cause trouble, but at least I could run for help if need be. The UC usually had a security guard or two drifting around. Usually.

I hurried on to class, Donnie Huggins's words circling around in my brain, mixing with the words Daniel had whispered in my ear as we'd made love the prior Friday.

I wanna be that close to you. Joined together, skin-on-skin…

As I opened the door to the Humanities building, I wondered how much more satisfied we'd be if we could have that. If we *could* get close enough. I thought of the intimacy in those photographs of my uncle taken by Harold, lovers before HIV ever came around. How much closer they'd been able to be, what had it been like for them to love like they did, and to be able to express it—skin-on-skin.

I plopped down in my usual chair near the front of the class with a sigh. It didn't matter, did it?

I'd never know.

✧　✧　✧

CREAM MY FACE was already going by the time I was able to hike across campus to the UC. Next to the sign proclaiming this a "Performance Pièce de Résistance," Minty was laying on his back, facing the sky.

He'd changed his clothes since I saw him last. Now he wore a dress. A pink, lacy dress that was open in a V over his pale chest, exposing his skinny ribs and collarbones. The frothy skirt of it came down to his ankles, and he wore ballet slippers on his feet.

His toes were pointed.

His blue eyes were closed.

He was covered already in melted white cream. It was a warm day. Sticky whiteness congealed on his face, dripped over his lips, and slid down his cheeks and into his hair.

A crowd had gathered. Mainly girls and some art students smoking their clove cigarettes, a few sketching Minty in their drawing pads. But there were some random guys too. Including Mo, sitting off to the side with his lunch, watching with cool eyes. My stomach knotted up at the sight of him, but worse, there was that Kyle guy, too. He was alone this time, standing with his arms crossed over his chest, and staring at Minty with murder on his face. My heart skipped and then started to race.

There was a big enough crowd, though. Surely nothing bad would happen? But why Minty felt like he needed to do this again, knowing that he was drawing attention to himself, the kind of attention that resulted in shit like that encounter with Kyle in the bathroom last time, I didn't know.

And yet, I was captivated, too.

Minty looked beautiful and debauched. Filthy and elegant. Masculine and feminine.

I wished I had a video camera to record him, because my camera wasn't going to do it justice. Still, I took a ton of shots, standing on a bench to get angles from above, and kneeling next to him to get close-ups of his face.

Glancing up, I saw Mo watching me, and I jerked my gaze away.

The minutes ticked by. I didn't know how Minty was still holding his hand up, unwavering and steady, as the cream fell to his face. My own arm ached just watching him.

Kyle shifted, moving a hand down to his crotch, adjusting himself. He licked his lips, not taking his eyes from Minty. Fuck. That was not good.

Mo stood up, threw his trash away, and walked toward me. I tensed, surprised when he paused and said, "Keep an eye on that one. He's got a death wish worse than Tad's."

I swallowed hard, turning to watch Mo walk away. When he turned the corner of the building, I focused my attention back on Minty.

The performance was taking a long time, the ice cream melting far too slowly. I kept flicking glances at Kyle, but he didn't notice, seemingly having eyes only for Minty.

After what felt like an excruciatingly long time, Minty announced, "Cream my face," in a calm, sultry voice, and dumped the melted contents of the cone into his open mouth. Like before, it splashed everywhere, getting on his dress, in his hair, and all over the concrete, too.

The audience clapped and whistled.

Minty gathered himself and rose, wiping the cream from his eyes with his skirt, revealing his biker shorts beneath. "Thank you, thank you," he said, pointing toward the tip jar he'd set up, and into which people were dumping bills and coins. "Please feel free to leave as much cash as you can reasonably afford," he called out. "I'm planning to use it to buy some good X from a local dealer I know and see where things go from there. Thank you." He nodded to an art student who dropped a quarter in the jar. "Thank you," he said prettily to a professor who put in a whole dollar. I could barely keep my mouth closed. "Thank you," he said, looking right at Kyle with a smug smile. "It's good to see *you* again."

Kyle's nostrils flared.

Minty put his chin up and waited for everyone else who had money to drop it into the jar, holding Kyle's gaze the entire time. When the last sorority girl had dropped in a few dollars, he grabbed the jar from the ground, and swung his attention toward me. "C'mon, Peter. Help me get cleaned up."

My eyes darted over to Kyle. My stomach ached at the hate shining from his face. Heart in my throat, I followed Minty into the UC and into the bathroom.

"Count it," Minty said, thrusting the jar at me and turning on the taps on the sink. "How'd I do?"

"Let's just hurry and go," I said. "And what are you going to do with all this money? You can't just walk around campus all afternoon with a big, jangling jar of change."

"Mm, there are a few dollar bills in there, too," Minty said, splashing water on his face, and then getting some hand soap from the dispenser to wash with. "But, dunno. I hadn't thought that far ahead. I'll take it back to my dorm room, I guess. It'll make me late to my next class, but so—"

The door swung open. My heart sped up.

Holy fuck.

That asshole walked in and stopped dead, staring at Minty in the mirror, arms crossed over his chest, and evidence of an erection pushing against the front of his jeans. I clutched the tip jar and opened my mouth, but nothing came out.

Minty smiled. "Hey, baby. I've been hoping you'd be back around. Last time, you went off too fast. Didn't get enough of that fat cock."

Last time? Was this just some bullshit Minty was spinning to goad this guy into killing us?

"You," Kyle growled at me. "Get out. Guard the door."

"What? No," I managed, before Minty took hold of my arm, and maneuvered me toward the door which Kyle had now un-blocked. "Go on, Heartbreaker. I gotta get this boy's nut before my next class. Make sure no one comes in."

"*What?*"

Minty shoved me out the door, closed it behind him, and, *fuck me*, he locked it.

"Minty," I called, banging on the door. "Let me in."

Just what I planned to do to help him, I didn't know. I breathed in and out through my mouth, my heart pounding, and spots circling in my eyes. When I was about to leave my post to go find a security guard, I heard the noises. Minty's high-pitched sounds, and what could only be Kyle's deep grunts.

"That's it, take it," I heard Kyle snarl. I pressed my ear to the door. "Open up like the bitch you are."

Minty let out a sound of joyous delight, and I flushed. He was…

He couldn't be, could he…?

"Fuck, your ass is tight. God*damn*."

Holy shit.

Then a smacking sound of flesh-on-flesh pierced the wooden door, along with a sharp cry from Minty, followed by another whacking noise and a grunt. "Take it, you bitch. Fuck."

I rattled the door, but neither responded.

The grunts and breathy moans were punctuated again and again by what sounded like an open-handed smack, but from time-to-time there was a hard *thunk* that was more like the sound of a fist on flesh, and then Minty's noises changed to grunts of real pain.

I didn't know what to do.

The rhythm of the cries and grunts escalated, and then Minty's vocalizations stopped. Kyle shouted, "Come on, fag. Come on my dick like the cum-hungry whore you are."

Then I heard a horrible, sucking gasp, like Minty had been without air for too long. Kyle shouted, "Fuck!" and the whole thing was over.

Within seconds the door was flung open, and Kyle marched out, still zipping up his pants. I fell into the bathroom, holding the tip jar and shaking all over.

"Oh God," I said, finding Minty bent over the sinks, his eyes glassy and his half-naked body quivering. "Did he hurt you?" It was a stupid question, I'd *heard* Kyle hurting him, and when I looked Minty over, I could see bruises rising on the sides of his hips in the shape of fingerprints. Worse, the same thing was happening around his throat.

Minty smiled at me in the mirror, his expression blissed-out and content. "So that's my new lover, Kyle," he said. His voice sounded scratchy from where that monster had choked him. "Isn't he hot?"

"What the fuck, Minty!"

In a daze, I watched as Minty cleaned himself up, washing the ice cream off his face and neck and using wet paper towels to wipe off the cum slipping down his legs. No condom. Of course not.

He knelt shakily to clean the semen from the floor beneath the sink. *His* semen, I realized.

"Thanks for watching the door for us, Peter," he said. "That was the best fuck he's given me yet."

I clutched my hair, heart hammering. "You've done this with him more than once?"

"Sure."

"He could *kill* you."

"Let him try," Minty said. "I can take care of myself. I know Aikido, remember?"

"Yeah, but—"

"Peter! I could take him, okay? He wouldn't even know what'd hit him. Trust me. I have it completely under control."

Minty grabbed the tip jar from me and walked out with a little less swagger than usual, but with a glowing, satisfied air that terrified me.

What the hell was he *doing* fucking a guy like that? And *like that?* Bare and rough and reckless.

I stood there shaking, trying to figure out who I could call for help with this. Windy? Antonio? Robert? I didn't know. Minty was disdainful of authority, and while he could be both sweet and loving, he was headstrong too. There was no one he'd ever consider the boss of him.

Well, there *was* one person Minty respected...

Groaning, I washed my hands and splashed my face with cool water. My head still spun, and I was getting a headache to match the dreadful stomachache I'd had since I'd spotted Kyle.

I sat through my next lecture in a daze. It felt like someone had taken a sledgehammer to my head and my heart. I'd been an accomplice to something horrible. I couldn't shake the feeling I'd somehow helped Kyle hurt my friend.

My friend who apparently *wanted* to be hurt.

Fuck.

Chapter Nineteen

"HEY," I SAID, pushing my hair out of my face, and peering up at Daniel standing in his open doorway wearing sweatpants and a T-shirt. "I needed to talk with you in private. Is it okay that I just stopped by?"

Daniel's surprised expression blossomed into a smile, and he grabbed me in a hug, kissing my cheek and squeezing me tight. "You're here. Back to your old magical ways, huh?"

"What?"

"I've been thinking about you all day. It's like you knew how much I wanted to see you, and—poof!—you appeared. Just like you used to over the summer."

I wished it were as simple as that, but rather than spoil his mood immediately, I let Daniel hold me, kiss me, and stroke my hair, because after only three days apart, I wanted it just as much as he did.

"Come in," he said, releasing me and looking up at the dark clouds crowding the evening sky before closing the door behind us. "There's a storm coming. I'm not sure if you'll be able to drive home tonight if it gets as bad as they're predicting." His eyes lit up. "But that's not a bad thing, is it?"

"Not a bad thing at all," I said, but I must have sounded impatient or stressed, because Daniel's eyes grew worried.

"What's wrong?" He tugged me close again, peering down at

me.

"It's a long story," I said, putting my head against his shoulder and listening to his heart. So soothing and calm. "Can we go somewhere comfortable? I'm tired. It's been a *really* long day."

"Of course."

He led me into the kitchen where he grabbed snacks and drinks, and then he took me downstairs to the living area and rec room. I hadn't been down there yet, and I took in the big projector TV, as well as the foosball and pool tables. Just as Kennedy had told me when I first met her. These marks of luxury and wealth now all had signs on them marked, "Best Offer—Estate Sale"—though the sign on the TV was off to the side so that Daniel could still watch it.

The couch, a sectional, was free of any such announcements. Daniel pulled me onto it, getting settled in with the snacks and drinks on the coffee table, and then he looked at me. "You're so far away," he complained, scooting closer.

I smiled, leaning in to kiss his mouth once before saying, "I really do have to talk with you. It's important."

Daniel frowned but didn't tease me anymore about how far away I was, nor did he try to kiss me again. "All right. Just tell me. It's okay. Whatever it is, we'll figure it out."

I wanted that to be true, but this wasn't something I had any control over. "I think Minty's in trouble."

Daniel's eyelids fluttered and he closed them for a moment, gathering himself. "What's he done?"

"An asshole named Kyle."

"What?"

"That's who and what he's doing. And it's bad."

"Fuck," Daniel breathed. He paused a moment, thinking. "Big guy? Treats him rough?"

"You know him?"

Daniel shook his head. "No, but that's the kind of guy Minty hurts himself with."

I blinked. "He's done this sort of thing before?"

"Yeah." Daniel wiped a hand over his face. "He got hurt pretty badly near the end with the last one. It escalated to a broken arm."

"I thought he could protect himself? He told me not to worry because he knows—"

"Yeah, I know, and he does. He can protect himself pretty well *if he wants to*…" Daniel shook his head. "He doesn't want to."

"So you're saying last time he decided to 'hurt himself,' he let some guy break his arm?"

"Basically, yeah." Daniel groaned and sat up straighter. I could see him pulling himself together, getting into hero mode. "So how bad is it now?"

"I don't know!" I felt frantic, my stomach twisting and my heart aching. "But we need to help him."

"Shh, we will."

"For all I know, he might be with the guy now."

"What do you know about this guy?"

"Not much. I didn't even realize Minty was screwing him until today. I thought it was another of his flights of fancy, you know? Just a more dangerous flight." I told him the whole story, including our first encounter with Kyle during the trial run of *Cream My Face*, and ended by saying, "It seems like this wasn't the first time they've…" I didn't want to say hooked up. What they were doing was *so much* darker than that. "Fucked."

Daniel groaned and stood up to pace. "I really hoped we were past all this."

"I left out one other thing," I said, in a small voice. I knew, if Daniel hadn't already blown his stack over this situation, and he hadn't yet, this was going to do it. "He didn't use a condom."

Daniel's jaw tensed and released as he turned to the wall and hit it with the flat of his hand. "Goddammit. Fuck."

"I'm sorry."

Breathing heavily, Daniel turned back to me. "It's not your fault." He tore a hand through his hair. "Why is he doing this now, though? He always has a reason, but every time I talk to him lately, he says things are great, fine, wonderful."

"Maybe he doesn't want to worry you." Like I hadn't wanted to worry Daniel after the first encounter with Kyle. "What can we do?"

Daniel flung himself down on the sofa beside me. "I need to think about it. When it comes to Minty, we have to approach things carefully."

"What if we don't have time to be careful? What if he gets with this Kyle guy again—tonight even—and what if Kyle hurts him, or even kills him?"

Daniel stood up. "Fuck, okay, yeah. Well, we should head up to campus now, go to his dorm, confront him about this before—"

Thunder crashed, followed by more rolling booms. The lights flickered and went out. The blackness was absolute.

"God," Daniel cursed. "Stay there. Don't move. Fuck."

I held still on the sofa, listening to him stumble around in the dark before a match was finally struck, and a long, formerly just-decorative candle was lit. He walked toward me and sat the candle and its holder on the coffee table.

Even down in the basement, we could hear the rain outside. A downpour of epic proportions.

There was no way either of us was driving in this mess.

"I don't know what to do now," he said, sitting down beside me again, sounding lost and defeated.

"I'm sorry. I shouldn't have told you about this." It wasn't his job to fix his friend. He already had so much he had to deal with. I was supposed to be helping him by *easing* his burdens, not bringing him new ones.

"No, it was the right thing to do." He pulled me close against his chest, kissing my hair.

"Was it?"

"Yeah." He brought me down to lie on top of him on the sofa. "I'm the only one he listens to. I know that. You know that. We all do."

"Sometimes he listens to Robert."

Daniel rolled his eyes. I couldn't see him well in the low light, but somehow, I just knew he'd rolled them. "Not really."

"Barry, then."

Daniel shrugged, conceding.

"We could call?"

"A phone call isn't the best way to handle this," Daniel said. "He'll just hang up and go find the guy to get himself even more hurt."

"Why is he doing this?" I asked after a few long minutes passed of us just resting together on the sofa. Daniel stroked my hair, as both of us considered it in silence.

"The last time he did this kind of thing, he told me it feels good," Daniel said. "He says it's never as hot as when he doesn't know if the guy he's with is going to try to kill him or not. Which is messed up as all hell, but there's more to it than that. He only does this shit when something *else* is bothering him. Usually, it's his father. Or at least that's how it's always been in the past."

"I thought his dad wasn't around."

"He's not. Anymore, at least. But he's always in Minty's head."

I winced. He was right. It was harder to shake someone free from your head than from your life. Adam was my personal proof of that.

"He was doing *so much better* before I moved back here," Daniel said. "When I was closer to campus and could spend more time with him, he—"

"You can't be everyone's hero," I said. "You can't be everywhere at once, Daniel. You just can't."

He cuddled me closer. "I know, baby. You're right."

The lights flickered on and went right back out.

"I hope the phone lines aren't down too," I said. "I should call my parents and let them know I'm staying the night."

"Yeah, let's do that," Daniel said, reaching to the side table by the sofa and pulling a phone across, the curly cord still tight and perfect.

I called my folks, and they were skeptical that I needed to stay the night with Daniel, but when I made it clear that I wasn't changing my mind, they backed off. I think the first part of the storm hitting their area of town might also have had something to do with their acquiescence.

"Be safe," my mom said before making kissing noises and hanging up.

I'd just replaced the handset when the lights flickered on and off, and on again. This time they stayed on. Relieved not to be bumping around in the dark anymore, Daniel headed over to a box of VHS tapes he'd half-packed and started going through movie choices. We settled on *On Her Majesty's Secret Service.* We didn't really watch it though, instead snuggling up together, letting our breathing sync, and calming ourselves by kissing, cuddling, and stroking each other gently. It was arousing, but sweet, and neither of us took it to the next level, content to bask in tenderness.

After the credits rolled, I sat up and stretched, jiggling my leg some since my foot had fallen asleep.

"Now what should we do?" Daniel asked, glancing at his watch. "Do you have homework? Or—"

Having had enough of sweetness, and definitely not interested in doing homework, I shut him up by pressing a kiss to his lips. "Well, I don't know about you, but I'm ready to find out how much of your dick I can fit in my mouth."

We'd done a lot of fooling around together already, but I hadn't blown him yet. He was big, just like Minty had said, and we'd always gotten each other off before I had a chance.

Daniel's eyes grew hot with interest, and I grinned. "I'm ready for that too."

"Right here, right now good for you?" I asked, leaning forward and kissing his jaw.

"If it's good for you," he answered breathlessly.

"It's perfect," I said, standing up, pulling off my T-shirt and tossing it aside, before I undid the button and zipper on my jeans. "I'm eager to show you my skills, Mr. McPeak," I said in my best James Bond-ish British accent, which was horrible. "Have you ever had your dick sucked by an inexpert guy with a relatively small mouth? It's an experience you won't soon forget."

Daniel laughed and tugged me down into a kiss. "I'll never forget it. I'm with you."

As it turned out, the size of my mouth didn't seem to be a problem. Daniel seemed more than gratified as I demonstrated my abilities.

"Fuck yeah, Peter. Shit, you're good at this."

I didn't know if that was true. I felt like his size impeded my skills, but if he was happy, so was I. Daniel touched my hair as I took him deeper. He fucked my mouth carefully, his girth making the corners of my lips ache.

Gagging, I pulled off and licked the spit from his cockhead, and then I returned to sucking, hollowing my cheeks as I worked.

"Fuck, Peter," he whispered. "Fuck, *fuck*."

I groaned around him and sucked faster, massaging his balls as they tightened. Opening up again, I took him in until the sides of my mouth felt too stretched, and I gagged around the head of his cock in my throat. He hissed.

"Unghnmngh," I encouraged him. Blood rushed under his skin

like a river beneath my tongue, and I worked harder, ignoring the urgency of my own cock.

"You're so hot," he said, his voice gritty and trembling. "This is so hot, fuck."

I moaned and wormed my hand under his balls into the sweaty cleft of his ass, and pressed my middle finger against his hole, just resting it there, not attempting entrance.

He groaned. "God, baby, I wanna do *everything* with you."

I released his cock and his fingers tightened in my hair as he let loose a small grunt of frustration. "Yeah. Tell me what you want to do with me."

Daniel tossed his head back against the couch, sweat dripping down the sides of his face. "God, Peter, so much. You make me want *so much*."

I jacked him, tonguing his slit, before pushing his shirt up and kissing my way to his nipples. He squirmed and hissed as I took the right one in my mouth and sucked it, moving my hand up and down on his spit-wet cock. I flicked my tongue over his nipple.

"I'll suck you off and make you come," I whispered, "but I want to hear what you want to do with me. Like last time. That fantasy. I want to hear about it."

Daniel squirmed. "We *can't*."

"It's just words." I blew on his nipple and went back to licking it.

"Baby, make me come," he whispered. "Please, Peter."

"I want to hear it first. What do you want to do to me?"

He groaned. "Wanna fuck you bare."

"Yes," I encouraged.

"*God*, wanna fill you up with my cum—"

"Yeah. I want to feel you come in me."

"See my jizz slipping from your ass..." Daniel's stomach tightened and he whimpered, twisting so that I had to latch on to his nipple harder. "Gonna come."

I blinked, surprised, and then moved my mouth back to his dick. I sensed the hot tension on my tongue—so close. He juddered, shooting into my mouth, his head back, neck straining and thighs quaking.

"Christ," he groaned. "Jesus fucking *Christ.*"

When I was done swallowing everything, I pushed against his splayed knees to rise up between them and kiss his mouth. "Daniel?"

"Hmmph," he answered.

"I know we can't, but I want all that too. So much."

"Fuck, Peter," he cursed, wrapping his arms around me, and holding me in a crushing embrace. "I need you so close. I want to breathe you in. I want to...I want you..."

"Me too."

Me too.

Chapter Twenty

THE NEXT DAY, Daniel went up to UT with me. I had classes and work, but he planned to go on the hunt for Minty. I wasn't sure of his schedule, but Daniel said he knew Minty took upper-level science courses for his major, so he asked to be dropped off near the Biology building.

We took the same car, even though that meant he'd be trapped on campus until I finished my shift at the library around nine. Then I'd need to drive him back out to Kingston and that big, lonely house, before driving back home again...

Unless I wanted to stay another night.

But no, I didn't have any clothes to wear tomorrow.

Unless I stopped by my house to get them...

But then he'd have to meet my parents, and I wasn't quite ready for that.

It was silly and superstitious, but both of my parents had liked Adam so much before they'd found out about the reality of our situation that I was worried about them *liking* Daniel almost as much as I was worried that they *wouldn't*. Either opinion seemed like a bad omen.

It was just a matter of time, though, before Daniel would have to meet the Mandels in all their dysfunctional glory. I took comfort in knowing he wouldn't even blink, given his own family situation.

But until it became unavoidable, I hoped to sidestep the issue for a while longer.

Dropping him off on the Hill near the main Biology building before heading out to try to find parking for the Volvo, I was pleased when Daniel leaned over and gave me a fast peck on the cheek. Public displays of affection were something I'd never had before, and he didn't even think twice.

"Bye. I'll meet you at the library near the close of your shift."

"Bye," I said, my voice a little tight.

He ducked back into the car. "What? You okay?"

"Yeah," I said, smiling and touching my cheek where he'd kissed. "I just…that was…"

He leaned back into the car and pressed a kiss to my lips. "Bye."

"Bye," I said again, watching him stride into the brick building ahead.

The day passed easily, but I wondered off and on whether Daniel had located Minty and what, if anything, he'd been able to get through to him.

Work went well, too. By nine o'clock, I was busy clearing up the front desk and preparing to hand the space over to April, who'd stay there until the library closed at midnight.

"Here comes your man," she said, nodding across the room.

"What?" I looked up and my heart thumped in my chest. It was Daniel, sure enough. I'd seen him just that morning, but somehow, he looked so good that I couldn't breathe. His blue shirt made his eyes look an even crisper brown, and his jeans fit so well that I had to refrain from fanning myself.

"Yeah," I said. "But how'd you know?" I'd never told April I was gay, much less introduced her to Daniel.

"I'm a little psychic," she said, in all seriousness. "But also, if he's not your man, he has no business looking at you like that."

I flushed. Daniel's eyes were set on me in a very appreciative way, it was true. Memories of all the recent naked times we'd spent together tumbled through my mind, and I watched him step up to the desk with a silly, almost bashful, smile on my face.

"Hey," he said. "Ready?"

"Yeah, um, let me just—"

"Go," April said. "I've got this."

Daniel slung his arm around me as I came around the desk and pressed a kiss to my temple, before releasing me. "How was your day?"

I glanced around to see who might have witnessed that display, but no one was looking our way. "Fine, good. But that's not important. How was yours? Did you find Minty? Did you talk to him?"

Daniel sighed as we walked toward the exit. He held the door for me to leave first. "I found him, but he saw me coming and went the other way."

"Are you kidding?"

"Nope."

"What'd you do?"

He snorted. "I didn't chase him. I went back to his dorm and waited there, but he never showed. I heard from Windy—I had lunch with him when I couldn't find you—"

"Sorry, I was with Jennifer in the UC."

"We should have made plans to meet up. Next time. Anyway, I heard from Windy that Minty's planning to be at Tilt-a-Whirl tonight, and I thought—" he glanced at me, a shy smile on his face, "maybe we should go? It's been a long time for both of us, hasn't it?"

It was true. I'd only been to the club once since school began. Between homework, classes, and being with Daniel—or wanting to get home so I could talk with him on the phone—I just hadn't had the urge.

"What about Milky Way?"

"She has a bowl of kibble in the kitchen, and I got her a little dog door set up last week. It goes out to a fenced dog run, too. She can come and go as she pleases now. The realtor said it'd be seen as a plus in selling the house."

"It's a weeknight," I said, thinking how much that eight o'clock Psych class tomorrow morning was going to hurt if we stayed out late.

"True. I can go alone and get Windy or even Barry to take me home?"

"No!" I said. "No, if you're going, I'm going."

"I'm not trying to pressure you. I just need to corner that brat, and Tilt-a-Whirl is a decent bet. He'll have his guard down."

"Meaning he'll be high?"

"Probably."

"We'll go."

Daniel glanced at his watch. "Well, it doesn't even open for another hour. Want to grab some food first?"

"Yeah." I said, bumping his shoulder. "I do."

He smiled down at me, and my heart squeezed in my chest.

The wind picked up as we sauntered down the hill toward Cumberland Avenue. Cuppa, the coffee shop I'd gone to with Millar, was overflowing with students, and the falafel place next to it was hopping too.

"Hanna's?" Daniel asked, as we turned the corner on the busy street.

"Yeah."

I wanted to grab his hand and hold it like the straight couple just in front of us, but I didn't. Not because I believed he'd rebuff me, but because I was still a little worried. Night had drawn down on us, and I didn't know who might decide to take it upon themselves to harass us for the fun of it. Better to save my affection for when we got to Tilt-a-Whirl with all the other queers. Maybe we could fit a dance or two in around Daniel's come-to-Jesus sermon for Minty.

The street was crowded with people, including a small band of homeless folks pooling money for a bottle. Daniel gave a woman a quarter as we passed by, and she called out a blessing.

As we walked, cars zooming past us, the wind buffeting us from time to time, and the moon shining from the inky sky, Daniel told me about his day. I laughed at the stories Windy had shared with him while they'd eaten lunch at Chalky 'N' Joe's and made appreciative sounds about his visit to one of his old professors.

"Then I stopped by the nursing school and talked with a counselor there. It turns out there are some classes I could take this spring to start the process of changing my major."

"That's good news, right?"

"Yeah. Probably." Daniel bit into his lip. "Speaking of the future… My mom was granted phone access this week. She called."

"Oh, yeah?"

"She's trying to talk me into moving to Florida with her, starting nursing school in Pensacola instead. She says the kids are having a hard time adjusting and that I should be close, so we can be a family."

My stomach tumbled. "You're moving?"

Daniel huffed. "If she had her way."

I stopped on the sidewalk and took hold of his arm. He faced me. "But what about *your* way? What do you want to do?" I held back from saying he *couldn't* go, that I'd just found him, and I didn't want to lose him now.

His expression softening, he lifted his hand and smoothed it over my hair. "I want to stay here with you."

I smiled, relief making my knees a little weak.

"And, well, I kind of have a plan for that if you want to hear it? You don't have to agree to it or anything. It's not dependent on you saying yes. I can still do it without you, or you can come in on it later, or—"

I soothed him with a hand on his arm. "It's okay. Just tell me."

"Well, you know Bobby left ARK everything in his will."

"Yes."

"And ARK's already arranged for the disposal of all of his belongings. Kerri saved me a few of his things that I asked for: the hunting cap he sometimes wore to keep his ears warm and the red socks he liked best."

"Those socks," I said, laughing, but my eyes stung with tears. I missed Bobby, and I knew Daniel must miss him even more. And yet our lives kept pushing us on, moving us forward, filling our days with so much more than thoughts of our loss of him. It was the prerogative of youth to be so caught up in ourselves.

"But the rest of his stuff will be taken by an estate auction house by the end of next week. Which means they just need to dispose of the house itself. And, well, I'm going to need a place to live pretty soon," he pointed out. "The movers will be here in three weeks to put our stuff in storage for my mom to sort out later, and the other things will be going to another estate auction house. I'll be homeless."

I took hold of his hand and squeezed it, dropping it when a drunk and oblivious frat guy bustled by us, knocking me aside.

"Watch it," Daniel called.

"Sorry, buddy," the guy said, bleary-eyed with drink. "Sorry."

Daniel lifted a hand, waving it off, and then we continued our walk. We were almost to Hanna's when I realized. "You're thinking of buying his house?"

Daniel smiled. "Yeah. It's a great old bungalow. Just needs a little loving care. The neighborhood's good if I'm going to start at nursing school. It's a much shorter drive to say the least, and it'd be a fresh start for me. Plus, I'd feel like I was honoring Bobby's memory, you know?" His voice grew tight. "Besides, I think Milky Way wants to go home. She's not accustomed to all the space. She prefers suburbia."

"Does she?"

"She does."

"I think that'd be amazing."

"And…" Daniel stopped walking to take my hand and swing me around to face him. "If you wanted…no pressure. I know it's early to even think about this kind of thing, but…if you wanted, you could move in with me, and we could start some kind of life together. Like what Barry and Robert have." He grinned. "Except with monogamy."

I laughed, my heart rising so fast I felt like it'd lifted up into the sky, fluttering like a bird. "I think that sounds amazing."

"Yeah?"

"I mean, *yeah.*"

He threw his arm over my shoulder and drew me in, kissing my forehead and then my lips.

"Gross. Fags."

The comment was tossed out without any real heat, and it said something about how happy Daniel's offer had made me that the nastiness didn't even dent my soaring spirit.

"Ignore them," I whispered.

We walked on, and I couldn't stop smiling. Daniel talked about all the ways we could fix up Bobby's house, and I laughed just imagining it all. We stopped at the door for Hanna's, and Daniel opened it for me. I stepped inside, feeling like a star, shining with joy.

"Two please. A booth if possible?" Daniel said to the hostess.

"Sure." She gathered two menus. "This way."

Daniel grinned at me, plucking one of my curls. "Boing," he whispered, and I rolled my eyes, smiling even as I did.

I turned to follow Daniel and the hostess to our booth.

Hazel eyes in a stricken face framed by dark hair and red highlights. I froze.

Adam.

With his arm around Leslie.

Seated at a table by the window with her parents.

Our eyes held and my heart fell to my stomach. A rush of anxiety replaced the elation.

I had no choice, though, Daniel was already being seated. I rushed to catch up, dropping into the booth across from him and taking the menu from the oblivious hostess.

Daniel was oblivious, too, peering at the offerings speculatively. "I don't feel like a burger. Maybe the burrito. But they have a better one at Sunspot. Hmm."

I felt frozen, my tongue caught in fear. Because it was definitely *fear* that I felt. Fear and sick anxiety, all lined with unresolved grief and anger and hurt. Lots of hurt. Dammit. How was he *still* ruining my life? I'd cut him out. I'd banished him. And yet he managed to crash one of the happiest moments I'd ever had and destroy it with just his fucking *face*.

Ugh.

"Hey," Daniel said, reaching out to touch my hand. "Are you okay?"

"Um…" Tears pricked my eyes, and I rubbed at them carefully so as not to dislodge my contacts.

"What's going on?" He started looking around, trying to identify what had upset me, and that's when he saw him, too. He'd never met Adam, never seen a picture of him even, but there was no missing the utter hatred and rage Adam arrowed his way from across the room. Nor did Daniel miss the blond girl on Adam's arm who was also gazing at us with a concerned expression. "Shit. Do you want to go?"

I shook my head. "No. Let's just ignore them." My jaw tensed. It'd worked out on the street and ignoring them could work again here.

"Baby, this is dumb. We can go somewhere else."

"If we leave then…" I trailed off.

"Then what? He thinks he got to you? He did, baby. He knows that already. And you got to him, too. He looks miserable. So, let's go and just save ourselves from all this tension, maybe salvage our dinner." He stood up, putting the menu down.

Across the room, Adam rose too, and Leslie grabbed his arm. Both her parents turned in their seats to see who or what was eliciting this odd behavior from their daughter's boyfriend.

"C'mon," Daniel said again, putting his hand out for me to take.

I did, leaving the menu on the seat of the booth, and letting him lead me out of the restaurant. A few heads turned at our hand-holding, but there were no nasty comments. The cool air outside was welcome on my hot face, and I sucked in a deep breath, realizing only then that I was shaking.

"Sunspot's just down the way," Daniel said, pulling me along. "We'll have a longer wait, but I'm not so hungry now. So that's fine. We can get burritos."

I went with him, my heart hammering, my entire body running cold.

"Peter!"

I stopped in my tracks, jerking Daniel to a halt, too. Light footsteps ran up behind us. I turned and was confronted by all my past mistakes. Again. Why couldn't I just get away from this? All I wanted was for it to stay in the past. For good. Forever.

"Hey," Leslie said, her tone gentle. "Are you all right?" She darted a glance at Daniel and then back to me. She touched my arm, and I struggled not to cringe away from her.

"Yeah. Great. Um, how are you?"

"I'm fine." She dug her fingers into my bicep. "Look, Peter, I'm sorry to chase after you like this, but you've been ignoring everyone, and I get it. I do. But Adam's sorry, you know? If you'd just—"

"Stop," Daniel said, stepping up beside me. "We were just on our way to dinner. So let's say goodbye and be done with this."

"Are you…" She looked to me, a hopeful kindness in her eyes. "Peter, is this your—"

Daniel talked over her. "Hey, look, I'm sure you're a sweet girl, and I know you mean well, but this isn't your business."

"It's not *yours* either," she retorted. "Peter's my friend, or he was, and he totally ditched me, and us, without any explanation."

"You were there," I said, my jaw so tight the words came out like a low growl. "You saw. You know exactly why." Though she didn't really know *exactly* why. "You don't need an explanation."

"Adam's sorry! He knows it was wrong, and he's grown up a lot in the last few—"

"Leslie!" a woman's voice called.

Leslie turned, her blond hair whipping around.

I glanced up to see her parents and Adam standing on the sidewalk. Adam's expression was horrible—jealousy plain as day wrestling all over his face. He leaned forward, like he was ready to stalk toward us, and I wasn't interested in that.

"It was good to see you, Les," I bit out. A lie, of course—just being in proximity to her and Adam made me a liar all over again. "Bye." I turned and took Daniel's hand, walking away.

"Peter!"

I forced myself not to flinch or look back. Daniel stayed in step with me, squeezing my fingers.

When we entered Sunspot, the place was crawling, wall-to-wall, with students and locals. We took a seat on a crowded bench to wait our turn, and I was glad it was so tight. I could sit pressed against Daniel and no one would look our way or think it was strange.

Daniel put his arm behind me, resting his palm against my lower back, rubbing there. We sat in silence for a while, the hubbub of the restaurant gradually crowding out the roar that had filled my head as soon as I'd spotted Adam. As time passed, the bench cleared, more couples and parties were seated, and we had a bit more breathing room.

"You all right?" Daniel asked, moving his hand away from my back now that there was no excuse to be right on top of me anymore.

"Yeah." I swallowed. "I didn't expect them to be there, is all."

"Nobody expects the Spanish Inquisition," Daniel murmured, getting a laugh out of me.

"Monty Python."

"Yeah, Monty Python."

We were quiet again for a moment until I said, "I hate that he still makes me feel like this. I don't *want* to have these feelings. I wish I could take them off, like…I don't know. Like a bunch of coats or something, and drop them on the street and walk away." I laughed bitterly. "Just unzip them. Boom. Done."

"That'd be great. I'd just unzip how mad I am at my mom and leave it behind, too, and all the bad memories I have of her drinking. Just a heap of coats on the street. Adios chaquetas."

"I don't love him. You know that, right?" I asked. "It's not about that."

"You don't have to explain."

"I just didn't want you to think I reacted like I did…" I squirmed a little. "That I got upset like that because I *care*. I mean, obviously I care, but not in any good way. Just in the way that he can still destroy my happiness just by being himself." I rolled my eyes. "Ugh. This sucks. I was so excited earlier. We were going to move in together."

"Are we not doing that anymore?" Daniel asked with a nudge.

I smiled up at him. "Yeah, we still are."

He leaned close to whisper in my ear, "Then let's forget him. Let's talk about the house and our plans. I want to plant roses in the backyard along the fence."

"Roses!" I laughed. "You sound like an old man saying that."

"Orange roses, like the ones you bought for me. Remember?" He boinged a curl again. "Oh. Sorry, the ones your *mother* bought for me, right?"

I bumped into him, giggling. I could still feel the experience with Adam and Leslie tugging on me, pulling at my sleeve to pay attention. But if Daniel kept my focus on him now, on the future we were fantasizing about, then who knew? It might even come true.

We brainstormed about the little ways we could improve Bobby's house and talked about the ways we could honor his memory there too. Like making sure that we always had impatiens on the front porch in the summer.

"Bobby loved zinnias," Daniel told me. "That's why Kerri was always so careful to make sure we potted them where he could see them out the windows. She watered them every morning, you know. Whether it was her day or not."

We'd been together for less than a full month. We were still waiting for our tests to come in before having anal sex. Maybe by talking about living together we were moving too fast, but everything about us felt right, healthy, and good. I dared to dream.

After forty-five minutes of waiting, we were seated at a table. Daniel ordered the burrito. When it arrived, he took a big bite, groaned with happiness, and said, "Yup. Still the better burrito."

I bit into my veggie burger and grinned at him.

Yup. Still the better boyfriend.

Chapter Twenty-One

THE WALL OF smoke smacked me in the face.

After a summer spent going to Tilt-a-Whirl, you'd think I'd have gotten used to it, but I never had. I coughed as I entered, waving my hands around, the smoke burning my eyes. Daniel patted my back until I stopped, and then led me straight to the bar to get some water.

As I sipped it, getting my lungs back in order, we scanned the room looking for any sign of Minty or the other guys. With no luck in that regard, we headed to the upstairs bar where Barry was both serving and monitoring the stage preparations for the upcoming drag show.

It wasn't starring Renée, who was in Nashville performing again, but a newcomer named Pearly Gates—a pretty girl with long black hair (a wig, no doubt) and glowing white skin.

"She's good," Barry said without much conviction, leaning against the bar and peering toward the dressing room reserved for the talent. I well recalled the dizzy, drunken night I'd spent back there trying not to puke. Until I had. "No replacement for my woman, but not bad, I guess."

"Can she bring in a crowd?" Daniel asked, tilting back his water and taking a sip.

He shrugged. "If you stick around, you'll see for yourselves."

I didn't know if we'd stay that long since it was a weeknight, and I still needed to drive Daniel back home at some point.

"Have you seen Minty around?" Daniel asked, leaning his elbows against the bar.

Barry frowned and rubbed at his forehead. "I've seen him."

"And?" Daniel asked.

"And something's not right with that kid. He's acting out. Trying to pick fights. Yesterday he came in here with some homophobic jock. The asshole jumped every time someone so much as looked at him. The dick threatened to punch that sweetheart Keith Shipley for asking him to dance. I kicked him out. Minty was pissed. The two of them left together."

"Fuck," Daniel muttered.

"I know. Nothing Windy or Antonio could say would stop him, and at that point, I kind of wanted to see him gone myself."

"You haven't seen him since?"

"No, but Antonio followed them to the jock's dorm and Minty came down again after twenty minutes with a glassy-eyed look. Antonio tailed him to *his* dorm then. Minty was out of it the whole walk there, didn't even notice Antonio. Nearly got run over by a car. Something's not right in a big way. Is it drugs?"

"I don't think so," Daniel said. "I think it's something just as dangerous, though."

"Do you think he'll be here tonight?" I asked, my stomach twisting. "Is he—"

"Ah, speak of the devil," Barry said, nodding toward the stairs where Minty was prancing up in a purple leotard and a green tutu, wearing multiple strings of purple and green Mardi Gras beads wrapped in layers around his wrists and neck.

"Minty!" Daniel called, waving him over. He wore a tight grin that fooled no one. Especially not Minty, who stopped, looked between me and Daniel, and then strode over, with his hands already clenched by his sides.

"What's up?" He held Daniel's gaze challengingly. "Did your little boyfriend tell you about my new lovey-bear, and you decided I needed your *guidance* or something?"

"Do you? Need my guidance?" Daniel asked, reaching out to take Minty's arm, but Minty flinched away. I couldn't tell if it was from pain or anger, maybe both. "Barry said you brought the guy here last night—"

"His name's *Kyle* and I'm happy with him, thank you very much."

"Okay, so you brought Kyle here. What's the story with him?"

"I told you. He's my lover."

"And you're happy with him?"

"Yeah."

"Why?" Daniel crossed his arms over his chest, a self-righteousness seeping into his stance that I knew would get under Minty's skin. And sure enough, it did.

"Because he doesn't treat me like I'm fragile. He's rough and mean, and he hates faggots," Minty said, putting his chin up. "Despite wanting to fuck them. Wanting to fuck *me*."

"What's that supposed to mean?" Barry asked, slapping a towel down on the bar and leaning over it.

"It means I have him by the balls. It means he wants me even though he *hates* wanting me." He smiled like a knife, sharp and cruel. "And I like that. I like it a lot."

"You *like* having him beat the shit out of you?" Barry asked, motioning at a visible bruise on Minty's forearm.

"He doesn't do anything I don't want," Minty said, sniffing. He rolled his eyes. "I told Peter that. He should have listened."

"And does what you want include being choked?" Daniel asked, reaching out to touch the Mardi Gras beads around Minty's throat. Now that he'd pointed it out, I could see they were supposed to cover up bruising.

"Yes," Minty said, lifting his chin even higher. "And I like to be hit, and fucked hard, and spit on when it's done. That's what I want. I love it."

"But why?" I asked before I could stop myself. This wasn't the Minty I'd met over the summer. The starry-eyed, romance-starved boy who'd longed for a true love of his own. This was someone else entirely.

Minty snarled, "Why did your pretty ex like being the Naughty Boy that one night? Why does *everyone* here get off on Renée's spanking routine? Because it's empowering. It's hot. It proves how strong we are. And what Kyle does to me? It's all that times twenty."

Until recently, when Renée had moved her shows to Nashville, Minty had been her Naughty Boy most nights. He'd liked being spanked like that, and Renée had never held back when hitting him. He'd always left with a hot, rosy ass afterward, and a big smile on his face, too.

"If you want someone to beat your ass," Barry said, resting his arms against the bar. "There are better ways to accomplish it. Much better ways."

Minty rolled his eyes. "What would you know about it?"

"Plenty."

"Right. Well, what if I *like* it this way? What if I like seeing how much he hates himself afterwards? What if I love how he just can't keep his dick out of my ass?" Minty crossed his arms over his chest, breathing hard. "What if *that's* what I love best about it? Is there a better way to get *that?*"

"Minty—" Daniel breathed out.

He put up his hand. "Don't go into your whole line about how I deserve to be treated with love and respect, because I don't. I never did. And I wouldn't like it if I was."

"This isn't you talking," Daniel said. "This is how you get

when…" He trailed off. "Did your dad come back to town? Did he contact you?"

Minty's shoulders tensed, and his face grew rigid. "What if he did?"

"That's no reason to—"

"It's plenty of reason," Minty muttered.

No one spoke for a long, bleak moment.

"But it's not the reason," Barry said, eyeing Minty. "Is it?"

Minty dug his fingernails into his own arms and clenched his jaw tight.

"So, what is it then? What's got you throwing yourself to the wolves like this?" Daniel asked. "I thought we were past all this, that you and I had an understanding—"

"We? *We* were past this? Good one." Minty wiped a hand over his face, his throat contracting beneath the beads.

"He could kill you!" Daniel said.

"If I'm lucky, he will."

"*What?*" Daniel reached for Minty, but again Minty stepped back. "What the hell are you saying?"

"Better than dying all wasted away and alone, better than suffering and hurting, and—"

Silence roared around us. My head ached. My ears buzzed.

Minty bit out the next words. "I'm positive."

"You're—" Daniel blinked.

"That's right. I'm not long for this world." Minty gave a feral, rageful grin. "So if I get taken out doing what I love most—getting fucked—so be it."

"Minty—"

"Fuck off," he sneered, glaring at me, Daniel, and Barry. "I don't have to explain myself to you. I can do what I want, when I want, with who I want. Don't you get it? I have nothing to lose. Nothing at all, anymore."

"You don't have to punish yourself," Daniel said, his voice gravelly. "This isn't healthy. If you're positive, if you're sick, then this—rough sex—is that much worse for you. The infection possibilities alone! You can get tears and… Minty, please. If you're positive, if that's true—"

"You think I'd lie about something like this?"

"—you should be treating yourself with love, with tenderness and care." Daniel reached out once more, but Minty evaded his touch again.

"Like how you treat Peter?"

"Yes."

"Pfft." He lifted a brow. "You haven't even fucked Peter."

"Minty—"

"Why? Because it should be special? Because it should be tender and sweet? Jesus, this glorification of penetrative sex is *very* heterosexual of you."

"This isn't about—"

"Oh, isn't it? At least a little? You and Peter haven't even *fucked*. Like you're both some sweet little virgins instead of the horny gay men you are! Screw that! I'd never want that!"

"Minty, this is a distraction. What Peter and I have or haven't done has nothing to do with—"

"It does! It has everything to do with it! Have you ever had someone fuck you blind while they choke you out? Because if you haven't, and you don't want that, then you can't *begin* to talk to me about what I should or shouldn't be doing with my body now that I'm dying. Got it?"

"You're not—"

"Shut up! I'm as good as dead!" Minty yelled, spinning on his heel and heading for the stairs again. "Fuck this!"

Daniel started to follow, but Barry grabbed his arm. "No. Don't. Let me handle it."

Daniel tugged his arm away. "He won't listen to you. He only listens to me."

"He isn't listening to you now," Barry pointed out. "Trust me." Barry locked up the register and tossed his apron on the bar. "I'll handle this. If the boss asks where I am, I'm taking my break. I'll be back in plenty of time before Pearly's show."

We watched Barry hustling down the stairs like a man on a mission.

"Wow," I said, sitting down on a barstool. My knees didn't want to hold me up any longer.

Daniel sat down next to me, leaning against the bar and burying his head in his arms. "I fucked that up so bad he's probably on the way to that Kyle asshole's dorm to get beaten to a pulp."

"Barry's on it," I said, stroking his back. "He said to trust him."

Daniel nodded. "I guess." A big swallow and then he choked out, "So. He's positive…"

"Yeah."

"*Fuck.*"

"I know," I whispered and shook my head.

"This doesn't have to be a death sentence for him," Daniel said, sitting up straight again. "If he takes care of himself, if he starts on AZT when the time comes—I can pay for it. I'm getting a lot from the settlement with the company—and if he doesn't put undue wear and tear on his body, then he can live—" His throat seemed to close up on him and tears filled his eyes. "Well, he doesn't have to die. Right *away.*"

I didn't say anything. So far HIV eventually led to AIDS in all cases, and AIDS *was* a death sentence. "Do we know for sure how it happened?" I asked.

"What?"

"How he ended up positive?"

"Who knows? After the last guy, the one who broke his arm, he promised to always use condoms. But it could have been that guy from last spring. The one whose condom broke."

"Yeah."

"But he sleeps around so much, and he's always refused to be tested." Daniel wiped a hand over his face. "He hasn't always been as careful as he could have been. I don't know why. It's not that hard to use condoms."

I didn't mention how much *he* seemed to yearn to be even closer to me, to be with me flesh-on-flesh. I cleared my throat, coming at it from a different angle. "In class my teacher told us about condom refusal in gay men," I said, and then proceeded to explain Donnie Huggins's take on it all. "Maybe what Minty's doing is related to that? Only…rough instead of loving."

"Maybe."

"But why would he crave it?" I asked.

"Some people just do," Daniel said. "His father abused him. When he was a kid, there was a lot of physical abuse. So, in his life, love and pain were mixed up, you know?"

I felt sick. "That's awful."

"Yeah. After Minty's parents got divorced, things got better. But he started to become more and more effeminate during middle school, and there was a day when—" He shook his head, rubbing at the center of his own chest like it hurt to breathe. "That's Minty's story."

"If you need to tell me so that you're not carrying that alone for him anymore, you can," I said. "I won't tell him that I know or tell anyone else either."

Daniel gazed at me, the need to let this out of his system plain on his face. "All right. You promise?"

"On my soul."

"All right. God. This is hard." He rubbed his chest again. "So…there was a day after the divorce when his father came by their house. Minty's mom wasn't home, and he caught Minty dressed as a girl."

"Oh God."

"Yeah. He told Minty he'd show him what girls were made to be used for if that's what he wanted to be so badly." He squeezed his eyes shut. "You can guess the rest."

"He…" I swallowed hard and whispered, "He raped him?" My gut churned.

Daniel nodded. "So you see the connection. In the past, Minty only fucked bullies when he ran into his dad or was forced to interact with him. But…this. This is new."

"I know." I felt sick all over.

"I let him down. I should have taken more care with him these last few months, made sure he was using condoms, and—"

"Daniel, you can't control everything. You can't make your mom stop drinking, or keep your siblings safe, or make Minty use condoms. You can only do what *you* can do and accept that it's not as much as you want to do. Believe me, I know what it's like to feel helpless, but it's not going to do anyone any good to blame yourself."

"Minty blames *him*self. That's why he's using Kyle as self-punishment."

"Minty is angry," I agreed. "But you can't do anything more than be his friend."

"I know what you're saying is true, but I'm so scared."

I slung my arm over his shoulders, squeezing. "I'm scared for him too."

"Yeah."

We sat in silence with my arm around him, our bodies close, and the thumpa-thumpa of the dance floor starting up downstairs. There was no return of Barry or Minty, and none of the other guys showed up either.

"He's too young for this," Daniel said after a long time. "He doesn't deserve it. Not after all he went through growing up."

"No one deserves it."

Daniel took hold of my hand and squeezed. "If it's okay with you, I don't think I want to be here anymore."

"Where do you want to go?"

"I *want* to go find Minty, but Barry said he'd handle it, and I don't want to get in his way. Minty's prideful, and if I'm there, he might decide not to listen to Barry out of stubborn spite." Daniel sighed. "So, I guess we should go home."

"Home as in your place?"

Daniel nodded. "If you want. I mean, if you can? I'd like to hold you tonight, to know *you're* safe at least."

I nuzzled his cheek. "Yes, I'll go home with you. But we need to stop by my house to grab some clothes first. I still have class in the morning." With Minty, no less. God, that was going to be awkward. I needed to plan what I was going to say to him when I saw him.

But what if he didn't come to class? What if he decided to skip?

Daniel took my hand to lead me out of the club.

Downstairs, I saw Jeremy on the now-busy dance floor, swaying with a twink, his head thrown back, laughing. My stomach knotted up remembering the reckless way I'd behaved with him, and the things I'd done while high on GHB.

I closed my eyes, and let Daniel lead me out of the smoke and into the fresh air outside the club.

The quote "There but for the grace of God go I," took on new meaning for me.

I didn't know how to process the news of Minty's diagnosis, but I hoped beyond hope that something would change soon to protect him. New science, new drugs. Anything to keep Minty—that lover of moonbeams and fairy stamps—from getting sick and dying like

Bobby.

Anything but that.

✧　✧　✧

THE FRONT PORCH light was still on at my house when we pulled into the driveway.

"Wait here," I said, unbuckling my seat belt. "I'll just be a few minutes."

Daniel unbuckled his belt, too. "But I want to see your room."

I glanced over at him and considered telling him that I'd invite him inside another time, but the sad, hollow look in his eyes made me decide that the last thing I wanted to do was leave him alone right now. "Yeah, all right. Come on."

As I unlocked the front door and eased it open, I heard the familiar loud clacking of Mom's word processor, and the less familiar strains of some 1970s love song wafting from the living room stereo.

"There you are," Mom said, turning from where she was dancing alone in a nightgown and robe, a wine glass in her hand, and her word processor going a mile a minute on the table, printing out her manuscript. "I was starting to worry."

"You're still up," I said, grimacing. I hadn't wanted Daniel to meet my mom just yet, much less meet her when she'd had a drink and was in her pajamas dancing to Billy Joel and crooning that she'd always be a woman to him.

"I am! And you're very late." Her eyebrows went up, seeing Daniel behind me. "And not alone." She walked toward him, hand out. "Hello, I'm Jessica. You must be Daniel?"

"Yes, ma'am. It's great to meet you, Mrs. Mandel," he said, taking her hand and shaking it.

"I agree. Abe would want me to express his deep sorrow that he's far too *asleep* at this, oh-so-late hour of one o'clock in the morning to come and greet you as well."

"Sorry," Daniel said meekly. "We were—"

"Don't apologize," I interrupted. "We were out with friends, and we're leaving again, Mom. I'm just grabbing some clothes and then we're heading to Daniel's house." I said, starting up the stairs, mortified that Daniel didn't follow. I jerked my head, trying to get him to follow me. Instead, he stood there, watching my mom with an odd expression.

Mom, for her part, didn't seem to notice. She sipped her wine and said, "It's really very late, Peter. I don't like the idea of you driving at this hour. Why don't you both spend the night here? I was just heading to bed myself. I can tidy up my manuscript pages, and Daniel can have the sofa."

"Daniel needs to get home."

"Why?"

"He has a dog to look after."

"Oh? What kind of dog?" Mom asked Daniel, eyes wide with interest. "We lost our dear old Harry this past summer. It was hard on us all, wasn't it, Peter? He was mixed-breed but had terrier in him."

"I'm sorry to hear that," Daniel said. "Milky Way is a shih tzu. She was my friend Bobby's dog, but he passed away and…" He shrugged. "Now I've got her."

Mom's expression softened. "Ah, you're a sweet one." The word processor stopped clacking and the room seemed a lot quieter despite Billy's crooning continuing in the background. "And that's my deadline met," she said with a grin. "Cheers!" She drank the rest of her wine in a gulp, and then whirled away. "I'll get this in the mail to Saundra tomorrow and that's one more romance down, a hundred more to go."

"*Lovers Reunited?*" I asked, still wishing Daniel would come up the stairs with me and leave her behind. "You finished it?"

"*Lovers Returned*," she corrected. "And yes."

"Congratulations, Mom," I said, reaching my hand toward Daniel. "We'll celebrate tomorrow or the next day."

Daniel put his foot on the first step, and I wanted to cheer. "Yes, congratulations, Mrs. Mandel. I know Peter's proud of all you've accomplished."

Was I? Had I *ever* said that? I didn't think so, but it was true enough, and it made my mother smile.

"Is he now? I have my doubts." She waved us off. "Go on then. I wouldn't want you driving even later because I kept you, and we don't want to keep your dog waiting."

"No, ma'am," Daniel agreed, and finally followed me up the stairs to my bedroom. "She's great," he said, shutting the door behind us, and looking around the room. "You're lucky."

I blinked, a memory of Adam saying something quite similar racing through my brain, but I dismissed it. "She's okay," I said. "Could be worse, could be better. At least she's not popping pills these days. Okay, so, let me just…" As I searched for and found a duffle bag and stuffed a few shirts and a couple of pairs of jeans, some socks, and underwear inside, I watched Daniel walk around the room, looking at my things.

He paused by my desk, looking at the pinboard there, and with a small smile he reached out to touch the picture I had placed in the middle—the very first shot I'd ever taken of him, a blurry one from the Hill at UT after he'd jump-started my car.

"Wow, you still have this, huh?"

"Our origin story," I murmured, coming up behind him and wrapping my arms around his waist. I was too short to hook my chin over his shoulder the way he did to me, but I rested my cheek against his back and held him, listening to his breathing and his heart. It was steady, strong.

"I wish I had a picture of you the way you looked that night, too," he said. "You were…"

"I was what?"

"Beautiful." He turned then and wrapped his arms around me, too.

"No," I whispered. "Not me."

"Yes, you." He kissed me then and the room melted around me; I went soft in his arms, and his tongue moved against mine, making my head spin.

"Let's go," I said, ending our kiss. "My mom will wonder what's taking so long, and I really want to get back to your place."

"Why's that?"

"I just want to be alone with you," I said, nudging my nose against his and pressing another kiss to his jaw. "I feel like we need that tonight."

"Yeah," he said.

I released him. "Let's go, then."

Daniel paused again by the pinboard and put his finger on a picture of Minty.

"He'll be okay," I said, sliding a hand down Daniel's back.

"No, he won't," Daniel said. Grief slumped his shoulders. He put his arm around me and tugged me close again. "But you and I will be."

After that, we left my room and headed back downstairs. Mom was still awake, looking over some of the printed pages, and smiling. Billy Joel was now movin' out, and the music was no longer romantic. She rose as we reached the last steps and started toward the front door, past the Disney World picture that Daniel had admired on his first visit.

"It was good to meet you, Mrs. Mandel," Daniel said again, lifting a hand to wave goodbye.

"Of course. When are you going to have dinner with us? Soon, I hope?"

"Mom," I said, trying to head that line of questioning off at the pass. "Daniel will have dinner with us when the time is right. Don't be pushy."

"And by that you mean Friday?"

I groaned. "We'll talk later. I love you."

"Love you too. Drive safely. Use condoms."

"Oh God," I said, shutting the door a little harder than I needed to. "For fuck's sake."

Daniel took hold of my hand as we headed toward the Volvo again. "She doesn't need to worry. We'll always use condoms."

I nodded, but some part of me wanted to argue. What if there came a day when we were sure enough of each other to go bare? What if we trusted each other enough to be together like that, raw and real, not at all like what Minty was doing and had done, but something so much more beautiful than that? What if Daniel and I could have everything one day? Did we dare to love like that?

I kissed Daniel's hand before we separated to get into opposite sides of the car.

Only time would tell.

That night, at Daniel's house, we slept spooned together. We'd been far too tired to talk or screw around by the time we'd gotten back. We'd made sure Milky Way had kibble and water and then settled down in Daniel's bedroom together. I'd wondered if the echoing, empty house felt like a grave of memories around him, but I hadn't asked.

I let Daniel hold me tight, breathing in his scent as he breathed in mine.

Before I drifted off, I remembered Minty's angry voice. *"You and Peter haven't even fucked! Like you're both some sweet little virgins instead of the horny gay men you are!"*

We hadn't done that particular act together yet. Ostensibly we were waiting on our tests, but we were planning to use a condom anyway. Sometimes I wasn't sure what was holding Daniel back. It made me wonder if there was more going on.

I remembered how Adam had put it off for a long time, too, claiming he'd want it all the time once we started. And he had. But then I had too.

And, of course, once I'd thought of Adam, I couldn't dismiss the agony I'd seen on his face earlier that evening, or the way he'd managed to fuck up my head without even trying. Sometimes I thought Adam was my biggest mistake. Other times I still felt a twinge of affection for him. But mostly he left me swamped with regrets.

The night had been far too full of emotion and stress, and while both of us were exhausted, I'm not sure either of us slept well.

At not even six o'clock in the morning, we were both startled awake by the sound of the doorbell. Jumping out of bed, pulling on sweats, and shaky from interrupted sleep, Daniel and I walked through the long, empty hallways, and down to the front door, hearts pounding and confusion mounting.

"Who do you think it is?" I asked.

"I don't know," Daniel said. "But it can't be good news."

Chapter Twenty-Two

"**I** WAS JUST so scared," Minty told us, sipping his hot coffee, and gazing with wide, shocked eyes at our reflections in the dark kitchen windows.

He'd been bedraggled and sobbing on the doorstep before Daniel had pulled him inside and held him tight. The light of dawn had cracked on the horizon and slipped over the lake before he'd stopped crying enough to talk to us. We'd made coffee and listened, holding Minty's hands. It was cathartic and necessary. It was hard as hell.

I checked the clock over the oven. Minty and I had missed our Psychology class. But what we'd gained was so much more than that. Each other.

"I'm *still* scared. It's real. It's happening. I'm going to die. And it's all the fault of one asshole and his fucking broken condom. I *know* it was him. It had to be."

"You don't know for sure," Daniel soothed. "You'd never been tested before."

"No, and I wish I hadn't gotten tested now either."

"You can't mean that."

"I do mean it! I only did it for my mother, not for me. I was going to give it to her as a birthday present. You know, ta-da! I'm negative! And now..." Minty's face crumpled. "What am I supposed to tell her? Happy birthday, Mom, I got that test you wanted me to have and, guess what, I'm dying? Should I tell her that my father was right and—"

"Fuck your father."

"Ha," Minty wiped at his face. "Already did that." He gulped, eyes cutting to me. I kept my face as impassive as possible, not wanting anything to slip, not wanting to let him know that Daniel had told me. "He said I'd get AIDS and, look, Pa, I did, and with no hands, too." He waved his arms around like he was balancing on a bike.

"You don't have AIDS," Daniel corrected. "You have HIV and that's…" he choked, but managed to go on by saying, "Manageable. Or it can be for some time. There are guys who were diagnosed early on who still haven't developed full-blown AIDS yet. We'll just need to get you on AZT as soon as your T-cells—"

"No way."

"I can help you pay for—"

"No. The cost is too much. Besides, don't you see what that shit does to people?" Minty asked. "It makes them look like shit."

"Minty—"

"Don't," Minty said, holding his hand out. "If I'm going to die, I'm going to be as beautiful as I can for as long as possible, and then I'll go out quick and fast. Step in front of a train or jump from a building. I'm not going to waste away. I won't."

Daniel seemed to sense it was better to lose this battle right now than to lose the whole war, so he dropped that line of discussion. "What did Barry say to you? He told me he'd handle you."

"He said…" Minty blushed, actually *blushed* and looked down at his coffee mug. "He said if I needed pain and punishment to get through this, then he'd help me get hurt."

"Barry?" I asked, confused. "Barry wouldn't hurt a fly."

"Not him personally, but a friend of his who specializes in hurting people, but, like, safely."

"Like what? BDSM?" Daniel asked.

I winced. A memory of the scene I'd gotten into with Adam in the spring came to mind. It'd been upsetting and sexy, hot and conflicted.

Minty nodded. "He said that if I need that, then there's a better way to get it, not with…not with people like my…my lover, Kyle."

"'Your *lover*, Kyle.'" Daniel lifted a brow. "You do realize that the term 'lover' implies love, and nothing he does to you is love."

"He loves the way it feels to come in my ass," Minty said with another of those sharp, scary smiles. "He loves that."

"And he hates it," Daniel said, repeating what Minty had told us at Tilt-a-Whirl.

Minty nodded. "He'd probably kill me if he knew I was positive, even though getting it that way is…" He shrugged. "Whatever. He'd kill me anyway."

"And you like that feeling?"

"No? Yes? I don't know. I just want to forget," Minty said. "When I'm rushing on that adrenaline high, when he's hitting me hard enough it really hurts, and he's got his hands around my throat—" he touched the mottled bruises on his white skin. "When he fucks me so hard I just see stars? I can forget *everything* but that moment. I exist only there. It's like heaven."

"And when it's over?"

Minty's shoulders slumped. "Then it's like heaven beat the hell out of me. Which feels right, you know? God would do the same if He had the chance. And He will. When I die, He'll punish me forever."

"He wouldn't," I said, even though I didn't believe in God. "Don't they teach that God loves everyone?"

Minty rolled his eyes. "That's a lie they tell children so they'll fall asleep quicker at night. The truth is, God—if there even is one—is a sadist who enjoys seeing people suffer. Because that's the only thing that can explain this world and all the bad things that go on in it. Like what happened to me back when I was a kid." He caught my gaze again. "What happened to you, too, right? The times you got beaten up? What kind of loving God allows for that?"

"I don't know," I said. I wasn't the right person to be having this conversation with him right now. "I don't believe in God."

Minty laughed for the first time since he'd arrived. "Then why are you defending Him?"

"I just don't like seeing you think such terrible things about yourself. If there is a God, he'd love you. You're very lovable, Minty. If there is a God, he'd be the one who sent you here to earth made of magic moonbeams and covered in fairy stamps, right? It doesn't make sense that he'd do that if he didn't love you and want you to be like that."

"I told you. God's a sadist." Minty's lips quivered, and he took another sip of coffee to hide it. Putting the mug down, he rubbed his fingers over his eyes, smearing mascara and makeup. "Holy shit, I'm going to die."

Daniel took hold of his hand. "How long have you known?"

"A few weeks."

"And you didn't tell anyone?"

"No. I thought I could handle it on my own." Minty's eyes filled with tears. "But I can't. I'm scared and mad. But mostly scared."

"I am too," Daniel said, holding his hand and rubbing the back of his knuckles with his thumb. "But we can hope for a miracle. We can't stop believing. You're not even sick."

"Yet."

"We'll hope better medicines are developed soon. I'll take you to consult with one of the doctors ARK keeps on call. We'll figure this out."

"And pray for a miracle," Minty murmured, his lips trembling and tears spilling over. He took hold of my hand and squeezed his fingers. "Peter, you too. Pray to that God you claim you don't believe in. Will you?"

"Yeah, of course," I said, taking their hands and closing my eyes.

"Then let's pray now," Minty said.

And we did. My first ever purposeful and out-loud prayer to a god I didn't believe existed.

But it was for a good cause. It was for Minty.

Part XI

October 1991

My dearest love,

The days grow darker as the year turns the corner from summer into autumn, but my love for you shines brighter than ever. I remember you in my arms, the joy of union, the small despair of sliding free from your body after the passion waned… I remember it all with clarity that can only be rivaled by the photos I took of you then, flushed with love and wet with our spendings. Is there any intimacy greater? Come back to me. Leave everything else behind. Our love can outshine all darkness, if you'll just allow it to take its rightful place in your life.

But let's not fight. Just come home to me.

Your very own,
Harold

Chapter Twenty-Three

THE BEGINNING OF October rolled around and between classes, my job at the library, his work on his house and attempts to help Minty, and all my studying, I spent less time with Daniel than I would have liked. Though I'd stayed over on two different Saturday nights, and Daniel had met me on campus twice just to hang out while I studied, it didn't feel like enough. When I wasn't with him, I was thinking about him. I felt jumpy and impatient, or dreamy and needy, and it all added up to *yearning*.

As for Minty, he wasn't making it easy for Daniel to take care of him. After our prayer together, he'd seemed ready and willing to go with Daniel to ARK, find out more about eventually getting AZT, and figuring out how to live with the disease.

But after he'd left, things had changed. He'd stopped reliably returning Daniel's calls, failed to show up when Daniel came to take him to a meeting at ARK, and was giving enough push-and-pull to remind Daniel way too much of his mother.

All in all, it was a mess, and Daniel had been advised by Barry to let Minty figure himself out. Daniel had struggled to give up control, but when Minty told him in no uncertain terms to back off and let him figure things out on his own, calling him "Dad" in a tone that dripped with disdain, Daniel had taken a step back.

He'd said, "There's only so much I can do. If a person doesn't want help, I can't force them to take it. Ask me how I learned that lesson."

Speaking of, Daniel's mother was still in rehab and had had her phone privileges revoked for some infraction or other. Daniel said he should be worried about it, but instead he was relieved. Her nightly calls did nothing but upset him. I agreed he was better off without her making promises he had no hope she'd ever keep.

Instead, *I* talked to him every night, dreaming of the future we'd make in Bobby's house, talking over furniture plans and vegetable gardens. It was all very fanciful, and some part of me whispered that I was too young to move in with someone, but most of me just danced in the dream of it all.

Sitting with Jennifer and Minty in the UC cafeteria, I listened to them talk over the details of Donnie Huggins's latest lecture. This one was on Bettelheim's theories on autism and the "refrigerator mom." Again, another topic I felt certain was not on the typical Psych 110 syllabus.

"Blaming the mother is always bullshit," Jennifer said, putting a forkful of salad in her mouth and crunching down.

"Agreed," Minty said, taking a bite of his chicken and rice. He was eating a little better lately, and I made note to report that good news to Daniel. "They blame moms for everything—autism, depression, gay kids, AIDS."

Jennifer snorted. "Yeah, and if they have straight kids, guess who gets the credit? The dad. For being a good role model as a man, for being someone the boy could emulate and the girl would want to marry." She rolled her eyes. "It's all bullshit. I think Donnie needs to get his head out of those crack-ass books and back into what he's supposed to be teaching us."

"I like his crack-ass books," I said. "His lectures are always interesting at least. Unlike most of my classes."

"My mom's birthday is coming up," Minty said, changing the subject. He caught my eye and then looked away. As far as I knew, he hadn't told Jennifer about his HIV status or why he'd gotten tested, and his tension around the subject of his mom's birthday went over her head. "I'm thinking of getting her a gift certificate for a fancy salon to celebrate her day. Where do you recommend?"

"You like my stylist's work?" Jennifer said, fluffing her hair and grinning. "Let me get my planner out. It has her number in it." While she sorted through her backpack, I studied Minty.

The bruises he'd had around his neck had long ago faded, and I hadn't seen any evidence that he'd returned to fucking Kyle since we'd all prayed together. Not that I trusted Minty to be honest with me if he had, but the lack of fingerprint marks around his pale throat was reassuring.

I followed him out of the cafeteria when lunch was over. Usually, we parted ways outside the UC, but this time I turned to walk with him. He cut a glance toward me, shoulders stiffening as he asked, "What's up?"

"I just wanted to check in on you."

"What? To see if I'm still 'acting out?' Daniel got you spying on me now?"

"No. I just care."

"Right, well..." He sighed, and the tension dissolved. "I cut things off with Kyle." He laughed and looked at my slyly. "But I'm still considering going for one last fuck. I hate to walk away from that without another hit for the road."

"Minty..."

"Don't scold me," he said, shooting me a dark look. "You don't get to judge me."

"I'm not judging. I just want you safe."

"Too late, dollface. I'm far from fucking safe. I'm a lost cause." The sun sparkled in Minty's blond hair, and even on his skin, which still had some glitter stuck to it here and there from his last trip to Tilt-a-Whirl. "I miss it. Being treated like that." He smiled, and his expression was so sad it cut me to the quick. "But I guess Daniel's right. The risk of infection or worse is too big. I need to be more careful."

"What about Barry's suggestion?" I didn't understand this need of Minty's to be punished and hurt, but if Barry recommended that he see this other guy, if it was safer or better for him in some way while still meeting his needs, then I'd rather he did that than go back to Kyle the next time he was feeling desperate.

"I'm still thinking about it." Minty and I started the long climb up the stairs to the top of the Hill. I was panting by the time we reached the top.

"What's stopping you?" I asked.

Minty huffed a laugh. "Well, I'm afraid for one thing. Barry said this guy knows how to hurt a person without doing real or lasting damage. Like screaming-crying pain. That's exciting *and* terrifying. At least with Kyle or someone like him, I know what to expect."

"Oh."

"And I don't know if it will even work," Minty went on. "Because part of what I like about guys like Kyle is knowing that they hate me, that they hate wanting me, and yet they can't resist. It's a huge power trip. With this guy, that element wouldn't be there."

"I see." But I didn't, because none of this was anything I'd ever want for myself, but I could see Minty craved it. Maybe not the Minty he'd been when I'd first met him, but the Minty he was now—post HIV-diagnosis, all self-destructive, hurt, angry, and scared. *This* Minty needed that kind of treatment almost like a fucked-up version of therapy. I didn't get it, but I could see that it was true.

"So, I don't know," Minty said, grimacing into the sun as it came out from behind a cloud. "What do you think?"

"I think if Barry suggested it, then it has to be safer than Kyle."

"But I don't *want* safe, Peter."

"I know. What about the other thing then? Like Daniel's been asking of you?"

"The ARK counselor?"

I nodded.

Minty sighed, hitched his backpack higher, and squinted into the sun again. I knew that look, and that hesitation. "I'm not ready for that." I opened my mouth to argue, but he motioned toward the other side of campus. "Go on. There's nothing else to say right now. I'm fine."

He wasn't fine, and neither was Daniel, but he was right that there was nothing else to say at this moment, not to someone as stubborn as Minty. He had to get there in his own time.

I headed back down the steep stairs and crossed campus, but not toward my class. I had somewhere else I needed to be, and talking with Minty only reminded me of how much I needed and wanted the information.

It was important to not be late.

✧　✧　✧

"NEGATIVE," I REPEATED, looking at the sheet of paper in my hands, and then back up at the Health Services nurse delivering the news. I'd waited six weeks for this, and I wanted to be certain I'd heard correctly. "You're sure?"

"Absolutely." He smiled at me. "False negatives are incredibly rare. Congratulations." He opened the door to the room, and said, "Exit's this way to the right. Now, play safe and stay safe."

I nodded and headed toward the first pay phone I could find. Putting in my quarter, I punched in the number and waited through four long rings before Daniel picked up.

"Hey, guess what?" I said, breathless.

"What?"

"I got my test results back. All negative. I'm fine." I didn't say that either Adam *had* used a condom that last time just as he'd claimed, or he hadn't given me anything at least. Daniel still didn't know about my worries on that front, and I didn't want to ruin the good news. "So what about you? Have you heard back?"

I waited with bated breath. We'd made out, gotten off rutting together, and given each other blow jobs, but we hadn't fucked yet—and I hoped now that I had a clear test, we could proceed to that next step sooner rather than later. With condoms, of course, but I figured the test must have been what was holding him back. Unless Daniel didn't like anal, and in that case—

"I have," he said, excitement coursing through the line. "Negative. And no other diseases."

"Finally."

Daniel's voice lowered. "Are you saying what I think you're saying?"

"Yes. I want to," I said. "I've wanted to for a while now."

"Me too." Daniel made a sound that was almost like a growl, and I laughed, spontaneous excitement turning to joy in a heartbeat. "I've wanted to do that with you for a long time. Longer than we've been together."

My breath came in sharp gasps, and I twisted my fingers into my hair, pulling enough to hurt and center myself *and* make sure I didn't get an erection. "When?"

"Soon. Definitely soon."

"I could come over tonight," I offered. It would mean getting up at an ungodly hour to make it to class, but it would be worth it to get to be with Daniel like that.

"No, I want it to be special."

"It can't be anything *but* special."

"I know, but I want to make it…extra special."

I laughed. "Minty would say that's very hetero of you."

"It's very loving of me," he said, and my heart skipped two beats.

"Yes," I whispered. "It is."

I remembered the first time with Adam, how much it'd hurt, the issue with the sheets, and the sense that I'd lost something important, and how nothing—absolutely *nothing*—had been made better by that act between us. It'd just complicated things even more. With Daniel, it would be different. *He* was different.

We were different together.

"So when?" I sounded impatient and horny. I was, and I wasn't ashamed of that fact.

"This weekend," he said. "What day do you work?"

"Saturday opening shift again."

"Great. I'll pick you up at your house after, and we'll go somewhere nice for a date. Afterwards, I'll take you somewhere special, too. Somewhere you've never been with anyone else, and I haven't either."

"Where's that?"

"A hotel."

I laughed. "That's…you're going to take me to a *hotel?*"

"I want a clean slate for our first time. A place with no memories and no parents in another room."

And no empty house reminding him of how many responsibilities were on his shoulders either, I supposed.

"What about Milky Way?"

"I'll leave her with Kerri. She'll take her if it's just for a night."

"Okay," I agreed. "That sounds great."

"And in the meantime, we can talk about what we want and how we want it."

"I'm at school," I whispered, as a girl walked up behind me, standing a few feet back, waiting for a turn at the phone.

"We can talk later then. Make a plan."

"A plan?"

Daniel laughed. "A sex plan."

I plucked at the front of my shirt, trying to cool off. I could blame it on the hot weather lingering into October, but it was all the excitement, nerves, and desire bouncing around inside me, revving me up, and making me sweat.

After we hung up, I started toward my photography class with my mind already crowded with potential positions that Daniel and I could try. The open-ended freedom of the kind of trust I had with him was mind-blowing. We were going to fuck—make love—*both*, and there was nothing to be ashamed of.

I almost started running, feet light, and heart even lighter.

Light enough to rise into the sky.

Chapter Twenty-Four

BY THE TIME Saturday afternoon rolled around, I was so high on our days of sex planning that I hadn't been able to concentrate at all during my work. I got sent up to the stacks multiple times looking for misplaced books, and I ended up wandering around for much longer than I should have. Not because I didn't want to come back downstairs and do my job, but because I was so distracted that I kept getting lost.

April asked what was going on with me today, saying I was never like this, and I had to agree. But I couldn't share what Daniel and I were planning. Everything about it felt private and important. Possibly because he'd made me wait all week to see him while teasing me on the phone with questions about what I liked and suggestions for things he was sure would drive me wild, and possibly because he'd planned something just for us therefore *making* it special with his intentions, and possibly because it just *was*.

I knew it wasn't true for everyone, but fucking or being fucked felt like the highest level of intimacy for me. It meant something serious and profound that I was going to do that with Daniel, and that he was going to let me do it to him, too.

As the day progressed and my workday drew to a close, I felt like a flip-flopping fish inside. Giddy like a kid who'd had too much candy. I couldn't stop smiling, amazed at what was ahead, but more amazed at myself. Compared to where I'd been a year ago, or even two months ago, my relationship with Daniel had taken my life to a whole new level of wonderful. I felt dizzy, and I knew for sure that I was in love. I wanted to tell him.

Tonight.

I chose a new short-sleeve, button-up shirt that Daniel had complimented once over the summer, and new black jeans that I knew hugged my ass well. I took out my contacts to give them a good soak while I got ready.

From beneath the sink, I pulled out a box I'd bought during the week, removing the bulbous item and reading the instructions. They weren't hard to follow, and for the first time, I douched in preparation for anal sex. Every other time, I'd just crossed my fingers and hoped for the best. But tonight, I wanted to be clean for Daniel.

Then I showered, cleaning everywhere I thought Daniel's lips might touch. Afterward, I put my contacts back in, I ran a comb through my hair, trying to get some of the crazier parts to lie down, but it was useless.

Then I put together an overnight bag. My glasses, saline solution, a change of clothes.

"Peter!" my mom called.

After one last glance in the mirror, I slung my bag over my shoulder and took off down the stairs to greet Daniel.

He stood in the entryway with a bunch of wildflowers in one hand and my mom's fingers clutched in the other. Seeing me coming down the staircase, his eyes lit up.

"Hey," I said, a smile tugging at my lips despite my attempt to look calm and collected in front of my mom.

"Hey," he answered.

"Daniel brought these flowers for me," Mom said, taking them from him. "They're wonderful, sweetheart."

"I'm happy you like them," he said. "I picked them from the field by my house."

She raised a brow meaningfully at me. "You picked them yourself? My goodness."

"Well, I'd have bought some, but these were prettier than many at the store, so—"

"They're lovely," she said, sniffing them. "Thank you so much."

Daniel's eyes were back on me, and I couldn't take my eyes off him either. He wore a navy shirt and well-fitting dark-wash jeans, and the thought that before long I'd take them off him and get to touch his skin, rub against him, and pull him down on top—and inside—of me was amazing.

"Where are you headed, and when will you be home?" Mom asked.

I almost snorted. There was no way she was getting to play the mom role tonight. Oh hell no. "I'm not sure, but I won't be home tonight. So don't wait up."

She blinked at me. "When are you going to have dinner with us, Daniel?" she asked. "I think you told me 'soon' the last time you swept in and stole my son for the night."

He blushed, and my mom looked victorious. "If you invite me, I'll make sure I'm available."

She was happy with that answer, and I was too, because I knew as soon as she got her head stuck back into a new book, she'd forget about inviting him until the next lull in her creative process.

I glanced at Daniel and said, "All right, well, we're off."

Mom cocked her eyebrow again and then said, "Okay, have fun. Use condoms."

"*Mom!*"

She gave me an innocent smile and then looked at Daniel and said, "I'm very keen, as the Brits say, on you boys *always* using condoms."

Daniel's expression ran through shocked to amused. "So am I, Mrs. Mandel. I promise."

"Good," she said, and then turned to take the flowers into the kitchen.

"Oh my God," I breathed, flames of mortification burning my cheeks as I turned to go. "I'm so sorry. She has boundary issues."

"Didn't we already agree to forgive each other for our families?" he whispered, and then said, "Besides, she loves you. That's a good thing." Daniel's hand rested on my back as we walked out the door toward the driveway. The warmth of it penetrated my shirt and tingled against my skin.

"My mom loves the flowers," I said. "Thank you for them."

"Well, I did owe her for the ones she bought me," Daniel teased as he opened the door. I climbed in and let him shut it for me, too.

Once he was in the driver's seat, he turned, his eyes glowing as he looked me over. "You look amazing. I want to kiss you."

My grin nearly split my face. "Go for it."

He laughed and leaned in, and his lips were warm, and his mouth tasted like mouthwash. When the kiss started to grow heated, and my hand had grabbed a fistful of his short hair, Daniel pulled away. "Let's go. I've got reservations."

Naples was a tiny Italian restaurant and a staple of the Knoxville restaurant scene. It smelled of garlic and spices, and the tables were pretty much on top of each other, but off to the side, in a separate area, there were several booths recessed into the wall with curtains hanging in front of them for added privacy.

On prom night, a lot of kids vied for reservations in the curtained booths, hoping the added romance would increase their chances of getting laid. I mentioned it to Daniel as we sat waiting for our table to be ready.

"Did you go to prom?" I asked.

"I had a bonfire at my place instead," Daniel said. "Most people didn't harass me at my school because, you know, my folks had money. Fair or not, that changes things."

I nodded.

"But Kevin and I decided we'd be better off skipping the prom anyway. Too chancy. What about you? Did you go stag or just skip the whole thing?"

I sighed. "I took Susan."

"Who?"

I gawped at him a moment, shocked that I'd never shared with him the fact that I'd had a "girlfriend" for the last part of the fiasco that had been my senior year in high school. But why would I have? Susan and I hadn't dated, or kissed, or done much more than attend the Kingsley group parties together and sometimes hold hands for show. Half the time, I'd forgotten that she and I were even supposed to be an item. I told him about it as quickly as I could.

"Wow, just when I think I have a grasp on how things were for you last year, there's always more," Daniel said, leaning against my shoulder.

"Last year was…"

Not what I wanted to be thinking about on our date tonight. Not when we were planning to…

Not fuck. That wasn't what we were going to do. It was so much more than that. Make love. I had no doubt that was where the night was going to end up going. I wanted to tell him how I felt about him, but I wasn't sure now was the time or the place. It'd be better to say it when we were alone.

"Last year was rough," I concluded, lamely.

"Where did you take Susan for dinner on prom night?" Daniel asked.

"Regas," I murmured. It was a posh place that teens could never afford except for very special occasions like prom. "We met some other people there. Let's not talk about it. It's depressing." I shrugged away the memories and smiled up at Daniel. "By the way, I love this place," I said, touching his arm. "My parents used to bring me here sometimes when I was a kid. Their lasagna is my favorite in town."

"I know."

"You do?"

"Yeah. You suggested Renée bring Barry here for their anniversary."

I grinned. "I can't believe you remember something like that. That was months ago."

"Why wouldn't I?" Daniel smiled. "I remember everything about you."

"No you don't." A tingle rushed through me, sweet and pure.

"I do. It's frustrating sometimes." He nudged me again. "Especially back when I was trying to forget you existed after Nashville."

"So, you admit you tried to forget I existed?"

"Yeah, but it didn't work. Even when I was dealing with all that stuff with my mom, I'd see, I don't know, a takeout packet of *ketchup* and remember that you'd said you only liked Heinz."

I wrapped my arms around my torso, trying to get the butterflies in my stomach to settle, and grinned. "I don't even remember saying that, but it's true."

"We were at Chalky 'N' Joe's with Windy and Minty, waiting on Renée after a show."

"That's right! For some reason, they had a random bottle of Hunt's brand sitting out on our table. I had to go ask them for their usual Heinz."

"McPeak? Party of two?" the hostess called out.

Daniel and I stood up.

We followed her to a curtained booth. She pushed back the red velvet and said, "Your server will be right with you," before pulling the curtain closed again after we sat.

Daniel and I settled in, grinning at each other.

"Wow," I said. "I've never sat in one of these booths before."

"Me either. But I wanted something romantic."

"Do…do you think the other people here think it's weird, though?" I indicated the closed curtains. "You know, two guys in here together?"

Daniel's eyes softened. "Does that bother you?"

I peeked through the small crack in the curtain and saw that no one was even paying attention. And, to answer his question, I didn't think I'd care even if they were. I didn't want to hide. Not anymore. "No. I'm not ashamed to be with you."

"Being out is about being visible sometimes," Daniel said. "I don't want to live out our entire relationship in our houses. I want to be a couple in public, too."

I looked down at the red, cloth napkin placed just at my right hand, and I blinked. He was right; since dumping Adam and putting an end to all those secrets, I was truly, fully *out*. I chuckled. Damn, it felt good.

"I think by mentioning prom, and talking about Susan, all that old stuff came rushing back up. It made me forget for a second that I'm not hiding anymore."

Daniel reached over and touched my hand, running his fingertips over my knuckles. "It's not always easy. Sometimes it's scary."

"I know, but I want to be a couple in public with you, too," I said, turning my hand over and squeezing his fingers.

He squeezed back before pulling away and opening his menu. "I've never been here before. So which lasagna is it that you like?"

My skin tingled where his fingers had touched my hand, and I wanted to kiss the spot, or pull him across the booth and kiss his mouth instead.

"Um, I can never remember what it's called. Let me look." I

opened the menu and scanned the dishes. "I always get the spinach lasagna, but I think I'm going to stick with one of the lighter salads tonight instead."

We shared a meaningful look. Daniel cleared his throat. "I think I'll do the same."

My heart quickened.

After the waitress took our orders and brought back our drinks, Daniel sprawled on his side of the booth and sighed, dark golden lashes lowering against his cheek. "God, it's nice to be here. Not at that big, rambling house with no one there but me and Milky Way." He opened his eyes fully and smiled in a relaxed, tired way. "She was excited to see Kerri, by the way. Nearly licked her face off."

"She's such a friendly girl," I murmured. "So, I don't know if this is something you'd want to talk about tonight, but how are Paul and Kennedy doing with your grandparents? Are things getting better?" We hadn't talked about them in a while.

Daniel sighed, running a hand over the back of his neck, easing the tension that came up as soon as I'd asked the question. "They're trying to adjust. Every time I call, Kennedy wants to know when she can come home, or when I'm moving there, too. It's hard to tell her that I'm not, but I plan to see them at Thanksgiving. I've decided I'm going to fly down for that."

"That's a good idea."

"But I'm going to spend Christmas here. If everything goes to plan, I'll have closed on Bobby's house by then, and I'll be in the process of getting settled in there. I kind of thought..." He hesitated. "No pressure, but I thought it'd be fun to spend the holidays together. Get a tree. Decorate it. That sort of thing."

"I'd love that."

"One day I can have the kids up to visit. I can make up the guest room for them. But for now, I'm trying to help them understand that we're never going to live together again. This is the new reality."

"That's gotta be hard for them to hear."

"Sometimes. Paul seems happier though. My grandmother is spoiling him rotten, giving him all kinds of love and attention. I think he needed that."

"I'm sure."

"As for my mom…" He shook his head. "I don't know. If she can't stay sober, my siblings would be better off if she just stayed out of their lives. But *if* she manages it, I guess I want them to all be together." His brows dropped low, and he added, "Away from me, preferably. Too much has happened for me to want to be around my mom on a regular basis. This is probably as good as our relationship can hope to get. But the kids? Maybe they can still have better."

"At least they have that with your grandparents now."

"Yeah." Daniel leaned closer and went back to playing with my fingers before saying, "You're a good person to care about them. You don't even know them, and you don't have to ask."

"But I know you, and you love them, so of course I care. Besides, you know I haven't always been a very good person. You make me want to be better."

He took a shallow breath, his teeth biting into his lower lip a moment. "You too."

I scoffed. "How could you be better than you are? You worked with ARK and only stopped to take care of your brother and your sister; you put them first. You're there for Minty and the rest of our friends. You're there for *me*. You didn't judge me this summer when I was an idiot, and you took me back after I hurt you. Minty's right. You're perfect."

Daniel shook his head. "I'm not even close."

"Prove it."

He snorted a disbelieving laugh. "How?"

"I don't know. Just…prove you're not perfect."

"Okay, fine. I'm an asshole to my mother."

"Some would say she deserves it."

"Maybe. Or maybe no one deserves the things I've said to her in recent days. I'm a dick to her. You've seen it for yourself."

I rolled my eyes but had to concede the point.

"And then there's you."

"Me? I'm a failing of yours?"

"Hardly. But you make me realize how damaged I am." I didn't understand, and my face must have shown that, because he went on. "You make me realize how bad I am at trusting other people. I'm very good at being the responsible one, but when it comes to letting someone *else* be the responsible one? That's hard for me."

"I don't get it." I tilted my head. "You don't trust me to be responsible? What does that mean?"

"No, it means… How can I put this? I'm choosing to trust you. But it's hard. I want to trust you, and let myself love you, but I'm scared."

I put my hand out and he took my fingers.

"If I let you all the way inside…" He swallowed. "Don't get me wrong, I want to do that, but…am I making sense?"

"Of course." I did get it. Even if I didn't love what it meant. He still didn't completely trust me. "Trust has to be earned."

"But you trust *me*, even after what Adam did to you," he said. "I admire that. You just walked right back to me and let me in again."

I didn't want to bring Adam back into the conversation, but I had to clear up his idea that I was somehow a guru at the trust thing. "It wasn't like that. *You're* the one who taught me that someone can be responsible and loving. You showed me how to have high standards. You *made* me trust you by being who you are."

"And you made me decide that I had to *risk* trusting you because of who *you* are."

I laughed. "I'm glad. But, why, though? I'd understand if you didn't want to risk it with me. I've made a lot of mistakes."

"First, to be shallow, have you looked at yourself? I mean, have you looked in a mirror lately? Because you're one of the sexiest guys I've ever laid eyes on."

I remembered my naked body in the pictures Daniel had taken and felt my cheeks start heating up. "Maybe it's pheromones? Your attraction to me? Because I'm not *that* hot."

"You are that hot."

I took a sip of my soda, not sure what to say and settled on, "So are you."

"And then there's how I feel when I'm alone with you, which is the best feeling I've ever had," he said. "Maybe I should have mentioned that first instead of your looks. And maybe I *shouldn't* tell you that I'd already rather have you over just about anything else in the world." Daniel frowned. "I worry my feelings for you are so strong I'll do something we both regret."

"Like what?"

He looked away. My cheeks flooded with heat as I recalled his desperate words whenever we'd gotten off together—wanting me closer and closer, wanting to be inside me, wanting more than we could have.

I pressed on instead of demanding an answer. "So, you want me more than you think you should, and you have a bad attitude with your mother. You're a nightmare, Daniel McPeak. A total nightmare of a human being."

Daniel's lips quirked up into the smile that I already loved so much. "It doesn't make you afraid? How much I care about you already?"

I remembered how fast Adam and I had fallen for each other, the vicious need followed by sudden raw, intense emotions that we hadn't been able to control. "Isn't that how it works?"

Daniel frowned, like he was thinking it over. "I don't know. Maybe."

"For what it's worth, I think about you all the time. It's messing up my schoolwork. I sleep like crap, because I want to be at your house, in your bed. So, if wanting me like that makes you a bad person, then I'm a bad person, too." I reached out and took hold of his hand. "We can be awful people together."

"Are you sure?"

"I'm sure."

Daniel nodded and looked down at his lap for a long time. When he lifted his gaze again, his eyes were mischievous. "Now, with that out of the way... Truth or dare?"

"Seriously? Right now?"

"Yes. C'mon, choose."

I paused thinking about it. "Um, dare?"

"I knew you were a risk-taker."

I shrugged and gave him a flirtatious smile. "Go on, what do you dare me to do?"

"I dare you to tell me what you want me to do to you tonight."

I laughed. "We've gone over that a million times this week. I think you know."

"Yeah, but it's hot to hear you say it."

I bit my lip. "For a minute, I thought you were going to dare me to blow you or something."

Daniel glanced around. "Because of the curtains?"

"Isn't that the whole point of them?"

His handsome eyes crinkled at the edges. "Probably."

"Should I?" I waggled my eyebrows before lifting the tablecloth and looking beneath. "There seems to be plenty of room under the table."

Daniel sucked in a breath, and his eyes dilated even more in the low light.

The curtain drew aside, and the waitress brought in our salads, putting them down in front of us. "Any parmesan?" she asked, holding up the grater.

Daniel accepted some and I did too. We ate a few bites as she tidied the table and then, when she closed the drapes again, we started to laugh. I wasn't sure if I'd have gone through with it, or if Daniel would have wanted me to, but it'd been fun to tease and play.

After dinner, I buckled myself into the front seat of Betty Blue and waited for him to cross to the driver's side. Daniel smiled at me as he started the car and put his hand on my knee, removing it only to shift the gears.

"Excited?" he asked.

"Beyond excited," I whispered. "Edging into delirious."

"Me too." Keeping his eyes on the road, his right hand moved to my crotch, rubbing until I was so hard that I thought I'd come in my pants. He adjusted his own cock a few times, too. I kept my hands to myself, trying to pace my excitement and not distract him from driving—at least not any more than he was already distracting himself.

Even though my hands were shaking and my legs felt jittery, as we pulled into the parking lot of the downtown Hyatt, I had no doubt this was where I wanted to be. I couldn't wait to be alone and naked with him again.

This time we'd go as far as we wanted to, with nothing and no one to stop us, no memories or empty houses full of responsibilities weighing us down.

"Is this all right?" Daniel asked, peering up at the hotel. Concern tilted his mouth and brows. "I wanted to do this somewhere special. But…maybe a hotel is too impersonal?"

"Daniel, this is the nicest hotel in town."

"Well, the Radisson is nicer."

I snorted and stared up at the modern, A-shaped building. "Believe me, if this place has a bed, it's going to be just fine."

We got out of the car and Daniel pulled a key out of his wallet. "I checked in earlier before I came to get you," he said. "So, we can just go up to the room without…" He trailed off. "But if you want, we can stop by the restaurant? Get some dessert?"

We'd left Naples as soon as our fancy salads were cleared away and the bill had been paid, both of us eager to get to the hotel and make good on our plans. I grabbed hold of his hand as we walked to the entrance and said, "No way. I wanted to be naked with you ten minutes ago."

Daniel laughed and followed me into the hotel. My head went up, taking in the intricate stacking of the floors, the opulent décor of the lobby, and then I found what I was looking for: the glass elevators at the end of the lobby that would take us up to whatever room was waiting for us.

Daniel pressed nine and my stomach fluttered as the elevator lifted from the ground floor and the lobby below grew smaller below us.

"Have you ever been here before?" I asked.

Daniel shook his head. "My dad used to host important out of town clients here, but until today I'd never been inside the place. You?"

"No. It's cool."

Daniel's smile glimmered and his eyes shone. "I can't wait for you to see the room."

As we walked down the hallway, I leaned over the railing to look down, and Daniel grabbed my shirt, tugging me away from the drop. "This is us," he said, and opened the door to a big, clean room with red carpets, white duvets, fluffy pillows, and a view of the river out the wide windows.

I hadn't brought a camera with me, having anticipated being far too absorbed in getting laid to take photos, but my fingers itched for my Leica to record the room, the red roses on the table by the windows, and the gray river flowing past outside.

"This is great."

Daniel walked around the bed and turned on the bedside lamp, then hefted up his leather overnight bag, opening it. "I brought this and the flowers up when I checked in earlier," he said. He pulled out an unopened box of condoms and a new container of lube. He opened them both and tore off two condoms, putting them on the nightstand.

I swallowed, watching him reach inside and pull out two dildos—a smaller one that would be easy to take, and a thicker one that made me sweat even imagining opening up for it. Though I wasn't sure it was any bigger than Daniel's cock.

He spread a napkin open on the table beside the roses and put the toys on it.

Daniel caught my eye then and said, "I thought we might need these to make it work." He approached me and wrapped his arms around my waist.

I slid my fingers into his hair and tilted my head for a kiss. Daniel's lips were soft and damp from where he'd licked them, and his tongue slid against mine, making my nerves sing and my knees go weak.

"Besides," he breathed, breaking away to whisper in my ear. "Playing with toys can be hot."

"It can be," I agreed. "But I want to feel you inside me."

"I want that too, but tonight is about doing something special together, something intimate, and I don't want to hurt you."

"You're right. I just—" I didn't want to pressure him. "I'm excited."

Daniel's lips tilted up at the edges and then he pulled away, drawing the curtains partly closed and flipping off the lights I'd turned on when we entered. He cleared his throat and looked around the room, like he was making sure everything was flawless. "Did I miss anything?"

I closed the distance between us and took his chin in my fingers. "Yeah. This."

I kissed him, the slick heat of his mouth and tang of his tongue was perfection, and I gripped the back of his neck, tugging him in closer to get a better taste. His hands scrabbled at the fastening of my jeans, wrenching the button free and being a little more careful with the zipper.

I undid a few buttons of his shirt and then pushed the bottom up, pulling back enough to yank it over his head and off his arms, and then I threw it somewhere behind me to the floor. For his part, Daniel got us both naked with my enthusiastic help, kissing me the whole time like I was oxygen, and he was starved for it.

His hands gripped my hips as he moved me backward. I held his face in both hands and kissed him hard. Feeling the edge of the mattress and the softness of the duvet brush against the back of my knees, I fell onto it, dragging Daniel down on top of me.

"Fuck, Peter," Daniel muttered against my mouth, rolling his hips, and digging his dick into my abdomen. My own dick strained up toward him. "Gotta get you ready before I come and ruin it."

"S'okay if you come," I said, panting and grabbing his ass, pulling him down hard against me and squirming under him. "We have all night, don't we?"

"Yeah. Yeah, we do." Still, he knelt up, and I reached to grab him back down, but he rolled onto his back. "Get your dick up here, please. I want to suck you off."

My heart pounded in my throat as I positioned myself with my achingly hard cock over his face and leaned forward to take what I could of his dick into my hand and mouth.

"Get me wet," he whispered as I licked the pre-cum that had already surged up to bead on the crown.

I studied the head, followed by the even thicker width of his penis behind it. I didn't know how many guys had cocks shaped like Daniel's, but I didn't think it was common for the head to be smaller than the entire shaft.

I opened my mouth and slid down as far as I could, the pressure against the side of my lips growing uncomfortable. I slurped up to kiss his cockhead, and he took my cue, sucking me hard and fast. Almost immediately, he brought me to the brink of orgasm with his intense, focused deepthroating.

"Daniel!" I warned, but he just slid his hands over my ass cheeks, separating them and rubbing a spit-slicked finger over my hole.

As he prodded my rim, I gripped his cock hard, threw back my head, and cried out as I unloaded into his mouth. It was fast and primal, and the orgasm left me weak, but I didn't have time to think about that.

As soon as I'd stopped spurting into Daniel's mouth, he released my cock and flipped me over onto my back, reversing our positions. While I was still gasping in shock from the sudden about-face, he moved to kneel between my legs. With a growl, he gripped the back of my thighs and pushed them up to my chest, burying his face between my ass cheeks.

"Fuck," I cursed, as he rimmed me hard.

Daniel went to work on my anus with his tongue and teeth, which should have hurt, but instead sent sharp jolts of amazing pleasure up my spine. That's when it hit me: Daniel wasn't just licking me for fun but working to prepare my ass to be fucked. My cock jerked back to life, rushing with blood and growing tight again. I reached down and squeezed myself.

"That's it," Daniel muttered, pressing a rough, sucking kiss to the muscled, fleshy part of my ass cheek. "You're already hard again. Christ, Peter."

My anus fluttered and flexed under his ministrations, and then two of his fingers pressed against me.

"Come on," he whispered before kissing my inner thigh. He moaned in appreciation as I bore down and took his fingers in. "Damn, Peter, you're so sweet and tight. I have no idea how this is going to work tonight."

"It'll work," I gasped, willing my sphincter to relax and release.

Daniel kissed my inner thigh again before reaching for the lube on the nightstand. After coating his fingers and drizzling some of the cool liquid on my asshole, he started to finger-fuck me for real. The pressure and intensity he used to stretch and work me open soon had me moaning. And when he jammed his tongue into the small gap his fingers left behind, I used my fist to muffle my loud noises.

My hard dick throbbed against my stomach, and I jerked it slowly. Ticklish streaks of pre-cum slid down the sides of my dick and slicked my palm.

Daniel's fingers found and exploited my prostate until I was sweating and dizzy with sensation. It shimmered through my whole self in an endless ramping up that didn't quite go as high as I needed to climax. I squirmed on his fingers and edged close to orgasm and back several times. Finally, unable to take it anymore, I choked out, "Fuck me please, Daniel. I'm not a virgin. I can take it."

Daniel's response was to kiss my inner thigh and say, "Quiet. You're still too tight."

He did, however, pull his fingers free and sit up. I drew my knees up even tighter to my chest, exposing my spit-slick asshole, hoping he'd take the hint. Daniel studied my face, looking for something, his brows slightly furrowed. Finally, I whispered, "I'm not too tight. I can take it. Please, Daniel."

He glanced toward the table with the dildos on it, and then back down at my asshole. I knew what he was considering, and I didn't want that. I shook my head. His eyes flashed hot as he leaned over—the long line of his back, ass, and thighs on display—to grab a condom from the nightstand. He fell to the bed beside me, reclining on his back, and handed the condom over.

"Put it on me." He gestured toward the tube on the bed. "Lube it up and lube yourself. Then you get on top. You control it."

Lust-addled and shaking with need, I got onto my knees and managed to roll the condom onto his dick. After I'd put a lot of lube on both it and my asshole, I straddled him. Daniel held his cock steady for me to lower myself onto it, gazing up at me with hot, gleaming eyes.

Just as I was in position, I froze with his cockhead pressed against my asshole, a thought holding me still: I'd only been fucked by Adam, only *he* had ever been inside me this way. Thinking of Adam right now was the last thing I wanted, but I was acutely aware of how he'd feel about what I was doing. He'd be devastated. He was so possessive. So jealous. I could still see his eyes burning into me from across Hanna's, full of rage and jealousy.

Fuck, I didn't need these thoughts right now.

My anxiety must have shown because Daniel put one trembling hand on my hip and said, "Hey, we don't have to do this."

"I want to."

"Are you sure?"

I gazed down at Daniel's face and took a few deep breaths, banishing Adam once again. I peered into Daniel's clear brown eyes, shining up at me with so much want and affection, maybe even with love. "I'm sure."

"You okay?" he whispered.

"Yeah. I'm fine. You're really damn big. I got nervous."

"We could work you open more first? We can be patient."

"Not me. I want to do this now." I pushed down and felt the tip of his cock stretch me. I closed my eyes, put my head back, and concentrated on opening up for him.

"Oh, *fuck*, baby," he muttered, voice tight and rough.

He was huge. The crown of his cock felt like it wasn't going to go in for a moment, and then I took a deep breath and *bore down*. The burn ran up my spine to my eyes. I kept them shut, squeezing them against the rush of shocked, stinging tears.

God, he was big. The head of his cock was in, and I breathed in and out shallowly, trying to keep it together, while my ass gripped and released around him. My heartbeat pounded, and I felt it pulse in the tight stretch of my asshole around his girth. Once again, I broke into a fresh sweat. The biggest part was still to come.

"Take it easy," Daniel whispered, his hands rubbing my thighs. "Not a virgin. But I bet you're feeling like one right now." His joke made me laugh, which kind of hurt, but also let me slide down on his cock a bit more.

"It's okay, Peter. Take your time." Daniel's voice was strained, and I could sense the tension in his hips as he struggled not to thrust up and just bury himself in me.

It *did* feel strangely like the first time. I was too vulnerable, a little insecure, and I felt like he was opening me up in ways I'd never been opened before. The resistance of my asshole was hard to get past, and I lifted until he popped out.

"Want a break?" he asked. "I can get the dildo and—"

I shook my head, positioned his cock again and pushed down onto it. This time it went in easier, though my ass stubbornly refused to let me slide down more than a few inches, tightening on him hard. Daniel's breath came in fast pants as he rubbed my ass cheeks, loosening my muscles there.

I sweated and moved my hips in slow circles, breathing in and out, lost already in a hum of sensation. He didn't thrust at all, just stayed there, poised in rigid want, until I could slide down a little more.

I forced another deep breath, trying to relax against the size of the intrusion, trembling nonstop. My own cock had gone flaccid, and I didn't care. The sensation at my hole was all-consuming. I took him in slowly, lifting and lowering myself in long drags, each ending with me bearing down to take more of his dick, feeling like I was on the razor's edge of a whole other continent of pleasure.

I hadn't known what to expect our first time. Maybe something softer, sweeter, and more like our other encounters, but this was perfect. Me, determined to take him in, and Daniel letting me work out my needs on my own—slow, easy, and hot as hell.

Daniel moaned and whimpered, talking to me through gritted teeth. His fingers dug into my hips and thighs, hard enough I knew I'd have bruises. I didn't care. Seeing him trying to hold back, seeing him trying to be a good, patient lover for me and almost failing was incredible. "Fuck, *Peter*, oh, fuck…this…you're… Baby, oh my *God*."

One of his hands drifted from my thigh to work my soft cock. It rose into hardness between us as I rode him up and down.

When I felt his pubic hair tickling my ass, I knew I was almost flush against him. I paused, feeling unbelievably full, my asshole stretched tighter than it had *ever* been, and marveling at the pressure on my prostate—still so intense without me even having to move.

"Fuck," I whispered, eyes squeezed tight, taking in how extremely and thoroughly full of Daniel I was. "*Fuck*."

Daniel was patient a little longer, letting me just feel him inside, until it seemed he couldn't take it another moment. "I need to move now, baby," he said, desperation in his voice. "Is that all right?"

"Gentle," I whispered, still afraid to open my eyes.

"Just…gentle."

He shifted up, and I felt myself stretch just a *little* more, taking the full length of him, feeling the scratch of his pubic hair press tight against my ass. My nipples ached, and my cock pulsed between us.

"Good?" he asked.

"Yesssss," I hissed.

And then came the slow drag out as he used his hands on my hips to lift me up and off him. My head fell back, and my breath came in near sobbing hiccups.

"Oh, oh, *oh*…" I shuddered as he slid out of me until I felt my gaping hole tighten around the head of his cock like a kiss. He pushed me down again, sliding back in with a gentle, sure stroke that stretched me open wide. My nerves roared and my hips strained as the pressure against my prostate grew and grew and *grew*. I let my head drop back again.

Daniel stilled. "Am I hurting you? Are you okay?"

I nodded, afraid to speak, my breath coming in hitches and starts.

It was too much, too *good*, and I felt like he'd opened me up, shown me something I hadn't known existed before, and I didn't know why. I didn't understand why I was reacting like this. I wasn't a virgin. I wasn't *supposed* to respond like this.

"Too intense?"

I flashed back to my first time. Adam saying, "It can be intense. I know." I bit down on my lip to keep from nodding. The sensation *was* too intense, but not in the same way as that first time, and what I felt was totally different. I didn't want it to stop.

"Peter, look at me." Daniel had paused mid-thrust, his hips taut and tense.

I did as he asked, gazing down at Daniel's face. His warm brown eyes peered up with affectionate intensity, and I was caught in them. Safe. Whole. Seen. Adored. Bright heat flared in my chest and grew in my groin, as I pushed down and took him in again.

"Is it good?" I asked him, though I knew the answer from the wonder in his eyes and the flush of his cheeks, the way his breath came in stutters and his cock throbbed against my stretched hole, threatening to erupt.

"So good, baby," he whispered. "Holy shit, better than I ever thought it could be." His fingers shook as he reached up and brought me down close to him, changing the angle of his cock in my ass, making it hit my prostate even harder.

I whimpered as I rubbed my cheek against his, nuzzled his neck, and then brushed my lips against his.

"Wanted you like this for so long. Worth waiting for," he murmured before kissing me.

The heat of his mouth, the intensity of our joining, it melted me, and I clung to him as he lifted his hips, fucking into me with slow, steady thrusts that made my eyes roll up, and my cock spurt pre-cum between us.

When I broke the kiss to sit upright again, I kept my eyes on his. His pupils were dilated, and his irises had softened. He was so beautiful, and my heart ached with tenderness for him.

"Daniel," I murmured, my nipples taut, feeling so full of him, and needing even more.

"Mm?"

"I love you," I whispered. It was cliché and maybe the worst time to declare myself in some ways, but in others it was perfect. I couldn't hold back. Not when I was stretched out on him and shaking like a leaf, alive and full of electric feeling.

"I love you," I said again, curling over him. I buried my face in his sweet-smelling neck. His hands moved desperately over my back and hips, his dick growing even stiffer inside me.

"Peter," he groaned. "Fuck."

I squeezed around him, and he quivered. "I love you," I whispered in his ear, not because I wanted him to say it back, but because now that I'd said it, I couldn't seem to stop. I needed him to know. I needed him to accept my heart. "I love you," I murmured. "I *love* you."

"Peter," he said, smoothing his hands up and down my back. "I love you too."

I groaned and sat back, needing to see his eyes. "Tell me," I demanded.

He took hold of my hands, holding them between us, and then pressed them to his chest where his heart pounded madly. "I love you."

I fell down over him again, kissing his throat, his collarbones, and his ears.

"God," he groaned, taking hold of my ass and plunging up into me. "Fuck, baby. Just…*fuck*."

His breath rose and fell with mine and his heartbeat vibrated against my chest, answered by the thunder of blood rushing in my ears.

"That's it, Peter. So good. You're so fucking gorgeous." He slid his hands between our bodies, rubbing and squeezing my dick and balls. I moaned, the sensation too much with him so big in my ass, and I pushed his hands away, shaking my head, but unable to utter any words as I hovered close to orgasm.

"It's all right," he whispered, gripping my ass cheeks and squeezing slightly, while grinding up into my hole. The pressure on my prostate grew more and more overwhelming, until I felt like I was going to burst into a dazzle of light and stars from the jolts of ecstasy coming from there.

I hung on the edge of coming for so long that I grew desperate, shifting every which way on his cock, whining, and finally just riding him as hard as I could, feeling turned inside out and strung out on urgent need.

I couldn't hold off another second.

"That's it," Daniel whispered. "Come for me."

I jolted, muscles seizing as I cried out. Heat roared through me. Sweat broke over my body. My eyes rolled back as ecstasy claimed me, and I surrendered to it blindly, spurting hard and rough. "Daniel," I moaned, dragging my gaze back to his hot, desperate eyes for a dizzy moment. I ran my fingers through the white streaks of my cum splashed all over Daniel's heaving chest and trembling stomach. I pressed the mess I'd collected to his lips, and he sucked my fingers clean with a hot, hungry tongue. I groaned and shuddered again, an aftershock rocking me.

"Yes, Peter. God, yes." Daniel's eyes glowed with lust as he grabbed my hips, thrust into me, and cried out, jerking again and again as he came. His eyes screwed closed, and his lips trembled as he whispered, "Fucking hell, that's so good, baby. This…you…I need you."

I clung to him, sweaty and panting. I needed him too.

Daniel stayed buried in me as long as he could. I shook on top of him, impaled on his thickness, and then hunched over, breathing in the sweaty scent of his neck. Moments later, after pulling out and removing the condom, Daniel tugged me close and held me tight. He whispered again and again, "I love you," between still-fevered kisses. My skin sang as I lay on my back beside him, my legs still shaking from the intense orgasm.

Once he'd caught his breath, Daniel disposed of the condom in the trash can by the bed and cleaned us up. Given that I'd douched before leaving the house, that wasn't as bad as it could have been. Sitting down beside me, he ran his hand over my hair, boinged a curl, and traced my mouth with his thumb. His brows knitted together, as he asked, "You okay?"

I gazed up at him, shuddering with aftershocks of shattering pleasure. Laughter bubbled up, and I curled into his arms, trembling against his warmth.

Daniel said, tentatively, "I think that's a yes?"

I nodded and then kissed his neck and shoulders, kissed his collarbones and his Adam's apple and his chin. "Yes," I huffed against him. "Yes, I'm fine. No. Amazing. No. Awesome *and* amazing, and more words like that."

Daniel grinned. "You're not sore?"

"Don't worry."

My ass did feel a little used—more than a little—but it'd been more than worth it. I wanted to do it again, for a longer time, though I wasn't sure how I could handle that kind of prostate stimulation for much longer than I had. At the end, just before I came, I'd felt like I was going to break apart.

"That was amazing," he whispered. "Being with you. Touching you. Feeling you from the inside. Watching you."

"Mmm," I couldn't say more than that.

"You're sure you're okay?"

"Yeah." I shifted and grimaced. "My asshole's a little achy, but I think it's fine."

"Let me see it."

I waved his concern off and slipped my arms around his neck, rubbing my cheek against his. "Just hold me."

Daniel's hand crept down my back, slipped between my ass cheeks and touched my asshole, prodding it with the pads of his fingers. "You feel okay. A little open, still, but okay." He nuzzled me and pulled me close. "Peter, thank you."

"For what?"

He went hot all over, a full-body blush. "You know…for…letting me. Thank you."

"You're welcome. I mean, I liked it too, you know."

He chuckled. "I'm just grateful to be here with you. Thank

you."

A silly smile spread over my face, and I kissed him.

"And I really love you." He sounded gruff, like he was choked up.

I kissed his nose. "I love you too." I kissed his chin. "Thank you for making tonight special."

"I could have done a better job. I'd planned to. I was going to give you a massage and draw out the foreplay, but…"

I kissed him again. "I liked it like this. I didn't want to wait any longer."

He snorted and, after a few moments of contented silence between us, I slipped my arms around his neck and toyed with the hair at the back of his head. "If that offer of a massage is still on the table, I wouldn't object. I've never had one."

"Really?"

"Nope."

"Not even from—"

I put my hand over his mouth. "Nope."

Daniel waggled his eyebrows and sat up, his skin still glistening with drying sweat. "Well, then, let me show you what you've been missing." He laced his fingers together, stretching his arms out and cracking his knuckles. "You'll love it."

I rolled onto my stomach, ignoring the wet, slimy places on the sheets where our cum had landed, moaning when Daniel sat on my ass and started to work on the tight spots in my shoulders.

Before long, I took him inside me again. I rested on my side as he thrust in from behind, holding me close and kissing my neck. It wasn't long before I was sweating, half-sobbing, and begging for release. He jerked me off this time, too, and the dual sensations of his hand on my cock and his cock in my ass were mind-blowing. When I came again, I cried out against the safety of his palm over my mouth, trying to keep quiet as I shattered with pleasure.

Afterwards, we rested and called room service. Daniel even ordered champagne, but we just drank one glass each before we started kissing again. Beard burn grew between us, and we got hard again. This time he rolled over onto his back for me. There was no hesitation, no resistance or angst like there had been with Adam.

I pushed into Daniel with more ease than he'd pushed into me. And when it was over, he held me, shaking in my arms, cum smeared all over his front from where he'd come before I had. I felt an unbelievable pride and affection suffuse me from head to toe at the evidence that he'd enjoyed me fucking him too.

"I love you," I whispered, after I'd disposed of the condom, and pulled him in to cuddle. "Did you like it?"

"I loved it," he whispered, still trembling. "Did you like it?"

I grinned. "Yeah, it was incredible."

He rolled over, touching my face and drawing me in for a kiss. "Why do I sense a 'but' at the end of that sentence?"

I kissed him again before answering. "I do want to do it again, but…"

"Go on."

"I think I like you inside me best of all."

Daniel grinned and kissed my jaw and the edge of my ear. "Anything that makes you happy, baby, I'm up for it. Anything at all."

And I believed it was true. I had no doubt. I even thought that one day, far in the future, when it had been just the two of us for long enough that trust was second nature, that maybe…just maybe…we could make Daniel's deepest wishes come true.

Because the thought of having him even that much closer, raw and real inside me? That was the most beautiful thing I could imagine, and I yearned for it in a way I never had before. I wanted to give Daniel that experience one day. I wanted us both to have it.

We deserved it.

✧   ✧   ✧

THE NEXT DAY we checked out and drove into the midmorning sun, our faces covered in beard burn and goofy smiles. Daniel held my hand as he urged Betty Blue forward onto the highway, pointing the car toward my house.

Daniel needed to pick up Milky Way from Kerri's place before noon. I didn't have to go into work, and could have gone along with him, but I was behind on several assignments for school, and I also felt woozy with exhaustion after our long night.

The silence between us was easy, and I relaxed into it. He turned on the car's built-in CD player and the opening notes of "Only You" started up. I grinned.

"This is our song, right?" I asked.

"Yeah," he agreed. "Only you."

"Yeah, only you," I agreed.

He squeezed my fingers before putting his hand back on the wheel to get a little more control as he maneuvered around a slower car. My mind wandered, and I came back to a question I'd been pondering for a while now ever since Daniel had brought it up.

"So, I think I might do it," I said. "I think I'm going to contact Harold Seville."

"Yeah?"

"I'd like to know more about my uncle, and Harold's a great photographer, too. I'd like to hear his story if he's willing to share it with me."

"I think that could mean a lot to him, too."

"What's the worst that can happen? He ignores me or tells me he doesn't want to meet."

He glanced my way and then back at the road. "What about your mom? Before, you thought you'd have to tell her about it, do you still think that's the way to go?"

"I don't know. Probably not. I could meet him on my own—or

with you there—and not involve her. Unless he's great, and I think it will help her in some way to meet him, then maybe I'd push for that. Otherwise, this can just be for me—and maybe for him."

"When do you think you'll do it?"

"I think the best thing to do is to write a letter to him explaining who I am. So, I'll start there. See what comes of it."

Daniel nodded.

That night, my mom and dad didn't resist heckling me about the beard burns on my face. After my mom's third attempt to give me burn cream, I stomped upstairs to avoid their embarrassing commentary.

I retrieved *Robin* from where I'd put it on the top shelf in my closet. I knew my mom wasn't snoopy, but I didn't want her stumbling on these photos by accident, so I'd hidden the book just in case.

I started reading it again from the beginning. It was a typical photography book for the most part, but the small write-ups Harold had done about George had all been executed with such loving care. I touched the words on each page, trying to absorb them through my fingertips.

The photos were gorgeous too. I wanted to take some of Daniel inspired by Harold's style. I wanted to capture the way Daniel laughed, the way he smiled when he was feeling shy, and the beautiful lines of his body. I hadn't been using the camera as often when I was with him. I'd told myself that, when it came to love, I wasn't as interested in living behind the lens anymore as I was in *living*. But maybe I'd given up something, too, by adopting that motto too fiercely.

I didn't want to miss my chance at putting together a group of pictures that could rival *Robin* with their devotion to documenting my feelings for and about Daniel. The purity of them, the lack of darkness. In the past, I'd used the camera to capture my despair, my shame, my self-loathing.

I now needed to make sure to capture the entirety of my joy, my love, my self-acceptance. My Daniel.

I got up from my desk, picked up the Minolta and filled it with new film. At the next opportunity, I'd train my lens on Daniel to capture the way he made my heart swoop and soar.

Chapter Twenty-Five

"SO, DANIEL, WHAT do your parents do?" my dad asked, and the mood around the previously jovial kitchen table dampened.

"Uh, Dad," I said, around a mouthful of chicken fried rice, using my fork to make slashing motions while shaking my head.

"What? Did I ask the wrong thing?" Dad's confused expression was as innocent as it was annoying. Why hadn't I told them about Daniel's parents in advance? I'd been too busy saying over and over, "He's great, so don't embarrass me." But look at that, I'd embarrassed myself by not thinking ahead.

"It's okay," Daniel said, wiping his mouth with his napkin before meeting my dad's eyes. "My father died during my freshman year of college, and my mom is…" He met my gaze for a moment and then went for it. "My mom's in rehab right now."

"Holy Mary of Blessings," Dad muttered. "Look at me putting my foot in my mouth like an idiot." He shot me a look that read, "Why didn't you tell us?" but it was too late now, so I shrugged and reached out to take Daniel's hand.

"In rehab?" Mom asked, glancing at the glass of red wine to the left of Daniel's hand. She'd poured it for him when she'd poured a glass for herself. She'd denied me any since I was still underage, but Daniel was twenty-two and legal. "For what?"

"Mom, that's rude," I interjected, just as Daniel said, "Alcohol."

"*Mom*," I said again, under my breath.

"It's okay, Peter," Daniel said, putting his hand over mine. "I don't intend to keep secrets from your parents."

He covered the facts of the situation: his father's death, the company, how he'd changed his mind about taking it over, his mom going to rehab, the kids moving to Florida, the sale of the house, and his intention to buy Bobby's old place. It was a long story, so it took most of the rest of the meal, even though he cut out most of the details.

By the time he'd finished, my father was nodding his head and my mother seemed less worried. I wasn't at all surprised that they liked him, but it was clear to me that neither of them was as charmed by Daniel as they'd been by Adam. I'd both feared that and hoped for it in equal measure. Now that I had evidence, though, I didn't know how to feel.

My parents had adored Adam, but they'd been fooled by his façade, the wonderful, shiny, amazing person Adam pretended to be, while being blind to and shielded from the darkness that he lived in and had dragged me into as well. They knew about it all now, but I could tell they still missed Adam's shine. Daniel was prosaic in comparison.

This was confirmed for me after I'd walked Daniel out to the car, kissed him in the moonlight, and sent him on his way to deal with Milky Way. He had to get up early the next morning to meet the first set of movers, who'd be taking most of his mother's things to be put into storage before they would be shipped to Florida in November.

Back in the house, Dad wiped down some dishes, and Mom sipped wine while chewing a string of cheese.

"So," I said, deciding to get it over with. "That was Daniel. You wanted to meet him, and now you have."

"He's nice," Mom said, peering at me with her dark eyes.

"Didn't you think so, Abe?"

"Quite nice," Dad agreed.

"*But…*" I prompted, crossing my arms over my chest. "I know you have one, so out with it."

"But nothing," Dad objected. "He's a great young man who seems to have your best interests at heart. What could we be worried about?" He gave my mom a stern glance, which told me everything.

"Okay, then," I said to her. "What about you? What's your 'but?'"

"I just think he's not quite as special as Adam, honey. And you deserve special, don't you think?"

I snorted. "He's *so* much more special than Adam."

Mom sighed. "It's possible you're blinded by the newness of—"

"That's just it. I'm not blinded at all. Adam was, and is, an asshole. You've said it yourself. You hang up on him when he calls. He hurt me—emotionally and physically—and you *know* that. How can you say Daniel's not as special as Adam? Do you want me with someone who treats me like crap?"

"Of course not!" she exclaimed. "I'm happy you're out of that mess. I agree. Adam had me and your father fooled for a very long time. But I just wonder if this Daniel has what it takes to keep your interest. He wants to be a nurse? That's not very creative. You're an artist! You're more interested in artistic men."

"Nursing is very creative," I countered. "And I know what kind of man I like."

"But he's got so much family baggage, honey. Maybe it'd be better to wait and—"

"Jessica, your son is nineteen years old," my dad interrupted. "Let him date who he wants. You certainly did at his age."

She swirled her glass of wine before taking another sip. "I'm not saying you shouldn't date him. I'm just saying don't let it go too far.

He's the kind of guy who gets serious fast. He'll want you to move in with him before too long. I don't want you getting hurt or hurting someone else just because you're on the rebound after—"

"This is not a rebound situation," I bit out. "I love him."

Mom shot Dad a glance and raised her hands in surrender. "All right, you love him. That's fine. You're young and—"

"Daniel is the best person I've ever met. He's always trying to do what's right. He might not be as charming as Adam, and his love might be less of a roller-coaster ride, but I'm happy when I'm with him. I like who *I* am when I'm with him. And I'm sorry if you think I need 'more' than that in some indefinable way." Rage pricked my heart.

"I just think you don't have the chemistry you and Adam—"

"You're not there when we're alone together. You don't know what it's like."

She put her hands up again, and Dad sighed when I met his gaze. "What? Do you agree with her?"

"No, son, I think you're happy, and I liked him very much. Who am I to have an opinion other than that? I made an error in trusting Adam, but I *do* trust you. If you're happy, then I'm happy." He lifted his brows at my mom.

"Your father's right, of course," she said. "I've been writing romance books for too long. Just because I don't see a spark—"

"I *feel* a spark," I said, sighing. "I'm happier than I have been in a long time, and I don't know why you can't see that."

"He's a nice young man," Mom said. "I'll say no more."

But her words rankled all the same.

I'd always tried to keep myself from playing the comparison game in my head, but that night I climbed into my bed with *Robin* and another one of Harold Seville's books of portraits. I compared the pictures he'd taken of George to the ones he'd taken of other men—other lovers.

There were differences, of course, but who could say if one set of pictures was better than another? The existence of an entire book dedicated to just George did say something, but the publication was after George's death. For all I knew it was only put out because he was gone, whereas the other men...

I got out of bed and went to my files. I pulled out the few photos and all the negatives I'd kept of Adam, as well as the Jobar's negative viewer I'd gotten for my birthday. I looked at the handful of photos I'd decided were worth keeping months ago, and, one by one, tossed them into the trash. Viewing the illuminated negatives through the Jobar's magnifying glass was like a punch in the gut, and, at the same time, like observing something from a dream.

This smiling Adam, that laughing Adam, almost didn't seem real. As if I'd made him up. This boy couldn't be reconciled with the liar I knew him to be, or the rageful, jealous dick I'd seen at the restaurant, or the desperate, miserable person who'd followed me in the car not even a full month ago.

I got out the files that held the photos I'd taken of myself during senior year, most with timers and some with mirrors. They were ghastly. I was too thin, with sad eyes and a nervous tension throughout my body. I remembered Dr. Landry telling me it was clear from some of these photos that I understood what it might be like to kill off the poetry in your soul. And that had been on Adam—well, on both of us. Our choices, the way we lived and lied. The poetry in me had almost died from all that filth.

But it hadn't.

I pulled out my files of Daniel. The most recent ones, taken three days after our night at the hotel, were gorgeous. A smile spread over my face as I gazed at them. I'd taken them by the river next to his house as the sun was coming down, and he'd agreed to let me photograph every part of him. He was naked, coated in coral light, and as relaxed as the water rippling behind him.

I'd also taken pictures of him with his clothes on, looking rumpled but easygoing, and calm in a way that always made my heart unclench.

If Mom didn't see what I saw, that was fine. She didn't need to.

Daniel was beautiful, inside and out, and being with him didn't make me feel like I needed to take photos of myself curled up in corners of abandoned buildings, or haunted and alone in mirrors, documenting love bites from a guy who would never love me in public.

I took out my latest set of self-portraits, taken the day after the hotel, and I gazed at them. I was relaxed, casual, and my eyes glinted with joy. I was a whole person in them, and maybe that wasn't as interesting, as edgy or intense, but it was just as real. More importantly, it didn't *hurt*.

The last pictures I looked over were ones I'd taken using a timer and a well-placed camera on the bookshelf by Daniel's bed. They were erotic, and once again I was grateful to Marta for her tips on when to sign up for darkroom times. I needed that access to develop these private, intimate pictures.

In the photos, I was on my back, legs spread, with Daniel over me. I'd loaded the camera with a thirty-six-count roll of 400 speed film and set it on autofocus with a click rate of every minute. The results were beautiful.

Me taking Daniel in, face twisted up with ecstasy and lust, and Daniel, holding me open, moving into me—the gradual escalation, the raw passion as he drove into me near the end, the way my toes curled, the vulnerability in my eyes as he'd taken me to climax. It all added up to plenty of chemistry, and it was all there in picture-proof for me to relive over and over.

Some might call it pornographic, but it was too beautiful for that.

I took one photo with me back to the bed, holding it as I contemplated my mother's assessment.

If the last year had taught me anything, it was that truth was more important than other people's opinions. And the truth was Daniel did *this* to me, he made me come undone, and afterward he made me dinner and told me he loved me and was, without a doubt, faithful and devoted.

I trusted him with my heart and my soul. That was something I'd never had with Adam.

Rolling onto my back, I stared up at my ceiling and let myself wonder, for just one moment, where Adam was and what he was doing, how he was feeling, and then I let him go again.

It didn't matter. I was here without him, and I was glad to be. I had my Robin, my George. My Daniel.

I got out of bed, pulled out a sheet of paper, and began to write a letter to Harold. When I was done, I sealed it into a plain white envelope and wrote out the address I'd uncovered during some downtime in the library the week before. My writing was neat. My hand and heart steady. The next morning, I stuck a stamp on an envelope, and shoved it into the mailbox alongside a letter from Mom to her editor.

Time would tell what would come of it. For now, I was satisfied I'd done my part.

Chapter Twenty-Six

THE SLIDE WAS every bit as gay and glorious as it had been when we'd first seen it over the summer. But now Renée was a headline act, and we, as her friends, were being treated like VIPs.

The theme for the night was *Costume Party–Halloween 1991*. The holiday had technically been the day before, but partying on a Friday was always preferable. Daniel was dressed as the song "Smooth Criminal," wearing a cream-colored suit found at Repeat After Me, a matching tie and fedora found in his father's old things, and a blue button-up. On the back of the suit jacket, I'd sewn the lyrics "Annie, Are You Okay?" in silver sequins, the skills I'd acquired by working for Robert/Renée coming in handy for once.

I was dressed as Andy Warhol. I'd put white hair spray in my hair—which just made me look gray—used my mom's dark eye makeup to make my cheeks look hollower, kept on my glasses, and wore a cream-colored turtleneck over black jeans. Most people seemed to think I was a yuppie ghost, but I didn't mind.

As for the gang, Antonio was dressed as a surgeon, in a cap and scrubs he'd borrowed from his older brother. Windy was dressed in a skeleton suit, and Barry wore his old cruise-ship uniform with a captain's hat.

Minty was there, too, and in surprisingly good spirits. The best mood I'd seen him in since before his diagnosis. He was dressed as Raggedy Ann, which surprised me since he so often enjoyed looking pretty. But with a red yarn wig and a homespun dress, he looked cute instead. A lot of the guys seemed to want to shake him like a rag doll, too, but, in another oddity, he wasn't even trying to pick up anyone. He stuck with me and Daniel when he wasn't dancing with Antonio or Windy.

Daniel and I were happy to have him around, but we were too caught up in each other to be the best company. Dancing together, kissing, surrounded by other queer men, it was wonderful. No tension existed between us. We didn't need to hold back. I wasn't fighting my feelings. He wasn't keeping me at arm's length. We were in love, and everyone around us knew it.

We'd arrived later than everyone else, so we hadn't seen Robert or Renée before the show. I'd heard she'd made a few changes, and I couldn't wait to see what they were.

When the time came for Renée's act, Barry sought us all out and brought us to a table near the stage. We were going to be up close and personal with Renée's shaking ass. In the few minutes we had left, Daniel fetched beers for us both, and as the music began, we took each other's hands, ready to be dazzled.

Renée looked amazing in her shimmering, silky dress for the opening number. As always, I marveled at the way she managed to make everything look so smooth and her chest seem so natural. Her crowd work had always been good, but it'd gotten even better, and soon she had everyone dancing, stuffing dollars into her bosom, and calling out adoration for her.

Then the chair came out.

Whistles and screams erupted.

The Naughty Boy routine. I turned to Minty, expecting him to climb onto the stage. He generally loved being the naughty boy for Renée. But he stayed still, sipping his non-alcoholic ginger beer.

"Tonight, my babies, I have some very special guests in attendance."

Applause broke out like that was the most fantastic news they'd heard all night.

"And one of those guests is going to be my naughty boy." She grinned. "Or at least I hope he is."

I looked around the table. Was it Windy? Surely it wasn't Daniel? Barry, maybe? Though I'd never known him to participate in one of Renée's performances.

"My very own Sweetie. Peter, come on up."

I choked on my beer. Daniel patted me on the back. I shook my head and slashed at my neck. What was she up to?

"Peter! Peter! Peter!" the crowd shouted, whistling and stomping the more I delayed.

"If you don't want to go up, you don't have to," Daniel shouted in my ear over the ruckus. "I don't know what she's playing at."

I met Renée's gaze, and she beckoned to me. "Don't be scared, Sweetie. You trust me, don't you?"

I narrowed my eyes at her, a flare of annoyance rising in me. I hated being put on the spot, and I'd never agreed to this. I didn't even want to.

"Go on, Peter," Minty urged. "Don't be a pussy about it."

Barry's brows were up as he looked between me and his woman. He shook his head at her scoldingly.

"Peter! Peter! Whoo, whoo!"

I groaned and rose, heading toward the stairs that led up to the stage. Hands helped me along with pushes and pats. As I reached Renée, she sat on the chair and patted her lap.

"Bend over," she commanded.

I shook my head.

The crowd booed and shouted encouragement both.

"You need your spanking," she said, eyes twinkling. "Rumor has it, you've been a very naughty boy."

I reached out for the mic she held in her left hand. Tilting her head, she handed it to me. Sweating, I flashed back to being on the stage at Kingsley, preparing to give my dull-but-adequate speech on my photography. I tried to summon the courage of Millar instead.

"I don't need a spanking," I said into the mic, gazing first at Renée and then out into the audience. "Because I haven't done anything wrong. I'm gay, and I like dick, and I'm in love with a guy, yeah. But I won't be spanked for that. I'm not ashamed."

The room had gone quiet as I spoke, but as soon as I handed the mic back to Renée, the room exploded with shouts. Renée stood and applauded as well. "Well, well, look at that. My Sweetie is taking after his boyfriend in the best way."

"How's that?" Minty yelled. "Being a party pooper?"

The crowd laughed.

"Being self-righteous?" Antonio shouted.

Renée shook her mic at him, and I flipped them both off. "By showing us all what it looks like to be a brave, out, queer man." She looked me up and down. "In a terribly ugly Halloween costume. What are you even supposed to be, baby?"

I leaned in so the mic caught my words. "Andy Warhol."

"Well, baby, this was your fifteen minutes—" she pretended to glance at a watch, "—no, make that three minutes of fame. You have twelve minutes left over for some other time in the future. Take a bow."

I obeyed.

The audience clapped and hollered.

Once they'd quieted, Renée said, "Now, who wants to get their ass busted?"

The number of volunteers was enormous, hands swinging in the air, and shouts of "me, me, me" coming louder than the chant of my name had been.

By the time I was seated by Daniel again, she'd chosen a twink with sparkling dark eyes and a pert bottom.

She proceeded to spank him while shouting out her usual pejoratives, until he was biting his lip, near tears. The crowd roared. The room shivered with energy and excitement. She looked at me, raised her hand, and ended her performance with, "This one is because you're not as proud as Peter."

Slap.

Part XII

November 1991

Chapter Twenty-Seven

DANIEL AND I fell into an easy, happy routine. Sunday through Friday I stayed at my folks' house, and he came to campus twice a week to hang out with me over lunch or to read next to me while I studied.

On Saturdays, though, I went out to his place—which was becoming more and more empty by the day in preparation for the sale and his move—and we had sex most of the night. Sunday morning, we'd wake late, eat brunch, and then I'd drive home so I could get any additional homework done that I'd neglected during the week.

It was everything and not enough at all.

I couldn't wait until he moved into Bobby's old place so I could spend weeknights with him, too. The drive from Daniel's new house to school would be shorter than the same drive from my parents' place, and, just as my mom had said, I *did* plan to move in with him—more or less—before the year was out.

It'd be easier on both of us. For a lot of reasons.

Not just because we'd get to have sex more often—which I was looking forward to—but because Daniel could go back to school in his new field, and we could drive to school together with just one parking pass.

"So, when I get back from Florida," Daniel was saying over the phone, as I sat on the kitchen floor and listened as hard as possible, trying to get the soothing sound of his voice even further into my ear. "I can move into Bobby's house. By then the Kingston house will be sold—they expect it'll go fast—which will give my mom a good-sized nest egg."

"How's she doing, by the way?" I asked.

Daniel's mom had gotten out of rehab two weeks ago and gone straight to Florida where she was living with her in-laws for the first time in her life. Daniel had flown down to spend Thanksgiving with them.

"The same," he hedged. "Not drinking at least. Not yet. But given the way she bristles at every word out of Grandma's mouth, it might not be long."

"But she'll lose the kids if she does that, right?"

"She needs to get her own place, near enough that Grandma and Grandpa can keep an eye on things, but away from the constant caretaking. Grandma's very loving, but very overbearing. I think she's trying to see if she can feed me an entire grocery store while I'm down here. Paul's gotten a little chubby from all of her feeding, if you can believe that."

"He was so skinny. That's crazy."

"Grandma's loving care and some stability has worked that problem out."

"Wow."

"Yeah." We were quiet for a long time and then he said, "I miss you. I want to be with you. I hate being this far away."

"I hate it, too," I murmured. "When will you be back?" He'd already told me earlier in the call, but I wanted to hear it again.

"Sunday."

"I'll pick you up from the airport."

"And we'll go straight to Bobby's."

I wondered when we'd stop calling his new house 'Bobby's.' I'd thought it would be when he redecorated, but he'd already started that. I'd thought it might be after he spent the night there a few times, but he'd already done that, too.

All that was left was for us to christen the place with a few orgasms here and there, and after that I wasn't sure what would need to happen for him to feel like it was his home. Maybe he'd just have to live there a while.

"Yeah, we'll go to your new house," I said, trying to see if I could get him to switch over if I did. "Milky Way will be waiting."

Kerri was going to drop her off in the morning, so she'd be there when Daniel arrived. It was easier for her to bring Milky Way to Daniel's new place than for her to drive all the way out to Kingston, or vice versa.

"And I'll have you all to myself."

"Did you buy lube and condoms?" I asked. The last time we'd been at the new place we'd gotten a little frisky, but we hadn't gone as far as we'd wanted because we'd forgotten to bring essentials.

"Yes, and a bed."

"A bed!"

"And a rug for in front of the fireplace."

"You're getting all kinds of ideas."

"And a washing machine that's just the right height to bend you over it."

"Daniel!"

"What?"

"What if your grandparents hear? Or the kids?"

"I'm on a phone extension in the guest room. They won't hear a thing. The real risk is someone hearing *you*."

I grinned. "My folks are away visiting some college friends for the rest of this weekend."

"So, you're alone, and I'm alone. What should we talk about?"

"Tell me more about the washing machine…"

He laughed.

We spent the rest of the call spinning out fantasies about where we'd fuck and how we'd fuck, and by the time the call ended up I was beyond horny and ready for him to come home. Unlike with Adam, though, it hadn't gone beyond talk and into the realm of phone sex. Not because I wasn't willing, but because, sure, Daniel might be alone in a guest room, but there were still kids that could barge in at any moment.

The doorbell was an unexpected interruption to my solitary relief from the agony of blue balls. I decided to ignore it, but when it rang four times, and then someone began to knock, I leapt up from my bed, straightened my clothes and headed down to deal with it. By the time I'd reached the front door, my dick was under control even if my temper was not.

I flung the door open, not sure who to expect, but hoping it wasn't Leslie or someone from Kingsley deciding to make an appearance since it was the Thanksgiving weekend. It wasn't. But I didn't know what to make of the tall, almost gaunt, man I found on the front porch.

He wore a dark suit beneath a long wool trench coat, a flamboyant scarf and a head of white hair. I blinked at him, waiting for him to tell me he was a Jehovah's Witness or something, and he blinked right back.

In the end, he broke the silence first. "George?"

I tilted my head. "No, I'm Peter."

The man's voice shook. "Of course. Yes, of course you are. My God, for a moment…" He put out his hand. "Harold Seville. You wrote me a letter last month."

It took me a few more seconds to recognize the man. He'd aged after the last photo of him I'd seen on the jacket of one of his books. "Right. Wow, yes, I did. I didn't expect you to drop by, though." I was flustered. "Don't you live in Nashville?"

"Indeed." He waved at his face as if he were too hot, despite the cold air that crisped the grass around us and wafted in puffs from his mouth. "I'm sorry. It was incredibly rude of me to arrive with no notice at all."

I wanted to agree with him, but instead I backed up into the house and said, "You should come in. It's cold outside."

Harold nodded. "I'd like that." He looked around as he stepped over the threshold. "Are your parents home? Your mother, perhaps?"

"No, they're away visiting family."

Maybe it was foolish to let a stranger into the house like this, but I did recognize him as the photographer Harold Seville, and he was elderly. I didn't see any reason why he'd want to hurt me, and if he tried…I could take him.

I collected some author copies of my mom's books from the sofa, moving them to the coffee table, and then shoved aside the blanket and the empty bag of chips I'd left out from the night before.

"Perhaps I should leave," Harold said. "I don't know that your mother would like you inviting me in when she's not home." Still, he took a seat on the sofa where I indicated, crossing his legs as he went on, "She might misunderstand my intentions."

I sat down in the chair across from him. "It's fine. Please, stay. I'm sorry if I've been rude. I wasn't expecting you, and I'm going about this all wrong. Can I get you something to drink? Water, tea, coffee?"

"No, thank you." His eyes were watery. "I'm not here for that, I'm here about your letter."

"Right." I wiped my palms over my jeans and wondered if I'd put on deodorant that morning. I wanted to sniff my pits but restrained myself. "I wrote it back in October. I'd given up hope of hearing from you."

"It took me some time to digest," Harold said. "George always told me his family was homophobic, you see. That they wouldn't understand about us. So, I had assumed that after what'd happened to him—" he broke off and seemed to collect himself. "I'm sorry. Even after all these years, I struggle to face the enormity of what he must have gone through that night."

"I try not to think about it either," I offered. "It's too much."

"Yes." He regarded me for a long time. "You resemble him. When you opened the door, for just a moment, a split second, it was as if I'd gone back in time. But I see now, looking at you, that your nose is a bit different."

"My dad's nose," I offered.

"And your voice is not the same."

"What was his voice like?"

Harold smiled. "You'll think I should say something romantic perhaps, given what you know of our relationship, and how I felt about him. I assume from what you've read in the journal and letters you mentioned, you know everything?"

I nodded.

"The truth is he had a quiet, scratchy, rather high-pitched voice. He sounded hoarse even when he was perfectly healthy. A little like Donald Duck without the dithering."

"Really?"

"His voice didn't fit his face. I remember the first time I heard it, I almost laughed in surprise. But as time passed..." He shook his head. "I yearned for it. Our phone calls were what I lived for. They were so few and far between."

"In my letter, I asked some questions about my uncle."

"Yes, you did." Harold sighed and wiped a hand over his face. He looked older than when he'd first walked in. "Would you mind getting that water now? I think I'm a little parched after all."

I rose and went into the kitchen, getting out two of Mom's nice glasses, the ones she saved for guests. I rinsed them out before filling them with fresh, cool water and adding some ice cubes.

When I returned to the living room, Harold was holding my Leica. I'd left it out on the side table by the sofa the day before, after I'd taken it down to campus to grab pictures of the new holiday decorations going up and the students walking around with cold-red noses and heavy coats.

"This is a fine camera," he murmured. "I took many of the photos in my Leisurely Lovers collection with one just like it."

"I like to use the Summilux Aspherical thirty-five millimeter lens with it. It's great for pushing in low light. It gives the photos a creamy, organic feel."

"Yes, that's a good lens." He put the camera down and accepted the water, taking a sip. "You asked in your letter how George and I met. Believe it or not, we met in a very normal way for two gay men back then—at a house party of a friend. Bill Bryant was his name. A fine fellow. George knew him through his trade school, and I'd met Bill in a public bathroom, but the less said about that the better."

I chuckled and sipped my water.

"I saw George across the room at that party, and it was everything they say a moment like that will be. Thunderstruck, wonder-filled, glued to the ground with certainty that this, *this* was someone special, someone I needed to know."

"I know that feeling," I said.

"Do you?"

I nodded. "I've had it twice."

"And how did those turn out for you?"

"One badly, and the other is good so far."

He nodded. "I never got the good. Though perhaps that's un-fair. For me, with George, it was heaven except when it was hell. He was married and committed to his family back home. Through the years, I convinced him to come stay with me for a week at a time. Beautiful, priceless weeks. That's when I took my photos of him."

Harold sipped his water. "He was jealous, though. That was part of our trouble, too. Part of the horrible end."

"Jealous of who?" I didn't get it; it was plain as day from the photos and everything Harold had written or said about George that he'd been deeply in love with him.

"My other models, of course. And the other men I slept with."

"Oh."

"I'm not going to lie and say I would have been the very picture of monogamy had he stayed with me, had he lived in my home as my dearest companion the way I'd wanted, but it would have been so much easier. Just seeing him once or twice a year? Other men were what I needed to survive, to not feel so alone."

I nodded.

"In your letter you said he wrote in his journal about me."

"Yes."

He leaned forward. "Can I...would you allow me..." His eyes filled with tears.

"You want to see it?"

"Please."

"Of course. Yeah. Hold on." I left him again to go up to my room, grabbing the manila envelope from my backpack and carrying it down to him.

I poured the items out on the coffee table, and he snatched a photo of George out of the stack. "Oh, love. Look at you. So young. So handsome."

I picked up the journal and handed it to him. Harold flipped through the pages, touching the handwriting like it was precious, and then he skimmed through, clearly looking for his name.

"Ah, that trip to the seaside. He writes that he was happy. I was happy too, George, I hope you know that."

He read on, and I felt like an interloper, but I didn't know what to do. Should I go upstairs and leave him alone with the journal?

Give it to him and let him keep it? But what if my mother did want to read it one day? Still…she'd given it to me. It was mine to do with as I saw fit.

"You should have that," I said, as he flipped to another page. "He would have wanted you to have it."

"Would he?" Harold asked, his voice thick with what sounded like tears. "I see this last entry about me gives me no grace. He lays it all so bare. Not the horrible, florid writer that I am, always making things prettier than they were. No, he just wrote it out bare. The truth." He wiped at his eyes. "I really did say these things to him."

"I'm sorry."

He shook his head. "These were the last words I ever said to the man I loved more than any other."

"I'm truly sorry." The weight of it was so heavy, I felt it pushing on me, though it wasn't my burden to bear.

His shoulders shook and tears fell. I reached out to take his hand, but he didn't let me, saying, "I'm sorry. This is all more than you bargained for. I shouldn't have come." He pressed the journal into my hands, rising. "I should have written you back like a sane, measured man, the kind of man that George was."

He snorted. "Instead, I fought against giving you any kind of response, pushing it out of my mind, and then this morning I got up and dressed, pulled your letter from the pile, and mapped out the roads to your home. On Thanksgiving weekend, too. I'm sure you have better things to do than to watch an old man break down."

"I don't," I said, putting my hand on his arm to forestall his leaving. "Take off your coat. Stay longer. There are some more pictures, and I'd like to know more about him."

"Do you have stories of him, too? Things your mother told you that you could share?" He sounded so hopeful, so eager to get more scraps of his long-dead love.

"I don't," I said. "I wish I did. But my mother can't speak of him much. She…" I swallowed, not sure I should say it, not wanting to bring up the horrible images again, but perhaps it would help him understand. "She found him that morning in the yard. So, she can't think about him too much." I motioned at my face. "Having me as a son—a gay son at that—has made it harder on her."

Harold studied me. "I'm sure it has. Your eyes, especially. It's uncanny."

"Sit down," I offered. "This is hard, but I think we both want to talk about him."

Harold nodded and took his coat off, handing it to me. I went to hang it up by the door, and when I returned, he was back on the sofa, another photo of George in his hand, caressing it with the tips of his fingers. "He was funny, did you know?" Then, realizing that of course I didn't know, he said, "He always made me laugh."

"I'd love to hear about that."

Harold nodded, and I listened to him talk for a long time. It wasn't the way I'd imagined meeting him, but it was real and honest, and when the afternoon started to grow dark, he decided it was time to find a hotel in the area. "I'm too old to drive all the way back tonight," he said. "Time was, I'd do day trips to anywhere in a five-hour radius. But now…"

"I'm glad you came," I said, walking him to the door.

"Me too, Peter. It was good to meet you." He paused on the steps outside and turned back around. "Wait, about your photography…"

"Yes."

"I'd like to see some of your work. Can you send some samples to me? At my address?"

"Ah, I don't—"

"I'd like to see what you're capable of. I can't make any promises, but I do happen to know people in the field," he teased. "If you have a unique eye, then perhaps I can make some introductions. George would want me to do that for you, and it would be a pleasure to do something I know would make him smile."

I shook his hand, and he pulled me in for a hug. A spicy cologne surrounded me. Was this the scent George had breathed in all those years ago? Or had Harold changed his fragrance? When I broke away, Harold's eyes were teary again.

"Goodbye," he said. "Even if we meet again, it won't be like this. Thank you for writing me and giving me a chance to say goodbye to him." Harold brushed his hand over my hair, smiling. "I hope this isn't too strange, but looking at you, I feel like I can finally lay him to rest. A part of him lives on here—" he touched both my eyebrows and slid his fingers down my cheek "—and here." He patted my chest above my heart.

On that note, he turned and walked away, leaving me contemplating the strongest, most bittersweet feeling I'd ever wanted to capture. I headed back inside, took our glasses into the kitchen, and sat down at the table.

A few moments later, I got up again and picked up the phone. There was just one voice I wanted to hear now.

"Hello, may I speak to Daniel?"

Chapter Twenty-Eight

P ICKING DANIEL UP at the airport, my heart thumped. I waited by the gate he'd be exiting from and fidgeted with my camera. I couldn't wait to see him, and I knew he couldn't wait to see me, either. He came through the door from the ramp, eyes searching the crowd, and then lighting up with sheer joy at the sight of me.

I snapped the shot, and then another.

"Hey," I gasped when his arms came around me, and lifted me into a big hug. The camera clunked against his shoulder, and I clung to his back. "You'd think you'd been gone a year," I laughed, as he swung me around and then dropped me to my feet. People gawked, but we ignored them. "Not just a week and a half."

"It felt like a year," Daniel said, pushing a hand through his messy hair, and then grinning at me again. "It's good to see you. It was a long trip."

"I want to hear all about it," I said, putting the camera's lens cap on, and picking up one of Daniel's bags of luggage. I hefted the strap over my shoulder and wobbled under the weight.

Daniel grabbed the other piece, and we headed down past the checked-luggage carousel, both of us glad he'd managed with just carry-ons so we didn't have to wait.

"Are you hungry?" I asked, as we put his stuff in the trunk.

He didn't answer until we'd both climbed in the front seat and put on our seat belts. "I could eat," he said. "But why don't we go on home first? We can order pizza."

I pulled out of the parking lot and headed toward the payment booth and then drove down Alcoa Highway, pleased that our destination was a hell of a lot closer now. It meant I could get Daniel out of his clothes a hell of a lot faster, too.

Pulling into the driveway, I realized that though it wasn't the first time I'd spent the night at the house since Bobby's passing, it was the first time since Daniel had bought it. The sound of barking came from inside as we walked toward the front door. "Aww, Milky Way sounds excited."

"Kerri left her this morning with bowls of food and water. I hope she's glad to be home. Her real home."

When Daniel got the key from behind a strategically-placed loose brick and opened the door, we were greeted by a ball of white fur and excited yipping. "Hey girl, hey," I murmured, squatting down to pet her, and let her lick my face.

Daniel petted her, too. After she'd peed by a bush, he lifted her up to carry her squirming body into the house.

When I stepped inside, Daniel turned on the lights and I let out a low whistle.

"One of the guys from McPeak Construction got the phone, water, and electric handled while I was gone with some help from an attorney and many faxes."

The place looked so different with Daniel's furniture; some was brought from Kingston, but most of it was new stuff he'd just purchased. I still remembered meeting Bobby for the first time in this room, and how different it had looked and smelled then. I wondered if his ghost lingered, and if he was happy with Daniel moving in here.

"That's the sectional from the basement?"

"Part of it. It was too big to bring in full."

"And the TV and stereo."

"Yeah."

We walked around, making sure everything was still where Daniel wanted it to be. The one thing he'd changed from Bobby's layout was the placement of the bed. Bobby had had his facing the south wall and windows, so Daniel had put his bed on the opposite side. It made the room feel less haunted.

"It needs a lot of work," Daniel said, turning and looking around. "But I love it."

"Me too. Let's make up the bed," I said, opening the linen closet by the hallway bathroom.

"In a hurry?" He laughed.

"Maybe."

As we tucked the sheets under the mattress, Daniel said, "Kerri told me she unpacked some stuff when she was here with Milky Way. Not just the linens, but the dishes too."

We went into the kitchen, and while Daniel investigated what Kerri had put where, I called in an order for pizza delivery. Then I touched base with my parents, letting them know where I was for the night.

"The spices should go in the spice drawer," Daniel murmured. "But otherwise, she did a great job. I'll have to pay her extra."

"You paid her?"

"Of course! She kept Milky Way for me and did some work around here. I wasn't going to just say thanks."

I grabbed his arm and turned him around. The bright light in the kitchen highlighted the tan he'd gotten in Florida. "I missed you," I said, pulling him close into a big hug. "After we eat," I said, looking up with a sly smile, "Do you want to test out whether the mattress you chose is comfortable or if you'll need to search for a different one?"

"Testing mattresses with you is something I'm always ready to do."

When the pizza arrived, we ate it on the sofa, using an unpacked box as a makeshift coffee table, and talked. I told him more about Harold coming over to my house, my classes, and how Minty seemed to be doing. And he told me about his brother, sister, and grandparents, and about his mom.

"She's better, but then she always is when she's right out of rehab." He chewed a bite of pizza and swallowed. "She's devoted to sobriety right up until the moment she's not, and there's no way to know when that will be, or what will cause it."

"That sucks," I said, never knowing for sure how to respond to his problems. They were all so serious and long-standing.

"It does. Especially for the kids. They've got their hopes up that she's going to be all right. She's told them they're going to get a house together and be a normal family again." He groaned.

"Shit."

"Yeah. At least they're liking their schools now. Paul's even on the chess team and doing well with it. Kennedy's made friends. My grandparents…" He sighed. "They're tired, you know? They raised their son already and thought they were finished with all that. I was afraid they'd ask me to move down and help out, but they told me not to, actually. They said I needed to get away from the dysfunction." His voice grew thick. "I almost cried."

I squeezed his thigh. "I bet."

"They get it, they really do, and I'm glad to have them, but sometimes I still get so angry with her, you know? The way we've all had to make our lives fit around her sickness. But I'm working on accepting that she can't help it, that it's not by design. My dad was good at that. He loved her so much."

"He must have seen through to the real her," I offered, not sure it was the right thing to say, but going with it.

"He forgave her for a lot. He wasn't always a good father or even a good man, but he was truly in love with my mother. When it came to her—and her alone—he had a loving, generous heart. I don't know if my heart is that open."

I put my pizza down, and crawled over to him, straddling him on the sofa. I put my hand over his heart, feeling its steady beats. "You're incredibly generous and loving. You're forgiving. I see it all the time."

Daniel clutched my back and leaned forward, dipping me a bit, to put his pizza back in the box, and then he wrapped his arms around me, nuzzling my cheek. "I don't know about that, but I know when it comes to you, I'd forgive just about anything."

"Would you?" I asked, breathless.

"Mm-hm. I'm whipped for you, Peter Mandel. Wield your power over me carefully."

"I'm whipped for you, too," I said, kissing his brows, his cheek, and bending down to press my lips to his.

The heat escalated. After a week and a half apart, and no Saturday sex-a-thons to keep us sated, we were eager for each other within minutes. We'd made the bed, but we didn't make it past the kitchen counter anyway. Kissing, stumbling, clothes coming off in a heap, Daniel bent me over the counter, ate my asshole until I was shaking, and then flipped me around to suck me off while he jacked his own cock.

The second time was in the shower, and it was slower. Making out until our chins were stinging, and then humping against each other beneath the warm water until we both came with breathless grunts.

The third time was later and *much* longer. We'd put away the remaining pizza in the refrigerator, thinking that we'd save it for breakfast, since there was nothing else to eat. Then we'd fallen into bed and cuddled up, spooning together while Milky Way got comfortable in her dog bed in the corner. I'd thought we were done for the night, but then Daniel went out to the living room and came back with his overnight bag from Florida.

"Condoms," he said, pulling one from the link and putting it beneath his pillow since he didn't have nightstands yet. "Lube." He put the tube in the same place. "Bought them at the drugstore before leaving."

"You think we can go again?" I asked, pulling him back into bed, our naked limbs intertwining, and his lips dancing over my neck and down my chest. I hadn't douched, but Daniel didn't seem to care.

"Let's see," Daniel said, rubbing his face against my chest, all over the minute amounts of chest hair that grew there. He reached down and touched my already-hardening dick. "That's a good sign."

I laughed, and he kissed my neck, the heat between us growing, as we moved and touched, licked and nipped, and finally rocked together. I breathed heavily, shaking with lust and effort, as I took him in.

"Fuck, baby," he whimpered. "You're so tight."

"No, you're so big," I chuckled, and then gasped as he pushed deeper into me. My asshole stretched around his thickness. "Slow," I whispered. "Slow, please."

He took his time, and eventually my ass gave up all resistance, letting him in. With the stamina earned from two prior orgasms, he dragged our lovemaking out, until I was a whimpering, sweaty wreck. My heart was pounding so hard he murmured in my ear about feeling it against his own chest.

After a while, he knelt up, hooked my legs over his elbows, and started fucking me like a piston. In and out, hard and steady. My head lolled on the pillow. I shook like a leaf, and when the building pleasure from his dick against my prostate grew to be too much, I convulsed and cried out. The now-familiar feeling took my breath away.

"Breathe through it," Daniel murmured, kissing my mouth, and then ducking down to lick my nipples. "Just let it go, baby."

I had "let it go" for him before, and it always ended the same way, with me keening and coming like a mad person, and him begging to be inside me raw just before he filled his condom and came to his senses.

This time, though, things broke from form. Daniel took me to the intense, wild heights of near-orgasm three more times before he collapsed on me, rolling his hips, trying to get in deeper. His breath came in sharp pants, and his shaky hands clasped me tight.

"Peter," he whispered. "I need you."

I moaned and let him fill me again, convulsing beneath him as his breathing went ragged and messy.

"I want to feel you. Just once, baby. Just one time."

"Do it," I urged, my heart pounding, my body running with sweat and want, and the needful urge to have that with him. That closeness. That moment of being as connected physically as two men could be. "Do it, please, do it."

Daniel groaned, twitched on top of me, and roughly pulled out.

For a moment, I thought he'd come. I clutched his shoulders, wanting more and yet sure I wasn't going to get it. But he moved his arm sharply, an empty condom flew away from the bed, and I felt his dick at my hole again. Just the head of it.

He lingered there, rubbing against my lube-slick asshole. I reached up, wrapped my arms around his neck and pulled him down for a kiss, whispering, "Do it." Another kiss. "I want you." Another. "Closer."

"Closer," he answered, and I felt him push. "Just for a minute. I won't stay inside long," he gritted out. "Just to feel you."

I wrapped my legs around his hips, using my heels to dig into his ass, pulling him in as he thrust. I moaned. The difference between condom and skin was immediately evident, though not so great as to make me think I could never survive if Daniel and I never did this again. And yet…When he pulled free of our kiss, and stared into my eyes, his raw cock buried in me, our breaths merging as we panted, I wasn't sure I wouldn't find myself begging for it, for this intimacy.

"Oh, wow," I whispered. "It's beautiful."

His face crumpled. That—*that*—was gorgeous, breathtaking, and heartbreaking. His wide-eyed wonder, his dilated pupils, his tears spilling over, and his whispers of, "Baby, oh, oh. I love you. Oh, *fuck*, Peter!"

In a panic he pulled out, his chest heaving as he shot against the sheets and my legs. He shook, eyes rolling back in his head, as he groaned and jerked, his noises desperate and his pleasure undeniable.

After, he fell on top of me, still quivering all over. I clutched him, breathing in his sweaty scent, and hunched up to rub my dick against his hip. It just took a few thrusts until I came, too. Not as forcefully as he had, and not as intense as earlier in the day, but strong and beautiful.

I panted as he held me tight, and tears welled in my eyes. It'd been so sweet, intimate, and special.

"You okay?" I whispered after he lay there awhile, saying nothing, and not moving to clean us up the way he normally did. He shook against me, and I rubbed his back. "Daniel?"

"I shouldn't have done that."

"Hey, it's okay," I murmured. "We've both been tested. We're faithful to each other. We didn't do anything wrong." Daniel's breath was hot and hard against my neck and shoulder, like he was sobbing. I kept comforting him, repeating, "We didn't do anything wrong."

When he rolled off me, he lay on his back, his wet eyes on the ceiling. I went up on my elbow and touched his face. "Daniel? Talk to me?"

"It felt so good," he groaned, wiping at his face. "I thought if we did it once, I'd get it out of my system. But I'm going to want it again. I already do."

"That's all right, though. Because we can have it," I said. "We can, because we're honest with each other."

Daniel squeezed his eyes shut, and his throat seemed to clamp up on him. He struggled to speak. "It's hard for me to trust people. I need to trust you."

"You can," I assured him. "I'm with you. Only you." Rubbing my nose against his, I whisper-sang the words of the song.

That made him laugh, and I was relieved. Still, he insisted "We shouldn't have done that, and we shouldn't ever do it again. After what I've seen in ARK…"

"We're *in love*," I said. "We're true to each other. Aren't we?"

"Yes."

"And I want it, too." Daniel stiffened like I was pressuring him. "But if you don't want us to—"

"I want us to!" he said fiercely. "That's the problem."

I stroked his chest. "It's all right. We're all right."

He drew me into his arms and held me tight.

When we fucked again, sometime in the middle of the night, he used a condom. I didn't protest or try to talk him out of it. It was still good—*so* good. If wearing a condom was what he needed to do to feel safe, I was okay with that. I had to be.

✧   ✧   ✧

THE FOLLOWING MORNING, I woke up to Milky Way panting in my face.

Daniel laughed. "Wanting breakfast, Miss Milky Way?" he asked.

She went berserk, jumping up and down on the bed, landing on my legs, my stomach, and my chest, making me shout and laugh and roll over to protect myself.

Daniel rose from the sheets, naked and gorgeous. I let my eyes roam over his body as he stretched. I remembered the intimacy of having him inside me raw the night before—it'd only lasted a few strokes, but it'd been mind-blowingly hot, and surprisingly emotional.

The tears in his eyes as he'd moved in me had been heady, and even the panic that had replaced the sweetness as he'd pulled out had been meaningful. I wanted to drag him back into bed, open my legs, and tug him into myself again, and again, and again.

Instead, I let him walk away. He put on some boxers and headed out to the kitchen to feed Milky Way before she lost her mind.

Standing up to go take a piss, my legs trembled as I walked. The night had been undeniably intense, and I was still shaky even after sleeping. There was little chance of me getting "over" Daniel's cock anytime soon. I didn't know if fitting it in was ever going to be less of a challenge, but every time it was worth it. Beyond worth it.

I brushed my teeth and rinsed, and then turned on the shower, feeling for the cold to turn warm. Distantly, I heard the back door open and close, and Milky Way's excited barking as she encountered a squirrel, or a bird, or a chipmunk. I climbed into the warm water. It was a dream on my back, and I leaned forward, letting it wash over my tender hole too.

I'd just washed my hair when the bathroom door opened. Daniel brushed his teeth, too, and took a piss. He moved the soft, green curtain aside and peered in at me. "Room for one more in there?"

I beckoned him in, turning to face the stream.

He slipped in behind me, cooler air stirring as the curtain fell back into place, leaving us in the quiet shelter of the bathtub. It wasn't that we hadn't showered together before, but it'd always been at Daniel's old place, in his big shower there. This tub-shower felt more intimate, closer, and altogether ours instead of a wet oasis in a big, vacant home that was, essentially, no one's anymore.

Daniel edged up behind me, and I shivered as his hands smoothed around my torso and slipped up to touch my nipples. My cock took instant notice, rising against the water spray. "Hey," I whispered, my throat still scratchy with sleep.

"Hey," he replied, kissing the side of my neck.

Things escalated, the soap coming into play to make our mutual jerking even more slippery and wonderful. Our kisses became erratic as we clenched and held each other close. No sooner had we both grunted and come, shooting against each other's legs and torsos, than Milky Way started barking to be let in.

"That dog…" Daniel murmured, kissing my cheek.

"I'll get her," I said, washing the cum off and stepping out to grab a towel. "I was almost done anyway."

I put on my glasses so I could see and padded to the back door to open it. Milky Way bounded in, skidding to a stop by her water bowl and lapping at it. I was exhausted and wished I could slide back between Daniel's soft sheets and spend another day in a daze of physical pleasure and emotional contentment in his bed.

But I couldn't.

I had classes all today, and I had a test on Friday on the six chapters from our Psychology text, none of which Donnie Huggins had ever covered in class. I also had a paper due in English Literature, *and* a photography group project that was not coming together well. Both due by Monday—the last day of the semester.

I opened my overnight bag, and I was dressed and had put my contacts in by the time Daniel came out of the bathroom, still slick and pink from the hot water.

"No, don't go," he pleaded as soon as he saw me. "I just got home."

"I know. I don't want to." I crossed over to him and wrapped him in my arms. "But I need to. I've got class."

He nuzzled my ear. "Is it considered kidnapping if I tie you up and keep you here?"

"It depends on how many times you make me come," I whispered. My traitorous dick was already on board with this plan. "I won't press charges if you make it worth my while."

Daniel sighed and released me. "I don't have any rope."

I laughed. "Better get some for next time then."

In the kitchen, eating the leftover pizza, Daniel said, "Oh, by the way, word is Robert and Barry are hosting their annual Christmas party Friday. The last one in their current house."

"Oh wow," I murmured. As I chewed, my mind flashed back to the year before. I'd been there with Adam, and we'd run into his ex from Rome. It seemed like a lifetime ago. Had it really only been a year?

"I was thinking we'd go together," Daniel said. "And then we could come back here and put up a tree, decorate a little and make this a proper home for Christmas."

I hesitated. "Okay. It sounds fun."

"Does it? You sound unsure."

"It's silly."

"Tell me."

"The party..." I considered how to phrase it. "I want to go. It's just that last year, I went with Adam."

"I know. I saw you there."

"You did?"

"Yeah, but you didn't see me."

"No, I didn't."

Daniel nodded. "It was the first time I ever saw you, and I couldn't look away. You didn't seem happy with the guy you were with, but I had no idea what was going on."

"Oh."

Daniel blushed. "I asked about you afterward. Robert and Barry warned me off. And then I saw you again when I came to look at Robert's documentary work."

"That's when I first saw you."

"Yeah. And then we met for real a bit later that day with the house plans, and afterward I asked even more about you…" He breathed out, touching my cheek. "By the time I saw you on the hill by Ayres Hall, I already knew I wanted you, but I had no idea how to have you."

"Here I am."

"Here you are." Daniel slipped his hands under my shirt. "Are you sure you can't stay?"

I breathed in the scent of his neck and kissed his collarbone. "I want to stay, but…" I groaned.

"But what?"

"I might beg you to do something you don't think is right. I don't want to pressure you."

Daniel stiffened. "God, baby, you know I want to, but we can't. We shouldn't have."

"It felt *so right*," I whispered.

"It did." Daniel's voice was tight. "Right up until I knew I was going to come and then I panicked."

Against my better judgment, I whispered, "You can always pull out again, if that relieves your anxiety about it. I trust you."

Daniel rocked me back and forth, his breath coming heavy against my hair, and his heart pounding hard enough I could feel it too. "*I* don't trust me. I was so close to coming inside you. It was terrifying."

"But you're negative."

"I know—"

"And you're faithful to me, and I'm faithful to you. We could do this. We could have it."

"No," Daniel whispered. "It's too risky."

"You're not being logical."

He pulled away from me then, taking a step back. "I said no."

I rubbed my eyes, noting that my contacts felt a little gritty. I needed to take better care of them. "I'm not trying to pressure you to do something you don't want to do."

"Yes, you are!"

My voice raised. "You *want* to do this! You've said so! Over and over!"

Were we fighting? Were we really arguing now over *this?* Over the most beautiful thing I'd ever shared with another person? That skin-on-skin closeness, the knowledge that he was in me, nothing keeping us apart, our cells touching.

Daniel pulled on some boxers, then some pants, and stood across the room from me, the backlighting from the window making his face hard to read.

I tugged my hand through my still damp hair and sighed. "I don't want to fight about it."

"I don't either." He was still rigid, though, as if he wasn't sure he was safe, like I might yell at him or hurt him in some way.

"I'm sorry," I said, reaching for him. He stepped closer, still wary. When I had him in my arms again, I said, "I loved what we did. I don't want to ruin it by fighting about it."

"I…" Daniel ducked his head, resting it on my shoulder. I pressed my cheek against his damp hair. "I love you."

"I love you, too."

"You're right. It's been a fantasy of mine for so long." He groaned. "And I've fought against it so hard. I shouldn't crave this. It's not necessary to feel close. We can be just as in love and have great sex without ever doing that. We shouldn't have done it at all."

"Don't get mad," I said, pulling back so that we could look at each other. "But, seriously, *why* shouldn't we do it? We're both negative. We're together—truly together, right?"

"Yes."

"And you trust me?"

Daniel swallowed hard, his eyes darting away.

"You don't trust me?"

"I do," he said, but it didn't sound true. "I trust you."

I wished I didn't feel so gut-punched by how little I believed him. I knew why he had trouble trusting. I understood it. I got why I seemed like a bad risk to him—after everything I'd put him through, and everything he knew I'd lied about the year before—but I also knew I was faithful to him.

"I know your mom has made it hard for you to trust anyone. She'd tell you she was sober, promise you all kinds of things, and then go get drunk. But I'm not your mom."

"I know that." His voice was gruff.

"I want to be with you and *only you*. I want to feel you like that. You cried last night when you were in me bare, and I know it was because you felt the power of it as much as I did."

"Peter…" His voice sounded anguished, as if I were Satan showing him the most delectable of temptations.

"But I won't ask again," I said. "It'll be your choice if we ever do that—halfway like we did last night, or all the way like I'm willing to do with you."

"Halfway?"

"Not coming in me. All the way would be letting you come inside."

"Baby—"

"I trust you. I know you're dedicated to me. But if you won't or *can't* give that to me, then that's okay too. I'll be happy without it. I love you, Daniel. This isn't a deal-breaker for me. I just wanted to be clear about what I'm open to in this relationship. At its core, this is about trust, and I understand why you don't trust me."

"I do trust you."

"I know." Because he did. He trusted me in most of the ways that mattered day-to-day. But with this one thing, he didn't trust me. It hurt, but I understood. I didn't want him doing anything he didn't want to do.

I told him that.

"But I do want it," he whispered.

"Yeah, you do," I said, sliding a hand around to the back of his neck and bringing him down to kiss his lips. "It's all right. We're okay. Don't worry about it anymore." I pulled away. "I need to go. I have class and a test tomorrow, and that paper and project are due on Monday. I'm not prepared."

Daniel followed me to the front door, and when I turned to give him another goodbye hug, he looked miserable. My stomach twisted up. I hadn't meant to do that to him, to make him feel guilty and sad. What we'd done was so beautiful, and I wanted more of it, but not this way.

"I'll see you Friday? After my shift at the library?"

"You could stay here this week," he said. "It's closer to school."

"I could, but we both know I'd spend more time studying ways to make your dick fit into my ass than I would studying Psychology."

"Friday's Robert and Barry's party," he reminded me.

"We'll go to it," I said, gripping his chin and bringing him down for yet another kiss, trying to take the sting of the conversation away before I left him for four days. "Then afterward, we'll come home and decorate, just like you wanted."

I headed toward the Volvo, and when I looked back after opening the driver's-side door, I saw Daniel in the doorway, holding Milky Way against his shirtless chest. He looked sad, and I hated leaving him like that.

"Don't worry!" I called to him. "It's all right."

He waved as I drove away, and I hoped I hadn't lied. Everything *had* to be all right, because what we had together was too good to get screwed up over something like this. I didn't *need* to have him that much closer—the micrometer of a condom's width—to love him with all my heart.

I knew he felt the same.

Chapter Twenty-Nine

FRIDAY AFTER WORK, I met Daniel at his house, eager to see him and excited to be almost done with school for the semester.

He met me in the driveway and gave me a big hug, kissing my neck and cheek, and then my lips. That was one thing I loved about the new house. Unlike at my parents', the driveway was private, with shrubs on all sides, and no neighbors across the street. Instead, there was a private park with a bike trail that no one ever seemed to take.

"Long time, no see," he breathed, rubbing our noses together. "I missed you."

It'd just been four days, and we'd talked every night, but it was still true. "I missed you, too."

We kissed again, and he took my backpack from my hands, carrying it and my overnight bag into the house. "Milky Way!" I said, getting down on my knees to pet her and let her lick my face. When she calmed down, I stood up and marveled. "You didn't wait to get started, did you?"

The living room and kitchen were already strewn with colored lights, and the mantel had greenery on it, as well as a wreath on the wall above the TV. A big, fresh Christmas tree stood off to the side in what looked like a temporary location, with lights on, but no decorations, and a few presents beneath it.

"I figured I'd get some of it out of the way, so we'd have more time, just the two of us."

"But before it's just the two of us, we've got that party, right?"

"Yeah," Daniel smiled, gesturing at his button-up shirt. It was green and covered with candy canes. "Think it's hot?"

"Sizzling." I laughed. "What about me?" I tugged open my overnight bag and pulled out the reindeer antler headband I'd grabbed from April at work earlier in the day. She'd agreed to let me keep it because she said it looked cute as hell on me. So, that was a hopeful opinion. I put it on my head and looked at Daniel.

He grinned. "Adorable."

I turned around, shaking my ass, and saying, "Want to play Santa and his reindeer later?"

Daniel chuckled and grabbed me from behind. "I want to do lots of things to you later." He kissed my cheek, and spun me around, pressing our foreheads together. "Look, I've been think-ing…"

"Yeah?"

"I just need you to be honest with me about one thing."

"Okay?"

"If *he* showed up today, or tomorrow, or whenever, and said that he was out now, and that he'd chosen you, that he'd broken up with her—"

I scoffed. "Daniel, that's not going to happen."

"But if it did—"

"It won't."

He gripped my hips harder. "I know you love me, but you loved him too."

"Yeah, I can't deny I did."

"And you still do." He tried to step back, but this time I held him fast.

"No. I don't."

I didn't love Adam. I felt a lot of things for him: responsibility, guilt, remorse, lingering lust, annoying fondness, hate, and even more mixed-up stuff than that. But love? That sweet, honeyed emotion that wrapped me up when I was with Daniel? I didn't feel that for Adam. Not now, and maybe I hadn't ever? Almost from the start, what I'd had with Adam had been poisoned.

"Daniel, if it was between you and him, I'd choose you. I'd always choose us."

"You're sure?"

"Baby, I wouldn't be here now if I wasn't sure. You're not my second choice. You're *my choice*."

Daniel's lips trembled. "Baby?"

"Hmm?"

"You called me baby just now."

"Oh," I chuckled. "You call *me* that, don't you? Is it weird if I call you that too? Do you want me to call you something different?"

He pressed his lips together before saying, "Only if you called *him* that."

I shook my head. "No, never."

"Then I'm good with baby… Baby." He let me draw him into a hug, and we comforted each other, swaying back and forth. The room felt like warm and welcoming, a place where our love was safe to grow.

I wanted a picture of us, just like this, but I'd have to break out of his arms to attempt to set up the camera, and it wouldn't be real then, just posed. I committed the memory to my heart, my mind, and my cells instead.

One day, I'd take a photograph that echoed this feeling. Somewhere out in the world, whether in nature or in a city, I was sure I'd find it again. Love, I'd come to realize, lived everywhere if you just looked for it.

✦   ✦   ✦

WE PULLED UP to Robert and Barry's house to find the party was already in full swing.

Just like last year, there were people smoking on the front porch as we approached, but *not* like last year, I'd brought a simple point-and-shoot camera I wouldn't have to worry about all night. I'd *also* brought a guy who wasn't going to abandon me to catch up with an old boyfriend.

Even if Daniel's ex, Kevin, showed up at this party for some bizarre reason, he'd never make me wonder or try to guess where I stood with him. He'd never introduce me as his friend and then take it back just to prove something.

"Well, if it isn't my Sweetie and my darling, my lovely, my Daniel!" Robert—no, Renée—was drunk already and wobbling on her high heels. Her bright pink wig was amazing, and so was the pink Mrs. Santa outfit she was wearing. Blinding, but amazing.

"Hey there." I went in for a hug, and instead got squished into her fake bosom and cuddled hard. "Missed you, too," I squeaked out, trying to get a breath.

"I don't think you have," she scolded me, holding me even closer by wrapping her hand around my head and clutching me. "No calls, no visits. And after all I did for you last year."

"I'm sorry," I gasped. "If I promise to do better, will you let me breathe?"

She released me, mussing my curls, which were no doubt already a disaster. "Sweetie, if you do better, then I'll have to do better, and I don't have time for that. Let's just both agree that we love each other and leave it alone." She gestured over my shoulder and called, "Barry, baby, bring these two something to drink."

"And here comes the Puker jokes," I muttered to Daniel.

"So, have you two been screwing like bunnies and that's what's kept you so busy?" Renée grinned. "I see by Daniel's red cheeks that's a resounding yes. Well, good gracious, I'm glad to hear it. Ah, to be young and full of endless hard-ons again."

"Renée," I murmured, rolling my eyes, as Barry approached with the beers.

"Don't throw up," he said, handing it to me. "Good to see you, Puker."

"You too."

Renée broke in again. "So how are you handling Daniel's dick, baby? Do you need any pointers?"

I blushed. "We're fine. Thanks."

Barry turned to Renée, putting a hand around her waist. "Woman, let these kids dance and relax. They don't want to tell you about what they've been doing with the lights out."

"I hope you've been doing it with the lights *on*," she said to us, grabbing a drink out of a passing guest's hand and commandeering it. "You're only young and gorgeous for a few years, and then the pot bellies grow and wrinkles set in."

"What pot belly?" Barry muttered, rolling his eyes. "You've got a six-pack under there." He turned to Daniel. "Hey, can I ask you about something in the kitchen? It's about the new house. They've started on the foundation, but I just want to make sure…" His voice trailed off as he and Daniel made their way into the kitchen where, I had no doubt, there were still plans for the house rolled out on the table.

Music thumped and laughter rang out all around. I wondered who all the people in attendance were. I felt like I'd seen some of them last year, but others were new.

"I saw your Naughty Boy," Renée said, taking hold of my arm and drawing me in close.

"He's not mine, and I don't care."

"He was at Tilt-a-Whirl."

I covered my surprise with a sip of beer.

"He was looking for you."

"That's creepy."

She snorted. "I thought so too. But our little fool Minty thought it was romantic."

I snorted. "Did he?"

"Well, he pretended to think so while pumping Naughty Boy for information about why he was there, what he wanted, and how long he was going to be in town."

"Hmmph," I said around my beer bottle again.

"The answers were: he was looking for you, he wants to talk with you, and he's going to be in town through at least the New Year." She ticked them off on her fingers.

"So what?"

Renée sighed. "Don't you think you should talk to him and just put an end to all this?"

"I've told him a million times, and my parents have told him a million times, it's *over,* and I don't want to see him. He's stalking me. Don't encourage it."

I wiped a hand over my lips, my heart skipping a beat. I half-expected to turn around and find Adam in the room, staring at me with those hungry, rageful, possessive eyes. It made me shiver and feel sick at the same time.

"He said he's not with the girl anymore."

I closed my eyes and shook my head. "I don't care. It's not even about that."

"What's it about then?" Renée said, leaning close and putting an arm around my neck.

"It's about how I love Daniel, for starters, and also about how Adam ruins everything he touches, and he has ever since I met him. Including *me.*"

"Is that fair?"

"Are you really defending him?" I asked, taking a step back. Hurt stabbed through me. "After everything?"

"He looked miserable." Was that sympathy I saw in Renée's eyes?

"I don't care. He made *me* miserable. We made ourselves miserable. He needs to move on. I have." I turned on my heel.

In the kitchen I found Daniel, and I wiped the scowl from my face before he saw it. This was supposed to be a party, we were supposed to have fun, and I didn't want to think about Adam. He wasn't in my life. Not anymore.

"So, he's okay?" Daniel was asking Barry as I approached. I realized they weren't talking about the house anymore. The subject became clear with Barry's reply.

"He's still positive, nothing will make that go away, but Luke has him in a better place mentally. Has Peter mentioned noticing a change in him lately?"

Daniel shook his head.

I shrugged. I'd had a few conversations with Minty about his situation, but while he hadn't outright asked me not to tell Daniel about the details of them, it'd been implied. So I'd kept it to myself.

Barry frowned. "I didn't think it was private. He was talking about it at Tilt-a-Whirl the other night, and he's expected to be here with Luke tonight."

"Maybe he didn't feel comfortable talking to *me* about the details of it, then."

"I don't know why not," Barry said.

"Maybe because he thinks I'm judgmental." Daniel turned to me as I slipped beneath his arm. "We were just talking about Minty. How's he been at school?"

"Good," I said, holding on to his arm and tucking myself in closer to his side. "He's been freaking out about finals, but he hasn't done any more stunts like *Cream My Face*. I haven't seen any indication of that Kyle guy, or anyone else like him, in his life. He doesn't ever want to talk with me about the diagnosis, though. He and Jennifer—our friend from class," I explained to Barry, "just talk about shopping and shoes most of the time."

"Good," Barry said, nodding. "I'll let Luke know he seems to be doing well at school too."

"And Luke is?" I asked, confused.

"The Dom that Barry hooked Minty up with," Daniel said, sipping his beer.

"Oh, right. His Sir."

Curiosity had gotten the better of me at the library one day after Minty had confessed some of his situation to me. So, when someone had returned a copy of *Story of O*, I'd read it over the afternoon, half-horrified and half-titillated. That was all I knew about the lifestyle.

Barry raised his pierced brow. "Ah, Puker, you're still so innocent. Stay that way." Then he walked away to greet some of our library coworkers, and I was left blinking after him.

"Do you think that's safe?" I asked Daniel as he slipped an arm around my shoulders. "Minty with a Dom?" I knew what Minty said, but I was curious what Daniel thought.

"Barry swears this guy is a good person. Luke likes to keep things safe and sane and makes sure to get consent for everything." Daniel sighed. "Minty isn't open with me anymore."

I hugged him. "He's missing out then."

"I think he feels judged by me, even though I've tried hard not to make him feel that way." Daniel's brows were drawn low.

"How could he think you judge him?"

"Because I've said too much in the past about condoms and AIDS and being safe."

"What happened to him was an accident."

"Probably. But if this guy can help him, then that's all I want."

"Yeah." I pondered what "helping" might mean in that context. "Do you think he whips him?"

"With Minty's HIV status, he needs to avoid injuries that could get infected. I don't know what that means for what they do together. But if he's not being beaten and taken roughly by that asshole anymore, I guess I can't be too picky about what and how they do what they do. Not if he's doing better."

The music drifting in from the other room, some Motown song from the '60s, switched to a familiar beat and rhythm. Daniel's grin was immediate and infectious. "Hey, Peter," he said, turning to me. "Do you want to dance?"

"Danny, are you okay?" I replied, giggling, and we moved back out to the living room to dance together to "Smooth Criminal."

The song had just come to an end when Renée stood on the coffee table in her gold, strappy heels and shouted, "Babies! I have an announcement!" The room hushed, and she plowed on, *"Drag Dolls* was accepted! Atlanta Film Festival here we come!"

Claps and whistles erupted around the room. Daniel and I cheered and hugged. I'd had a hand in the making of the documentary, helping with edits and feedback, and this success felt like mine, too.

Barry cued up Kool and the Gang's "Celebration," and Renée popped the cork on some cheap champagne, having made sure to shake it first so it fizzed everywhere. Daniel and I didn't partake, but we laughed as others made a beeline to kneel by the coffee table and try to catch the falling foam in their mouths.

Later that night, Minty showed up on the arm of a tall, handsome blond guy who wore a fuzzy Santa hat and big black boots. This was, apparently, Luke. Minty was dressed in a gauzy red and white dress, with red glitter on his skin, and a carefree lipsticked smile that I hadn't seen on him in a long time.

Windy arrived with someone as well, surprising everyone but Luke and Minty, it seemed. This guy was also a bit older and seemed to be friends with Luke, but the dynamic between Windy and this new friend was the exact opposite of Luke and Minty's. When Windy said jump, the guy jumped, and when Windy said higher, the guy jumped higher.

As for Minty, he seemed to be in hog heaven. Luke treated him like a pampered princess, bringing him anything he wanted, whenever he wanted it, and dancing with him like they were the only two people in the room.

"Wow," Daniel said, holding me closer as the room swayed to "Endless Love." Renée had turned out the lights and shone a big flashlight at the disco ball she'd hung from the ceiling. A broomstick had gotten it spinning, and now the whole room sparkled, between the glittering lights and the sequins and baubles of the very queer crowd. "I don't know what I'm seeing, but I like it."

"They seem happy," I said, watching out of the corner of my eye as Windy told his date something, and the guy dropped to his knees and kissed Windy's fingertips. "I don't know what *that's* about either, but I guess they're having fun?"

"When I danced with Minty earlier, he told me Windy asked Luke to teach him about being a Dom. Who knew that was even a thing he wanted to try? But supposedly, he's gung ho about it."

"What's the guy's name?" I asked. "I missed it when I was in the bathroom."

"Ryan," Daniel said. "Barry said he's Luke's friend from, get this, the local dungeon."

I scoffed. "Knoxville does *not* have a local dungeon."

"You'll have to be wrong then, because it does."

I laughed and rubbed my face against his dumb candy-cane shirt. "Oh God, this year has been…" I shook my head. "This year has been the craziest ride. When I came here for last year's party, I never could have guessed what was ahead."

Daniel lifted my chin, and I peered up into his warm brown eyes. "Happy with how it ended up?"

"Yeah."

We kissed, and Daniel wrapped his arms around me, swaying faster as the music changed from the slow romance of "Endless Love" to the fast, joyful keyboard of "Take On Me."

The year wasn't through with me yet, though, I could feel it. There was something about the way Daniel held me, the way he kept whispering in my ear, and the heat of his breath when he said, "I need you closer, I want you as close as I can have you," that told me there was even more excitement to come.

I pressed against him, chest to chest. Breathing in sync, feeling his heartbeat.

"Closer," he whispered. "Closer."

I held him tighter.

Closer, yes.

Chapter Thirty

During the ride home from Robert and Barry's house we chatted about Windy and Minty and their kinky dates. We fiercely ignored Minty's HIV status and the fear it engendered in both of us for him. We didn't want to ruin the night ahead. When we ran out of gossip, we sang along to cheesy Christmas music over the radio, and discussed the Christmas Plan of Action, as I had dubbed it.

"We'll pop the corn," I said, sleigh bells ringing through the car speakers. "And then we'll string it with all those sequins Robert gave us."

"While we do that, we'll eat cookies and watch *The Grinch*. You brought the VHS tape?"

"In my bag at your house. And, after we get the garland made, we'll wrap it around the tree, and finish decorating with the new ornaments you bought." I lifted his hand and kissed the back of his knuckles. "Are you going to miss your family ornaments?"

I still had the Christmas tree—aka Hanukkah bush—at my folks' house to decorate later in the week, and I always looked forward to hanging specific ones that held precious memories.

"I kept a few of my childhood favorites, but I sent the rest of our old ones in a box down to Mom and the kids. They'll appreciate having them. And I like having new ornaments."

"All yours."

"All ours," he corrected, squeezing my thigh.

At the house, we dragged the tree across from Daniel's sectional sofa, laughing as it wept pine needles onto the wood floor. Wrestling it into the position I liked best brought even more laughter, and while I started munching on the popcorn we'd popped to string into garland, Daniel sorted through a box of mixtapes he hadn't yet unpacked.

"Where is it?" he muttered, and then came up with a battered-looking cassette case, triumphant. "Here! I made this from my mother's old vinyl records a few years ago. You can still hear the pop and hiss of the vinyl." He turned to the stereo he'd brought from the old house—sold for a bundle of money and forever gone from his life—and started up the music.

Nat King Cole's voice filled the room with warmth as Daniel went out to the porch and came back with an armful of logs. They'd been left there a few days ago by a neighbor who'd brought them over for Bobby every year, and had told Daniel he'd bring logs for him, too.

After Daniel got the fire started, he stopped the music and put *The Grinch* VHS tape in the player. We watched the movie as we put together popcorn-and-sequins garlands and sipped the champagne he'd bought and chilled earlier. It was relaxed, easy, and by the time the Whos down in Whoville had their happy ending, we had enough garlands to wrap around the tree's branches.

Once we had the ornaments up, we draped a bedsheet around the bottom of the tree as a makeshift tree-skirt, and Daniel sat beside me on the sofa, a little tipsy and very smiley, looking at our joint effort. "It's great, don't you think?"

I turned to him and straddled his thighs. "It's totally great."

Daniel laughed into my kiss, but his hands came to clutch my ass and tug me closer. "What else should we do to celebrate our first Christmas together?" he whispered. "Got any ideas?"

"I sure do."

"Me too."

Before long, we were naked on the sofa, the coverlet he'd bought the week before beneath his back, as I kissed and licked my way down his body to his cock. The blow job was messy and unfinished because he pulled me up to kiss me again. Then he flipped us over, me on my back, and him above me. He knelt between my legs before pushing them up to my chest to get at my asshole.

I gripped his hair as he licked and prepped me, feeling giddy with lust by the time he sat back on his heels, staring down at me with wide pupils and red lips.

I reached for him, but he turned away, sliding open the drawer in the coffee table he'd picked up recently. He took out a fresh tube of lube. As I watched, he slicked his cock…

No condom.

My heart pounded as I reached out for him, my already-shaky hands trembling even harder.

"This okay?" he asked.

I whispered, "It's good."

Quickly, he smeared lube on my asshole, and then, leaning forward to press the head of his cock against me, he whispered, "You're sure?"

"Are you?"

He nodded. "I trust you."

"Me too," I groaned, tugging him forward to kiss his lips. "So much."

"Merry Christmas," he breathed, as he pushed for entrance.

I bore down hard, my eyelids fluttering as he moved into me.

Just like always, it was intense and surprising to get no real relief from the stretch after his cockhead entered, just another stretch, and then even *more*. But he was gentle, moving inside me with the steady press we'd perfected over the last few months. Before long I had him wrapped up in my arms, my heels resting on his ass, and his cock lodged deep inside me.

I breathed in and out, just feeling him there, big and thudding. Daniel lifted up on his elbows to watch me, and the dreamy delirium in his eyes set me on fire with adoration. His lashes fell against his cheekbones, and when they lifted, his eyes were wet with tears. His lips trembled as he pulled back and thrust into me again.

Gazing at him, I wasn't sure what he saw on my face, but I hoped I was radiating the love and lust and pure wonder I saw in his. "I love you," I murmured. "I love you so much."

"This feels like nothing else." He touched his hand to his chest, over his heart, and rubbed. "Here, too. I feel it here."

"I feel it everywhere," I said, hiccupping a small laugh. "Because you're so damn big."

He laughed, too, thrusting into me again. Suddenly, he went still, his eyes going wide. "Peter?"

"Yeah?"

"I'm not going to pull out."

"Okay. Don't," I said, reaching up to push my fingers into his hair, tilting my pelvis to take him in just that much deeper. "I want you to stay in me."

"I want to come in you," he whispered, his hips flexing on the words. His face flushed even more with need. "I want to give you my cum."

"I want to take it," I whispered. "Please let me keep it."

"Keep it?"

"Make it part of me."

"Oh, baby," he groaned, and his dick seemed to swell in me even more. "Don't say that, or I'll come now." He wrapped his arms around my back, buried his face in my neck and clung to me hard. I held my legs back by the knees to give him better access as he lost control, fucking into me hard and fast, his need overwhelming his desire to take his time.

"I'm gonna come," I whispered. "Please, please, *please*, Daniel…" I tossed my head back, his hips stuttering just as I reached the peak. Cum pulsed between us as I shouted. Pleasure peaked and pulsed through every cell.

Daniel groaned. "So beautiful," he whimpered, and then took his final thrusts before going rigid and shouting against my shoulder. His cock throbbed hard against my stretched hole as he came.

"Oh, fuck," he whimpered when the aftershocks released him. He collapsed with all of his weight on me, his cock still in my ass. "Oh, baby, that was…fuck. Baby…*fuck*."

He was at a loss for words, and so was I. All I could do was clutch him close and kiss his sweaty neck as I shuddered around his still-hard cock. I felt blissed-out thinking about how he was inside me, skin-to-skin, cell-to-cell, and the even greater wonder of it was that, when he pulled out, he'd leave part of himself behind.

This was for only me. He'd given this special gift to no one else ever. And I wanted it from only him.

"I love you," he whispered.

"I love you too."

After he pulled out, I expected him to panic, like last time. But he didn't. He held me tight and used his fingers to push his cum back inside me when it started to drip out. "Merry Christmas," he whispered, serious and sober. "My present for you."

I kissed him, heated and needy, until the tenderness passed enough for me to breathe again. It was the greatest present I could have ever imagined: love, trust, and Daniel.

Later that night, we did it again, this time in the bed. We took our time, and I reached that amazing anal climax I craved before Daniel came too and left more of himself behind in me. It was so hot and just as beautiful as the first time. I'd never felt closer to another person. Open, receiving, trusting.

And the next morning, Daniel woke me with a kiss and a slicked-up asshole. While I was still hovering on the edge of sleep, he opened himself up to me, accepting me raw. The trust of being let inside, of being allowed to return the gift of this kind of intimacy, blew my brains out, took my soul, and shook it up. When I came, I left proof of myself behind, too, and when Daniel asked me to make sure it didn't leak out, I'd never felt so gratified.

So trusted. So close.

So in love.

Chapter Thirty-One

WE WERE HALFWAY through our pancakes when the morning went to hell.

The phone rang and Daniel startled. "Huh. Not many people have this number yet. Just you and your parents, Minty, Robert, Kerri, and my family in Florida."

That seemed like a lot of people to me, but I said nothing as I buttered the brown circles of cooked batter. As Daniel hustled to the extension on the kitchen wall next to the counter and picked up, I avoided making eye contact with Milky Way where she sat hopefully at my feet.

"Hello?" His eyes first went wide and then vibrantly angry. He squeezed them closed and his expression hardened into stone. Our tranquil, postcoital morning dissolved into strain and anxiety.

"She's okay, though?" He pressed two fingers to his temple and shook his head. "How long will they keep her?"

Shit. Was it his mom? Kennedy? His grandmother? It had to be his mom given how angry he seemed.

"What does *that* mean?" He turned, resting his shoulder against the wall, as if he needed the support. "It's that bad?" He paused, and then with a hint of shame in his voice, he went on, "Did she hurt anyone else?"

I abandoned any pretense of buttering my pancakes and crossed to him, putting my hand on his arm. He didn't move or acknowledge me, but he didn't shake me off either, so I didn't withdraw my support.

"Will there be a court date?" He let out a shaky breath.

I tilted my head, trying to understand what was happening.

"Yeah, okay. I can testify. Sure." He let himself fall harder against the wall, and then slid down to the floor, as if his knees were giving out on him. I followed him down. "And what does that mean for her? Long-term, I mean?"

I could hear the rumble of a deep voice through the earpiece, but I couldn't make out any words.

"No, no, don't apologize. I should be thanking you. Because if not for you…" He choked up, pinching his thumb and forefinger at the bridge of his nose. "I wish…" He let out a rough laugh. "I just wish everything was different. For all of us."

I leaned against him, trying to give him comfort, not sure he even felt it through whatever he was processing.

"Yeah, I know. I love you too. Tell the kids…" He cleared his throat. "Tell them I'll be there for Christmas after all. Yeah, it's all right. They need some normalcy after this. I'll be there. Love you too, Grandpa." He pressed the handset into my grasp, and I stood to replace it on the hook, before sinking down beside him again.

We said nothing for a long time. I held his hands, and he played with my fingers, his chin shaking and emotions moving over his face like clouds in a storm.

"My mom got drunk."

I nodded. I'd figured out that much already.

"She decided to drive to another bar when the first one cut her off."

I stiffened and drew myself even closer, as close as I could get to him while still leaving him space to breathe.

"She didn't make it there. Her tolerance wasn't as high because, you know…" he waved his hands around. "A few months of sobriety and all. She got into a wreck, and she's in the hospital."

"Oh my God."

"Yeah. She's injured, but she's going to be okay, they think. Spleen and kidney bruising, some lacerations to her face and hands."

"I'm sorry."

"She hurt no one but herself, thank God." Daniel's lips twisted. "But this was it for my grandparents. They aren't going to let the kids continue to be exposed to this, now that they've seen it for themselves. They've kicked her out, and they've filed for custody. They have an emergency court date this week and have asked me to come testify about why she can't continue to have custody of them."

"That's..." I didn't finish. What was it? Good? Bad? Awful? The right thing to do? I didn't know.

"I'm sorry. I hadn't intended to go back to visit until spring break, but..." He pressed my hands to his mouth, kissing my knuckles and then turning them over to kiss my wrists. "I wanted to spend Christmas with you. Get to know what the Mandels do for the holidays. See that Hanukkah bush you told me about."

"It's just a Christmas tree with a menorah on top. Honestly, it's kind of offensive if you're not, you know, part of my actual family. My dad's ridiculous. So don't worry," I said. "You can be there next year."

He nodded, and then pulled me into a hug. We sat there on the floor, our pancakes going cold, and Milky Way snuffling around the kitchen table, hopping up and down on her back legs, ignoring us.

This wasn't how I'd imagined our winter break or first Christmas either, but I understood.

Eventually, I asked, "When do you need to leave?"

"There's a flight this afternoon, my grandfather said." Daniel sighed and hefted himself up, before reaching down to pull me up as well. "Let's eat, and then I have something to show you—well, to *give* you—before I need to pack."

"To give me?"

Daniel smiled, and it was sweet and loving, but still tinged with the grimness of the news. "Yeah, for Christmas."

"But I don't have your present! It's at my house. Let's wait until you get back."

"No," he said, shaking his head. "This is a useful gift, and I want you to feel free to use it right away. Okay?"

After cold pancakes made their way down our throats, Daniel bundled me up in his big, thick coat hung up by the kitchen door, and then pulled a sweater on, over his long-sleeve T-shirt. "C'mon," he said, tugging me out into the backyard. Milky Way scampered after us into the gray Tennessee winter.

I followed him to the detached garage that had, when he'd started the process of moving in, contained the remnants of broken pots and planters. Now I noticed there was a small side door built in that hadn't been there before.

Daniel led me to it. "Ready?"

I laughed, trying to figure out what could be inside. "A lawnmower? To make this summer easier on both of us? A puppy?" I guessed.

"See for yourself."

He opened the door and let me go in first, flicking the light on as he stepped inside, too.

"Oh." I couldn't think of what else to say. I was breathless with surprise and affection, and a horrible feeling of embarrassment. Because my framed photo of the two of us and the mixtape I'd made for him were woefully inadequate. Because within the garage was an even smaller room, and it was perfect. "A darkroom? This is…it's just…Daniel! You didn't have to do this!"

"I know. And I know you have access to the darkroom on campus, but it's always at awkward hours, and some of the subject matter is more risqué than should be developed in a public place. So, when I had the people in to outfit the bathrooms with new fixtures, I asked them to price out a darkroom, too. It wasn't too much. And I did a ton of research on what I should buy, but you're welcome to replace anything that isn't what you need." He walked over to a small heater and turned it on. "This is an oil convection heater. It doesn't generate dust. We'll have to solve the problem of cooling it down in the summertime later. I'm still looking for air-conditioning units that are dust-free. I'm not sure they exist."

"When did you have time for this?" I asked, finding the room was stocked with all the supplies I needed. He'd been thorough.

"I was lonely and bored out in Kingston before the old place sold. Once I decided on this, I bought a bunch of photography magazines and took some books out from the library. The local one, so you'd never know." He smiled. "Do you like it?"

"Do I like it?" I asked around a lump in my throat. "I love it. This is—" I threw my arms around his neck. "This is perfect. I love it so much. I love you so much. I'm so happy, and I'm so grateful. And I also need to buy you a better present now."

"Don't you dare," Daniel said, rubbing his nose against my cheek and taking a deep breath of my scent. "I did this because I could afford to, and I don't want you buying me anything other than what you already got. I know I'll love it."

"I hope so," I murmured.

"Now," he said, pulling away. "Why don't you explore out here, and I'll go pack."

I started to argue that I wanted to help him, but he kissed me, and turned me around to face the equipment and shelves of chemicals. "Make sure you have everything you need. I want you to be able to use this while I'm away."

I didn't argue and got to work examining everything, marveling at Daniel's generosity and love for me. He was definitely going to get more than a framed photo and the mixtape. Maybe I'd gift him another sexy photo session and make a private album just for him.

I wished I could give him the gift of a healthy mother and a trouble-free family. I wanted to give him that more than anything else in the world.

Chapter Thirty-Two

AFTER A LONG but far too short goodbye in Daniel's driveway, Milky Way and I started off toward my house. The sun had set already, and that distinctive winter darkness was closing in. At least it was punctuated by the bright lights of homes and stores decorated for Christmas. I remembered some photos I'd taken when I was younger of lights reflected in the lake. I knew now those had been some pretty shabby photos, but I'd been impressed with them at the time.

I shrugged and petted Milky Way, who panted in the passenger seat. She wasn't sure what was happening, and I didn't blame her for being anxious. She must be wondering if she was going to the vet, or to Kerri's, or to somewhere new. Her life had been turned upside down when Bobby had died, but at least she was well-loved and had many people who cared about her. Well, three people. Me, Daniel, and Kerri. Though shortly it would be five, because my parents loved dogs, and they were going to adore Milky Way.

When I reached my street, I turned off the Christmas tunes I'd been listening to and pulled into my driveway. I couldn't wait to tell my parents about the darkroom, though I was less enthused by having to report that Daniel's mom had gotten into an accident after falling off the wagon again. I knew, despite her own issues with pills, my mother worried Daniel had inherited the "alcoholic gene," as she put it, and could end up like his mom.

"C'mon, girl," I murmured to Milky Way, clutching her to my chest and exiting the car. "Let's go meet your new favorite people."

I started toward the front door only to stop in my tracks halfway up the sidewalk.

"Peter."

I blinked. Rage flared inside me, hot and cold at the same time. A horrible pain stole my breath like a sucker punch. "Adam."

Milky Way twisted in my arms, sensing my distress. I held her tighter.

Adam rose from the front stoop and walked toward me, his shaking hands outstretched, and his expression lost. "Peter, please listen to me."

I shook my head. "Stop stalking me."

"But I chose you," he said, his voice strained with emotion. "No, I *choose* you. It's over with Leslie, forever and for good. She knows everything now. She knows I'm in love with you, and that I've chosen you."

I blinked at his delusion. "You haven't 'chosen' me. I'm not available. You need to leave me alone."

"Peter, I know I did a lot of things wrong. I'm going to be a better person, I promise. I *know* you still love me. You never stopped. How could you stop? We're a masterpiece. There's nothing out there like us." His voice broke. "Just say you'll take me back. I'll be so good to you. You'll be so happy. I promise, Peter. On my honor."

I almost laughed. His honor? What was that worth? But my heart hammered in fear. He was blocking the entry to my house, the way to safety. I backed up, deciding to return to my car. He strode toward me, and I ran. I got my keys into the car door just as he reached me, but I couldn't turn them in time.

"Don't be afraid," he said, not touching me, but reaching out and putting his hands on either side of me against the roof of my car, boxing me and Milky Way in. His eyes traveled down to her and grew soft. He murmured, "Is this your new dog?"

"She's my boyfriend's dog," I gritted out, wanting him to get it. I wasn't available.

"What's her name?"

"It's not your business."

"She's pretty."

"Go home."

"I will, but I just need you to understand. You have to believe me. It's over with Leslie."

"Great. It's over with Leslie." I doubted it was even true.

"No!" he said, vehemently. "It's *not* great. It hurt her a lot. But I couldn't stop loving you, Peter. I couldn't forget you no matter how hard I tried, and I know you feel the same about me." His voice softened, wheedling.

I couldn't believe he thought he could convince me to come back to him. Once, I'd loved him with my whole heart. I'd have done anything to hear him say these words a year ago. But not like this. I'd never wanted it to be like this.

"Adam, move your hands off my car."

"Tell me you believe me."

"I believe you."

"You believe me about what?"

"That it's over with Leslie." Milky Way panted with anxiety. "I believe you."

He stepped back, but not far enough that I could make a break for it. He was stronger than me. Physically, he always had been. Emotionally, though? That was another story.

"Do you believe me when I say I love you? That I've always loved you?"

"I guess."

"What does that mean?" His voice pitched up. "I've never wavered."

I took a steadying breath. "I mean that you *think* you love me." Milky Way whined. "You love me the way you know *how* to love. But that doesn't matter, Adam, because I don't love you." I shoved against him, surprising him enough that he lost his footing. I ran toward the front porch. I hoped the door wasn't locked. My parents were fifty-fifty on locking it, and I hoped beyond hope that tonight was one of the times they'd forgotten.

"Peter," he said, grabbing the back of my coat and hauling me toward him. "We need to talk."

"Adam, no." I yanked free of his grasp. "I don't love you. I have a boyfriend. Don't touch me again."

He raised his hands as if in surrender, but I needed to make it clear. "If you touch me again, I'll tell everyone—*everyone*—including your parents, what you and I did. I'll publish it in the paper. I'll scream it every time I run into someone from Kingsley on campus."

"No, you won't."

"What makes you think I wouldn't?"

"Because it would hurt Leslie even more, and she's the victim in all of this. You and me, we made her the dupe."

"Adam," I growled. "Go home."

He stepped away from me, shoving his hands into his pockets, and that's when I realized he wasn't wearing a coat, just a button-up open over a black T-shirt and some jeans. "You need some time to process this. I'm here for Christmas, and you can come over to my house anytime."

"I won't be coming over, Adam. And you won't be coming back here either," I said, stepping quickly toward the front door. "Stay away from me. All you've ever done is hurt me and ruin my life."

He stared at me as I wrenched the door open—it was unlocked, thank God. Darting inside, I shut and locked it behind me, panting like Milky Way. I half expected him to start banging on the door with his fists.

But he didn't.

Silence descended, and I realized my folks weren't home. They'd left the front door unlocked while they'd gone out. That was so dangerously like them. I put Milky Way down, but she didn't stop cowering at my feet.

I glanced at the clock over the living room mantel and realized it was well past her dinner time. At that same moment, I remembered her bag of food was out in the car. There was no way I was going back out there tonight to get it. What if Adam hadn't gone home? What if he was out there waiting?

I went around the downstairs closing the blinds and pulling the curtains to keep any spying eyes from watching me. Then I went to the kitchen, checked that the back door was locked, and pondered what to do for Milky Way. There were some cans of Harry's dog food in the pantry. They weren't expired yet. I put some in a bowl for her, and she ate it with gusto, happy now that she'd been fed.

When I let her out back to do her business, I stood in the door, shaking from both the cold and anxiety. What if Adam was out there? What if he shoved his way inside? What if he wanted to do more than talk to me? My stomach twisted. I felt dizzy and nauseous. "Hurry up," I called to Milky Way. "Come on, girl."

She finally trotted back inside, oblivious to how scared I was. I took her up to my room, locked my bedroom door, put on pajamas, and cuddled with her on the bed. The whole while my heart hammered, and my head whirled.

I chose you.

I chose you.

I chose you.

I groaned and pulled the pillow over my head, trying to settle enough to go to sleep. But when I did, I dreamed that Adam and I were back together. We were at a beach resort, drinking champagne, and I toasted him, saying, "I love you, and I'm so grateful you chose me."

And Adam replied, "Eater, don't you get it? I'll always choose you."

I woke up in a sick sweat.

✦ ✦ ✦

THE NEXT MORNING, I took Milky Way downstairs and introduced her to Mom and Dad over breakfast. As I'd suspected, she was a hit, and by noon my dad had taken her into his office and stolen her affections forever.

I didn't mention Adam's visit to them. I should have. I knew that. But I couldn't bring myself to tell them I was feeling threatened by a boy I'd once loved. As far as they knew, Adam had stopped calling me a few months ago and had moved on with his life. Given my mother's stance that Daniel was too "dull" compared to Adam, I suspected that, despite how things had ended, and how angry she'd been that first night when I got back from Atlanta, she'd always held a place for him in her heart.

Given my dream from the night before, I seemed to hold a place for him, too. It was disturbing and frustrating to be so betrayed by my own sleeping mind. Since Dad had Milky Way under control, and Mom was working on making a countess fall in love with a baker's son, I grabbed my Leica and headed out into the grim day.

Drizzle slapped my windshield as I drove, looking for the right place to take pictures. I wanted to match my mood to the scenery, needing to process my feelings on film. The quarry was a great location. The water, blue and perfect on a summer's day, looked as gray as the rocks and clouds ahead.

I took some nature shots and then set my camera up on a rock, stripped my shirt, and posed with my hands over my face, my shoulders hunched, my spine bowed. I was on the fifth or sixth equally miserable pose when I stopped.

I was doing it.

All it had taken was one encounter with Adam, and I was using my camera to show how much I could hate myself.

I wiped at my eyes. This was why we were bad together, sick and twisted. I remembered Adam telling me we were glorious, beautiful, and all sorts of adjectives that I couldn't put together with the sickness in my chest. That wasn't love. I knew that now.

I knew love.

I felt it. Every day with Daniel I felt the clarity, the joy, the honesty of love.

This feeling? Was bullshit.

I stood tall, put my shirt back on, chilled to the bone, and walked back to my car. Turning the heater on full blast, I pulled out my wallet, and gazed at the photos of Daniel I'd tucked inside. He was warm, tender, generous. He never asked me for more than I could give. He always gave as much as he could. I trusted him.

And he trusted me. Enough to have given me a piece of himself, and to have taken a piece of me. Vulnerable and open. The kind of love that I'd always dreamed of.

I noticed a white edge of a photo sticking out from a hidden pocket in my wallet. My stomach dropped again. The last time I'd thought about this compartment was when I'd placed the photo there almost a year ago.

I pulled it out with shaking fingers.

Adam and I smiled, clutching each other, tangled in the rough sheets of a Florida motel room. I remembered the pleasure, the fleeting happiness, the shame.

Rolling down the car window, I held the picture out in the sharp, winter wind. I let go and didn't bother to watch as it was swept away from me.

I started the car and pointed it toward Daniel's house.

I had new photos to develop. Not these I'd taken today, but the ones from the week before Daniel had left again. Naked Daniel, laughing Daniel. Bundled-up Daniel wearing a scarf and glowing with cold. Sweet Daniel, half-asleep in bed. And photos of me, too. Laughing, smiling, glowing—with cold *and* love.

I wasn't going to be this person. I didn't want to be. Tearing the half-used roll of film from the back of the Leica, I ripped it from the spool and exposed the shots to the sun. Light would drive away darkness. It had to.

I drove away from the quarry. It was best to leave it behind, in the past. With Adam.

Now, if only he'd just stay there.

Chapter Thirty-Three

BACK HOME AGAIN, I was greeted by a note in my mother's handwriting saying, "You missed a call from Daniel. He got to Florida safely. There's a story there. I'd like to hear it." Then farther down the pad, she wrote. "And you missed a call from an odd man named Harold? He asked that you call him back regarding the pictures. He said you'd know what that meant. Cryptic. Should I even ask?"

The number was written at the bottom of the note, so I made sure Mom was locked away working, and Dad had Milky Way in his office still, before calling Harold back.

"Peter," he said after we'd exchanged hellos. "It's good to hear your voice. It reminds me that he really is dead and that the boy in these self-portraits is someone else."

I'd sent Harold a packet of prints, including a varied selection of some of my best shots. Mostly portraits, since I knew that was his specialty, but also some self-portraits and nature shots, some Tilt-a-Whirl madness, and some of the pictures I'd taken of Renée behind the scenes, getting her face on.

I didn't quite know what to say, but I decided to go with, "I'm glad to hear from you, sir. I'd hoped I would."

"Don't call me 'sir.' What a load of paternalistic nonsense, my dear. Just call me Harold. And, yes, it took me some time to get up the courage to open your package. I had a lot of worries about it."

"Yeah?"

"Yes. What if you were a terrible photographer with no eye for composition or subject matter? Or what if you were a good photographer, plenty talented, but I hated your work? We can't all love what we know is good, can we?"

"I guess not."

"I worried I'd be letting George down if I didn't look, and I worried I'd be hurting his memory somehow if I did and hated the photos. It was all very fraught."

"It sounds like it."

"In the end, I opened the package."

I held my breath.

"You're good. Very good. I'd like to see even more photos from you. This time with a theme. Imagine that you're curating a show of some type. And, should you send these to me, and if I agree that the selection is worthy, then perhaps I'll give you half a wall at my next gallery show this summer. It'll be a small, but valuable place to put up some of your work."

"What?" I gasped. This was so much more than I'd imagined or dreamed.

"But only if I like it," he said sternly. "And only if it complements my own show, of course."

"What's your show about?"

"The theme is the male nude."

"Oh."

"Is that something you're capable of complementing?"

"I can do nudes." I swallowed hard. But who would be my model? I could take portraits of my own body, and I had many times before, but was that what he'd want to see? More importantly, was that what I wanted to show? "Are we talking erotic or tasteful?"

"Both, darling."

"Right." I had a lot of erotic pictures I hadn't developed yet, but

I'd taken the photos thinking just of the moment. I hadn't gone into it trying to work with a theme, or to present the naked body in any particular way. "I'll have to think it over."

"Models must consent, of course."

"Yes, of course."

"Do you have a release form?"

"No?"

"I'll send one to you and you can make knockoffs."

"Thank you."

"And Peter?"

"Yes?"

"Your mother…" he hesitated. "It was nice to talk with her for a few seconds, even if she doesn't know who I am."

"I'm glad."

"Thank you."

"I'm the one who should be thanking you!"

"Well, you can thank me by sending me solid work. None of the student stuff that my agent is always thrusting at me, as if I can't tell art from shit."

"No student work," I breathed.

"You're capable."

I hoped I was. Marta seemed to think so at least.

When I put the handset back onto the hook, I danced a jig in the kitchen. Worries about Adam floated away from my mind. I needed to think. I needed to make a plan.

I always did that best with a camera in my hands.

So back out on the road I went, and the day flew by along with the click of my camera's shutter. When the evening rolled in strong and dark, I decided to head back home.

✧ ✧ ✧

AFTER TAKING PHOTOS for hours, making mental plans about

where and how I wanted to take pictures of myself, deciding on the theme of "joy in the male form," I felt challenged, scared, but also certain that I could pull it off, and also that *I* was the right model for this project.

Finding joy in myself, my body, my gayness, and my pleasure was something I was determined to do, and the idea of photographing my journey made me feel proud and strong.

As I pulled into my driveway, the sun having long set, I remembered Adam. I'd managed to push him from my mind, but now it all came flooding back. I hesitated before opening my car door, worried that he might be waiting in the shadows again. I didn't like to admit his persistence scared me, but it did. What did he need to hear before he believed it was over?

I walked into the house with my senses on high alert for movement or sound, and then quickly locked the door behind me. Milky Way came running and I scooped her up, rubbing my cheek against her fur. She wriggled in my arms, struggling to get around to lick at my face.

"You're home. Good," Mom said, coming out from the kitchen with string cheese. Milky Way renewed her struggles, but this time to get down and hopefully score a treat. I put Milky Way down and she scampered to Mom.

"What's up?" I asked, worried that maybe Adam had harassed *her* today.

"Daniel called again. He wanted you to call him when you got back," Mom said, sighing at Milky Way. "She's sweet, but a demanding little thing. I already gave her cheese earlier. You can't have more," she said to the white furball at her feet. "Peter, deal with the dog, please."

I called Milky Way into the kitchen, giving Mom a chance to escape into her office. "It'd be better if she didn't give you any cheese at all," I said, stooping to pet Milky Way's head.

Daniel picked up on the second ring, almost as if he'd been sitting by the phone, which, as it turned out, he had been. "I've missed you," he said. "I didn't want to miss your call, so I've been reading in my room next to the phone."

"I keep forgetting there's a phone in the bedroom."

"In *every* bedroom," Daniel said with a laugh. "My grandparents believe in the power of communication. They had to disconnect the one in Kennedy's room, though. She was placing random outbound calls for fun."

"Oh, man."

"Yeah." He laughed. "She's something else. Anyway, hi."

"Hi."

"Like I said, I've been missing you. I regret not stealing one of your sweaters for this trip, so I'd at least have something that smelled like you."

"I could mail you one. Get it good and sweaty first and then send it down."

He laughed again. "See? You're good for me. I needed to laugh right now."

"How are things?"

"Rough. The kids are upset, of course. Mom looks like hell." He sighed. "She keeps begging me to talk my grandparents out of going for custody, but, God, Peter..." I could almost hear him raking his hand through his hair anxiously. "I just can't. I can't put them through this anymore. I grew up with it, and they shouldn't have to go through it too. I know she loves them, but she can't do what it takes to mother them. I know it's the addiction. It's not that she's a bad person, or even a bad mom, but I won't let them live the way I lived."

"I'm so sorry."

"I feel like a traitor, but I love my brother and sister. I have to do this, even if it hurts my mom."

"You do. It's hard, but it's the right thing."

"Is it?"

"Yeah," I reassured him. "I think it is."

"Thank you. I know it's true, but I just needed someone who isn't involved in this mess to say it. So thank you."

"Always."

Daniel let out another heavy sigh. "But enough about that. What's going on with you?"

I hesitated, the recent memories of Adam on my front stoop rearing up, stressful and ugly in my mind. I decided to lighten the mood with the good news first. I told him about my conversation with Harold.

"That's amazing," he said. "I'm not surprised at all. You're such a talented photographer. That's why I got a darkroom for you. Have you had a chance to use it yet?"

"Yesterday," I told him. "It had everything I needed. I developed some great pictures of you. I'll probably go back tomorrow. I was out all day today grabbing shots."

"Your mom said you were out yesterday afternoon too?"

"I was, but…those shots ended up…I didn't want to develop them after all. I destroyed the film."

"Destroyed the film? That sounds dramatic. What happened?"

It was my turn to let out a heavy sigh. "Well, when I got home the night before last, after leaving your place, Adam was waiting on my front stoop."

A heavy beat of silence fell before Daniel said, "Oh? What was he doing there? Wait, are you okay?"

"Yeah, I'm okay. He was here because he wants to get back together."

Daniel's silence was loud.

"I told him no way, of course," I said, my breath coming in funny little pants. I giggled nervously, as if I were lying. My heart jolted, and my palms went sweaty. "I told him to leave."

"Good."

"But he didn't go right away. He told me he'd ended things with Leslie, that she knew everything about us, and he'd chosen me." I laughed again, and this time it sounded painfully tight. "Right. He'd chosen me. Like I'm a piece of candy he can just pick out of a batch."

Daniel stayed silent.

My scalp and armpits broke out into a sweat. I felt like I couldn't breathe. "Crazy, isn't it? That he'd think he could just show up, and I'd fall into his arms."

"Is it crazy?"

"Yes!" Everything was coming out strange. I took a slow breath, trying to calm myself. Daniel wasn't angry. Everything was fine. It was all going to be okay. "I don't love him, and I don't care if he's come clean with Leslie. All I know is he makes me miserable. Just seeing him for a few minutes yesterday made everything go dark, and when I went out to take pictures, I found myself taking all kinds of ugly, sad shots. It was just like last year. Being near him? Remembering it all? It just makes me hate myself."

"Peter..."

"I'm sorry. You've got so much going on in your life. You don't need this, too."

"What is 'this,' though?" Daniel asked, his voice quiet. "Is there a 'this?'"

"No. The only 'this' is just how stressful it was to see him. That's all there is."

"I know that." He didn't sound like he did, though. "You're right. I'm going through a lot right now, and I'm..." He paused, like he was gathering courage. "I'm scared. Because of my mom, because of what I'm doing here, the testimony I'm going to give against her." He took in a shaky breath. "And I'm also scared because of what we did together the other night, what we shared, and how vulnerable that makes me feel."

"Daniel," I breathed. "What we did was sacred to me, but if you never want to do that again then—"

"That's not the issue. It's trust. Right now, I'm torn up about what it even *means* to trust someone. My mom thought she could trust *me*, and now I'm helping her lose her kids. I've always *wanted* to trust my mom, but she's proven to me so many times that I can't."

"Daniel…"

"I want—no, I *need*—to trust you, and I do. *I do.* But right now, with everything? I feel like, I feel like—" He broke off and I wanted to crawl into the phone, down the line, and into his brain to take out whatever horrible thoughts he was having.

"I know you're scared," I said, sliding down to the floor to sit with my back against the wall. "But I'm not going anywhere with anyone. Not Adam. Not anyone else at all. Understand? I'm not even tempted. Not even a little."

"I know. I believe you. But you loved him so much."

"Loved. Past tense."

"He was your first love."

"*You're* my love," I said. "You. I love you. Please don't let this come between us. It'd just be letting him ruin something else in my life, and he doesn't deserve that power."

"You're right. I'm sorry." He huffed. "For a minute, I was being selfish."

"It's okay," I said. "You get to be selfish sometimes. You can't be strong for everyone, and it's okay to show me your weakness. I love you."

"I love you too."

After that we were able to talk more objectively about Adam and what he'd said and done. Daniel advised me to keep on being careful. We couldn't know the state of Adam's mind right now. Not if he'd told Leslie everything, like he claimed. "I wonder, though," Daniel said, and then didn't go on.

"Wonder what?"

"How she felt? What she must be going through right now? She was a nice girl. I could tell that when I met her."

Guilt slammed into me. "I was so caught up in how it made me feel when he showed up that I didn't give her even a minute of thought." I let out a rough laugh. "You're a much better person than me. Again."

"You're a good person. He's hurt you a lot. Hold on." There was a voice in the background, muffled and masculine. "Yeah, Grandpa. Sure. I'll come help." Daniel sighed in my ear. "Hey, so Grandpa needs me to inflate some new rafts for the kids. They love the pool. Can't get enough of it. Paul burns like a lobster, though. I wish they made a stronger sunscreen."

"Go on then," I said. "Talk tomorrow?"

"I'll try."

"I love you."

Daniel sighed again. "I love you too. Stay safe."

"I will."

The sound of the line disconnecting hurt. I wanted to keep on talking with him, being close to him, until all the anxiety that'd been introduced between us at the mention of Adam dissolved. But life didn't wait for healing. It just carried on whether we were still hurting or not.

That night, with Milky Way asleep at my side, my mind turned over the events of the last few days instead of sleeping. Now that Daniel had brought her up, I couldn't stop thinking about Leslie, the real victim of what Adam and I had done.

How was she feeling? What must she be going through right now? How much hurt was she enduring? And who could she get comfort from? Her best friend was Sarah, and first and foremost Sarah was Adam's sister, his twin. Worse, Sarah had been in on the whole thing. Even Sarah's *boyfriend* knew the truth.

Leslie must be wondering if she could ever trust anyone again. Her world must have been turned upside down when he told her.

Groaning, I shifted, trying to get comfortable. But it was impossible. The discomfort wasn't in my body, it was in my heart and soul.

As ugly as it was, as scary as it would likely be, I knew what I needed to do. If not for Leslie, then for myself. Even now, even in this, I was a selfish jerk.

I just hoped I was being selfish in the right way for a change.

Chapter Thirty-Four

LESLIE'S HOUSE WAS in one of the nice new neighborhoods that had been going up in Knoxville over the last ten years or so. These consisted of brick homes and very little aesthetic variety. I didn't love the sameness of it all, but I knew the style was considered the latest sign of being "high class." Leslie's parents were both psychologists, and they did quite well. I remembered her house reflected that, both inside and out.

Not that I was going to be invited inside today.

Ringing the doorbell, I waited. My heart throbbed, and I was dizzy with nerves. I rubbed my cold hands together and tightened my scarf around my throat.

Footsteps sounded from within. "I'll get it, Mom!" Leslie's clear, calm voice.

I almost ran. The only reason I didn't was I knew I'd never make it back to my car and down the drive before she opened the door. And the only thing worse than what I was about to do to her would be running off before I actually did it.

The door swung open. "Oh."

I opened my mouth to speak but choked on the words and ended up coughing and gagging a little at the same time. I thought for a second that she'd slam the door in my face, but, instead, she came out onto the front porch, closing the door behind her.

"You." Her voice was pitched quieter and deeper than I'd ever heard it before. "The whole time. You."

"I'm so sorry," I got out. "I'm so fucking sorry."

Leslie crossed her arms over her chest, anger flaring her nostrils. "You're sorry? That's all you have to say?"

"What else can I say?" My desperate breaths puffed between us. Hers puffed right back into the same space. "Nothing will make it right."

"Why are you here?"

"Because I'm truly sorry, Leslie. I hurt you, and you never deserved that. It's been over with Adam since..." I waved my hand. "Well, you know since when, but it never should have been the way it was. That was on me. Not just him." I felt like I might puke. "I was part of that. I need you to know...I'm sorry."

She laughed bitterly. "You think that's enough? That I'll forgive you?"

"No." I shook my head. "I don't think you'll forgive me. I don't even know if you should. But I can't forgive myself if I don't tell you that I know what I did was really fucking wrong, and tell you how sorry I am about it. Even if that makes me another kind of asshole, it's at least the kind of asshole I can live with being." My voice trembled. "The asshole I was last year? Being that guy? I can't live with that anymore."

Another hostile laugh escaped her lips. "Great, so you come here and say you're sorry so you can go home with a clear conscience. You get to leave feeling so good about yourself, and I get what?" She tossed her hair, eyes hot with anger. "*Nothing.* I get to just *live* with the fact that my boyfriend, the guy I loved and thought I would marry, was *sleeping with* his best friend the whole time—his best *guy* friend, mind you—and even when he wasn't, even when you ended it, he still wanted to be with *you,* or someone like you. I was never enough."

"I'm sorry."

"Do you know how humiliating this is?" Her eyes filled with tears. "How embarrassing it was for me when Adam's lab partner, his new 'best friend on campus,' came to me and told me Adam was coming on to him? That he'd kissed him, and…" Her voice broke. "How *stupid* did he think I was? When I confronted him? He denied it. But I knew. I *knew*. It all clicked into place in an *instant* when Sammy told me what Adam had done. *Everything* about how his 'friendship' with you ended suddenly made sense." Her lips twisted with pain. "Did you laugh at me? For being so stupid? Did you both laugh at me?"

"No. Never."

"I don't believe you."

"I guess I haven't given you a reason why you should, but I promise, Leslie, I *promise*, it was a lot of fucked-up things, but it was never like that." My hands shook as I brushed them through my hair and tried to catch my breath. "Adam loved you. That's part of why I ended it. He *did* love you, I swear, but I couldn't do it anymore. I didn't want to. It was all too gross. I'm sorry."

Tears fell from her eyes.

"What made it so confusing for me was that he loved us both."

A sharp sound of hurt burst out from her.

"I'm truly so fucking sorry." There was nothing I could do or say. Because I *was* the asshole here. Whether I want that to be true or not. "We never laughed at you. And I loved you too, for what it's worth. You were a wonderful friend to me. One of the first I'd ever had in my life. And I repaid you by lying to you and hurting you in the worst way. I'd hoped you'd never find out. I really thought that once I left him, he'd be happy with you."

"He wasn't," she bit out. "Sammy came along." Her lips twisted in a snarl. "Are you going to try to tell me he 'loved' Sammy too?"

"No," I said. "I don't think he did. But even if he had, it wouldn't make it okay. Nothing about what happened was okay."

"You think I don't know that?"

"I just wanted to tell you that I know it too. And I'm sorry. I'm deeply, deeply sorry. I keep saying it, and I know it won't change anything, but I am. I truly am. I'd go back and undo it if I could."

She studied my face. "I believe you would."

"Thank you."

"But I fucking hate you, Peter," she burst out. "So go now, okay?" She pointed at my car. "Go and never come back."

The echo of the very words I'd said to Adam not too long ago slapped me in the face. But unlike Adam, I intended to obey her command.

"Bye, Leslie," I said.

And that was that. I'd done what I needed to do, cut open the wound and sucked out the poison. I felt sick and dizzy as I climbed into my car. I probably shouldn't have driven in that state, but I needed to get away from Leslie's house, to grant her wish that I go.

I drove to Kingsley. The campus was eerily empty over the winter break. I got out and walked over the gray grass, stood in the place I'd been when I first saw Adam, relived that lurching, amazing moment when we'd met. I remembered the dazed infatuation, the thrill of his attention.

All the buildings on campus were locked up for the break, but I walked down to the flagpole and remembered Leslie and Adam striding toward me and the rest of our group, their hands clasped, and that horrible, sick feeling I'd had then—so close to what I felt now.

Leaving campus, I drove back to my neighborhood and walked to the pool. The place where Adam and I had first met up, where he'd read *Lolita*, and I'd fallen straight into lust.

I wandered over to the playground and the industrial-sized tire where we'd had that intense confrontation—the one that'd made me just as guilty as him in everything that came after; the one where

I'd told him I wasn't giving him up, and if he wanted to end things with me, he had to do it himself.

Sickness roiled in my gut. If I'd ended things back then? If I hadn't been selfish and addicted to my first all-consuming love?

Maybe everything would have gone differently for Leslie.

Or maybe not.

Since, despite Adam telling me he'd chosen *me*, that he'd broken things off with Leslie for me and told her *everything*, there was some guy named Sammy in the picture. So maybe things were always going to end in heartbreak for Leslie. Who knew?

I hoped there was a universe where it had played out in another way, and she'd gotten her happy ending. Because there were so many what-ifs that could have changed things. What if I hadn't switched to Kingsley? What if I hadn't let Adam convince me to go to Tilt-a-Whirl that first time? What if we'd never met Renée?

It was endless.

So many possible places an alternate universe could break off, and each would have changed everything. For all of us.

It didn't matter though, I thought, as I headed back home again.

In the end, none of us were together anymore, and all of us were hurt and damaged. Possibly forever.

At least by taking responsibility for my part of it, by facing Leslie, I could start to heal that wound in myself. If nothing else, I could say I respected myself again. I'd owned up to my part of the mess. I'd expressed my regret to the victim. I would never do anything like it again.

I wondered if Adam was out there right now struggling with the same horrible guilt and self-loathing that I'd labored under whenever I thought of him or Leslie or what we'd done.

In one way I hoped not, because I didn't like the idea of him suffering. But in another way, I hoped he was *aching* with guilt, because only if he had a conscience and real self-awareness would he ever be able to change and find a way to treat people right.

To do love right.

Milky Way greeted me again as I opened the front door. I bent to let her lick my cheek before petting her and saying, "Today was a hard day, but it's over now. It's done."

And it was.

My part in Leslie's pain was finally, truly finished.

Chapter Thirty-Five

CHRISTMAS EVE WAS when our family celebrated the holiday my father called Secular Winter Fest. As a kid, I'd always called it Santa Night. I'd grown out of that, of course, though my dad still stuffed a stocking for me, and my mom always put a few wrapped gifts under the tree. Last year there hadn't been any, but then last year they'd bought me the Volvo. It'd been too big to fit.

Over the last week, I'd added to the small stack of presents with gifts I'd bought for them. I'd found three early 1980s Johanna Lindsey romance books in like-new shape. The covers were some of her most racy and yet beautiful, and I'd had them framed for my mom's office.

For Dad, I'd also gone down the framing route with two photos of him at his university desk, taken earlier this semester during one of the lunches I'd shared with him. I loved both shots. He looked amused in one and patient in the other, peering up at me from behind reading glasses in both. I could imagine those were the expressions his students saw most often during his office hours, too.

I also had Daniel's presents tucked under the tree. A bootleg of one of Sting's performances, the mixtape I'd prepared, and the framed photo of the two of us.

I wanted to get him something even more special as a thank-you for the darkroom. I was considering having some of our more intimate—but not graphic—photos framed for his bedroom walls.

He still hadn't put anything up in there, having decided all the stuff from his old room—aside from the photo of his family before his father's death—needed to go to the trash with the rest of his stuff from his past. He'd even gotten rid of the *Danny, Are You Okay?* banner, which had made me a little sad. It might've been a gift from his ex, but it was such a cute story, and the reminder of it always made me smile.

But I'd had no time to accomplish that. It was Christmas Eve now and the stores would be closed on Christmas Day, and Daniel was returning in the afternoon of the twenty-sixth. I couldn't wait to see him, hold him, and go back to the new house with him. I planned to take a box or two of my stuff so that I could "move in" without alerting my parents to the situation.

It wasn't that I didn't want them to know. I just wanted to ease them into it. They might not have paid a ton of attention to me over the years, but I was an only child. I figured telling them I was moving in with my new boyfriend would trigger a bunch of *talks* and *emotions* that could just simmer on the back burner instead.

Eventually, I'd achieve a tipping point of things at Daniel's versus things at home, and I could just say, "Mom, Dad, I already live there anyway," and they couldn't dispute it.

I'd spent more time in the new darkroom Daniel had put together for me. He really had thought of everything, and the photos I'd developed out there were good, but not great. I needed to keep working. Going from my old self-portraits of misery to new ones of joy was a bigger change than I'd expected, but I knew I could do it. I didn't want my art to resonate because it was sad. I wanted it to resonate because it was happy. Gay joy. It was possible, and I wanted to prove it.

"Peter!" Mom called from downstairs. "Come set the table!"

I put a few photos I'd been considering sending to Harold into a file and shoved it into my backpack to take to Daniel's. I'd start a new filing cabinet over there, and this would be the first file in it.

In the downstairs hallway, I ran a few steps in my socked feet and launched into a long slide on the slippery wood before hopping over the threshold into the kitchen.

"At your service!" I said, snapping a salute.

"You're in a good mood." Mom opened the microwave to zap the green bean casserole. She'd picked up the holiday dinner from a local restaurant yesterday, and it was now heating up in various pots and pans on the stove. The pre-cooked tenderloin warmed in the oven.

"Hungry," I said, with a smile. "And my boyfriend comes home in two days." I slid across the kitchen, singing, "Twoooo dayyyys!"

"See? Petey-boy *is* my son," Dad said, from where he stood plating the sufganiyot and the latkes. One of his Jewish colleagues made them for him most years. "Singing with happiness."

I grinned. "He's really cute, and I miss him."

"Really cute, he says. He misses him, he says," Dad teased.

"What does your colleague think of you asking for his sufgani-yot and latkes on the twenty-fourth when Hanukkah was earlier in the month? Does he know we did nothing for it?"

"He thinks I'm a man who makes his own choices," Dad said. "And no."

"Blasphemer is more like it," I said.

"That's what your friend Robert's father, Dr. Michaels, thinks of me." Dad shrugged. "If the others think it as well for different reasons, so be it. I'm happy with how we do things. Aren't you?"

"I just think we should pay more attention to Hanukkah, too."

His eyes lit up. "Are you finally interested in learning about your heritage? We could do it differently next year. Use the menorah for real instead of tying the pre-lit one to the top of the tree—or we could do both!"

I hadn't meant that at all, but the light in my dad's eyes made my happiness bubble over. "Sure, let's each buy a menorah. One for you, and one for me, "I said. "And, yeah, maybe I am interested in learning."

The idea of being at home with Daniel next winter, and lighting the menorah for eight nights was cozy actually. I thought I'd like it. Though I didn't know if I could stand to learn the prayers. Maybe I'd just want to send good wishes into the universe for eight nights straight. I thought Daniel would like that, too.

After we sat down, Mom and I let Dad bless the food in his multireligious way before we dug in. We chatted, laughed, and talked about plans for the new year, enjoying each other's company, until a clatter came from the kitchen door leading out to the backyard.

Milky Way barked. Mom twisted in her seat to look over her shoulder.

The door opened.

Dad thrust his chair back, rising quickly. Milky Way went berserk. I jumped up too, and all three of us stared, hearts racing, breath coming in gasps, as Adam sauntered into the kitchen.

Milky Way stopped barking and started dancing around his feet.

Despite a bloody lip, a rapidly swelling eye, and a dazed expression, Adam tried for his usual charming smile. "Merry Christmas! Mind if I join you for dinner?"

Words were caught in my throat, and Mom and Dad just gaped, too.

Adam walked around the table, dropping into the chair he'd always sat in when he'd eaten with us last year. He started to fill the plate I'd put there for symmetry.

"Adam? Son?" Dad asked, still standing with his napkin in his hand, and a white-knuckled grip on the steak knife he'd been using to cut the tougher-than-expected tenderloin. "Are you all right?"

"Great. Just had a big talk with my dad." He grinned, his swollen eye squinting, and his lip bleeding again as the smile spread it wide. He licked the blood away and went back to spooning corn onto his plate with a shaking hand. Corn fell onto the table, but it didn't deter him. "It didn't go so well." He laughed. "I didn't really expect it to, though, you know? So…" he shrugged. "Yeah."

"He hit you?" Mom asked, her eyes shifting from Adam to my dad and back again, as if trying to gauge what either, or both, of them might do.

As for me, I was motionless, standing there with a slack jaw and my pulse rushing so hard I felt faint. Adam had just—

And he was here and—

There were bruises.

From his father.

I remembered the one time I'd met Adam's dad, the dark expression, the intensity of his energy. I had never forgotten how frightened Adam had always been of his dad, and how he'd confessed to me that his father had hit him the last time he'd suspected Adam of being gay.

"Please, sit," Adam said, like he was the host, and we were the guests. It was unnerving. Everything about the situation was. My mother reached across the table and took the steak knife from beside Adam's now haphazardly full plate. Adam didn't even seem to notice.

I looked toward my dad and found him looking at me. His eyes darted to the phone on the wall and then back to Adam. After a moment, he caught my eye again before sitting down. I followed his lead, my knees wobbling and hands shaking as I placed my napkin back across my lap.

Milky Way snuffled around Adam's feet. She lifted up on her hind legs to press her front paws against his thigh, panting up at him and expecting pets. Adam released another strange-sounding laugh and then petted Milky Way's head, speaking to her in the voice he reserved for animals—soft and sweet. "Hello, I met you the other night. Remember me?"

Mom and Dad both looked toward me, and I shook my head. Now wasn't the time to talk about that. What was happening right now was weirder than that entire prior encounter.

"So, what was the conversation about?" Mom asked, going back to her food, though she was still visibly shaken. She put a small bite of casserole into her mouth and chewed unnaturally, as if it was something she had to remember how to do.

"I told him the truth," Adam said, putting his chin out and wincing as he did. I noticed the additional welt blooming on his cheekbone and another along his jaw. "I told him I'm bisexual."

I blinked. Adam had never identified with that word at any point before. I'd tried to get him to embrace it as an identity, but he hadn't wanted to, or felt it was quite right. But now, here he was saying it as clear as day, as if we all knew, as if we'd all known for a very long time. And I supposed we had.

"I told him Leslie dumped me because of it."

I held back a snort. *That* wasn't quite true. But again, timing was everything and it wasn't the time for that discussion.

"And your father didn't take that well," Dad said, repeating Adam's words from earlier.

"No," Adam said, as if from far away, his eyes going distant and blank. "He didn't."

"What did your mother do, sweetie?" Mom said, her voice softening.

I felt a weird fissure open up inside between what I wanted from her—to stay on my side, to see Adam as the villain of the piece— and what I knew was right for Adam. He'd just had the crap beaten out of him by his own father. He needed solace from people he could trust. People he knew wouldn't hurt him.

That was us.

He'd come to *us*.

Even after everything, I didn't think he'd made the wrong choice. He was safe here, whether I liked his presence or not. The table had room for him tonight—and tonight only.

"Should we call an ambulance? Or take him to a hospital?" Mom asked Dad, her voice low, as though that would prevent me or Adam from hearing her.

"I'm fine," Adam said, taking a bite of tenderloin and chewing painfully. "It's not a big deal."

"The police—"

"No," Adam said a little sharper. "Don't. It won't happen again."

"But it's happened before, hasn't it?" Dad asked. "And if it's happened before, it *will* happen again. There's always a next time."

"No," Adam said. "Because he's thrown me out."

Mom blinked.

"No car, no clothes, no nothing. No school. No money. He told me to never come back. He never wants to see me again." Adam swallowed his bite of meat. Tears rose in his eyes. "I never want to see him again either. So, there won't be a next time. I won't let there be."

"Adam…" Mom's voice was tender.

Adam looked to me, and I realized I'd said nothing. I'd done nothing. I hadn't reached out a hand to comfort him. I hadn't asked questions or even felt tempted to hug him. I'd just sat there, dumbfounded, scared, and worried.

Adam whispered, "I told him I love you."

"You shouldn't have done that."

"Why not? It's true!"

I fought a weird rush of guilt. Adam had gotten beaten up because of me, he'd lost it all because of me. He'd lost his home, his family, his girlfriend.

I had to shake it off. It wasn't my fault. I hadn't asked him to do this, and I didn't owe him guilt or any other feeling because of it.

But I couldn't bring myself to tell him again that we were over and that I didn't love him. It remained true, but he was so shaken up right now. I didn't want to twist the knife or kick him while he was down.

"No one should be beaten up for who they love," Dad said firmly.

Mom grabbed her wine glass and drained it. Her hand was shaking and the horrified expression on her face told me her old trauma had resurfaced. And there were no pills in the house anymore to help her face it. I reached out and took her hand. She squeezed my fingers.

"Tomorrow, I'll talk with your father," Dad said. "Give him a piece of my mind, and we'll find a way to make this right."

"No, Mr. Mandel. I don't want him in my life." Adam took another bite of corn, stood up from the table, and said, "I'll be upstairs."

Then he walked out, just as strangely as he'd walked in.

We sat, staring at each other over the remains of dinner, trying to process what had just happened. Trying to pluck the answer of what we should do now straight from the ether.

Trying. And failing.

✦　✦　✦

DAD WENT UPSTAIRS and found Adam in my bedroom, on my bed, crying into my pillow. I stayed in the living room with Mom and Milky Way. The presents under the tree remained wrapped. The strings of lights glittered as the muffled sounds of Adam's sobs and Dad's voice drifted down the stairs.

I stroked Milky Way with one hand, and Mom held my other as we sat together on the sofa. She rested her head on my shoulder. I kissed her crown and tried to stop my whirling thoughts, but they just spun around wildly. A tornado in my mind.

When Dad came down and sat in the chair opposite us, he leaned back and stared up at the ceiling for a long time. "I told him he could stay tonight, but not in Peter's room. In the guest room. He's moved across the hall now. I think you should lock your door tonight, son. Just to be safe."

I nodded, my throat thick, my heart rabbiting against my ribs.

"Tomorrow we'll reassess the situation," Dad went on. "I would have liked to call the police and an ambulance, but he refused again. He's legally an adult. He doesn't seem to have a concussion." Dad clucked his tongue. "I don't know. I just don't know."

"His own father," Mom murmured. "Hurt like that by his own father."

"And not for the first time," Dad murmured.

Mom looked at me. "Was this a regular thing, Peter?"

I shook my head. "Not as far as I know. I think it just happened once before. When his dad found out about another boyfriend of his, a guy he was seeing in Rome."

"And the other kids? Are they safe?"

I swallowed. "I think so?" How could I know for sure? "They're adults, too, though. And they all manage their father's moods. Their mother does, too." I sighed. "I don't know."

We sat and stared at the glowing tree, all three of us a wreck of worry.

The menorah mocked me from the top. The original had given light for eight days without any oil, but tonight it shed no light at all on what we should do or what to expect now.

"We'll open the presents another night," Mom said, rising. I held on to her hand as she stood. "I can't say I don't wish I had some Valium around. This has been quite the Christmas Eve."

Dad rose too, ushering her back toward their bedroom. But he paused, glanced upstairs, and asked, "Do you want me to go up with you? Until you're locked in your room?"

I shook my head, still patting Milky Way. Adam had frightened me over the last few months, but tonight I was certain he wouldn't hurt me. Tonight, I thought if he asked for anything at all, it'd be to climb in my bed and cry in my arms.

There was no way that was going to happen.

Instead, I took the stairs on my tiptoes with Milky Way in my arms. I tried to miss the steps with telltale creaks until I was safely in my bedroom. I locked the door behind me. Paranoid, I checked under the bed, in the closet, and in the bathroom. Adam wasn't hidden anywhere. He'd stayed in the guest room.

That night, I couldn't sleep. I'm not sure any of us could. But as dawn rolled around, pearly and pink, unconsciousness tugged me under. I got a few hours of rest, and then rose, jittery with worry over what was ahead.

In the kitchen, Adam sat at the kitchen counter, wearing a pair of my sweats—too short—and one of my T-shirts—too tight. He ate from a cereal bowl, with jerky, mechanical movements and a hollow expression in his eyes.

My father was on the phone. Sitting down across from Adam, I poured myself a bowl of cereal, too, and listened in to the conversation. It became clear that my dad was talking to Adam's older brother, Mo.

"I see," Dad said. "Well, that's good. Yes, he can stay here one more night. And after that?"

Adam's gaze landed on me.

My heart wrenched. Bruises, swelling, despair, and yes, shining at me from beneath that sadness, was love. Raw, hopeful, yearning love.

I looked away, wanting no part of that. Not ever again. "Why is Dad the one talking with him?" I asked. "Why aren't you?"

"I can't." Adam shook his head. His voice sounded like he'd sobbed all night. "I don't want to hear what he has to say."

"Adam, he's not going to abandon you."

Adam shrugged. "He's always hated me."

"That's not true," I said. Even I knew that was a lie. "He doesn't hate you. And Sarah would never let him do that, even if he did."

Adam rubbed a hand over his eyes, his lips trembling. "I ruined everything for him. I can't ask him for help he doesn't want to give or to risk his relationship with our dad. I just…I can't talk to him. I can't."

I knew his fears were unfounded, but I understood. He'd put all of them in the path of a volcanic explosion with his confession. I could imagine Mo and Sarah didn't understand what had led him to admit it all in the first place. Not when they wanted him living in the closet, repressing everything, shoving it down, making it easier for the family. For them.

"I'm sorry." I held myself back from taking his hand. "You were brave."

"I was stupid," he spat out.

I pressed my lips together. Part of me thought he was, especially if he thought he could be with me. If that had factored in any way into what had happened with his dad last night, he *had* made a terrible mistake.

But I also knew what kind of strain it was to be living like that, hiding myself, afraid every moment of every day that the wrong people would "find out" and hurt me. I understood the temptation to just get it over with.

If that was what had happened, I understood.

I didn't ask.

Dad's conversation seemed to be wrapping up.

"I'll tell him," Dad said, his tone softer now. "And, let me just say, Mohammed, I'm terribly sorry things ended up like this." He replaced the phone and turned to us.

"That was Adam's brother."

Obviously.

"He was calling from the gas station down the road. He said he figured Adam was here because we're within walking distance, and Sarah said he'd be here."

I swallowed.

Sarah. How must she be feeling this morning? She'd always tried so hard to protect Adam. She'd done her share of awful, asshole things to help him keep a lid on his bisexuality and male lovers. She must be feeling like a failure. Though she shouldn't. She didn't bear any more guilt than I did. If anything, she bore less.

I'd been the one who—

No. I shut off that line of thinking. I wasn't going to let myself get suckered into believing I needed to save Adam. Just like Daniel, I couldn't be everyone's hero, or even *anyone's* hero. I was still trying to save myself, and I was succeeding. I wasn't going to get pulled back down into a pit of pain.

"Mo also said Adam's representation of the facts is true. His father won't allow Adam access to their house, car, or tuition money, or any other kind of maintenance. His mother has been arguing in support of him, but Mo thinks, if his father capitulates at all, it'll be some time in the future. For now…Adam's been cut off."

Adam didn't flinch. He'd known. He must have known even before he'd confessed the truth to his father. How painful had it been for him? To speak his truth aloud and know it was going to cost him his relationship with his dad, his place in the family? His relationship with his *mom?*

"Mo also said to tell you this is all bullshit."

Adam's head came up.

"He said as soon as your folks have left, you can come live with him. They're leaving on the—"

"The twenty-eighth," Adam said. "Yeah. I know."

"Mo said once they are out of the country there's no way they'll know if Mo and Sarah are still interacting with you." Dad reached out and patted Adam's hand. "They don't plan to let you flounder."

Tears came to Adam's eyes.

"And in the meantime, you can stay with your brother's friend Sean, but he won't be back from visiting family for the holidays until tomorrow. Sean will call to make arrangements. So…" Dad met my eyes, seeking my objection or approval, I didn't know, but he went on. "You're welcome to stay here another night. In the guest room. So long as Peter's okay with it."

I shoved my hands into my jeans pockets. I wasn't okay with it, but where else was Adam going to go? I already knew that if Leslie knew everything, then all our old Kingsley friends would take her side—rightfully—and Adam would be persona non grata in their lives. There was one other option. "What about Mike?" I said, turning to Adam.

"He's in Puerto Rico," Adam said. "His family wanted a tropical Christmas this year. Sarah was supposed to go, but she wanted to see Mom instead. I bet she regrets that now."

I chewed on my lip, crossing my arms over my chest.

Watching me, Adam stood. "It's okay, Eater. I'll find somewhere else to go."

I rolled my eyes. "Don't be an asshole. Sit down. We both know there's nowhere else to go. You don't even have a car to sleep in now. So just…sit. Stay. It's one night. It's fine."

Even so, I turned on my heel and walked out. Guilt tugged at me again. I should comfort him. I should hug him. I should stroke his hair and tell him everything was going to be all right. What kind of human being wouldn't do those things?

But I couldn't be that person.

He loved me, and I didn't love him. I couldn't give him false hope when he'd lost *everything* else in his life. That'd be unkind, unloving, and cruel.

I went up to my room and turned the lock again. I sat on my bed, stroking Milky Way's soft ears, and wishing Daniel were here. I perked up. That could be an answer. I could spend the night at Daniel's. My parents and I clearly weren't doing presents today either, and I didn't want to stick around and make things worse for Adam.

I grabbed my keys and the dog and opened my bedroom door.

Adam stood outside, his hand raised to knock, and his messed-up face growing darker with bruises by the minute.

Fuck. My escape thwarted, I resigned myself to what had to come next.

I stepped back and motioned him inside, taking a seat at my desk when he sat on the bed. Milky Way squirmed in my arms, and I let her down. She left the room, trotting downstairs, no doubt hot on the trail of something aromatic in the kitchen.

Adam got up and shut the door.

My heart thumped, but I didn't make a move to stop him.

Leaning back against it, he turned to me. "Peter." The desperation in his voice tugged at my heart. "Please. Give me another chance. I did it. See? What you always wanted me to do. I did it."

I shook my head. "Adam, no. I wanted a lot of things from you, but I never wanted this."

"I know you didn't want me to get hurt, but I thought if you understood how much I really love you, enough to tell my dad, enough to—"

I raised my hand, stopping him mid-sentence. "Adam, no. If you did all this for me, then that was a mistake. I'd rather you said you did this for yourself, or *anything* other than that you did it for me."

"Why?" he asked, sinking down to the floor, back still against the door. "Why not?"

"Because I don't love you anymore. I love someone else."

Adam winced liked I'd decked him on top of all his bruises. "But you haven't stopped loving me too," he insisted. "You couldn't. You'll never stop."

I sighed, tore my hands through my curls, and stood up so that I was towering over him. "I *have* stopped. I'm not built like you. I don't love multiple people in that way at the same time. Sure, I care about you. I didn't want anything *bad* to happen to you. I'd hoped you'd be happy with Leslie, or at the very least, happy without me. But I did stop loving you. I'm not quite sure when, maybe it started in Florida, maybe it started as soon as you started dating Leslie…" I took a shaky breath. "It'd definitely started by the time you went to Rome. And by the time you got back—"

"You'd fucked him," Adam gritted out.

I shook my head. "No. Well, not back then."

"You have? Now?" His fists balled up, and I took a stumbling step back, almost falling over my desk chair. He must have seen the fear in my eyes because he unclenched his fists, shook them out, and took a long, deep breath. "All right. It's okay. I thought you had. And it doesn't matter in the end. What matters is we can be together now… I love you. None of that other stuff matters, no other person matters."

"It does matter, because I love him," I repeated again. "And I *don't* love you."

"Peter, just—" He broke off. "You can't mean it. We're beautiful together. You and me? There's *no one* like you for me, and no one like me for you. We're a masterpiece. You know it's true. Maybe I messed it up at first, maybe I hurt us, but we can still fix it. We can be all that we were supposed to be. You just have to let us."

My heart twisted for him. Empathy I didn't want to feel body-slammed me. He looked so devastated. So miserable. And he really had lost it all. But that didn't mean he could have me.

I sat down by him on the carpet. I took up one of his hands, running my fingers over the knuckles, feeling the skin on the back, so subtly different from Daniel's in texture.

"Look at me," I began. "This is important."

He dragged his eyes up from where he'd been watching my fingers dance over his hand. "All right."

"Do you remember telling me about the trip you took with your family from Rome to Florence back when you were younger? You went to see the *David* there?"

"Yeah." He blinked, confused.

"And you know this past fall, someone took a hammer to the *David*'s foot, damaging it, right?"

"Yeah…"

"It can't ever be repaired. But he's otherwise still beautiful and perfect."

Adam tugged his hand out of mine, suspicion clouding his eyes. "Where are you going with this?"

"Just listen to me. I've told you a lot of things over the last few months—mainly to stay away from me—but I've never told you this."

He nodded. "Okay, go on."

I took his hand again. "I also remember you telling me about these other sculptures you saw in Florence. Unfinished works of Michelangelo's that were kept near the big room where the *David* stands."

"Yeah. *The Prisoners*." Adam wiped at his eyes, pushing the tears off his cheeks. "What about them?"

"I remember you described them to me so well, I could see them in my mind's eye." Adam always had such a way with words.

A writer through and through. "Then a few months ago, I came across a book of photos, a collection from the museum where the *David's* kept. I looked through it to study how the photos were taken, what angles were used, and the lighting. All of that. I thought it might be helpful one day. Photography jobs come in all kinds of shapes and sizes."

I realized I was stalling at getting to the point. Once I'd said what I needed to say, I'd have to let go of his hand and I'd never touch him again. Yesterday, I'd been more than all right with that. But now…

I cleared my throat and pushed on. "I got sucked in beyond just studying the photography work. The close-ups of the *David* were incredible, but that was no surprise." I licked my lips. "But those weren't what held my focus. You see, I couldn't stop looking at the photos of *The Prisoners.* I just kept coming back to them."

He looked up from where I held his hand, and our eyes caught.

"I loved how they were unfinished, forever frozen and incomplete," I said.

"It's sad."

"Is it? In the book, the write-up talked about how no one knew just why the sculptures weren't finished. They posed questions like, had Michelangelo been distracted from his work? Had he been pulled away to another project and just never made it back? Or maybe, as he'd worked, he'd seen a fatal flaw in the marble. Something he couldn't fix, and that was why they remained incomplete."

Tears filled Adam's eyes. "Why are you talking about this?"

"Because I remember you told me once that *The Prisoners* troubled you because you could see how beautiful they were supposed to be. It seemed a pity to you, a waste of time and marble. You said they could have been beautiful. You wished he'd finished them. But when *I* was looking at the photos, I thought of it differently. To me, they were *already* beautiful. Unformed, half-made, with a fatal flaw that even a great artist couldn't overcome. Left forever like that, complete in their unfinished way."

"Peter, something can't be complete if it's unfinished, and—"

"Shh. Adam, I think you imagine us as being like the *David*, nearly perfect with just a little damage to the toe—easy to overlook because the rest is so flawless. But I see us as being like *The Prisoners*—there *was* potential for something whole and complete, but there was a flaw that kept us from ever reaching that potential. Whether that was your family, or your ability to love more than one person at the same time, combined with my inability to be all right with that, or if it was our homophobic culture, or so many other things that went into the formation of the marble that made our relationship, but—"

"Peter, please, stop."

I shook my head, pushing on, "But whatever the case, we were *never* going to work. We don't have to look back at this as a failure. Our relationship had something beautiful about it, too. Like *The Prisoners*. That's why it's valuable to us both, even though it ended like this. But that's also why we need to stop it here. Now. Because if we tried to continue, we'd strike that fatal flaw at the wrong angle, and it'd break us both into pieces that couldn't ever be put together again."

"But I've already done that, don't you see?" He gripped my hand hard, and I felt his desperation radiate up my arm. "I've already struck that blow, and, without you, my whole life is ruined."

"You're only nineteen years old. Your life can't be ruined. Not yet." I touched his wet cheek. "And if I did what you wanted? If I took you back? We'd ruin each other for sure. This is your best chance to be happy, and mine too. Let's take it. Let's learn how to be better to the ones we love, how to not hold grudges or take our pain into our next relationship. Okay?"

"No."

"Adam, nothing you say will change my mind, so you need to change yours."

"Peter…"

I shook my head. "If I take this metaphor in another direction, I could say you have a choice now. You can let go of this and become the *David* yourself with just a small bit of damage on his toe. Or you can hold on to us and stay trapped in unyielding marble forever, because that's your choice. Move on and grow or stay stuck. I'm going to grow."

"But you just said *The Prisoners* were beautiful. Stay in this with me. Please."

"That was the metaphor about our relationship. We can only look at it as beautiful if we move on. If we keep hammering at it, we'll destroy every last bit that was ever good. But this other metaphor is about us, as men. As gay men—"

"I'm not gay."

"As a gay man and a bisexual man, then. We have to be better than we have been."

"We could be better together!"

I released his hand and put my fingers on his lips to keep him quiet. "We can't. Because *I don't love you*. Not anymore."

"This is about that guy, isn't it?"

"No. It's about me. If Daniel left me tomorrow, I still wouldn't come back to you. We're over, Adam. Accept that, so you can move on. Maybe even with Leslie if—"

"She hates me now!"

"Okay, then with some other person, or people."

"People?"

"Yeah, there are folks out there who are open to having more than one person in their relationships. Look at Robert and Barry.

There are probably girls like that, too."

"No, Peter… Please. *Please.*"

I sighed and stood, picking up my keys again. "I'm sorry, Adam. I've said everything there is to say. Now you just need to accept it." I tugged on the door behind him, opening it against his back, forcing him to move.

As he stood, I walked out, down the stairs, and out the front door.

My Volvo was waiting for me, and I drove straight to Daniel's, with tears running down my cheeks.

Chapter Thirty-Six

"WHAT'S WRONG, BABY?" Daniel's voice came down the line. "You sound upset."

When he'd first answered the phone, he'd greeted me with a hearty "Merry Christmas" but after I'd returned the greeting with a lot less enthusiasm, he'd known something wasn't right.

I stood in the middle of his kitchen, thinking that we should get a phone extension for the living room. It'd be a lot more comfortable. "It's a long story. I don't even know where to start."

"Long since yesterday?"

I groaned. "Yeah, pretty much. Hold on." I'd been so overheated, both from being upset and the aggressive heater in my car, that I'd opened the kitchen window when I first got to his house to let in a cool, fresh breeze.

After I closed the window, I picked up the phone again. "Sorry. Like I said, I don't know where to start."

"Is everyone okay?" Daniel asked.

I laughed a touch hysterically. "No. Not everyone."

"Minty?" Daniel asked, worry in his tone.

"No," I reassured him. "No, as far as I know, he's okay. It's Adam. He's not."

Daniel was silent for a moment, but then asked, "In what way?"

"His dad beat him up."

Daniel let out a rough breath. "Thank God." I must have made a shocked noise at that because he rushed to explain. "No, it's just that I thought he might be dead, from the way you sounded, so I was relieved. Not happy."

"No, he's alive," I said, pacing back and forth through the kitchen. I paused to look out the kitchen window at the gray backyard that I knew would be bursting with color in spring, but which was miserable-looking right now. "Sorry. I didn't mean it to sound so dramatic. Not that getting the hell beaten out of him by his father isn't dramatic." I tore a hand through my curls.

"Okay, let's start at the beginning," Daniel said.

I took a slow breath and let it out, leaning against the kitchen counter. "So yesterday was normal. Completely normal. Mom and Dad and I had gotten dinner from the same restaurant as always. And we'd just sat down to eat when he walked in."

I explained everything that'd happened, and when I was done, I let out another wretched little laugh. "I'm the reason he got beaten up, the reason he's been kicked out of his house and disowned, the reason he has no car and no money and no school anymore."

"No," Daniel said softly. "It's not your fault."

I'd known that already but hearing it from him made all the difference. It was like someone releasing an iron band that had crushed tight around my chest from the moment Adam had arrived. "He wants me back," I said, wiping a hand over my sweaty upper lip. "He wants us to get back together."

Daniel was quiet again. "And what did you say?"

"I said no. I told him that was never happening. I told him I'm in love with you."

Daniel remained silent.

"I told him that he shouldn't have come out to his dad if I was the reason, because I'm never going back to him."

"Peter..."

"I'm not."

"I know you aren't."

"You sound unsure." I couldn't stop the hurt in my tone.

"No, I'm just…" Daniel sighed. "This is a lot to take in. And there's been a lot going on. I'm here for you, though. And I believe you."

I groaned. "I'm sorry. I hate adding to your problems. How are things there? I haven't even asked."

"No," Daniel said. "We're not talking about me. We're talking about you right now. You're important to me, and this is a whole load of crazy bullshit that's been dropped onto your shoulders. Let me support you."

"You support too many people."

"I love you. Let me do this."

I sighed. "I'm at your house. I couldn't stay there with him."

"Stay where?"

I snorted. "Oh, yeah, I guess I didn't say. My folks let him spend the night last night and are letting him stay again tonight. He has nowhere else to go. Nowhere else to stay."

"A motel?"

"No money."

"Your parents could—"

"He's pretty traumatized," I said. "They didn't say as much, but I think they want him to stay somewhere he feels safe. And…not alone."

"Is he a danger to himself?"

"Possibly. His brother and sister can't see him until his parents leave the country again, and he doesn't have friends anymore. Not since Leslie found out, and they took her side—which they should have. Her side was always the only honest side."

"Peter, don't be so hard on yourself."

"Did I tell you I saw her? I went to her house. I told her I was sorry. She said she hates me. That seems fair. She told me to go, and

I left. But I did it. I took responsibility, and I'm not sorry about that, even if my apology hurt her." I was rambling now. Maybe seeing someone I cared about beaten up like that had shaken me more than I realized.

I sank into a chair at the kitchen table, laid my head down on the cool wood and took slow breaths.

"Baby, that was brave."

"I don't know. It just seemed necessary."

We were silent together for a few minutes, and then I went on. "Maybe I'll stay here tonight instead of going home. I don't want to be there if he's in the house."

"Why not?"

"I don't want to give him false hope. I mean, I've told him flat-out that we're over, and I explained it with this complicated metaphor about Michelangelo's sculptures—"

"What?"

"It's complicated, like I said, but I think he understands. You know…that I'm not going back to him. So, I think I should stay away until he can go be with his brother's friend tomorrow. Besides, I wanted to see if the sheets still smell like you."

"You can do that without spending the night, you know."

"You don't want me to?"

"You're always welcome in my house, baby. It's going to be your house too before long. But I also think…" He sighed. "I think you need to help him right now. I don't love the guy, and I don't want you putting yourself at risk for him. If he seems angry, or unpredictable, or dangerous, then stay at my place. But if you're just running away from having to feel something you don't want to feel about him? Then I think you should go back home. Deal with it."

"You want me to spend time with him?"

"Unless there's a reason you shouldn't for your own safety, I think maybe you should. Not for him, though it would probably help him, like you said, to not feel alone, but for yourself. Running away from whatever you still feel for him isn't healthy. It won't make things better for us, either, when I come home. Confront it now. Put it to bed. Come back to me when you're done."

"I won't be 'coming back to you,'" I said. "I'm not leaving you."

"I know. That's not what I meant. I just don't want to think there's anything you can't face when it comes to him, because that scares me more than anything."

"Why?"

"If you can't face what you feel for him, maybe it means there's still something there."

"No."

"People can love more than one person at once," he said, softly. "Some part of you might still love him."

I scrubbed a hand over my face. "I don't hate him. I care about him. But I don't love him."

"You're not *in love* with him," Daniel said. "But maybe you love him."

"I don't know. Everything with him has been so out of control since the day I met him. When I'm with you, things are peaceful, and I like how that feels. I love you so much. I wish you were home. I'd feel safer."

"You think he's going to hurt you?"

"No. But I'm going to hurt him. He still loves me and being near him? It's going to hurt him."

"It's going to hurt him more to feel abandoned by everyone he ever loved."

"For two days," I reminded him.

"Even one day of that kind of loneliness is too long. Look, I have no affection for him, and no reason not to want to see him suffer after what he put you through... But being here, dealing with this shit with my mom…" Daniel groaned. "It's too ugly to wish pain on anyone at all. Even my rival for your heart."

"He's not your rival. He has no chance."

"I love you," Daniel said. "I want you to be happy. Please, baby, deal with all of this now. Be a person you can look back on in ten years and not wish you'd done it differently. For any reason at all."

I didn't want to go back to my house and face Adam again. But Daniel was right. I was running away from feelings I didn't want to face.

"All right."

"And if he threatens you, call the police."

"He won't."

"Well, if he does…"

"I will."

We sat on the line in silence again, and I whispered, "I miss you. I love you so much. I want you home."

"Me too, baby. I want to be home."

"Soon," I said.

"Tomorrow."

"Yeah, tomorrow."

I took a long nap in Daniel's bed—the sheets did still smell like him—before heading back to my parents' house. I drove into the sunset, Christmas Day ending with a red-coral sky, and the threat of rain.

Chapter Thirty-Seven

I RETURNED TO the house right as dinner was being put out. Ragu spaghetti sauce and some noodles Dad had located in the back of the cupboard.

Mom met me at the doorway. "He's upstairs. He has been all day. Your dad's checked on him twice, and he's all right. See if you can get him to come eat, will you?"

I took the stairs slowly, trying to compose myself. When I realized what I was doing—shoving my feelings down, hoping to avoid them—I stopped in the middle, looked down, and remembered being fucked hard and fast there when Adam first returned from Rome.

Ghosts of us cluttered this house.

Our first time in my bed. Meals in the kitchen. Watching movies in the living room. Getting rimmed in my bathroom.

I started walking again. Ghosts would linger forever. But that's all that was left of us now.

The guest room was relatively free of memories. We'd never done much in there.

I knocked, and when there was no answer, I peered inside. Adam was on the bed, curled in a ball that almost made his tall form look small. "Hey," I said. "Can I come in?"

He unrolled at the sound of my voice, turning over to look at me. If it were possible, he looked even worse than he had that morning. "Have you thought about it?" he asked. "About us?"

I sighed and sat at the edge of the bed. "Adam, stop. There's no us. If you can put all that aside, I can be your friend. You don't have to be alone right now."

He swallowed hard and nodded.

I scooted closer to him and opened my arms. He fell into them with a sob, and I rubbed his back and smoothed his hair, shushing him. His scent flooded my senses and, with it, more memories hit me, too.

The feeling of him inside me, the way he kissed, the terrifyingly intense passion I'd felt for him. Even the way I'd learned to come on his dick, and the feeling of his cock thudding against my asshole. Inappropriate thoughts for such a sad time, and yet there they were. All my firsts were with Adam. All except for one.

But, my mind reminded me, *maybe he had that first, too.* I still didn't know for sure if he'd used a condom that last time. My heart thumped—part rage, part grief.

I took a shaky breath. Now was a terrible time to ask. But I had to know. I needed to know.

"Adam," I whispered, rubbing his back, my hand shaking so much that it jittered up and down his T-shirt. "The last time, in the middle of the night—*our* last time—did you use a condom?"

He stiffened against me.

"It's okay. Tell me the truth."

It wasn't okay, but I had to hear it from him. I needed to know. I'd tested negative, but I still wanted to believe that what I'd shared with Daniel was the first time anyone had ever had that with me.

Adam grabbed me tighter, his breath coming in hiccupping sobs. "I did," he whispered. "I'm a lot of bad things, but I'd never do that to you."

"You're sure?"

"I don't have anything to lose by lying now. You're gone, you're not coming back to me—right?"

I squeezed my eyes shut. "Okay. Thank you. I believe you."

He held me even tighter. I held him back. When I let go this time, it really would be the last.

"I know we're over," Adam said again, his voice breaking. "But I hate that I don't remember our last kiss. I hate that I didn't know it was the last one."

My throat went dry.

"Could we, I mean, would you kiss me now? One last time? With everything out in the open like this. No more secrets, no more lies. Just us."

I considered it: his lips on mine, the taste of his tongue. "No," I whispered and pulled out of his embrace. I'd never kiss him again. "Mom said dinner is ready. You should come down and eat."

He gazed at me. "Because of your boyfriend?"

"Because I don't want to kiss you. Come on. You need some food." I stopped by the doorway and turned back. "The next kiss you have can be with someone you've never lied to or hurt. It can be an honest kiss with no baggage or history. I want that for you."

"Is that what it's like with him?"

"Everything with him is honest."

I turned and started down the stairs, the scent of spaghetti sauce luring me down. My stomach growled. I was hungrier than I'd realized, after not eating much all day.

I sat at my spot, the same place I'd been sitting when Adam had barged in the night before. My parents were in their usual places, too.

"Is he coming?" Dad asked.

"I don't know. I guess we'll see."

I'd just finished filling my plate from the bowl of spaghetti in the center of the table when Adam joined us.

"Thanks for this," he said, quietly.

"The Mandel family's secret recipe," Dad joked just like always.

Adam gave him a wry, tired smile.

We all began to eat, all of us tired, all of us damaged.

Part XIII

Chapter Thirty-Eight

THE NEXT MORNING, while Adam and I ate a quiet breakfast at the kitchen counter, and Milky Way begged her new buddy for a piece of his toast, my dad came into the room with a half-full black garbage bag. With a sad frown, he placed the bag beside Adam's feet.

"Some of your clothes. Mo dropped them off just now while I was out getting the paper."

Adam stared at the bag and then nodded. He'd been wearing the same clothes he'd worn when he came in on Christmas Eve, except when he wore my too-small things while he washed them.

"So," Dad said, dusting off his hands and trying on a more cheerful air. "What's the plan for today? A movie, maybe? A comedy to get your mind off things?" He reached into his back pocket for his wallet. "I'll be happy to pay."

"Thank you, sir, but I think I should be getting to Sean's place." Adam caught my eye and then ducked his head.

I pushed my glasses up the bridge of my nose and said nothing. He was right. It was time to move on.

"Ah." Dad glanced between us. "What time is he expecting you?"

"Anytime. He told me where to find the key to his house. I can let myself in if he's not there yet."

"I see." Dad put his hands on his hips, studying Adam for a

long moment. "If you ever need us, we're here for you."

"Thank you, sir."

"Take care of yourself."

"I will." Adam stood then, and Dad gave him a hug.

Turning to me, Dad said, "I'll be in my office. You'll be taking him?"

I nodded.

Dad patted my back. "That's good, Petey-boy. That's good."

"When do you want to leave?" I asked.

He glanced down at the garbage bag. "I've got my things. Whenever you're ready."

"Where does he live?"

"Off John Sevier Highway."

I stood, pushing my unfinished toasted PB&J away. "Let's go. I wanted to drop Milky Way off at Daniel's house and take a box of stuff over there."

Adam nodded, grabbing the garbage bag. He followed me up to my room and watched in silence as I added my point-and-shoot, my Leica, some camera lenses, a few pairs of jeans, a couple of T-shirts and sweaters, and multiple rolls of undeveloped film to a box. He waited in the bedroom while I was putting in my contacts in the bathroom. I added my toothbrush, toothpaste, glasses, and contacts kit to the box as well.

It was only when we were on the highway, the Volvo pointed toward the airport, that he asked, "So you're staying with this guy a lot."

"Yeah."

"What's his name again?"

"Daniel."

He nodded, shifting. The bag at his feet crinkled, and it occurred to me that it was fitting that he was carrying around a garbage bag. Adam didn't just have baggage, he had garbage to deal with. His garbage, our garbage.

He also had Milky Way in his lap. She cuddled up close to him like he was her new favorite person.

"So, let's talk about Sammy…" I said, leading him to a topic I'd wondered about since Leslie had brought him up.

Adam's jaw worked. "How do you know about that?"

"Leslie. I went to her place. Apologized."

He rubbed his face with both hands. "How did that go?" There was a tiny note of hope in his voice. Did he hope he could be forgiven?

"Not well. She told me she hates me. She told me she never wanted to see me again."

Adam nodded again. "Yeah," he croaked. "She told me the same thing."

"And Sammy?"

"He was a mistake."

Obviously, since he had gone to Leslie. But I didn't say that. "But you cared about him?"

"I don't know. He looked like you, but blond with green eyes, and straight hair, and he was almost as tall as me."

"So, he looked nothing like me."

"He reminded me of you."

"He was nerdy? Wore glasses?"

Adam winced. "Am I that predictable?"

"I think you might be. Yeah."

"I didn't love him," he said. "Not the way I—" He stopped himself, and I was grateful.

"Was it about sex?"

"It was about wanting to replace you in my heart, because I missed you and what we had. I thought maybe, if he was someone like you…" He choked. "But that's impossible, and I fucked myself over."

"You didn't choose me," I pointed out. "You put yourself in a situation that forced the issue."

"I chose you when I told my dad."

I wanted to laugh and cry at the same time. Even now he couldn't be honest with me or even with himself. "Yeah, I guess you did."

"And I fucked myself over a second time." He petted Milky Way's soft fur, his voice subdued. "I wish I'd never met you."

"Do you?" I couldn't say the same. For everything horrible that had happened, there'd been a lot of wonderful moments, too, and, despite all the pain we'd caused, I'd finally learned to love myself and be proud of who I was.

"I wish I didn't want men. Why can't I just want women?"

"I don't know. I think it's just how you're made. I don't think it's something you can change."

"I ruined everything."

I wanted to reach over and take his hand, reassure him that he hadn't, take the pain out of his voice. But the fact of the matter was he'd screwed up. We both had, but he'd taken it so much further with Leslie. "You're going to be okay. You'll move in with Mo, and you'll figure out what to do about school. Maybe get a job."

"I don't think I can stay here in this town."

I pressed my lips together. I didn't want him to stay here. I couldn't stand the idea of running into him while I was doing something mundane like getting groceries, or worse, seeing him at Tilt-a-Whirl on a night out with our friends.

"Marcus told me about a job teaching English in Japan. The JET program. Have you heard of it?"

I shook my head.

"He's doing it next year."

"Ah."

"Or I could apply for the Peace Corps."

"What about a degree?"

"I want to write books. I should live life before anything else, don't you think?"

I didn't know what to say. It sounded to me like Adam wanted to escape—not only Knoxville, but the consequences of his actions. But I couldn't blame him. There would be nothing for him here but memories of what he'd fucked up.

We pulled into Daniel's new neighborhood, and Milky Way jumped to her hind legs, paws against the passenger window, panting happily. "That's right, we're almost home," I said to her.

"Home," Adam whispered.

I heard the note of envy threaded with jealousy.

Pulling up to the house, I wondered at myself for bringing Adam here. I could have taken him to Sean's house first. I could have waited to drop off Milky Way. But there was a part of me—a petty part—that wanted him to see what I had now.

"This is it," I said, climbing from the Volvo. I zipped up my jacket, the winter wind cutting into me.

Adam put Milky Way down on the concrete, and she took off scampering over the driveway, sniffing everything like it'd been a month since she'd last smelled it. He stood with his hands in his pockets looking at the house. He still didn't have a coat. Mo hadn't included one in the garbage bag.

It hit me that I didn't want him in our house. There could be no ghosts of him in the rooms I shared with Daniel. Not even a hint.

Leaving the box of my stuff in the back seat, I said, "I just want to put some things in the darkroom, and then leave her in the house."

Wordlessly, Adam followed as I opened the gate to the yard, and Milky Way darted inside. He stayed silent as we walked up the path.

Unlocking the darkroom door, I threw it open and stepped inside. "Daniel gave me this for Christmas." It was petty, a brag, but I needed him to see. I wasn't leaving him for 'nothing.' I was leaving him for *everything.*

"It's nice," he whispered, looking from the doorway, but not coming in behind me.

I left the film canisters I'd brought in a bin and exited, shutting the door. Another cold wind blew.

Adam shuddered, and I thought about offering him a scarf. I had left one in the house before Christmas.

"C'mon," I said. "Let's put her inside and then I'll take you to Sean's."

Milky Way had done her business in the yard and bounded up to the back door. She raced inside, and I motioned for Adam to wait. "I'll be right back. I just want to make sure she has food and water."

He didn't budge.

Inside the house smelled of Daniel. The scent of his laundry detergent and the new shampoo he'd taken to using recently. I checked Milky Way's provisions and glanced around to make sure everything looked good for Daniel's arrival in the afternoon. Being in our place calmed me down.

Home.

Strange that I had two when now Adam barely had one.

As I returned to the kitchen door, I stopped by the wall rack and pulled down the blue and green scarf I'd left behind. It was soft. Lifting it to my nose, I wondered if it smelled more of Daniel's house or of me. I didn't know what I hoped for.

"Here," I said, holding the scarf out to Adam as I turned back to lock the door. "It'll help keep you warm."

Adam hesitated, his throat working, but he took the scarf. He wrapped it around his neck, before lifting the tail of it up and sniffing. His eyes filled with tears, and when he looked at me, I knew.

It smelled more like me.

"Let's go," I whispered, turning back to the gate.

"Peter..."

I shook my head. I didn't want to know what he had to say. I shouldn't have given him the scarf. I should have let him shiver.

"Peter, please..."

"This way." I opened the gate, and he passed through. I'd just gotten the keys out of my pocket to open the Volvo when a blue car turned into the drive.

Daniel. My heart thumped. What did it look like, me being here with Adam? What would happen now that they'd meet? My stomach tightened. There was no stopping it, though.

Daniel pulled up next to the Volvo, put his car into park, and climbed out.

"Hey," I said, a helpless smile washing over me at the sight of his tanned face. I went to him. "You're early."

"I am." He opened his arms, and I hugged him tightly. "The airline changed my flight time. Who knows why?"

"Oversold," Adam offered. His voice was gruff, and I was shocked to hear him speak.

I broke our hug and turned to him. "Daniel, this is Adam. Adam. Daniel."

They regarded each other with a tense interest that didn't seem to know what to do with itself. Neither of them looked angry. Both just looked...sad. For different reasons, and in different ways.

"Hi," Daniel said, stepping forward with his hand out. "I've heard a lot about you."

Adam's lips twisted into an approximation of a smile as he shook Daniel's hand. "All horrible, I'm sure."

Daniel shrugged. "Well, you know. My father told me once 'no one leaves happy.' That was about employees quitting, but I'm sure in relationships it's the same."

"Yeah," Adam agreed, his eyes straying to me, miserable and lost. "No one leaves happy."

Awkwardness fell hard between us. I toed the concrete, trying to think of the right thing to say.

"I should get going," Adam said. "It's about time I got to Sean's."

"Right," I agreed. "Um, I'm taking him to stay with his brother's friend for now. I left Milky Way inside…"

Daniel nodded. "I'll be here."

Relief swept me that he wasn't going to insist on coming. He trusted me enough to go alone with Adam.

"Great, and I'll be back."

As I started toward the car, Daniel grabbed my hand and tugged me back to him. I went easily, and he kissed my temple. "I missed you," he whispered.

"Me too. It won't take long. I promise."

Climbing back into the car with Adam, the atmosphere between us had changed again. There was no more pleading from him, no more vague hope in his eyes that I might change his mind. And no more attempts for us to be "friends."

"He treats you well?" Adam asked, as we pulled down the drive, and I started toward John Sevier Highway.

"Yes."

"He loves you?"

I nodded.

"He better."

I didn't dignify that with a response.

We didn't talk the rest of the way to Sean's house, except for Adam to give me directions. As he got out of the car, garbage bag in hand, I got out, too. I wasn't sure what I wanted to do. This was it.

Our final goodbye.

"Hey," Adam said, coming around to my side of the car. "I'll always love you."

I cleared my throat. Didn't say anything.

"I'm sorry for how I hurt you."

"Thanks," I whispered.

"Thank you for last night. For holding me."

"You're welcome."

"Peter?"

"Yeah?"

"You're a great photographer. Don't give that up."

"I won't."

"Take care of yourself."

"I will."

As he walked up the sidewalk to the front porch of Sean's small, blue-shuttered house, I felt a strange need grip me.

I opened the back door of the Volvo, grabbed my point-and-shoot camera from the box, and aimed it at him. He turned back, raised his hand, and gave me a small wave.

Click, snick.

I captured it.

My last photo of Adam.

Chapter Thirty-Nine

"H EY," I SAID, coming in through the front door.

Milky Way acted like she hadn't just seen me thirty minutes earlier.

Daniel sat on the sofa, his elbows on his knees, and his head in his hands. He looked up, brown eyes darker than usual. "Hey."

"So that's done," I murmured, toeing off my shoes, and hanging my jacket on the coatrack Daniel had put by the door. The Christmas tree lights were off, and so I went over to turn them on. It was pretty shabby-looking after days without water. It might even be a fire hazard. I pondered it a moment before turning back to Daniel. "How was your trip?"

"It was all right."

I sat by him on the sofa, but he was tense. "The airline didn't change your flight time, did they?"

He huffed a laugh. "No. I did."

"Because of Adam?"

"Because I was jealous," he admitted. "And the part of me that my mom's damaged started whispering to me that maybe I shouldn't trust you."

I nodded and took his hands in mine. "Nothing happened with him."

"You're sure?"

I put his hands to my chest, letting him feel my steady heartbeat. "There was never a moment that I was even tempted."

Daniel cleared his throat. "He's handsome. Hot, even."

"Sure. I have good taste in men. Go look in the mirror."

He gazed into my eyes, searching for whatever it was he needed to see. "I'm sorry I'm like this."

"I get it."

"With all my heart and soul, I need to believe and trust in you. It came to me last night when I was sitting by the pool with Grandma. If I lose this, if I stop trusting everyone, then she's stolen the most precious thing from me. My ability to be vulnerable and be loved. Because you can't do one without the other."

"I love you."

"I got on the earlier plane anyway. Even though I tried to talk myself out of it."

"I'm not mad."

He sighed. "I kept picturing...all kinds of things."

I shook my head. "I hugged him a couple of times because he was crying. That was it. He asked me to kiss him, and I said no."

"Thank you."

"I didn't say no for you," I said. "I didn't want to kiss him because I love you. There's a difference."

I curled up to his side, and we held each other, watching Milky Way snuffle around on the floor looking for crumbs.

Eventually Daniel asked, "What's going to happen to him?"

"Adam?"

"Yeah."

"I don't know. But it's not my responsibility." I sighed. "He was talking about going to Japan to teach English. Or entering the Peace Corps. I don't know what he'll end up doing. But I feel like he'll be okay. He's Adam. He always charms his way to the top."

Or was that Sarah? I didn't know anymore. But I couldn't invest my heart and mind in worrying about him. I hadn't asked him to come out to his dad. I hadn't asked him to turn his life upside down. He did that all on his own, and I'd helped him as much as I could without getting myself ensnared in his web again.

"So, what's for lunch?" I asked, sitting up straighter. "Want to order a pizza?"

Daniel took hold of my hand. "I need to go to the grocery store. We can't survive on pizza delivery alone."

"Tomorrow. Today, let's stay in." I waggled my eyebrows. "There are some photos I wanted to show you. And some Christmas presents I need to give you."

"All right. Pizza it is."

Before we could place the order, we ended up in his bedroom with the door shut and the lights off. Our clothes hit the floor, and we rolled onto the mattress. Daniel's kiss was sweet and soft, and my heart felt squishy in my chest, as he rose over me.

"Condom?" he asked.

"We have plenty in the drawer." I wriggled toward the nightstand.

"No, I mean, do we need to use one?"

"Oh." My chest went tight. "No. I can't think of any reason we should."

He nodded, smoothed a hand down my cheek, peered into my eyes and kissed me again. "I love you, Peter."

"I love you, too."

"I'll be right back." He moved off the bed and over to the stereo system he'd put in before he'd left for Florida. Pressing play on the CD player, the sweet, almost saccharine, opening notes of our song came on.

"It's like a story of love," I sang softly, reaching for him.

"Only you," Daniel whispered, crawling toward me over the mattress.

No one else had ever touched us like this. We'd never shared this level of trust with another soul. It was powerful and beautiful, and we whispered promises as we moved together with nothing between us.

Only us.

✧　✧　✧

THE NEXT DAY Daniel and I took Milky Way on a walk through the green space opposite the house, and then I headed back home to check in with my parents and to grab more of my things.

Being with Daniel so openly and honestly the night before left us both resistant to being apart for long. We were eager to start a new life together. I was young, I knew, and so was he, but we were ready to dive deeper into adulthood. Living together seemed like the best next step to advancing our relationship and our lives.

Sitting at the kitchen table with Mom and Dad, I fessed up to planning to more-or-less live with Daniel during the upcoming semester. "His place is closer to school. You're welcome to come see it and visit anytime. It's really nice."

"How does he afford this house?"

"He bought it with his portion of the inheritance from his dad and the sale of his dad's business and the house. He's got a decent amount put aside to get through school."

"And after that he'll be a nurse?" Mom said.

"That's his goal. Yeah."

Her attitude toward Daniel continued to be tepid. She agreed he was a good guy, that I seemed happy, and that he didn't cause me pain like Adam had. But she still seemed to think I needed someone more artistic to be satisfied. I had no idea why she couldn't let that idea go, especially given that she and Dad were happy together, and Dad wasn't an artist of any kind. A dreamer, maybe, but not an artist or a writer.

"What about you?" she pressed. "How will you afford to keep

up your share of expenses?"

"I can take on more shifts at the library," I said. "And I don't eat that much. Between what I make at work, and what Daniel has saved, I think we should be fine."

"What if there's an emergency?"

"That's what we're for," Dad said. "To help out if he needs us while he's getting on his feet as an adult."

Mom sighed, her shoulders curving.

"It's not that different than if I were moving into the dorms. I'll still come home to visit."

Her eyes were damp as she pulled at her string cheese distractedly. "But you won't even need to come home to do laundry," she whispered. "I'm sure he has a washer and dryer."

"I can bring laundry home if that's important to you, Mom."

She rolled her eyes and tossed a bit of string cheese at me.

Dad sat back and crossed his arms over his chest. "It's a big step, Petey-boy, but you know you can always come back if things don't work out."

"I know. Thank you."

"Well, we knew this day would come, Jessica," Dad said, taking her hand. "It's part of the parenting gig."

"But you'll see him at school. When will I see him?"

"I'll visit once a week for Ragu night. I'll bring Daniel every other week, so you'll get some time with me alone, too."

"All right," Mom agreed. "Any night but Fridays. I get my best work done on Friday evenings."

I agreed. I didn't tell her that between my job, getting naked with Daniel, and hanging out with our friends at Tilt-a-Whirl, our Friday nights would be booked. "I could do it on Wednesday," I suggested. "A midweek meal at home."

That seemed to satisfy her. She gathered up her remaining string cheese, threw it in the trash, and said, "On that note, I have a castaway to reunite with an heiress." She kissed my cheek, touched my chin, and gazed into my eyes. "I love you."

"I love you, too."

She nodded. "Will he keep you safe?"

I swallowed a sudden lump in my throat. "Always."

"He'll take care of you?"

"And I'll take care of him, too."

She seemed to ponder that, and then she said, "Will you bring that envelope with the photos of George for your first dinner alone with us?"

"Yes," I whispered.

"Good. I'm ready to see them now, I think." She smiled. "You do look so much like him."

I nodded. If she was ready to go through the photos in the envelope, maybe soon she'd be ready to know about Harold and *Robin*.

"But you'll be happy, Peter. Won't you?"

"That's my plan."

Another kiss on the cheek, and off she went to help her characters fall in love.

"Speaking of someone coming home," Dad said. "I waved down Mo today. I saw him driving toward his house while I was out front taking the Christmas lights off the bushes."

My throat tightened.

"He'd been to visit Adam at his friend Sean's place."

I pressed my lips together.

"Do you think he'll be all right, son? In the end?"

Strange for Dad to be seeking my reassurance, but in another way, it was gratifying. He trusted me and saw me as a man whose opinion was valuable.

"I don't know. I hope so," I said. "He's not a bad person. He just wasn't the right person for me."

Dad patted my hand. "I'm proud of you."

"For what?"

"For knowing when to walk away."

"I should have broken up with him a lot sooner."

Dad sighed. "That's part of life, Petey. Woulda, coulda, shouldas crowd the room sometimes. That's part of the reason your mom hasn't warmed to Daniel, you know. She sees he's the real deal, and if he's it for you, then our job as parents is almost wrapped up. She missed out on a lot, and she sees that now. There's no going back, but she projects her disappointment in herself onto Daniel."

I lifted a brow. "Moonlighting as a Psychology professor these days? Hanging out with my TA Donnie Huggins?"

"Oh, that Donnie kid," Dad said. "Jesus, Mary, and Joseph save him. He's a mess."

"He is." I chuckled.

"But no. I just know your mother, and I've met your Daniel and seen how he lights you up. If she can't see it, the problem is with her eyes, not with him. Her eyes don't want to see."

"That's always been the problem for her, hasn't it?"

"She's healing, Petey. But time doesn't wait for anyone. She's lost her chance at more time with you, because now it's Daniel's turn. She resents that, but don't worry. She'll come around."

"It doesn't change anything even if she doesn't. I love him."

"I'm glad to hear it." Dad smiled again. "You're being safe?"

I swallowed, a flutter of feeling in my chest. If he knew, what would he say? If he knew that I trusted Daniel with my heart, soul, and body so entirely that I'd allowed him to do things I'd never let anyone else do. In fact, I'd begged him to. "He's safe," I said. "The safest man I know."

Dad's eyes changed just enough that I knew he sensed the evasion, but he nodded. "Good. I trust you to know what you're doing."

"Even after all the mistakes I made last year?"

"Because of them," Dad said. "I watched you learn and grow. If you say Daniel is safe, then I trust you to know if that's true. Nothing's foolproof. No condom, or seat belt, or fire alarm. But if you can't trust the person you love…" Dad shook his head. "Where does a relationship go from there?"

"I trust him."

"That's all I need to hear."

After that conversation, I went upstairs to my room to pack up some of the things I wanted to take to Daniel's. I started with more clothes and shoes, stuffing them into the old green suitcase Mom and Dad had taken with them on the Disney World trip where I'd posed disco-style in front of the castle.

I moved on to my boombox, mixtape collection, and books. Daniel's mixtape gifts went right into the cardboard box I'd brought up from the garage to pack what didn't go in the suitcase. I smiled at his solid, steady writing on the first tape he'd given to me on my birthday. "Losing My Religion" by R.E.M., being the soundtrack of my summer, and the song I most associated with him from before we got together, was our honorary second song in my heart. It was surpassed by "Only You" of course. A song that now held so many intimate memories for me, I wasn't sure I could hear it in public without blushing.

I turned to the mixtapes Adam had made for me. I hadn't listened to them in a long time. All the songs reminded me too much of that time. I picked up the last one he'd ever given to me, a few weeks before our spring break trip to the beach. His handwriting looked so strong and confident.

Song titles and band names leapt out at me: "Why Can't I Be You?" by The Cure, "Enjoy the Silence" by Depeche Mode, "How Soon Is Now?" and "I Started Something I Couldn't Finish" both by The Smiths. Placed at the end of several mixtapes was another Smiths song, "Please, Please, Please Let Me Get What I Want."

Adam had told me more than once he related to that one. I'd

never understood why. From my perspective, he'd always gotten what he wanted: me, then Leslie, and then us both.

But had he ever gotten what he *really* wanted from either of us? Unconditional love and acceptance? He'd hidden so much of himself from Leslie, she might as well have not known him at all. I'd known him better, but I'd scorned a core part of who he was—someone capable of loving more than one person at once. Closeted, rejected by his father, pressured to stay hidden by his family…

Had Adam ever gotten what he truly wanted? From anyone? I doubted it.

Sunshine sifted through the window and glinted on the edge of the cassette case. I put the tape in my box and moved on.

Over to my filing cabinet.

There I pulled out files of photos and negatives. All labeled so I knew what I'd find inside. I flipped through the pictures I'd taken at Kingsley the prior year. Mike by the flagpole with his arm slung around a brooding Van. Allison kissing Van's cheek outside of Dr. Landry's classroom while Dr. Landry smiled in the background. Mike hoisting Sarah up and tickling her at the beach. The group, sans Adam, sitting at a table in Beans, steam rising from their coffee cups.

They were good photos. Nicely framed, competent. I'd learned in Marta's class and from the critiques over the semester how to look at my own work more objectively. There were criticisms I could make, but even so, to me these photos were their own brand of perfect. Juvenile, but natural. Topical, but revealing.

I put them back in the drawer. I didn't need to take them with me.

Opening another file, I glanced through pictures of Sarah. That tiger's-eye shot I'd taken the first day of school. A nice one of her legs in her cheerleading uniform. A rare one of her genuine smile. I remembered Mike had cracked a joke just as I'd snapped the picture.

I didn't need those either.

I hovered over the files containing the negatives of Adam's photos. There were some beautiful shots of him in there. I'd developed them and destroyed them, but they remained safe in their primitive state. I'd taken so many of him. Naked, dressed, bundled up for cold weather. In a bathing suit. Kissing me.

I knew there were some amazing shots mixed in with banal or sentimental ones. I could conjure them up in my mind. There were pictures that might even complement the "joy in the male form" concept I was trying to pull together for the potential show with Harold, and with which I wanted to impress Marta.

But I put the negatives back in the file. I didn't need them either. Not anymore. Not in any way.

I had plenty to look forward to in experimenting with taking nudes of myself and whichever of my friends might agree to pose. I figured Robert was a definite yes, and I wanted to take photos of him with Barry. Nothing pornographic. Gay love, two men naked and unashamed. Something that could go in a gallery or on their bedroom wall.

Minty might pose for me, and maybe even Windy. I didn't know about Antonio, but I'd be curious what he looked like under all the plaid and flannel he'd taken to wearing lately. A new Nirvana fan, he'd embraced grunge.

I shut the filing cabinet drawer.

And that was it. I could always come back for more stuff if I needed to. This wasn't goodbye. It was just see-you-later. I'd be back next Wednesday for the promised dinner.

I carried my portfolio, the box of my things, and the suitcase down the stairs, stepping over the ghosts of me and Adam there, and into the hallway where I remembered Daniel smiling over my Disney World pose and heart-shaped glasses.

I stopped by the kitchen and glanced toward the corner where Harry's dog bed used to lie and smiled at the counter where I'd banged my head over my crush on a "straight boy."

The same counter where I'd held Daniel's hand while making the most stressful phone call of my life. Speaking of… I turned my head. On the wall was the phone I'd waited beside in agony, and called Daniel from in excitement, and listened in surprise as Adam, across the world, had jerked off thinking of me.

I shook my head. That last seemed so long ago. Another lifetime. Another person.

Backing out of the kitchen, I passed through the living room where I'd played on the floor with my childhood friends' Strawberry Shortcake dolls. Where I'd opened presents every Christmas Eve. Where I'd sat beside Mom while she'd marked up her manuscripts as I'd watched TV.

Would this ever be my home again? Or was I leaving it behind the way I'd left Harry, and Adam, and Strawberry Shortcake in the past? The way I'd left Leslie and my most horrible mistakes?

Was this growing up?

I stood in the doorway, listening to the loud clacking of my mom's word processor from behind her office door, hearing my dad start to sing a Gaelic hymn from their bedroom down the hall.

I closed my eyes and collected the moment like a living photograph.

Locking the door behind me, I stepped out into the cold December light.

In the driveway, I put my suitcase into the trunk and the box tapes and trinkets into the passenger seat of the Volvo. As I backed out down the drive, I turned on the radio. A university DJ announced the next song was a personal favorite. The song began. I smiled and aimed my car toward my new love and my new home.

Windchimes. Robert Smith's voice.

Pictures of you.

THE END

Letter from Leta

Dear Reader,

Wow! What a journey! Thank you so much for taking it with me and Peter. There are no words to express my love for him and for readers who also love him. It's been emotional coming to the end of this twenty-year-long project, and I'm grateful to every last one of you. I hope you carry his story in your heart forever.

I'm sure many readers are left with worry for Minty. I'm happy to let you know he's going to have his own book. You can grab *My Skin Begs You Please* to find out more about his life during and after this time period. Unlike Peter's books, which are predominantly Coming of Age, Minty's book will be a Standalone Erotic Romance with some big content warnings (as you might have guessed,) so do take care with that.

As for Adam, many have expressed their love for him, and want to see him get a redemption arc and a happy ending of his own. While there can be no official promise for a book like that right now, there's also every reason to hope for it in the future. So keep an eye out for that possibility.

If you loved the music mentioned in Peter's book, and want to hear those songs and others that inspired his story, you can go to my '90s Coming of Age Spotify Playlist and have a listen.

Don't forget to join my newsletter for snippets of the day-to-day writing life, new release information, important announcements, sales, and more. And be sure to follow me on BookBub or Amazon to be notified of new releases. Also, to see some sources of my inspiration, you can follow me on Instagram.

If you enjoyed following Peter on his journey, please take a moment to leave a review on all the books in the *'90s Coming of Age* series. Reviews not only assist readers in determining if a book is for them, but they also help books to show up in site searches.

For the audiobook connoisseurs out there, the entire *'90s Coming of Age* series will be available by the end of summer 2023 narrated by the amazing Michael Ferraiuolo. Look for that on Audible.

Thank you so much for being a reader!
Leta

Acknowledgments

Normally, I put acknowledgments at the front of the book, but after twenty years, there are so many thanks to give to so many people that I hardly know where to start. This list will no doubt be chaotic and strange, atypical of my usual pages of thanks. Even so, I'll likely forget someone, and for that I apologize. Every person in my life for the last 20 years supported me with these books in one way or another.

We'll start with the technical folks, move to research and personal, and then finish the list with inspirational.

The Behind-the-Scenes Gang who edit, copyedit, proof, beta, and make sure everything flows just right: Willow, Mel, Keira, Mia, Cecily, Sharon, Amy, and Anne-Marie.

Research Helpers: Melanie (who found and took me to the NYC Library for the Why We Fight: AIDS Activism exhibit which set me on the path of researching condom refusal among gay men during the height of the AIDS crisis—to fascinating results), the Metro Pulse Archives (which now seem to have vanished from the internet) for the 1989-1993 era interviews and information about AIDS Response Knoxville, AIDS treatment in Knoxville, and interviews with local AIDS victims. The archives were also a fantastic source for research on the history of drag in Knoxville, as well as interviews with several local drag queens which served as inspiration for Robert's documentary. The HIV.gov site which hosts a timeline of the HIV and AIDS epidemic from 1981 through to the present. I referred to it constantly. My own experiences at The Carousel II in Knoxville, TN as a college student and young adult, which provided me with the inspiration for Tilt-a-Whirl (including seeing a drag queen spank a blond, bare-assed twink on stage—though without the titillating commentary I added for Renée's show.) In more recent years, the Knoxville Drag History Facebook Page has served as a helpful source. My years working at the University of Tennessee library in the early 1990s served as all the knowledge necessary to know how the place worked in 1991 (yes, we had a computerized system with barcode readers! High tech!) Shout out to Becky and Julie, my bosses there. I hope they're doing well.

Family and Loved Ones: Brian (who was there for all the inspirational moments, and who's loved me through it all), Cecily (who grew up hearing about Peter and then grew into the best beta reader a mom could ever have), Mom (who always reads with love), Dad (who loves and supports even if he doesn't "get it"), Sean, Cynthia, Clara, Shel and Lo, Hannah, Heather, Maxine (most supportive mother-in-law ever) and Bob.

Dear Friends: Kim, Liza, Punny (& Charles, for the love, support, place to stay), Keira, Danielle, Cynthia, Holly, Sabrina, Denine, Wendy, and Cara. Whether you read these books (or any of my books) or not, your friendship gives me the love and stability to write.

Ye Olde LiveJournal Support System: Aimee (for loving Peter the most), Brigid, Sharon, Anne-Marie, Alice, Lisa, Other Lisa, Ragna (for her early Peter fandom), Haley, Jeanette, and so many others. I couldn't have grown as a writer without all of you. Thank you for supporting infant-Peter and baby writer-me.

Strangers-that-I-Used-to-Know: Jed (for the years I loved you best of all, we might be strangers now, but until I die in my heart I'll keep you alive), Jacyn (for the time when you were family, and for the look that told me to shut up and gave me confidence), Jodie (who gave me an inadvertent kick in the pants; it broke my heart, but got my priorities in line), Diana (who'll make it into a book one day for all the right and wrong reasons and who squeezed my hand when I needed it), Clay (who told me in no uncertain terms that the first draft of Peter's story truly sucked and was so, so right).

Inspirational Persons: David (because he was handsome and wrong in every way), Mark (because he was brave, the world was cruel, and I was there), Alan (who hated me and didn't love him either), Morrie (for photography and sweetness), Dr. Lippincott (my own Dr. Landry), Jeff, Leonard (RIP sweet friend), the boy in the tutu skirt at UT circa 1991, John Robert, the entire student body of my private high school, and especially the drag queens at The Carousel II.

Inspirational Musical: The Cure (especially "Pictures of You", The Smiths (especially "Please, Please, Please Let Me Get What I Want This Time"), Tori Amos (especially "Doughnut Song"), "Daniel" by Bat for Lashes, "The Whole of the Moon" by The Waterboys, REM (especially "Losing My Religion"), Casey Stratton (especially "You Were My Religion" and "Congratulations"), "Only You" by Yazoo (or Yaz if you're in the US), "Smooth Criminal" by MJ, "Don't Get Me Wrong" by the Pretenders, "You Make It Real" by James Morrison, and "They Weren't There" by Missy Higgins.

Plus, every single person mentioned in the acknowledgments of both editions of the first two books. I owe a debt of gratitude to all of you.

Other Books by Leta Blake

Contemporary

Will & Patrick Wake Up Married
Will & Patrick's Endless Honeymoon
Cowboy Seeks Husband
The Difference Between
Bring on Forever
Stay Lucky

Sports

The River Leith

The Training Season Series
Training Season
Training Complex

Musicians

Smoky Mountain Dreams
Vespertine

New Adult

Punching the V-Card

'90s Coming of Age Series
Pictures of You
You Are Not Me

Only You

Winter Holidays

North's Pole

The Mr. Christmas Series
Mr. Frosty Pants
Mr. Naughty List
Mr. Jingle Bells

A Boy for All Seasons
My December Daddy

Fantasy

Any Given Lifetime

Reimagined Fairy Tales

Flight
Levity

Paranormal & Shifters

Angel Undone
Omega Mine

Horror

Raise Up Heart

Omegaverse

Heat of Love Series
White Heat

Slow Heat
Alpha Heat
Slow Birth
Bitter Heat

For Sale Series
Heat for Sale
Bully for Sale

Audiobooks
letablake.com/audiobooks

Discover more about the author online

Leta Blake
letablake.com